FLORESH WINGS

Morton Faulkner

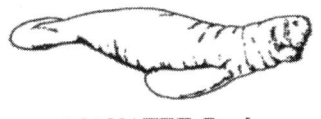

MANATEE *Books*

FLORESKAND: WINGS

Floreskand, where myth, mystery and magic reign.

The sky above the city of Lornwater darkens as thousands of red tellars, the magnificent birds of the Overlord, wing their way towards Arisa.

Ulran discovers he must get to Arisa within seventy days and unlock the secret of the scheduled rites. He is joined in his quest by the ascetic Cobrora Fhord, who harbours a secret or two, and also the mighty warrior Courdour Alomar, who has his own reasons for going to Arisa. They learn more about each other – whether it's the strange link Ulran has with the red tellar Scalrin, the lost love of Alomar, or the superstitious heart of Cobrora.

Plagued by assassins, forces of nature and magic, they cross the plains of Floreskand, combat Baronculer hordes, scale snow-clad Sonalume Mountains and penetrate the dark heart of Arisa. Here they uncover truth, evil and find pain and death.

"A fast-paced fantasy adventure as an innkeeper, a city dweller full of surprises, and a long-lived warrior, join forces in a race against time. Their quest is to save the red tellars, the giant birds, which are the wings of the overlord. Along the way even the weather becomes a powerful adversary and the three are tested almost beyond endurance. Tensions and evocative language keep the reader turning the pages to the very end!"- Anne E. Summers, author of *The Singing Mountain*

An expansive and well thought story, a must-read for lovers of magic and military fantasy. - Kate Marie Collins, best-selling author of *Daughter of Hauk, Mark of the Successor* and *Son of Corse*

FLORESKAND:
WINGS

The right of Morton Faulkner to be identified as the Author of the Work has been asserted by him in accordance with the Copyright, Designs and Patents Act 1988.

ALL RIGHTS RESERVED
No part of this book may be reproduced or transmitted in any form or by any means, electronic or mechanical, including photocopying, recording, or by any information storage and retrieval system, without written permission of the author or Manatee Books except for brief quotations used for promotion or in reviews.
.

This is a work of fiction.
Names, characters, places, and incidents are used fictitiously. Any resemblance to actual persons living or dead, business establishments, events, or locales, is entirely coincidental.

Manatee Books
ISBN-13: 978-1975907303
ISBN-10: 1975907302

First printing, October, 2017

Copyright 2017 Morton Faulkner

Previously published in a slightly different form as WINGS OF THE OVERLORD, 2014

Cover
Dreamstime stock-image-60432918

Dedication

To Maria for putting up with my obsessions decade after decade, and to Christine to whom I promised to mention years before I even put pen to paper – Gordon

To Jennifer for never losing faith – Nik

*Reviews of the previous version published
as WINGS OF THE OVERLORD:*

"A beautiful and atmospheric tale. The author has skilfully developed the characters in a way that you feel you are right there with them on their quest. I can say that I have read many fantasy stories I have truly enjoyed, but only a few have left that lingering haunting feeling within me. Can't wait for the next instalment."

"Started reading this genre like most people with Tolkien moving on to Feist and Eddings. Grand in scale, well written and certainly the start of the next series on my bookshelf. A gripping read..."

"It took a chapter or so to get into the world of Floreskand and process the characters, language and sense of place, then I was off! Great storytelling which carried me through quickly to its conclusion, making me impatient for the next book in the series. Well drawn characters with enough mystery about their back story to keep you interested. Well-written too... I could see this as a film - now you just need Vigo Mortensen for the hero and you are set."

"This story has a complex yet well-structured plot presented in a relaxed writing style which easily draws the reader into an alien landscape whose topography, vegetation and inhabitants are described in an almost affectionate detail….

As our three adventurers continue on their journey they undergo both natural and human disasters... The ongoing relationship between the principal characters is explored at some length; the strong, almost mystical presence of Ulran who could win an Iron Man contest without blinking, the superstitious fragility of Cobrora Fhord and the destructive violence of Courdour Alomar ... Such twists and turns in the presentation of the plot expand the telling of the tale and there are many duly woven into the pattern to enrich and excite the reader. The journey through the Sonalume Mountains has a strong element of authenticity to it, concentrating on the treacherous ice and snow coupled to an intense bitter cold. This seems to derive from an actual experience that must have been quite wretched at the time.

The final denouement by which our now familiar heroes, at great personal risk and cost ... is recounted intensely and is quite a page-turner. The body count is high and contains images of great cruelty.

This is quite clearly the first volume of what is intended to be an entire sequence of stories about the world of Floreskand, a very cultivated creation. Enough links have been established within this tale onto which further adventures, deeds and characters can be connected at later times. It is a well-worked story involving swords and sorcery which will have a very direct appeal to those who admire heroism, but who also like to wade through buckets of blood and gore combined with a dash of mystical sentiment added to provide a degree of sweetness to finish off the feast."

Morton Faulkner is the writing team of
Nik Morton and Gordon Faulkner

Nik Morton hails from Whitley Bay, Tyne and Wear. He joined the Royal Navy as, appropriately, a Writer and has travelled all over the world both privately or with the Navy. He gained his Open University BA Degree in 1987 and left the RN for a civilian career in computing.

Nik has sold articles and numerous genre short stories - espionage, science fiction, fantasy, horror, love, adventure and ghost; many of these have been collected in six themed books: *Gifts from a Dead Race, Nourish a Blind Life, Visitors, Codename Gaby* and *I Celebrate Myself*.

He has had 27 books published, among them the Tana Standish psychic spy series (*Mission: Prague, Mission: Tehran* and *Mission: Khyber*), the Avenging Cat series (*Catalyst, Catacomb* and *Cataclysm*), a vampire thriller set in Malta, *Chill of the Shadow*, and a romantic adventure set in Tenerife, *An Evil Trade*. Also he has 9 westerns published: *Death at Bethesda Falls, Last Chance Saloon, Blind Justice at Wedlock, The $300 Man, Old Guns, The Magnificent Mendozas, Bullets for a Ballot, Coffin for Cash*, and *Death for a Dove*.

His bestselling writing guide *Write a Western in 30 Days – with plenty of bullet points* has garnered good reviews and is considered useful for writers of all genre fiction, not only westerns. He has sold illustrations and cartoons and his artwork for hundreds of Tae Kwon Do sequences was featured in *Fighters Magazine*. Nik learned Chinese kung fu (*quanshu*) in Malta where Gordon was a black belt; he then teamed up with Gordon to write the first of a fantasy series set in Gordon's mythical Floreskand – *Wings*.

He is married to Jen and they live in the Alicante region of Spain; they have a daughter, Hannah and a son-in-law Farhad, and two grandchildren, Darius and Suri.

Gordon Faulkner was born and raised in the West Riding of Yorkshire. During an extended stay in hospital while young he developed what turned out to be a life-long passion for Oriental culture, especially Chinese after reading the travels of Marco Polo. He started training in Oriental martial arts in the late 1960s and after joining the RAF in the early 1970s he specialised in Chinese martial arts and Daoist philosophy. During his 22 year career in the RAF, he was one of the founders and General Secretary of the RAF Martial Arts Federation, a post he held until his retirement from military service, when he became a full-time Daoist Arts teacher. This resulted in extensive travel within Europe and North America where he was invited to run seminars and give lectures.

For more years than he cares to remember he has planned and developed the mythical Floreskand, its characters, coinage, history, geology, religion and myths. When he met Nik in Malta during martial arts training, they decided to work on a series of novels set in this colourfully imagined land.

Gordon is a member of the Society for Anglo-Chinese Understanding and a Fellow of the Royal Asiatic Society. In 1990 he had the first of what was to eventually become annual trips to China. These trips take students to study at the Beijing University of Physical Education (BUPE) and visit various research establishments, hospitals, temples, markets, bars, etc.

He is the Principal Instructor of the Chanquanshu School of Daoist Arts which he founded in 1983; it now has in excess of 300 registered students. At a ceremony held at BUPE he became Ru Shi Dizi (an outstanding and close disciple) of Professor Zhang Guangde, the creator of Daoyin Yangsheng Gong which is a part of the Chinese National Fitness Program.

And at a Ba Shi ceremony in a temple on Mount Wudang, Central China, he was initiated as a 15th generation Wudang Boxing disciple of Daoist Master You Xuande.

He is the author of *Managing Stress with Qigong*.

Gordon and his wife, Maria have two children and six grandchildren and live in the Scottish Highlands.

CONTENTS

Map 1 – Floreskand, 2050AC - 1
Map 2 – Arion - 2
Compass points - 2

Prologue 1 Sonalumes - 3
Prologue 2   Shadows over Lornwater - 6

Part 1
Third Sapin – Fourth Sabin of Juvous

Chapter 1   Quest - 31
Chapter 2   Inn - 45

Part 2
Fourth Sabinma of Juvous – First Sabinma of Fornious

Chapter 3   Portent - 54
Chapter 4   Orb - 66
Chapter 5   Seer - 73

Part 3
First Dekin – Third Dloin of Fornious

Chapter 6   Teen - 78
Chapter 7   Presentiment - 95
Chapter 8   Nebulous - 112
Chapter 9   Jaryar - 122
Chapter 10 Blighted - 133

Part 4
Third Sufin of Fornious – Fourth Durin of Darous

Chapter 11 Trial - 150
Chapter 12 Talus - 167
Chapter 13 Pre-ordained - 184
Chapter 14 Angevanellian - 198
Chapter 15 Irrea - 210
Chapter 16 Dissension - 221

Part 5
Fourth Sapin of Darous – First Durin of Lamous

Chapter 17 Palace - 235
Chapter 18 Iayen - 245
Chapter 19 Ash - 261
Chapter 20 Rite - 280

Epilogue
First Sapin –Sapinma of Lamous - 296

Glossaries
A - Names, places and meanings – 300
B – List of Characters – 307
C – Madurava: compass bearings – 310
D – The Arisan Calendar – 311
E – Lords and Gods – 312

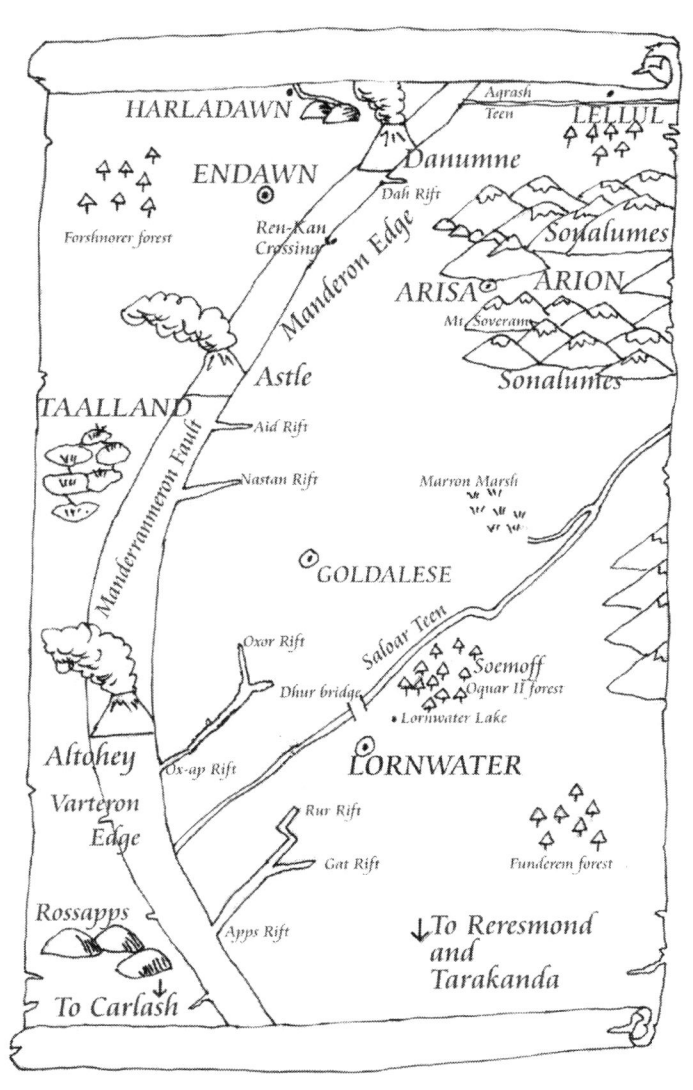

MAP 1
FLORESKAND 2050 AC
Not to scale

MAP 2
ARION

PROLOGUE 1: SONALUMES

No one can ever truly know or understand these magnificent creatures. How could they? For the red tellars are the Wings of the Overlord.
Dialogues of Meshanel

Snow-clad and ice-bound, the two peaks opposite rose in ragged splendour to pierce the egg-blue sky of dawn. Wisps of cloud gusted and swathed about the rock formations, occasionally obscuring the chasm far below. Scattered on narrow ledges and precipitous ridges, thousands of drab-clothed men stood or crouched, waiting.

Wrapped in an inadequate fawn-fur cloak which freezing gusts of air threatened to whip from him, General Foo-sep braced himself and, his clean-shaven chin set with annoyance, looked down upon his suffering men. His gums ached dully with the insidious cold, yellow teeth chattering. In vain he rubbed fur-gloved hands together.

An entire toumen! Ten thousand men! And they were to take orders from an accursed civilian! He seethed, casting an embittered glare to his right, at a black-clad man of slight frame, parchment-coloured skin and ebony pebbles for eyes.

The wind slapped at the man's fur cloak and whistled over the bare out-jutting rocks nearby.

Wind-howl was deafening on the outcrop up here, yet only a step back into the shelter of the overhang no sound penetrated; and from here the entire range of the Sonalume Mountains seemed enveloped in this same eerie stillness.

"They will be along soon," said the civilian, visibly tensing as he leaned over the sloping ledge. His bear-hide boots crackled as he moved, shifting ice from the soles.

Below – a dizzying drop that had claimed too many men already – the bottom indistinct in a slithering purple haze.

Foo-sep discerned the tiny motes of black in the sky and, as the shapes approached, he was struck by their immense size. Framed by the two grey-blue peaks, the birds were coming; he had to admit, grudgingly, as predicted.

"Now!" howled the civilian.

Hoarfrost encrusted brows scowling, Foo-sep lifted his arm and signalled to his men on both sides of the wide, gaping chasm.

Soundlessly, with military precision, the prepare signal was passed through the dispersed ranks.

Foo-sep raised his eyeglass, careful lest he touched his skin with its icy rim.

Stern-faced with the cold and, at last, a sense of purpose, his loyal soldiers were now unfurling nets and arranging stones for quick reloading of their sling-shots.

Foo-sep slowly scanned across the striated rock face.

Abruptly, the birds leapt into focus, their presence taking away his breath in cold wisps. Such an enormous wingspan! And red, O so red! He hesitated at the thought of the task ahead.

His momentary indecision must have been communicated to the other, or perhaps the civilian possessed even more arcane powers than those with which he was credited; "The King desires it," was all he said.

Foo-sep nodded and moved the eyeglass across to the other rock face where the remaining soldiers were trying in vain to keep warm, quivers ready, bowstrings taut and poised.

Now the birds were entering between the peaks.

Foo-sep waved to a signaller who blew three great blasts on his horn. The sound echoed among the peaks.

In a constant flurry, ice-coated nets looped out, a few attached to arrows, entwining many of the creatures' wings. Some birds swooped beneath the heavy mesh then swerved, talons raking the men responsible. Others used their wings to sweep soldiers from the ledges as though dusting furniture. Stones hit a few on their bright red crests and they plummeted, stunned, to be caught by outstretched nets beneath; nets that were slowly filling up, straining at their supports.

Watching through his eyeglass, Foo-sep was amazed at the weird silence of the birds: only their frenetically beating wings generated any sound; all other noise originated from his yelling and shrieking soldiers as they flung nets and stones or were dragged from precarious positions. He scowled as a group of fools forgot to keep clear of their own nets; entangled, they were wrenched to giddy, plunging deaths.

Pacing from side to side, Foo-sep watched helplessly as his beloved toumen was decimated. And for what? A few hundred birds!

His attention was diverted to an uncannily large specimen ensnared in nets, its feathers flying as it clawed at two soldiers on a ledge while they loosed sling-stones at the creature.

Yet the missiles had no effect, and the massive curved beak snapped through the brittle mesh as though it was flimsy plains-grass.

As the bird looped, Foo-sep noticed a distinctive marking none of the others seemed to possess – a white patch on its throat.

The civilian must have observed it also, because at that instant he gripped Foo-sep's arm, lips visibly trembling, black pebble-eyes shining. Then, in desperation, the idiot shouted an order that made no sense at all: "Let that one go!"

Numb with cold, bitterly aware of how many good men had suffered already at the talons of that gigantic bird, Foo-sep steeled himself against his better instinct and cupped gloved hands round his mouth.

"Let that one go!" he called.

And the words echoed, mocking: *"Let that one go!"*

PROLOGUE 2:
SHADOWS OVER LORNWATER

Lornwater, 2050AC*
*[see glossary at end]

I

Be wary, they have a life of their own,
Roaming across ceilings in moonlight,
Fleeing or slinking away in day-bright.
Yet, they hold feelings like me and you.
- *A Life of Their Own*, from
The Collected Works of Nasalmn Feider (1216-1257)
***
First Sidinma of Juvous

In striking contrast to the brownish spot on her forehead above her nose, Sister Illasa's complexion held a bluish tinge, despite the flickering torches in the shadowy stone-walled basement room. Deep green silk covered her thickset body, wrapped about her waist and draped over one shoulder. Her bosom heaved as she spoke, her voice demanding and yet sultry. "O, Tanemag, strong king of the Dunsaron, heed me in my conjuration!"

Her right hand comprised six fingers and held a bowl of dark water, which she moving in a circle over a crackling brazier. Her close-set olive green eyes flashed, almost luminous in this light. "Mussor, master of water, fashion me my melog!" She blew on the flames, purred, "Wrest from those I name the life-force that will drive melog, by ear and eye and nose and ear, animate my shadow assassin from out of darkness!"

With her free hand she pulled at her stringy black hair that was streaked with grey and blue. She yelped involuntarily and her fingers gripped a bunch of hair like twine, and then threw it on the flames, where it sizzled among the charred bones of sacrificed creatures.

An abrupt draught wafted through the dark shadowy place, even though there were no open windows or doors. "Winds of Lamsor, breathe life into my melog. Dark Bridansor, fashion me my creature to do my earnest bidding! Let the named ones lose the use of their limbs and become mere puppets for my melog."

Exhaustion stretched her nerves taut, her breathing rasped in her throat. This must work; she knew she would not have the strength to repeat the spell. Lifting the bowl to her lips, she drank the entire contents, every last vile drop. Fleetingly, her stomach threatened to rebel, but she held it down and smiled. Her dry throat was cured; the corners of her mouth dribbled blackly as she reeled off names, her lips moist and slavering: "Pro-dem Hom, Den-orl Pin, Cor-aba Grie, Fet-usa Fin – you all are spawn of Saurosen and thus deserving of my creature's dread ire!"

II

Their life is sucked from your bone.
But not only in obscure curtained night.
No, they draw strength from any light.
Barely the suggestion of a glimmer will do.

Of all, children understand them alone,
They know that the Unreal in Darkness breeds,
And their dread sustains all gloomy needs.
Oh, and children's tears enrich them, true.
- *A Life of Their Own*, from
The Collected Works of Nasalmn Feider (1216-1257)
***

First Durin of Juvous

Shadows danced in the room, a faint breeze from the open door wafting the flames of the shagunblend torches, casting stripes of darkness over the supine naked woman's corpse. Welde Dep stroked his black beard and cursed his bad luck as well as the gods. He removed his watchman's bronze helm and placed it on the wine-stained sideboard. Those same shadows flickered over the helm's vigilant eye, giving the absurd impression that it blinked. Kneeling beside the dead woman's head, he glanced at the two attending watchmen who hovered near the doorway of the House of Velvet. "Make sure nobody enters until I have completed my examination."

"Yes, sir," said Banstrike, the more reliable of the pair. Cursh appeared disconcerted, which was not surprising, considering the amount of blood on the floor and walls. Dep suspected that Cursh didn't have the stomach for the job; he bore watching. Watch the watchmen. As ever. The two men hurriedly slipped under the bead curtain and out the door.

The corpse was no longer recognisable. Her face had been expertly sliced off, baring bone. That accounted for the mess of blood. He shuddered and wondered if the mutilation had been done while the victim was alive. As Lornwater's chief special investigations watchman for eleven years, he'd seen all manner of sights and dealt with man's depravity, the cruelty meted out to men and women alike by disturbed individuals forsaken by the gods. Yet even now he was not quite inured to the grisly nature of his calling. He still felt empathy for the victims.

Stripping the skin from a person's face was a message. Usually, the messenger was an assassin. This particular message meant that the victim would be consigned to forever roam Below and never attain eternal rest with the Overlord. That raised at least two questions: who was the assassin, and who hired him? Yet more questions lingered, however. This disfigurement was slightly different: the woman's right eye had been cut out and placed in her left palm, and her nose was missing. Absently, he fingered the gristle that was all that remained of his right ear and let out a throaty mew of sympathy.

The dead woman's body was twisted, as if she had fallen abruptly, her right arm trapped under her. Gripping her cold shoulder, Dep eased up the corpse and released the arm.

The glint of a gildring on her finger immediately caught his attention. Most odd. There were not many female assassins registered in Lornwater. And what was a member of the assassin's gild doing here; and why was *she* killed? Was it a failed assassination attempt?

Clutched in the woman's right palm was the missing grisly nose. The placement of the eyes and nose signified something esoteric, he felt sure. He must solicit advice from someone adept at dealing with the Darkness;

his own dealings were concerned with ranmeron magic, involving personal power, and this was beyond his knowledge. He sighed. He had no choice but to approach Nostor Vata, the king's witch.

Dep stood and studied the room.

This was a place of leisure and pleasure. He expected to see scantily-clad nubile women, fruit of the gods and wine, plenty of wine. A goblet lay on the floor, its red liquid spilt, near the sideboard. No bottles, no more goblets. Wine mixed with blood. He noticed his own bloody footprints – and those of Banstrike and Cursh – *but there were no others*. Most odd, indeed.

Business-like, he fished out a small black leather pouch and bagged the eye and nose. Then he removed a thin sliver of coloured paper and dabbed its edge into the spilt wine; the colour changed, but not red, rather blue. Poison, then. That was the female assassin's method, though it clearly went awry and cost her life.

***

"I find it hard to believe that you've developed a sudden case of memory loss," Watchman Dep said, levelling his dark brown eyes on the proprietor of the House of Velvet, Ska-ama. The office was small, two walls filled with shelving. Only high narrow windows admitted daylight. Shadows abounded wherever Dep looked.

"I'm trying to remember, Watchman." He leant on his desk top, screwed-up his features. "But... it is the shock. Who was she?"

"I was hoping you'd tell me."

Ska-ama shook his balding head and his jowls wobbled. "I didn't recognise her. How could I, with... with..."

"What about her other features? They weren't defiled by her killer."

Ska-ama nodded hesitantly. "She – a terrible waste, she had a good body... but nothing that would identify her for me."

"Do you know who was visiting your establishment earlier today?"

"No, I can't keep account of..."

"The law says you should." Dep sighed. "I will have to close you down, since you're incapable of abiding by the law."

"But – some very important people visit here. They don't want their names associated with... with my house."

"I'll spare their reputations and blushes, providing you give me the information I require."

Reluctantly, Ska-ama got up, moved sluggishly to a shelf and removed a book. "My receptionist records every person who enters and when they leave."

"Really?"

"Yes."

"So, since the woman's body was found the place has emptied. And she managed to make a note of everyone leaving?"

"I imagine so. It's her job."

Dep took the book, leafed through its pages, found the most recent entries. "Seemingly not. A good half-dozen visitors are not logged out. Yet they certainly are not here now."

"An oversight. My receptionists are usually very conscientious."

"I'm sure they are. And doubtless being scared of vicious murderers, they abandoned their post." He wasn't going to get anything out of Ska-ama. "I need to interview your... staff."

"I'll arrange it at once. But please don't keep them too long. They have a job, you know. Time is money."

"Since you said 'please', I'll do my best."

"Thank you, Watchman." Irony was lost on him, clearly.

Dep sent his two men away to check on the whereabouts of today's visitors listed in the receptionist's book. In the meantime, he spent the next two orms interviewing the men and women "entertainers" who "catered for all tastes". Every one of them vowed that none of their company was missing. The dead woman was a stranger to them. This suggested that she had entered this place without being noticed, which wouldn't be difficult for an adept assassin, and was here on a killing contract.

***

First Durinma of Juvous

At about the same time that Dep's men returned to report that only one person on their list couldn't be located, a man of letters called Pro-dem Hom, a message arrived from his chief, Prime Watchman Zen-il. A man identified as Pro-dem Hom had been found drowned in a vat of red ink in the dye processing factory in sector five in the Second City.

Prime Watchman Zen-il met him at the factory. He was tall, thick-set with piercing slate-grey eyes and wrinkled features. His uniform was the usual plaid, tight-fitting; he wore knee-high black leather boots.

The dead man was unclothed and had been deprived of one eye and his tongue; which were clutched in the right and left fists respectively. 'S1' had been burned into his forehead.

Staff who found the wordsmith had recognised him as Pro-dem Hom immediately since he often visited for writing supplies.

"Welde, I want this murderer caught soon," said Zen-il, his voice grating. He gazed at the morticians who removed the corpse, splashing the floor in ink, making crazy patterns.

"As do I, sir." He bagged the eye and tongue in a separate leather pouch, tied it to his belt, alongside the other evidence bag. "It's not going to be easy, though."

"Your cases are not meant to be easy, Welde. That's why they're special investigations."

"Indeed, sir." Dep shook his head. "Nobody saw anything. The place was full of shadows, according to the night-watchman when he found the body floating face-down."

"Chasing shadows is not within our remit. Give me a flesh-and-blood killer. Soon. Before he strikes again!"

"Or she, sir?"

Zen-il growled, spun on his heel and stomped away, flinging over his shoulder, "Yes, 'or she'!"

***

She didn't appear too distressed at being made a new widow, Dep mused, sitting opposite Pro-dem Zimera. Maybe it was her upbringing, a reluctance to show emotion to strangers, especially if on official business? Good breeding, perhaps; she was the daughter of Xarop, one of the oldest nobles in the city. Her upturned nose twitched; maybe she'd caught a whiff of the contents of the evidence bags at his belt?

Wealthy just didn't describe Zimera and her family. They lived here in the Doltra Complex, which was perched upon huge stone-block pylons and, on his approach, he felt it looked obscenely bright and clean in comparison to the dark and sullied earth surrounds beneath it. Nobody walked near the foundations, where lay the caved-in remains of an older city, which had collapsed in 1823; city and King Kculicide had perished, falling into flooded mines and, myth told, into the dread hands of the Underpeople.

"I'm sorry to ask you at a time like this," Dep said, his tone soft, caring, "but have you any idea where your husband might have been last night?"

Her grey-green eyes flickered away from his face, but only for a moment and then she returned his gaze steadily. "He frequented the Red Tellar..." Her hands fidgeted in her lap. She was withholding some information, he felt sure.

"Really?"

Zimera nodded. "I know that was his favourite place. He was a close friend of the innman, Ulran, I believe."

***

"I find it strange that Pro-dem Hom was a target for assassination," Ulran said, running a hand over his short black hair. The innman was tall and commanding, even in the simple attire of a green silk shirt and loose-fitting cotton trousers. He stood at the window of his tenth storey office, gazing down at the inn's roof-gardens.

Established some 570 years ago on the occasion of the First Festival of Brilansor, the Red Tellar Inn was situated in Marron Square in the Three Cities that comprised Lornwater. The renowned Red Tellar was the only inn in all Floreskand equipped with duelling rooms. Its ten-storey height alone would draw attention, only overshadowed in Lornwater by the two minars and the Eyrie above the Old City's palace. There were many specialised chambers, among them music and shrine rooms, hotel rooms, staff residences, private duelling rooms, the beer-hall and the Long Gymnasium.

Ulran turned, faced Dep. "He was a man of words, and posed no threat to anybody."

"Pro-dem Hom was rich and had the ear of the king," Dep replied from his chair. "A powerful man, by all accounts."

"True." Ulran's brown eyes narrowed. "And powerful men have enemies."

Dep nodded. "Just so. Why did he come to your inn?"

"For the amenities it offers. He particularly liked visiting the storyteller rooms. He would write down their tales."

"I suspect he wrote down other things. Would he be privy to improprieties here?"

"Hidden knowledge can be powerful, I admit. It's possible he saw someone or something that might adversely affect a reputation, if you concern yourself with such matters."

"But you have a reputation that goes before you, Ulran," Dep countered.

"It is nothing that I foster or invite. It is the nature of a gossip-hungry public that they settle on certain individuals. I'm one of those individuals." He shrugged. "It means nothing. Celebrity is base coin."

"Do you know if Pro-dem Hom was working on a speech for the king?"

Ulran laughed. "He would need to write a fine speech for any of the king's words to be praised, I assure you." His face clouded, serious. "I do not talk sedition, it is just an observation. Our king is not widely liked by his subjects."

Dep sucked in through his teeth. "Have you any idea why Pro-dem Hom was in the House of Velvet?"

Ulran arched an eyebrow. "It's a pleasure house. I imagine he was seeking pleasure where he could find it, as it was no secret that his wife hadn't provided him with any for several years..."

That would explain her lack of bereavement. "It's puzzling. He went missing from the House of Velvet and turned up dead at the dye factory," Dep mused. "The room assigned to him was where we found the dead assassin. If Pro-dem Hom eluded his female assassin, why didn't he call out the watchman?"

"Yes, it is a mystery. Have you a name for the assassin yet?"

Dep shook his head. "Their gildmaster is my next call."

"Strange, isn't it?"

"What?" Dep asked.

"The assassin's gild is illegal, yet it is allowed to flourish."

Dep shrugged. "I've had a similar discussion with the Prime Watchman more than once. We consider that they will exist whether we proscribe them or not. Perhaps having a gild permits some kind of oversight."

"Perhaps. The killer of the assassin might have taken Pro-dem Hom, kidnapped him?"

"It's a slim possibility, innman. Surely they would have been seen by somebody. Yet none of those interviewed so far know anything."

Ulran pursed his thick lips, frowned. "Drowning in ink suggests something premeditated and vicious. Despite the presence of the dead assassin, it seems that Pro-dem Hom was singled out for an unusual death. The colour of the ink might be significant too."

Dep jotted down a note about checking on the colour red in magical rituals.

Ulran stroked his chin. "He was a good man with words, and I liked him. I'll make my own enquiries, I think."

"Have a care, Ulran, don't tread on my toes."

"I will tread so lightly you won't know where I've been," Ulran said.

III

Shifting 'tween supernal myth and every day,
They enjoy fearful images wondrously born.
And they thrive on these myriad feelings torn
By the dark deceit that suborns what is true.

Their world is unlike ours in every way.
It's spectral in aspect, where dusk's forever worn,
Always at the mercy of effulgent light shone,
Be they god-hewn or man-made in effulgent hue.

Morton Faulkner

- *A Life of Their Own*, from
The Collected Works of Nasalmn Feider (1216-1257)
***
First Sapin of Juvous

"Yes, this ring belonged to Aba-pet Fara," explained Gildmaster Jentore, turning the pages of a thick tome. "Now, we have only six female assassins on our books." His tone seemed to suggest that the woman's death was an inconvenience to the gild bookkeeping, rather than a human tragedy. He stopped, pointed to an open page and an illustration. "See, these small chevrons intertwined with berries. The fruit stalks twine from the left, indicating the wearer is female." He held the ring against the drawing; the images matched.

"Good," Dep said. "At least we now have a name for the victim. Was she on gild business?"

"Yes." Jentore indicated a column of dates and amounts of money below the illustration. "She registered two days ago, see... Of course, an assassin does not record who the target is, solely that there has been a commission, and the fee obtained, so that a percentage can be contributed to the gild's coffers."

Dep nodded, quite aware of the process and not a little irritated by the gildmaster's manner. It was not unusual, he knew. Most gildmasters felt they were above the king's law. The best of them was old Fascar Dak, gildmaster of precious metals and the city's Great Gildmaster; he was always gracious and honest in his dealings with the watchmen. More than could be said of Olelsang, the gildmaster of saddle-makers, who oozed corruption from every pore yet possessed an indefinable aura that drew allegiance to him like flies to manure. "Do you think Aba-pet was intent on a target when she went to the House of Velvet?"

"I would hope so. I mean, it would be demeaning for her to be there, otherwise. You know, I'm quite shocked to hear she was found there. Naked, you say?"

"Yes, Gildmaster. The mutilation goes beyond anything I've encountered."

Gildmaster Jentore shook his head, and his long white hair whispered over his narrow shoulders. "I wish I could help, Watchman. I agree with you, the signs are not good. It is of dark significance. You have little choice, I fear. You must consult Nostor Vata." As he spoke the witch's name his mouth twisted as if in distaste. Witches had no gild; they were above all that: the gods endowed them with their arcane powers.

"Thank you for your time, Gildmaster."

"I suppose you will have to report how Aba-pet Fara was found?"

"Yes, of course, I must."

"I would hope you would have no need to besmirch the gild. Perhaps you could mention that she was fully clothed?"

"I don't think so, Gildmaster Jentore. The facts are the facts and we cannot condone tampering with them."

"No, of course not, I understand…"

"Believe me, the manner of her death and the whereabouts will be old news and soon forgotten. Your gild's reputation won't be sullied."

"I trust not, Watchman Welde."

***

Zen-il reported to the king about Pro-dem Hom's assassination and stood patiently awaiting a response. Queen Jikkos sat on the adjacent throne, her gimlet sky-blue eyes glaring into his while she twirled a be-ringed finger round her long braids of blonde hair.

A nevus on Saurosen's left cheek, in the vague shape of a spider, grew inflamed. His almond-shaped eyes grew moist. "A dear friend and a wonderful speechwriter. He often knew what I wanted to say before I did." His voice was more rasping than usual. He was tall, thin, and wiry with narrow stooped shoulders. He gestured dismissal with manicured hands. "Excuse us, Prime Watchman, so that we may mourn his tragic loss."

"Sire, before I leave, I must point out that his killer is still at large."

The king fingered a small tuft of brown hair under his lower lip. "I understand that. So what are you *not* telling me?"

"It is believed that your speechwriter's death was invoked by magic. The assassin has killed twice already…"

King Saurosen's reddish-brown complexion paled as he croaked, "Twice? I thought…"

"The other death need not concern you, sire. Save that it was caused by the same baleful hand."

Saurosen turned to his queen.

Her alabaster features betrayed no emotion.

"Dearest," he said, "I fear… I fear we need to take action, don't you?"

She leaned toward him, the low neckline of her silver dress displaying a snow-white bosom separated by a gold necklace. "I agree, my dear." Her voice was sensuous; her rosebud mouth curved. "Whatever keeps you safe."

"Yes. Safe." Saurosen stepped down and paced in front of the thrones, his gold sandals slapping. Then, abruptly he glanced at Zen-il. "I have it!"

"Sire?"

"I will issue an edict. We must cancel the Kcarran carnival..."

"Excellent, my dear!" exclaimed his queen, clapping her hands, the rings on every finger clinking loudly.

He continued to tread to and fro, excited by his idea. "Yes, you must curtail free passage of strangers into the Three Cities – at least until the assassin is found..."

"But, sire, the carnival celebrates the crowning of Lornwater's first king, Kcarran.

The people have enjoyed their carnival for 1062 years..."

"You are so precise that it is tedious, Prime Watchman Zen-il!" Saurosen railed. "It is precisely because they love their carnival that I will outlaw it! If they wish to harbour an assassin, then they will *suffer*!"

***

King Saurosen's witch, Nostor Vata was a contradiction in many ways, Welde Dep believed. For someone of fifty summers, she possessed the complexion of an adolescent, with piercing blue-grey eyes; perhaps her looks could be attributed to her inscrutable powers. She welcomed him graciously enough into her chamber, her tall shapely figure gliding over the patterned floor tiles on rope-soled sandals. Her long black hair draped over her shoulders; the left shoulder was bare, as was that breast, which appeared scarred. Her gown was a deep ochre colour, tied with a black leather belt at her waist. Gold armbands and bangles jangled at her wrists. "I am flattered that you should wish to consult with me, Watchman Welde." Her voice was like surf sifting over sand.

He bowed slightly. She was a powerful woman in her own right, even if she hadn't had the king as her patron. Her friends were rich and influential, not least the Nemond family. "In matters of the unknowable, Nostor Vata, you are matchless. I seek your guidance on a troubling matter."

She gestured to a seat.

He sat and she lowered herself into a sofa opposite. "This would be the manner of Pro-dem Hom's murder?"

"You are well informed," he replied with a fleeting smile.

She didn't return his smile but tapped her forehead – a narrow vertical crease above the bridge of her long straight nose. "The third eye has its uses."

"I don't suppose it has seen who the murderer is, by any chance?"

She smiled now. "A fine jest, Watchman. If my power were that great, you can be assured I would have informed you at once."

"Can you explain the meaning of this, please? A female assassin was found with her face cut off and her right eye in her left hand, her nose in her right hand. I believe it's ritual magic of some kind."

She leaned forward. "Intriguing. But what has this to do with my king's speechwriter?"

"Pro-dem Hom's left eye was put in his right hand, and his tongue in his left."

"Balance in all things," she mused, fingering a curved knife at her belt. "You're not familiar with our manderon magic, are you?"

"How did you know?"

"You hark from Tarakanda, originally, I believe, though few know this."

Dep shifted in his seat. "I would rather maintain that secret."

"It will not go beyond these walls, Watchman." She withdrew her knife, flicked the blade at her bare breast. It was only a small nick in the flesh and drew blood; small droplets fell onto the marble tile at her feet. The blood spots spattered slightly. She sheathed the knife and her right hand absently dabbed at the little cut while she studied the bloody pattern. "I see," she whispered, licking her lips. "Yes, this is troublesome."

"In what way?"

"The transposition of those organs in this manner is part of a forbidden ritual. This ritual can conjure up a melog…"

"But that's pure myth, surely?"

"So some say. I am not aware of anyone who has been successful with this ritual. Often, it just results in several dead bodies and displaced organs – a messy business…"

Dep shuddered. "Thank you, Nostor Vata."

At that moment, King Saurosen entered. "Vata, I was not aware you had company." His deep almond coloured eyes glanced at the blood spatter. "Who are you to consult with my muse?" he demanded of Dep. His eyes narrowed and he gazed with suspicion at his witch.

Rising to his feet, Dep bowed. "I am Watchman Welde Dep, working for…"

"Zen-il, yes, of course! What are you doing here? Shouldn't you be in the city tracking down the assassin? Even now, my assassination could be plotted already!"

"There are special factors that…"

"Never mind, man. Be gone!"

Bowing again, Dep made for the door. "Thank you, Nostor Vata!" he called and left.

Before Dep moved away from the door, he heard the king

remonstrate, "I'm disappointed in you, Vata. Can't I trust anyone now?"

***

Ulran left his inn and walked the streets of the city, moving from the House of Velvet to the dye factory, asking questions of the people along the way. He knocked on doors of houses that overlooked the roadways and alleys and slowly he constructed an image. A most unusual picture emerged.

Pro-dem Hom was a well-known figure in the area. Many had glimpsed him walking rather awkwardly. Some felt he was deep in his cups. Others wondered if he were ill. Almost everybody who saw the writer felt confused because his entire body seemed bathed in a freakish gray miasma. There was no other description. A grey mist enveloped Pro-dem Hom as he walked.

The dye factory was locked, the night-watchman vowed. He could not explain how Pro-dem Hom and his murderer could enter and drown him. "I did my rounds as usual and he certainly wasn't in the ink vat when I left; when I returned, there he was. Such a shock, I can tell you…"

Ulran then checked the home of the murdered assassin, Aba-pet Fara. She lived alone, over a leather-goods shop. The smell of leather permeated everywhere. It was evident that Watchmen had searched the place, but it had been cursory. He soon found a secret cache under the floorboards beneath a sideboard. The hiding place contained money and a parchment notebook with figures and names scrawled, detailing her contacts, contracts and her fees. Some fees were clearly freelance, as she didn't deduct gild dues, while others showed a proportion allocated to the gild. One name in the book leapt out at him and he smiled. Welde Dep would be pleased. Though, in fact, what charges could he muster? Since Aba-pet Fara did not assassinate Pro-dem Hom as planned.

***

First Sapinma of Juvous

Illasa completed her scrying and sat back, exhausted. She was concerned. The innman Ulran was nosing around, getting close. Ulran has too much influence among the common folk and would do all he could to prevent an uprising, and it was the defeat of Saurosen she craved. If she could get the king's first cousin, Nemond Thand on the throne, she would wield the power, since dear Thand was susceptible to maladies of the mind. For the next two orms she waited impatiently. Finally, in answer to her secret summons, there was a knock on her door. She let Badol Melomar in, ensuring that nobody in the street had seen him.

"I trust this visit will be worth my while, witch," he said, his voice thick and throaty. He was an unprepossessing specimen of manhood, with a face covered in pustules, rheumy eyes of tarnished coin and moist thick lips seemingly always turned up in a scowl.

"Oh, it is, Badol." He was head and innman of the powerful Open House Combine and he'd had a running vendetta with the Red Tellar for an age. "I wish to finance an assassination. It would be to your benefit."

"Go on. I'm listening."

"Offer a hefty purse for the life of Ulran. I will pay."

He stroked his forked beard that was reminiscent of a swallowtail and grinned, exposing a saw-toothed mouth. "I like it. But why?"

"You don't need to know my reasons. Of course my involvement will remain secret." She described an incantation in the air with her sharp fingernails. "Or you will regret being born."

Badol hunched his burly body. "It will be arranged." He held out his hand.

She dropped a pouch of coin into his palm. "You will receive half again when the deed is done." She opened the door for him and he left.

She had been tempted to use her melog, but no, the conjuration was already complete, the runes cast, the names given, so the assassin would not directly kill anyone else – unless they got in his way, such as the unfortunate Aba-pet Fara. And she doubted if she could repeat the incantation successfully. It had taken much from her life source to accomplish. Anyway, Badol did not need to know about the shadow assassin, for conjuring a melog was blasphemous, and she doubted if the conniving man's scruples could be entirely trusted.

***

Second Sabin of Juvous

Prime Watchman Zen-il paced in front of Dep. The exotic floor covering showed wear, as if his chief made a habit of pacing up and down. This was only the fourth time he'd been in his chief's office housed here with the Royal Council in sector one of the Old City.

"Welde, I have been apprised of a rumour"

"Where from, sir?"

Zen-il pursed his lips then shrugged. "I was visiting – in an official capacity, I might add – the House of Velvet."

"But I questioned all of them. They told me nothing."

"Yes, but this is new – a fresh rumour."

"You're at pains to point out it's only a rumour, sir."

"Many of our watchmen rely on whispers for leads, Welde. You know that."

"True, sir. So... What is this whisper you heard?"

"There's a new assassin's target. It's supposed to be Ulran of the Red Tellar."

The innman. "Really? Whispers, you say? Usually, it's merely pillow-talk."

"Have a care, Welde..."

"Just an observation from experience, sir."

"I thought you should be aware of this... information."

"But, sir, my job is to follow facts, not whispers..."

Zen-il nodded. "I know," he responded with a grin. "Who'd be foolish enough to go up against the innman of the Red Tellar, eh?"

***

Ulran's son, Ranell, betrayed concern in his brown eyes. He ran a hand through his dark wavy hair. "Begetter, there suddenly appear to be too many assassins for comfort," he said, his voice husky.

Ulran grinned. "It is only gossip."

The innman was slightly taller than his son but, Dep noted, they were both slim and powerfully muscled; doubtless formidable opponents. "Your son has a point, Ulran. I think you should be cautious. It's quite possible that your enquiries have already stirred up something."

"What will you do with that evidence?" Ulran asked, changing the subject.

Dep held up the notebook. "This will convict Pro-dem Hom's wife of conspiracy to murder." He made for the door. "Thanks for finding it. I'll have words to say with my two men, be assured!" At the door, he added, "Listen to your son's counsel, Ulran."

After Watchman Welde had left, Ranell said, "Begetter, I insist that you must abide by the watchman's warning. You must be accompanied at all times by two of our men."

Ulran grinned. "At all times?"

"Yes. Wherever you go in the Three Cities." Ulran raised an eyebrow. "I know you can handle yourself, Begetter, but these assassins are underhand people."

"If the whispers are true," Ulran countered.

"I'd feel happier," Ranell said.

***

"This is most displeasing, Watchman," said the gildmaster. "Your evidence shows that Aba-pet Fara's fees did not always go through the gild."

"This could be worse, couldn't it?" Dep said. "Others might be doing the same..."

Jentore wailed. "We can't have assassins freelancing. It will be anarchy!"

"It might be the death of your gild," Dep suggested, hiding a smile. The gildmaster was going to have problems balancing his books.

***

Lornwater library was imposing, a tall austere gray building, its pillars and windowsills carved ornately with ancient symbols. The shelves were tier upon tier, some cloaked in cobwebs, others laden with dust. Only the books near the reception desk seemed to be dust-free. Dep wondered if reading might be a dying art. That would be sad, he reflected. Wisdom and knowledge resided in these countless tomes; just waiting for inquisitive minds to unlock their secrets.

He needed to read more about melogs. And brush up on manderon magic. The eye and nose in Aba-pet Fara's hands, and the eye and tongue in Pro-dem Hom's must mean something other than signifiers for a melog.

At the nearest broad table sat a young woman, leaning over a tome entitled *Songs of the Overlord*. At least she'd found what she was looking for; he gazed ruefully at the dusty shelves. Where to begin?

"The most secret books are those with the thickest dust layer," the woman offered, glancing up from her book, her angular and thin face framed by long lank black hair. Her voice was soft, pleasant. To one side of her was a satchel with faded initials engraved in the leather.

"How did you know I sought arcane knowledge?"

She shrugged, shifting her brown eyes away, seeming uncomfortable under his direct gaze. "I believe you seek knowledge of the seven senses, Watchman, though perhaps you do not yet know it." She indicated the next shelf along, on his right. "You'll find what you want in there – *The Forbidden Arcane.*"

"Seven senses?" He was not familiar with those beyond the normal five. He had heard of a sixth, and understood some folk could master it, and he thought it was fanciful myth. But seven?

The woman rose, her features abruptly pale, her forehead creased. "I'm sorry, I must leave. My head aches. I fear something is amiss... soon..." She grabbed her satchel and fled the library with her book under her arm.

"Amiss soon?" he wondered. When in fact, there was something very amiss right now.

It didn't take him long to find the tome the woman alluded to. He used a sleeve to brush off the dust, sneezed and opened the reedpaper pages.

"Ancient teaching propounded that the soul of mankind contains seven properties which are under the influence of the seven planets," he read. "Fire animates, earth gives the sense of feeling, water gives speech, air gives taste, mist gives sight, flowers give hearing, and the ranmeron wind gives smelling." He sat back, intrigued. "So," he mused, "the seven senses are animation, feeling, speech, taste, sight, hearing and smelling?"

By the time he left, he had gleaned some knowledge that might be of use; whether it was enough, only the gods would know.

IV

Theirs is a world where meaning has no sense,
Where evil is black and good is not grey but white,
Where darkness succumbs to implacable cleansing light,
Somewhere concealed, clouded in mystery and rue.

Here be spirits lost and full of offence,
A place of unknowing where imagery is all,
And the intangible takes form, where trust takes a fall,
Obscured, treacherous places, hidden from direct view.
- *A Life of Their Own*, from
The Collected Works of Nasalmn Feider (1216-1257)

***

Second Sabinma of Juvous

The streets leaned in on them, corners lit by torch flames. With Berstarm and Trellen flanking him, Ulran was on his way to see Fet-usa Fin, a trader in weapons and poisons. It was highly likely that the female assassin Aba-pet Fara acquired the tools of her trade there.

Out of the shadows leaped four men, all armed with swords and knives.

Berstarm was taken unawares and fell with a fatal sword cut cleaving his chest.

Trellen dispatched his friend's attacker immediately, and then was hard-pressed by another swordsman.

Two men closed on Ulran. One of them laughed. "Hey, Hun, he doesn't carry a weapon!"

Hun replied, "Easy meat, Phal!"

Ulran crouched, waiting, hands extended, the edges like knives.

Hun swung his sword and gaped. Ulran had somersaulted out of the way, spun on the ground and used his rigid legs to topple Hun. As Hun dropped his knife in shock, Ulran regained his feet, ducked the swooping sword blade of Phal.

Ulran jumped on top of the disoriented Hun, gaining purchase on the man's chest and dived at Phal. The move was totally unexpected. Phal stared and stumbled backwards, his weapons discarded, clanging on stone flags. The hilt of Hun's knife protruded from Phal's chest. As Phal's back crashed to earth, Ulran jumped clear and pivoted, ready for another attack.

It was all over, though. A death-cut having sliced his belly open, Trellen sat beside his fallen comrade and squinted up at Ulran. "I despatched the other two, innman."

Ulran knelt and gently rested a hand on Trellen's shoulder. "You fought well."

"But none live to tell you who bought them?"

Ulran shrugged. "It cannot be helped. Their attack was too sudden and vicious, without quarter. It was fight or die..." He let that thought linger, uncomfortably, as Trellen knew full well he was breathing his last. "I'm sorry, Trellen." He made the sign of the Overlord and an instant later closed the man's staring eyes.

"I see I arrived too late," Welde Dep said, turning a corner. "Six assassins who won't be collecting their fee, eh?"

Ulran cast a glance at the corpses. "Four assassins, Watchman. And two staunch men who worked and died for me."

***

Second Dekin of Juvous

Early in the morning, Den-orl Pin, the officer in charge of the royal stables, the man who organised the royal race meetings, was found dead by the stable lads.

By the time that Welde Dep arrived on the scene, whispers were filling the streets of the cities. Ulran joined him and observed, "Den-orl Pin was an inveterate gambler."

"Really?" Dep nodded. "That might explain his death, I suppose." He gestured at the corpse.

Den-orl Pin had choked on a mouth filled with coin of the realm. And his left eye and right ear were placed in his hands. 'S2' had been burned into his forehead.

"It's our assassin all right," Dep said, bagging the eye and ear. "Yet nobody saw anything, not so much as a glimmer of light." The royal stables were shadowy places at night. The king refused to pay for torches. His argument was plain: "Nobody needs to go anywhere near my horses at night. Anyone caught doing so must be on nefarious business!"

"Den-orl Pin was killed in this empty stall," Ulran said. "None of the horses were harmed? None are missing?"

"No. The purpose was to kill him, that's all."

"Another connection to the king."

"Do you think the killer is telling us something?"

Ulran nodded. "The message is clear: Be careful if you work for King Saurosen IV."

V

Phantoms are real in these places, in dim recesses.
Apparitions appear and vanish as the moon waxes and wanes.
Comely colours are dappled, blemished by their stains.
They darken faces in metaphor, and their feelings in grue.

Wherever you go, they will be there, ubiquitous, voracious,
Screened from the seemingly real world by false logic
And reason and excuses so untrue that it is tragic.
Pretending they are harmless, one day you will surely rue.

It is of shadows that we speak, intangible and caliginous.
Yet do not be fooled by children's silly rigmarole,
For indeed shadows are evil and eat your soul.
Impalpable they be, but heed them, before they kill you.
- *A Life of Their Own*, from
The Collected Works of Nasalmn Feider (1216-1257)

***

King Saurosen IV stormed into the treasurer's room. Three walls comprised ceiling to floor shelves, all crammed with scrolls of parchment. The wizened grey-haired treasurer sat bent over a desk, scribbling numbers on a sheet of columns.

"Treasurer," Saurosen snapped, "I have received cloaked demands from Lord Tanellor, Duke of Oxor. He requires funds for the mines."

Hesitantly, the treasurer stood. "Cloaked, sire?"

"Only a fool would openly demand anything of a king, fool!"

"Sorry, sire. Of course. Forgive my stupidity. What is the Duke's reason for asking?"

"He believes the mines are at risk. Require new supports, or something…"

"Are they faulty, sire?"

"I don't know or care! I turned him away, and I told him to make sure his miners don't slacken! Oh, sit down before you fall over!"

Obediently, the treasurer sat and hastily scrawled some figures on his parchment sheet, then glanced up. "But, sire, if there should be an accident, the revenue from the lost output would also be forfeit. As it is, there is no money in the coffers." He raised a sly eyebrow. "Much has been diverted to special projects, as you are aware, sire..."

"There must be no record of that, damn you!"

"Nor is there, sire. I merely point out the fact." He paused, mused, adding, "Yet, a mining accident would not be good. Not good at all..."

"Yes, I can see that now." Saurosen sucked air through his teeth. "So, you're saying I should finance Tanellor's mine maintenance?"

"It would be prudent, sire. As for funds, you could perhaps try your financier friend; he has agreed loans in the past. You can repay him at the next tax round, anyway..."

"Yes, Cor-aba Grie is usually most accommodating. Though he seems forever greedy for more land..."

"Greedy, yes. Isn't all of his kind like that? Personally, sire, I abhor financial people, but they seem an evil we cannot do without."

***

Dep and his men questioned the staff at the royal stables. Ulran told Dep that he was going to visit the financier, Cor-aba Grie. "He supplies Saurosen with funds and in return is given more land and power. I know that Den-orl Pin gambled too much and owed Cor-aba Grie money. Maybe that's a connection."

"That's a good thought. I'll join you." Dep turned to Banstrike, told him, "I'm going to the Doltra Complex. If you find anything of value, send Cursh to me."

"Right, Chief."

***

Cor-aba Grie studied his separate towers of coins on the desk; the metal glinted in the light of a guttering torch. It tallied. He hated it when his accounting and the money didn't add up. The king had already promised an entire street for his next loan, ostensibly to cover the maintenance of the Oxor mines. He smiled at the prospect of all those rent payments and then wondered how much would be siphoned off for the king's own ends. No matter. *Wealth and power accrued for me, regardless.* He ran a hand over his white gold-braided burnoose made from the finest cotton of Lellul. This attire hid his abnormally large size, he had to admit. Not that he had many callers.

The torch flickered but he had no need to replace it, since his counting was complete. He got up and put a fresh one in the sconce, then shook his head, annoyed with himself. The cost of shagunblend had continued to increase, yet he had failed to invest in their manufacture.

Out of the corner of his eye he glimpsed his shadow. Odd. It was moving, but it couldn't be caused by the flames from the torch as he hadn't lit the new one. Rather, it seemed to slip out of sight, behind furniture. Very odd behaviour for a shadow. Fanciful. I need a drink, he thought, when abruptly he felt something tug at his left foot and ankle. He glanced down, expecting to see a neighbour's cat – the damnable creature was constantly fouling his balcony.

His heart missed a beat. His foot was black, so dark he couldn't discern the pale leather sandal. It was a blurry shape. He sensed a vague tingling in his calf, then his knee, and then his thigh. Now the same troubling sensation was starting in his other leg. By the gods, what was happening?

He stood up, and found he couldn't control his legs. He stumbled back against the desk, his hip jarring, and the piles of coins toppled, spewing onto the tiled floor.

He lifted the hem of his burnoose and he gasped in dismay. Already, his legs up to his groin were blurred, black – like a shadow. Involuntarily, he dropped the material and gritted his teeth as the oppressive sensation moved up his body, beneath his clothing, constricting his vast belly, clamping onto his chest. Was he having a seizure, a heart-attack, was this a hallucination before death?

His eyes started. Some kind of dark latticework emerged from the hem of his clothing, from his sleeves, out of his chest opening, and engulfed him. He tried to move, to grip the desk for purchase, but whatever steps he took were ungainly, rigid, and terribly painful. He didn't seem to be in control of his body!

Gradually, he found that without his own volition, he was moving around the desk, towards the open doors that led onto the balcony.

***

Together, Ulran and Dep left the royal stables and made their way through the throng of people to the Doltra Complex. The financier owned a luxurious apartment near the top of a tall building. The stairs numbered in the hundreds. But Ulran knew it wouldn't bother the financier, who hardly ever left the building; he could afford others to do his bidding. Access using ropes and pulleys would be preferable, he thought, perhaps based on the same principle used at the Ren-kan crossing of the Manderranmeron Fault.

Ulran was in the peak of fitness, however, and ascended quickly, soon leaving Dep behind. "Go on, don't mind me! I'll catch up, probably tomorrow!"

Even so, Ulran arrived at the financier's floor a little breathless. He stopped, suddenly cautious. The door was open, ajar. Not good.

Voices, far inside.

He slid in and crossed the lounge floor that was carpeted with a variety of Lellul rugs. The voices came from the balcony, outside the smaltglass window.

Soundlessly, he approached.

He eased the curtain aside.

There was only a single figure, standing on the parapet of the balcony wall. He'd seen Cor-aba Grie before, on those rare occasions when they attended infrequent royal functions. This was definitely him – but more gross. Some kind of dark lattice-work encased him, like an exo-skeleton. Cor-aba's arms jerked spasmodically, as if he were fighting himself. His voice emerged as a strangulated croak: "No, you cannot force me. I have free will!"

Then, alarmingly, Cor-aba's mouth twisted and a different voice emerged, deeper, sinister: "I take your essence and become whole! Your death serves me – and my mistress!"

Shadow flickered over Cor-aba's entire body, as if sentient.

Night, the shadow of light... He'd heard that before. Night shadow consumed him. Was this the melog that Dep spoke about? He glanced behind, into the lounge, and saw unlit shagunblend torches in their sconces. He rushed inside, fished out his flint from his belt pouch and hastily lit the torch. Light dispels shadow.

As the torch burst into bright effulgent flame, Dep staggered in the doorway. "Made it..." His eyes widened. "What?" Then he noticed Cor-aba struggling with the shadow entity that imprisoned his own body. "By the gods!"

"Is that the melog?" Ulran demanded.

"I – I don't know – I think so..."

"This torch light should banish it!" Ulran took a pace forward.

"No, wait! Stop!" Dep fidgeted with the evidence pouches on his belt.

"Throw the torch down here!" He pointed to the floor.

"You're sure?"

"If you scare off the melog, it will be free to kill again – and we don't know who else. Maybe even the king!"

Ulran nodded and threw the torch onto a fawn and red furry rug.

"Get ready to catch hold of Cor-aba!" Dep instructed.

Moving towards the balcony, Ulran noticed that Cor-aba was

unsteady, about to overbalance on the parapet. Abruptly, the financier raised a foot to step forward into space and tottered on one leg.

Ulran glanced over his shoulder. Dep had thrown the evidence pouches into the flames.

Cor-aba let out an eldritch yell.

Ulran lunged forward, grabbed the financier's calf; it was cold, like stone. The shout transformed, became high-pitched, female perhaps. The latticework of dark shadow shimmered all around Cor-aba. Ulran held on tight, leaning over the balcony wall.

Suspended upside down, Cor-aba stared up with a single eye, since his other had been plucked out. 'S3' had been burned into his forehead. He was screaming in pain, while the black entity danced up and down his body; it seemed baulked by the presence of Ulran, couldn't move up past him.

Finally, the dark shadow imploded and the financier split into several pieces and Ulran was left holding a single leg.

Scanning the building, Ulran was sure that no vestige of the shadow assassin had survived.

***

"Ulran, sudden death seems to haunt you wherever you go," Welde Dep said, stepping onto the balcony.

"Yes, like a shadow."

"Thank the gods the melog was somehow attached to those extracted body parts..."

"The torch might have been enough, but we'll never know."

"And," Dep added, "I suppose we'll never know who was behind the shadow assassin?"

"There are a few witches in Lornwater. And in every city beyond. It could have been any one of them... Who knows where their allegiances really lie?"

"I don't know how I'm going to write up this report."

Ulran clapped Dep on the shoulder. "Blame Cor-aba, the financier, for the deaths, perhaps?"

"Do you think this is the end of it, then?"

"I don't know. It depends on how easily a melog can be created. I would like to believe it is not so simple a task, even for a powerful witch."

"Well, I think that Saurosen's position has been seriously weakened. Those assassinated men were his backers."

"Then the king better tread with care."

Dep nodded. "My chief will inform him that the immediate threat is over."

"And the cancelled carnival?"

Dep ran a hand over his face. "I suspect the king will not revoke the edict. He'll feel threatened now that a number of his influential friends are no longer around…"

"The populace won't take kindly to his edict, you know."

"I know that, Ulran. We have to police thirty-three sectors of the Three Cities with too few watchmen as it is. We don't need this."

***

On his return to the inn, Ulran was met by Ranell and they embraced briefly. "News travels fast, Begetter. Whispers have already spread that the purse offered for your assassination has been withdrawn."

"That's good news. Until the next time, I suppose."

"Do you think Badol paid them to assassinate you, Begetter?"

"Probably, but there's no proof. I mentioned it to Watchman Welde and he says he'll keep an eye on Badol Melomar for a few moons, just in case."

"So, the deaths of those four assassins are the end of it?"

"For now. We can hope that the witch responsible will slip up in the future. We must see to the family of our two fallen men - Berstarm and Trellen."

"Yes, Begetter, of course."

"And then arrange for a recruitment drive – we need two good men to replace them."

PART ONE
THIRD SAPIN - FOURTH SABIN OF JUVOUS

The Song of the Overlord – Part the First:
How to explain the omniscient Overlord?
How shall I define what thing He is?
Chance is a word without reason;
Nothing can exist without a cause.
So it is with Him –
Wholly existent, and yet non-existent.
Whatever becometh naught out of entity
The meaning of that nothingness is He.

CHAPTER ONE
QUEST

> It is an unknown quantity veiled in a mystery within an enigma.
> – *The Book of Concealed Mystery* (Ascribed to Lhoretsorel)

After-morning sunlight streamed through the high windows to illuminate the Long Gymnasium and its polished wooden walls which were festooned with all kinds of physical training apparatus. The floor was a series of padded rush mats. The huge room dwarfed the seven people here.

The tension was almost palpable to the two onlookers as four prospective employees of the Red Tellar Inn advanced soundlessly, their eyes flashing warily at Ulran, the innman.

Behind Ulran, his son Ranell stood by the tall ironwood doors with Ulran's aide, the short black-skinned Aeleg.

Of the four enlistees, only Yorda and Krailek on the left gave the impression of being at ease; their movements were measured, eyes never leaving Ulran's.

Enlistment combat was traditionally unarmed and this day's would not deviate from the norm, though for reasons of honour no contender was ever searched. While these four wore their own colourful street clothes – breeches, boots and jerkins – Ulran, in complete contrast, stood barefoot, garbed in a single long voluminous garment of jet black, his left breast emblazoned with an embroidered white sekor.

Ulran studied the approach of the combatants. He nodded his head to indicate that the contest could begin.

Meetel was dark, tall and powerfully built. His long black hair streamed behind him as he rushed first, shrieking defiance. He had nerve – but no technique. With little effort Ulran skipped to safety. Close on Meetel's heels came Ephanel and the other two. Ulran ducked and weaved out of reach of grasping hands, flailing feet and fists.

By now all four must have realised there were no openings in the garment Ulran wore: he used neither arms nor legs to block or counter-attack: his speed was sufficient to avoid contact. They circled Ulran in a wary, predatory fashion.

As Meetel charged with rigid fingers lancing at the innman's eyes, Ulran lowered his head and Meetel's fingers shattered on impact with cranium-bone. Ulran swiftly moved away, leaving Meetel on one knee, tears of pain streaming as he clutched a broken hand.

Ephanel was squat and too muscular. His sallow features twisted as he delivered a tremendous kick.

Robes cracking with the sudden movement, the innman leapt high above the out-thrust leather boot and, as though from nowhere, the innman's legs whipped out from the material, full into Ephanel's stomach. The kick's force hurled Ephanel head over heels to land noisily among weights and dumb-bells. Ephanel was completely taken by surprise.

Without any openings save that for the wearer's head and feet, the garment's special properties were impressive. With the right force and inclination, the cloth could be penetrated easily and when the limb was again withdrawn into the folds, the opening would seal, leaving no trace. But if the right force could not be mastered, then the garment was little better than a burial shroud.

Krailek was short and wiry, his face careworn by weather and travel; his blue eyes darted to left and right, gauging distances. Yorda was tall with well-toned muscles, and deceptively light on his feet. Both, obviously determined on a joint action, simultaneously attacked Ulran from each side.

Ulran leapt in front of Krailek on his left, arms suddenly shooting out of the black garment; the surprise had hardly left Krailek's lined, weather-beaten face when he found himself grabbed, stunned and swinging in an arc towards the astonished Yorda. Both tumbled into the nearby wall, dazed and bruised.

Turning, Ulran reflected his son Ranell's fleeting smile: two would prove suitable for probationary employment, replacements of men recently slain by the shadow assassin. Yorda and Krailek. They would require a great deal of training to be a match for the rest of his men, but they had that special intelligent spark that –

Only one lightning-fast blow was necessary, delivered as Ulran pivoted on buckling knees: the punch, angled upwards, thudded into Meetel's solar plexus and seemed to travel through bone and flesh, rupturing the man's heart.

A small dagger fell from lifeless fingers and Ulran grasped it before the handle hit the floor.

A nasty weapon with serrated edges pointing to the hilt, it would extract entrails, flesh and muscle on withdrawal from the wound. Ulran knew it well: a tukluk, the brainchild of the Brethren of the Sword, the gild of the mercenaries. Ulran shook his head. "A man who would savour another's pain or misery," he mused, turning to the slowly recovering participants. "The test is not to win but to see how the fight is fought – and, indeed, how it is lost."

Without another word, he left the Long Gymnasium with his son and his aide close behind.

***

Looking down from his tenth storey office, Ulran gazed upon the vast variety of colour blossoming in the roof garden.

Decorative shagunblend lamps tinted sunlight in his office. Ulran divested himself of the Jhet-fibre garb and slowly his thick lips curved in a sanguinary grin. He pictured again the disconcerted look on Meetel's face.

Perhaps then, at the instant on the Edge – the moment between life and death – Meetel had comprehended that the cloth was the fabled Jhet-fibre woven by seamstresses from the Fane of the Overlord itself.

Ulran washed then dried himself on a small towel and donned a silk shirt from the wardrobe and a pair of loose-fitting cotton trousers which he tucked into brown hide boots.

In a rare moment of reverie, he idly fingered the large wall-chart that reminded him of the travels he and Ranell had made.

Ranell was quick to learn; yet after all his training he possessed a stubborn streak. Still, he'd done well, considering he had lacked a mother's warmth and love almost since birth. Ulran felt he could be justly proud of his son as the youth approached full adulthood.

A distinctive knock sliced into his thoughts.

"Come in, Ranell."

Though shorter than his sire, Ranell was otherwise in every way Ulran's progeny, from his dark wavy hair, alert brown eyes and almost classical facial features, to his slim yet powerfully muscled physique. He stood in the doorway that led into the anteroom; there, Ranell performed the duties of secretary to his father, in preparation for the day when he would succeed him to become Innman, Red Tellar.

Formally, he gave a respectful nod. "Begetter," he said, assuming the common family address for an esteemed father. "There's a strange silent fellow in the passage waiting to see you." His eyes gleamed, amused. "He speaks with an air of the arcane about him and is weighted down with countless talismen."

"And what did you say?"

"I expressed sincere apologies for having kept him waiting and requested that he be patient while I ascertained when or if you would be available..."

"But didn't you ask him his business here?"

"Yes, Begetter – I tried, but he just smiled knowingly and said his business was with you."

"I see."

"He's unarmed – and looks as though he wouldn't know which end of a sword to hold were he given one!"

"Very good. I'll see this mysterious visitor now."

At that moment Aeleg stepped in, his old skin creased in anxiety. "Ulran!" he said, breathless. "Thousands of them! Sky's full!" His eyes shone in excitement. "Never so many before – red tellars!"

Scalrin. Heart hammering though outwardly calm, Ulran brushed past his son and aide and, ignoring the seated stranger, he leapt the stairs three at a time to the roof.

***

The midday sky was brimful with red tellars. The entire populace of Lornwater seemed to be out – on the street, rooftops, city walls or at windows – looking at these mystical creatures.

Even Ulran's height was dwarfed by the bird's wingspan. With bristling carmine red feathers, yellow irises and darting black slit-pupils, the red tellar appeared a formidable bird, predatory in mien, an aspect completed with lethal talons and huge curved beak. And yet not one living soul, Ulran included, had once reported seeing a red tellar eat. To compound the enigma surrounding them, they were rarely observed landing *anywhere*. And apart from the muted whisper of their wings, they created no sound at all – unlike the local avians that infested most eaves, lofts and trees in the city.

Ulran burst out onto the inn's flat roof as a shadow darkened the area.

A solitary red tellar broke formation and dived down from the main body. Ulran instinctively glanced back at Aeleg and Ranell; but Scalrin's sharp eyes had spotted them and he veered over to the opposite side of the roof.

A slight crack of mighty wings, then the bird was down, talons gripping the low wall by a shrine to Opasor, lesslord of birds.

Ulran motioned for the others to stay where they were.

Aeleg and Ranell stared, as if thunderstruck that a red tellar should land on their roof.

Recognition flickered in Scalrin's eyes as Ulran knelt before the bird's great feathered chest. Without hesitation the innman reached out, gently stroked the upper ridge of the bird's beak and smoothed the silken soft crest.

In answer, Scalrin's ear feathers ruffled and he settled, pulling his greater wing coverts well into his body.

The innman exhaled through his nose, then relaxed, steadying his breathing till it was shallow. Ulran closed his eyes and slowly outstretched his hand again, palm flat upon Scalrin's breast. A rapid heartbeat pulsed under his palpating hand and transmitted sympathetic vibrations through his own frame.

Their rapport created a bridge and across this span came primitive communication, sense-impressions. Ulran gathered that something was seriously amiss in Arion.

Something terrible, something concerning Scalrin.

Ulran opened his eyes, surprised to discover moisture brimmed his lids for the first time since his wife Ellorn's death.

Then Scalrin was gone, powerful primaries lifting him up to the vast multitude of his brethren. As far as the horizon they still flocked.

But what did it portend?

***

"Trouble in Arion?" the stranger enquired as Ulran stepped from the stairs into the passage.

Ulran did not show the surprise he felt at this disclosure.

The wiry stranger was evidently chagrined at the innman's negative response but, poise quickly regained, explained, soft spoken, "I walk with Osasor." An offered hand.

Ulran's enfolded it completely: a gentle, yielding handshake. Not the usual type who would follow the white lord of fire, the innman thought.

"Cobrora Fhord," the stranger made the introduction, dressed sombrely in a grey cloak, charcoal tunic and trousers, colourless face angular and thin. "I can enlighten you a little on the behaviour of the red tellars. And I would like to join you on your journey to Arion."

Ranell appraised the stranger with quickened interest; Aeleg stared at Cobrora shrewdly.

Ulran, unblinking, said, "But I haven't mentioned that I'd go – though I was considering it."

Cobrora nervously stroked long lank black hair. Ulran noticed the glint of some kind of amulet beneath Cobrora's grey cloak. Big brown eyes suddenly evasive, Cobrora Fhord murmured, "My – er, properties might prove useful – should you decide to go."

In preference, Ulran always travelled alone, in this way being responsible for himself and nobody else. But, this Cobrora presented a conundrum. The roumers regularly and swiftly carried messages along their established routes complete with staging posts, unmolested by villains and Devastator hordes, but even they could not have carried news of Arion's dire affairs in such a short time. And, as conclusive proof of this psychic's ability, Cobrora knew of Ulran's intentions to travel to Arion. It was just possible that the strange powers of Cobrora's spirit-lord could be of some use on the long trek.

"All right," said Ulran decisively. "But first we must arrange equipment." And, looking at Cobrora's thin city clothes, he added, "We must dress you properly for the long journey ahead. It may be summer – but the nights are harsh and the mountains will prove inhospitable."

***

"I have no intention of using the accredited tracks or the Dhur Bridge across Saloar Teen," Ulran said. "We'll leave by the Dunsaron Gate, stay overnight at The Inn, then head for Soemoff – about five days from Lornwater." Ulran's thick index finger traced the parchment map; an impressive red ruby sparkled on a gold ring. "Then we'll leave the Cobalt Trail, crossing Saloar Teen at its narrowest point, the shallows – here..."

"But that way you miss the Goldalese road –"

"I don't want to go in by the front door. As you know, Arion is sealed off from all save a few necessary merchants. So, instead, we'll try getting into Arion over the Sonalumes. It'll take at least eighty days."

Cobrora's head shook. "You – we've only got seventy."

Ulran arched an eyebrow.

"I – I don't know the how or the why, but the red tellars are involved in some rite... which is to take place on the First Durinma of Lamous – seventy days hence."

Rolling up the map, Ulran grinned. "Then we've no time to lose – even if we shorten our journey by way of Astrey Caron Pass."

Cobrora blanched at that prospect.

Sturdier boots and tougher cloak and clothes were borrowed from the Red Tellar's ample stocks for Cobrora's use. Ulran loaned Cobrora a light sword and dirk, though one look at the city-dweller's face confirmed Ranell's first observation that Cobrora would have little inclination to use either even if life depended upon it.

Their transportation was obtained from the stables attached to the rear courtyard of the inn. "I'm afraid we've got little spare at the moment, save Sarolee, this palfrey," Ulran said, nodding at a roan the ostler was holding.

"I'm not proud." Cobrora smiled and hesitantly stroked the horse's muzzle.

Ulran's horse, Versayr, was a beautiful black stallion. Ulran also selected a pack-mule for carrying provisions: "We'll hire another mule and purchase most of our stores at Soemoff. I have no wish to alert anyone to the length of my absence."

As shadows lengthened with the approach of dusk, Ulran embraced his son in the courtyard entrance.

Solemnly, the young man said, "No harm shall come to the Red Tellar, Begetter."

"I know." The sureness of Ulran's tone impressed Cobrora. "Now, we'll be on our way."

Marron Square, named after the great battle of Marron Marsh in 1227, was bustling with people raising banners across the streets. The two travellers shook hands with Ranell, and mounted their horses. A gentle nudge and they set off across the square, Cobrora holding onto the pack-mule's reins. Neither looked back.

Cobrora scratched an irritating itch, unaccustomed to this heavier clothing. A faint hammering of trepidation churned within, which must be controlled. A city-dweller since birth, Cobrora, apart from an occasional picnic with the gild outside the high outer city walls, had not ventured further. In fact, many people never set foot beyond the square launmark of their city-sector. Now, Cobrora couldn't really blame them.

But it was surely too late to turn back. O, by the gods, what a capricious gift this Sight was!

They cantered along the Long Causeway, the only road that ran straight through the Three Cities.

From the Red Tellar Inn to the Dunsaron Gate was a good ten launmarks; Ulran intended to get out of the city before the gates closed at sunset.

For many weeks the gossip had revolved around the forthcoming carnival. And now Cobrora snatched snippets of dialogue from passers-by:

"Let his liver stew, I say!"

"I hear the Harladawn Players have some satirical comments on our magnanimous monarch!"

"Only yesterday a friend told me Saurosen's been hiring spies to report on our preparations and progress..."

"Typically underhand!"

"He'll ban sex next!"

"If you were wed to my husband, you'd wish he would!"

Even in adversity, some people retained a sense of humour. Perhaps it was the city's unease that affected Cobrora. Something *other* than the normal had drawn the city-dweller to accompany the innman.

Drawn was the right word. And to speak to Ulran like that at their first meeting! As though possessed, Cobrora thought, forthright and ironical, so unlike my true, docile self! Drawn, indeed.

"Three years since Saurosen replaced Kcarran II – three hundred it feels like!"

"Aye, he may be the fourth Saurosen, but if the Three Cities have their way, he'll be the last!"

"Hush, Lorg, that's seditious talk!"

Some mansions shone red in the sinking sun's rays, as though on fire; other adjacent dwellings were little more than timber-shacks and voluminous tents.

Many of the side streets carried on as normal, their entire length covered with awnings, the stalls vying for custom. Cobrora always thought they most resembled an underground city. Unpleasant smells suggested that the drainage system was not coping with the increased numbers.

A glance down adjoining thoroughfares revealed buildings on either side leaning inwards, conveying a claustrophobic atmosphere, deepening the shadows, greatly welcome in the summer heat though to be avoided at night.

Shouting from the left drew their attention.

Miners, still grimed with coal-dust, were leaving the Pick and Shovel Inn, a musty earthy place where they habitually congregated after work or before their next shift. Lornwater was built over many disused mines; now, mining continued in the suburbs, beyond the cultivated fields. Opposite this inn was a competitor, The Open House, one of ten so named and owned by Ulran's biggest rivals, a combine.

"Next shift's due back from the death-caves, soon, lads – let's meet them, toast their good health!"

"Health? Till the carnival, anyway, then we'll see who's left alive, let alone healthy!"

"Oh, be quiet, Moaner. We'll tell him what to do with his infernal edict!"

"Aye!" chorused the dusty-throated men.

Pausing at the Old Drawbridge, which had not been raised since the New City was built, Ulran twisted in his high tooled saddle, and waited for Cobrora Fhord to draw alongside.

"I'd say they're near the brink of rebellion," Cobrora observed.

"They'll have their carnival, regardless of any ~~stupid~~ royal edict. It's a pity the king's second cousin, Lord-General Launette is on his way to Endawn; he would mollify the crowds, I'm sure."

"You fear rebellion, Ulran?"

"I do. But I cannot tarry from this quest. Let's move on."

They crossed over the very old stagnant and evil-smelling moat that completely surrounded the Second and Old Cities, and passed into the Second City.

Saurosen IV had persistently deprived his people of their little pleasures; and now he had banned their annual carnival that commemorated the crowning of Lornwater's first King, Kcarran. Considering these festivities had taken place without fail annually for over a thousand years, Cobrora thought the people had taken the edict commendably well. But, as Ulran said, they intended having their carnival anyway!

On either side, the flat rooftops of varying heights presented a colourful display of roof-gardens and tents.

Because a large cart had lost a wheel on the Causeway and a huge crowd gathered to relieve the conveyance of its spilt merchandise, Ulran urged Versayr down a side street on a twisting turning detour over resounding cobbles amidst streets of washing and stalls.

It was a lengthy detour and Ulran didn't spare the horses or Cobrora. To their right towered the Doltra Complex – home of the wealthy – perched upon huge stone-block pylons and looking obscenely bright and clean in comparison to the dark and sullied earth surrounds beneath it.

The Second City, thought Cobrora with irony, evinced a conspicuous change. Markedly fewer preparations for the carnival ensued here; the inhabitants were more reserved and few freely expressed opinion on the monarch and his infamous Edict.

As speedily as possible through winding streets, they returned to the Causeway.

At the tall Old City gates, Ulran reined in.

The slave market was evidently closing; the bartering and ogling crowds had dispersed, apparently uninspired by the remaining merchandise: a willowy youth and a pregnant middle-aged woman.

Ulran hailed the Slaver: "You!"

Head jerking up, the Slaver grinned with a toothless mouth, "Me, Sir?" He fingered his flamboyant tunic then, his sixth sense seeming to apprise him of a potential sale, his hands rubbed oilily together. "You want to buy the boy, my Lord?"

Ulran shook his head. "The woman – how much?"

"But she can't do much work – not far off term, I reckon... Now, the boy, he may be slender – but a little work'd soon build his muscles. Why not –?"

"The woman, Slaver." Ulran withdrew the purse from his belt, unfastened its strings. "How much?"

The Slaver's face contorted in thought, then: "Shall we say two sphands?"

"You can say what you like, but I'm offering fourteen carsts – take it or leave it. No-one else will buy her – two mouths to feed and incapable of working for her or her brat's keep."

Sighing resignedly, the Slaver nodded. "As you say, my Lord."

Ulran handed down a small gold sphand and four silver coins. "When you've closed down for the night, take the woman to the Red Tellar. Say Ulran sent her. My son Ranell will make the arrangements."

At mention of the inn and the innman's name, the Slaver's artful eyes widened and he nodded repeatedly. "Yes, sir, yes, I'll do as you bid – straight away. You'll not regret doing business with me, sir."

Taking up the hastily scrawled bill-of-sale, Ulran beckoned the gravid woman.

Waddling a little with the weight of child, she stood before him in bare feet and, head held high, her eyes levelled on his, pupils glinting red in the waning sun.

"When you enter the Red Tellar," he said, "you're a free woman. What is your name?"

"Jan-re Osa."

"Well, Jan-re Osa, my son Ranell, will care for you in labour and after."

Shock showed but briefly in her deep brown eyes. There was unquestioning acceptance in her curt nod and she backed away.

Ulran turned to Cobrora who had watched the whole transaction with avid curiosity. "Come, Cobrora, let us move on. It will soon be dark."

***

Directly opposite the slave market stood one of many city fanes. Gold-coloured in the form of a pyramid, the Fane of Jahdemore, Great-Lord of day, burned in the vermilion rays of day's end.

Upon a plinth at the head of the wide shallow entrance steps sat the imposing statue of the great Meshanel, Jahdemor's prophet, his sightless eyes seemingly omniscient, a trick of light. Even at this early juncture in the carnival's arrangements, the fane pillars, doorways and arches were garlanded with sweet-scented crimson sekors, the flowers of the Light-bringer.

Blending with the shadows cast by the entrance columns stood two robed men whose stance and attention clearly had nothing to do with the worship of the god of light and strength, though the exquisite garb of one blatantly indicated that he was rich enough to do so.

Rashen Pellore wore tattered dun-coloured clothes and old sandals and silently cursed his companion for drawing attention to them. He had no difficulty recognising Badol Melomar beneath the thin disguise of false goatee, moustache and shadowy cloak-hood. The ruthless head and innman of the powerful Open House Combine was too distinguishable because of his ugliness to go unnoticed, Rashen thought unkindly, inwardly chuckling.

By the gods, Badol was simple! Yet, Rashen warned himself, this innman was also very rich and powerful: and, more dangerous still, he was incredibly greedy. No, he didn't really have to be a mercenary of long standing to guess why Badol had approached him: the vendetta between the Open House Combine and the Red Tellar was no secret.

"How did you know Ulran would be riding through here?" Rashen asked.

"I have spies even in the much-vaunted Red Tellar. Spies everywhere, in fact," Badol said, his tone containing an underlying threat. "So. Can I count on you, then?" he asked, peering down the length of his sharp nose. "To deal once and for all with that upstart?" Thick lips upturned in an unprepossessing scowl, he gestured with distaste towards the horseback figure bargaining with the sycophantic Slaver.

Pointedly ignoring Badol, Rashen silently appraised Ulran's powerful frame and effortless manner: not a movement wasted, wholly at ease. This was the first time he had seen the illustrious innman. He could see no talisman whatsoever dangling from the innman's person or horse. Obviously a man in complete harmony with the gods, an enviable state of mind indeed, he mused, fingering his own snakeskin necklace.

Rashen grinned. So unlike Ulran's companion, though! From both sides of Cobrora's palfrey and also from the tunic and belt, all manner of potion-pouches and talismans dangled and chinked.

"As you well know, the Kcarran Carnival pulls all sorts of people from all over the country," Rashen remarked icily, still studying Ulran. "There'll be plenty of opportunists and fellow mercenaries employed as bodyguards for the rich and fat travellers. Don't worry, I'll have my men hand-picked by sunset and we'll be on their trail at dawn."

Snatching a glimpse of Badol's moist lips forming a protest, he added, "Soon enough... I mean, you wouldn't want the foul deed committed on your own threshold, would you?"

Badol paled, shook his head vigorously.

"I thought not," said Rashen.

The Open House innman wrapped his resplendent cloak tightly about him and shakily proffered a small leather pouch; its contents jingled. "As agreed, then – half now, the rest when you bring me Ulran's ruby ring of the Red Tellar?"

Weighing the pouch thoughtfully, Rashen smiled darkly. He absently brushed his drab brown cloak. "What's to stop me teaming up with Ulran and taking his ring with his permission, just to fool you and get your money?"

Badol's lower lip trembled, saliva dribbled, and his brows knitted together. "You – you couldn't – I know Ulran. Nothing short of death would part him from that ring."

"For some men, even death has no power over them; remember that," snapped Rashen, ill-at-ease with his contract of hire. Sometimes, he wondered why his blood flowed in the way of a mercenary. Abruptly, Rashen turned on his heel, threadbare cloak swirling, and flung over his shoulder, "I'll be back within eight days... then you'll be able to take over the Red Tellar, lock, stock and barrel, Badol Melomar!"

The innman convulsed with a tremor of fear and stared coldly after the laughing mercenary who tossed and caught the purse of gold as though it were a mere plaything.

That morning's shaky resolve was now firm: the mercenary and his brood, whoever they might be, must be eliminated once the death of Ulran was assured. Mercenaries and creatures of their ilk knew no loyalty to employers, he was sure. No, he couldn't risk them living, no, not at any price!

Stroking the itching false beard and moustache, Badol Melomar glared at Ulran and his incongruous companion as they passed through the Old City gates. But his countenance softened as he pictured the vast revenues of the Red Tellar at last within his grasp.

***

"Why, Cobrora?" Ulran repeated as they rode to the Main Plaza, the largest square in Lornwater. "Let us just say I had a feeling of kinship with that unborn babe."

Cobrora nodded, not understanding, though it seemed there was some history concerning the innman and his origins. Perhaps all would be revealed on the journey.

Unlike the two outer cities, the Old City was formed on a strict grid plan. Here, there were no outward signs of the forthcoming carnival. The tall buildings of the palace would have something to do with that, thought Cobrora.

It was always the rich who stuck with Saurosen IV; and the rich lived in their mansions, here in the Old City or protectively closeted themselves in the Doltra Complex, cocooned, looking out at the world through the pretty smaltglass windows. But they didn't see the real world, Cobrora realised, surprised at such thoughts. Ulran's gesture with that slave woman had had quite an effect.

They rode past a solitary fane festooned with the appropriate sekors of its god. There was one brothel across the square, which seemed to be prospering, eagerly making welcome the many newcomers to the city.

The lowing of cattle and the stench of the livestock's excrement engulfed them. A cattle market was still embroiled in the business of auctioning. Torches were lit to combat the deepening dusk, naked flames flashing in the frightened beasts' eyes and upon their huge curved horns.

Once at Dunsaron Gate, they had to pull their mounts to one side to make way for three loaded wagons bringing in the old shift of feldspar miners.

The eyes of both male and female miners glared white and forlorn, bizarre sad contrasts to the theatrical black faces and pink mouths. Exhaustion was etched around their eyes and in the stoop of shoulders, bodies now permanently misshaped. They worked for a pittance and had little to look forward to, save their carnival which celebrated a good and memorable king's reign. And now the worst king in recent history decreed there would be no more play, only work and more work.

Cobrora suddenly felt all apprehensions disappear as they rode through the last city gate. To get away was like clearing the mind after a heady bout of mindsaur smoking, though that vice was only attempted twice.

The road straight on led to the mines, but Ulran took another, less used track.

Almost everyone kept clear of this road.

Fresh disquiet assailed Cobrora, clutching a talisman, then another, strangling each evil effigy in turn; then whispering a succinct prayer to the most sacred gods for protection, for they were heading towards The Inn.

Feeling at odds, Cobrora looked back at the exceedingly high outer grey-stone walls of the vast city of Lornwater.

Home, with its defensive towers, its sinister crenellations spreading as far as the eye could see; the palace minars, the dominating Eyrie, all now bathed in silver moonlight. The moon was approaching its last quarter, its surface without blemish or crater, intensely bright, transforming the land into an eerie ghostlike place.

Cobrora had never been outside the city when the gates were shut; now the sound carried, of the ponderous bolts thudding home.

Loneliness fell with complete suddenness.

A warm orange halo arched above the Three Cities' forbidding silhouette. A distinctive thin streamer of blue-grey smoke issued from the smalthouse and joined the many other smoke-trails of the great city.

Turning to look upon the vast night-sky, Cobrora shuddered involuntarily, wondering at the absurd relief felt on leaving the city a short while ago.

The road was a little uneven in places where the recent rains had collected. On either side crouched shapeless bushes of muskflower: threatening, sinister. The stridulation of night-devils sent an uncomfortable tingling down the spine.

Presently, the road curved gently downwards, to the shore of Lornwater Lake.

"The Lake", whispered Cobrora, unable to repress a shudder.

The roan's ears pricked and the animal shied.

The evil waters – where to drink even a drop meant hideous death.

Clasping talisman tightly, prayers tumbling from trembling lips, Cobrora looked down and across the expanse of still, dark water and noticed with unease that the surface bore no reflection, neither of the stars nor of the moon. No silvery ripples like the city ponds at night. No mirror-image of the window-lit Lornwater Inn by its shores.

Cold clammy panic swelled up into throat, hands tensed to jerk on the reins. Cobrora wanted to halt, to yell for Ulran to stop, unwilling to have anything to do with either Lake or Inn. Yet, no sound came out and Sarolee tentatively cantered forward.

"We'll spend tonight here," Ulran said, dismounting in front of Lornwater Inn.

Floreskand: Wings

CHAPTER TWO
INN

In any posture whatsoever he understands that he is so doing, so that, however his body is engaged, he comprehends it just as it is... he acts with clear awareness.
– *The Lay of Lorgen*

"I conjure and I invoke thee, O Tanemag, strong King of the Dunsaron, by the name of Quotamantir who was your Master! I order thee to obey me, or otherwise to send at once to me Assel, Mardiib, Entrespir and Ost, that they will clear the pool and aid my sight!"

Large dark eyes staring intensely at the shimmering stagnant pool, the alchemist licked his thin lips in concentration. He dropped the final ingredient – the viscera of a crested niedem newt – into the water.

The splash was slight. Scarlet ripples began, widening. Then an alarmed gasp issued from the only spectator, Yip-nef Dom, the seventh King of the Yip, tenth dynasty of Arisa. Moving pictures formed in the blooded water, indistinct but nevertheless identifiable.

Two men on horseback outside an inn.

Faintly, could be seen the black impenetrable expanse of Lornwater Lake.

"Are you sure the red tellar has brought them?" the king asked anxiously, his eyes gleaming in the light of the smouldering flames beside the pool. His glass eye glinted green, yellow, red and blue whilst his dark brown eye shone with a pinpoint of white in the pupil. A third eye, clearly a craftsman's aberration, dangled upon a chain on the royal chest.

Por-al Row nodded sagely while his insides quivered with fear.

Yip-nef Dom leaned forward to see better and coughed on the stifling fumes. "Why did you order –?" His fleshy jowls wobbled in petulance. "Why did you countermand our – my – order, Por-al Row?"

So, she has started sharing orders with him! Pretending not to hear his king, Por-al Row remarked, "See, my lord. They enter The Inn. I warrant come the dawn they'll be on their way here!"

Now Yip-nef Dom stamped his foot and upset a bowl of green slimy liquid. *"But why?"*

Fuming inside, the alchemist shrugged his shoulders. His narrow jutting bones gave an angular aspect to the black silk robes patterned with esoteric symbols. "There are still plenty of red tellars in the mountains, sire. More than enough for our own ends. They're bringing them in daily. Four hundred at the last count –"

"We've been to a lot of trouble to capture these creatures!" The king's glass eye moved slightly, threatening to pop out and fall into the Scrying Pool, as his face grew bright purple and his temple's vein throbbed.

"I was there at the beginning, sire, remember?" And Por-al Row shivered expressively at the memory.

"Yes, yes, *yes!* But why let *that* one go?"

Por-al Row could not even begin to explain; he could scarcely believe it himself. But the truth was that he had been mortally terrified: the bird had looked straight into his eyes, penetrating his very soul, and filled him with absolute dread. For in that moment he had seen –

"Why *that* one?" demanded the king again.

Damn General Foo-sep – the king must have learned of that incident through him! He emitted an exasperated sigh: "I'm only a Seer, my lord," he said, slipping smoothly into the explanation he devised whilst in the mountains. "I do as my gods invoke. Their voices, they said, 'Let one escape – the red tellar with a white patch on its throat – *let it go.*' It's almost the shape of a white sekor," he mused.

"But why do we need those men here? Tell me that."

"At the moment, sire, I can only guess –"

"Guess?"

Por-al Row hastened on before his liege had an apoplectic fit. "Perhaps we can enlist them in our cause against Lornwater. Everyone knows how unpopular Saurosen IV is. Or perhaps we can glean more knowledge of the city's defences."

The shivering picture between the now receding ripples was stilled, showing two tethered horses by The Inn's entrance steps. "Can't you see indoors, then?" the king asked peevishly.

A young ostler came out to lead the horses and mule to the stables.

"Not inside The Inn, no..."

***

Because The Lake was dark legend and this inn was associated with it, Lornwater Inn was not greatly patronised. Only travellers stranded outside the city after sunset found their way here, and then only with reluctance. In the summer moons, most would rather camp under the stars than sojourn at The Inn.

History books had apprised Cobrora that the names of the land and everything in it derived from the Early Kellan-Mesqa, Floreskand's original inhabitants. The City-Dwellers drifted up from Shomshurakand long before counting of years began. Yet the Kellan-Mesqa did not name

Lornwater Lake: they denied its supernatural existence, never venturing near its shores.

Ulran stood in the wide doorway, noted the solitary black cloak and black felt hat upon the peg to his left, then, expressionless, surveyed the interior.

By Ulran's side, Cobrora sensed some presence within the shadowy confines and briefly attempted to fathom the sensation, almost oppressive in its nature, but desisted at once as senses wavered, almost on the verge of becoming addled. Wiping a hand over damp brow, Cobrora looked around with eyes instead of mind.

A place indeed where superstition could flourish with little need of imagination as fertiliser. The whole room reeked of age; not years, but millennia. Though everywhere was spotlessly clean, Cobrora was convinced that cobwebs could be seen by the score out of the corner of an eye, yet, when looked upon directly, there were none.

By the fireplace was a row of trestle tables and ornately carved wooden chairs, where the only visible guest – a great hulk of a leather-clad man – was bent forward facing the hearth's roaring flames. His back to them, he was eating and appeared to have paid no attention to their arrival.

Floorboards creaked under the pressure of their feet; some creaked before they set foot upon them, as though other feet trod these boards – spectral feet...

Firelight had always fascinated Cobrora Fhord, having a great affinity for that primal element; but this log fire held no thrall whatsoever. Cobrora strangled the little manikin of Honsor, the evil lord of fire, futilely, for fire paid homage to either Honsor or Osasor. Against better instincts, however, Cobrora believed this room's atmosphere, palpable enough to rend with a blade, was neither good nor evil. Perhaps it was simply age, or something before either good or evil came into being.

Over 700 years ago the Second City had been added only to one side of the Old City because of the superstitious fear of The Lake. Latterly, the buildings had encroached upon the forbidding expanse of water: but still latent in most Lornwater breasts was an inordinate dread of The Lake.

As if in amplification of this, Cobrora's heart had been hammering loudly since their arrival, and the presence of the establishment's innman did nothing to dispel any trepidation.

"Here, give me your cloaks," the landlord said. "And sit you by the fire. Our friend here won't mind, I'm sure."

Ulran slid his frame into a chair opposite the stranger who had just finished a plate of bean stew.

Cobrora sat on Ulran's left, unable to desist staring at the eyes of the stranger.

Having given the landlord their order, Ulran said conversationally, "We're heading towards the Sonalumes."

The stranger grunted. He wiped his lips and long, drooping black moustache with the back of a hairy hand. Great bushy eyebrows cast shadows over his eyes but they sparkled even so, almost ironically, light blue, worldly and penetrating. His skin, creased round eyes and mouth, looked a great deal older than the eyes. The black hair streaked with grey suggested old age too. Fancifully, Cobrora thought there was something ageless about this man, as, in a subtle way, there was with this hostelry's landlord.

When the stranger spoke, his voice was deep, climbing slowly, contemplatively, from the barrel of his chest: "Two men with some sense, I see," he said, resting back. "But why should the owner of the Red Tellar be leaving the city just before the carnival?"

At that moment the resident innman brought them both a bowl of hot steaming rabbit-stew and a dish of fresh fruit for the stranger.

"You're rather inquisitive, old man!" said Cobrora, perhaps emboldened by the companionship of Ulran.

The Inn's landlord paused by the table, face paling as tension mounted between Cobrora and the stranger.

Picking up an apple, the stranger rubbed it vigorously against his sleeve and calmly waved the landlord away. "And you're a rather foolish boy," he menaced. "Your tongue could get you into trouble."

"It could, indeed," added Ulran.

Cobrora now wished common sense had stilled a foolish loose tongue: *by the gods, I'm out of my sector here...* Something in this stranger's manner suggested he was no ordinary mortal.

"But Ulran –"

"Be quiet, Cobrora, while I explain the journey to our friend here–"

"Friend–?"

A glance from Ulran commanded silence.

The innman of the Red Tellar addressed the stranger who at that moment discarded the apple core into the fire: "You heard of the flight of the red tellars this morning?"

Large white teeth with yellowed edges chomped into a peach. Juice drooled over his jutting chin. He nodded.

"We believe a great many more of them are in danger in Arion. Something to do with a magical rite–"

"Yip-nef Dom!" exclaimed the stranger. "I wonder..."

"Arisa's king?" Cobrora interrupted, still inwardly seething. "How is he involved in this?"

Looking askance at the pair, the stranger grinned and threw the sucked-dry stone into the flames where it hissed then cracked. "I have a very old score to settle with that pompous freak!"

Ulran's face remained unmoved, attentive.

Cobrora glanced at the two warriors eyeing each other.

"Quite a few years ago," said the stranger, then murmured to himself, "I forget the years so easily..." He sighed, went on, "I was tracking a giant yak in the Sonalumes when I came across a snowed-in encampment. From the tattered standard I could see it was a troop of Arisa. Three soldiers and a young woman and her baby were alive – only just. The rest had perished. They were ill-provisioned to travel into snow-laden mountains. The leader of the troop had deserved to die!

"I rigged a cart and piled it with tent-fabric and blankets and bundled the survivors inside, covered them up. Another died long before I arrived at Arisa's gate.

"But Yip-nef Dom wasn't pleased to see me, not at all. I was treated with the barest civility and urged to leave the city.

"I could tell when to take a hint and set out. Then – at the Palace Gate – I turned my horse Borsalac and saw Yip-nef Dom on his royal balcony with the infant raised in one hand, held upside down by its ankle. The gate doors were closing as I'd turned in my saddle so I think I hadn't been meant to see that – but I had – and by all the hoary gods I saw red! Before the gate completely shut I whipped out an arrow and loosed it at the king."

Cobrora swallowed thickly. Clearly this man was more than other men, but to attack a city's king so boldly amounted to madness!

"I didn't wait to see where the arrow hit but rode Borsalac as though the lord of whirlwinds were after me!"

Cobrora looked troubled; Ulran simply nodded and said, "Cobrora, meet Courdour Alomar."

Cobrora gaped and stared, having heard of this man. Stories only. Consternation showed. The stories had been handed down from grandfather to grandson.

"They were meant to perish in the mountains?" prompted Ulran.

Courdour Alomar nodded. "Yes. It seems the baby had been a girl, unsuitable as an heir, so Yip-nef Dom sent his wife and babe out on an expedition, ostensibly to visit an Angkorite in the mountains concerning ways to conceive a male, but in truth so they would both succumb. He doesn't want his cousin Yip-dor Fla as his successor when the time comes – he is obsessed with having a male heir of his own loins."

"I heard your arrow pierced his eye."

"If only it had, Ulran!" Courdour Alomar chuckled. "No, I believe the truth is more prosaic. The arrowhead simply glanced off the wall at his side. Some stone shards blinded him. My getaway was the more successful because nobody immediately associated my departure with the prostrate king. They managed to save one eye, by all accounts."

"But what of the child and her mother?" asked Cobrora.

"I haven't heard. Since my visit very few outsiders have been permitted within Arisa's walls, and even less within the palace confines. Rumours trickle out, of course. They say he's a veritable despot now. Has a harem, by the gods, just like the Ranmeron Emperor. But none of the bitches will give him his much-wanted heir! He has even risked civil unrest by jailing Yip-dor Fla, though even he dare not murder his cousin and rival – at least, not yet. But if his reason deteriorates any further..." Courdour shrugged meaningfully.

The question of the Arisan king's sanity hung on the air and the silence lengthened.

Cobrora looked from Alomar to The Inn's landlord who was returning with another bowl of fresh fruit. Cobwebs still persisted in appearing at the very edges of vision.

"This magical rite – have you more to go on?" asked Courdour suddenly, breaking into Cobrora's reverie.

"No," Ulran answered. "But the omens are bad."

Courdour shook his head. "Then if Yip-nef Dom is involved he must be well and truly insane now. Only a madman would threaten the birds of the Overlord."

Ulran and Cobrora nodded in agreement.

Rising from his bench and tucking his cotton shirt into his leather trouser waistband, Courdour grinned. "I'm heading in your direction, Ulran. Why don't we go part of the way together?"

"Agreed. I only hope Cobrora here doesn't get bored with all our talk of fighting!"

Cobrora forced a sheepish smile, more than ever feeling dwarfed by these two men.

***

Por-al Row's concentration strained over the cauldron of putrefying entrails that simmered around islands of fat. But the pictures that formed were hazy.

He was perturbed: he could not perceive the visages of those two men set on coming to Arisa.

He re-directed his spells, and was pleased to see that fogginess dissipated a little. He looked upon the royal court of Saurosen IV and liked the tenor of the happenings. Civil unrest was rife. Yes, Yip-nef Dom would be pleased, also.

**

By daybreak all three had eaten a substantial breakfast because they planned to eat light through the day, in order to cover as much ground as possible.

At the doorway, Courdour Alomar signalled farewell to the innman of Lornwater Inn. Even Courdour viewed The Lake with reverence, expressing no desire to go near. Cobrora was comforted by that.

Shortly afterwards, the woods appeared in front of them, beginning on the next gentle slope and stretching as far as the eye could see: Oquar II Forest, named after the king in whose reign the afforestation project began, in 1376.

By the roadside at the forest's edge were two shrines, one on either side – Chasor and Amasor. They were pointedly ignored by Courdour Alomar, to Cobrora's dismay.

Fumbling among the many amulets and potions, the city-dweller produced an effigy resembling one of the gods, Chasor, the evil lesslord of woods. Fleetingly, Cobrora passed a palm over both eyes, signifying no recognition of Chasor. Then, turning, Cobrora rode over to Amasor, the good counter-part of Chasor, and touched eyebrow and lips with a finger, informing that white lesslord that recognition and obeisance were offered.

Ulran nonchalantly acknowledged the presence of both gods; this upset Cobrora, as though the innman were merely going through the motions. Cobrora swore very quietly at the evil little figure of Chasor and looked up at Courdour Alomar with ill-concealed disdain.

The warrior sat astride his stallion, urging Borsalac: "Come on, we haven't time for this time-wasting cant!" But he wasn't permitted to go further.

A great black shadow descended out of the morning sun, impelling Courdour to draw his shortsword. Borsalac reared, alarmed.

Soundless, not a crack of wing in the air, the huge red tellar landed upon the head of the shrine to Chasor and Cobrora would have sworn that the shrine visibly shrank under the power of the bird.

"Scalrin!" exclaimed Ulran. He dismounted and ran to the shrine.

Already, the figurine of the shrine had aged, its ironwood shrivelling.

Intelligent eyes flashing, Scalrin jumped the small distance to the earthen track as Ulran knelt down.

Courdour Alomar's temper subsided. He had never seen one of these mystical birds land before. Everything about the giant creature seemed modelled by the gods – so big yet so serene. And the look of eyes was so human; it was as though the creature could talk.

After a moment, Ulran rose, dusting his knees with a hand. "Cobrora, Scalrin has decided to accompany us to Arisa."

"It is a good sign, Ulran – the wings of the Overlord will protect us."

Casting a doubtful eye over Cobrora and the charms, Courdour Alomar asked, "Can you really commune with this Scalrin?"

"Yes. It isn't talking, it's more like sense-impressions. All I pictured was Scalrin flying above us – along the way – he must wish to join us, then."

"I see." Courdour sat without any intention of moving. As if the thought had just struck him, he added, "I had planned sojourning at my toran but this quest of yours, Ulran – it's intriguing. I've a mind to join you all the way. Perhaps I could learn the fate of that woman and child as well."

Sliding his foot into a stirrup, Ulran leapt astride Versayr while Scalrin perched on the horse's rump. From the angle Courdour viewed them, Ulran looked as though two great red wings flicked and sprouted from his shoulder blades. "We'd be glad of your company, Alomar."

Courdour nodded. "If you will, I suggest we go through Marron Marsh. My toran's well stocked. A day's rest would serve us well and, besides," he added with a grin, raising the wide brim of his floppy hat, "I require my war accoutrements."

"Certainly. But – war –?"

"I always travel prepared, Ulran. That's how I've lived so long, *alas*!" He laughed, reared Borsalac round and raced into the dappled shadows of Oquar Forest.

PART TWO
FOURTH SABINMA OF JUVOUS - FIRST SABINMA OF FORNIOUS

The Song of the Overlord – Part the Second:
Sometimes a mote on the disc of the sun
At others, the ripple on a taal's surface
Now He doth fly about on Sormakin and Madarkin
Now He is a bird of the immutable world
By the name of ice He doth style Himself
Congealed in the winter season is He
He hath enveloped Himself in the infinity
He is the cloud on the face of the sky.

CHAPTER THREE
PORTENT

In the Overlord's all-seeing eyes, such men are like unto murderers and idolaters, less to Him than a mote.
– The Tanlin, 241.14

Dwarfing all others about them, ironwood trees stretched in uniform lines along the soft grassy track, refracting the sun's rays into myriad narrow slanting lemon and emerald beams; tiny insects seemed to be trapped in the streaming light. Different varieties of tree bordered one side of the track, providing a strange contrast as the three riders and the trailing mule made good time through Oquar Forest.

Ulran suggested they skirt round the usual road as a precaution, so they rode on through the undergrowth. Scalrin flew from Versayr's rump and, winging high into the narrow slice of sky, was soon gone from sight. "He probably feels hemmed in – caged," explained Ulran.

The deeper they penetrated, the more tangled and treacherous this track became. Thorn twigs lashed unsuspectingly, lacerating cheek or tearing leggings.

High aloft, where the taller pinewoods climbed into a heat-haze of wispy grey steam, the odd simian creature swung from fragile branch to liana, uttering a startling, thrilling screech. Multi-coloured parakeets cawed and flashed their plumage from high safe perches.

But Cobrora hardly had eyes for anything but the almost continuous welter of backlashing branches, and greatly appreciated the heavier clothing Ulran had provided. They might make me sweat in this humid forest, Cobrora thought, but at least they afforded some protection.

Courdour Alomar urged his horse Borsalac with a virtual obsession, his black hat all but concealing his eyes and nose, black cloak billowing in his wake. What madness drove that man?

Ulran and the mule brought up the rear.

Cobrora slowed to peer behind. The innman scoured each side of the track, seeming to take note of quite invisible features, then absently arrested a back-hacking branch before it could hit him. Nothing seems to disturb the innman, Cobrora Fhord thought not without envy. Urging the animal on, Cobrora was consoled with a prayer to Amasor.

Eventually they returned to the proper trail again which, after some time, opened out into a clearing, where lots of trees had been felled in regimented files.

To one side was a sleigh with two oxen for pulling and, upon the sleigh, defoliated trunks. Standing around the transport was a group of ten leather-clad people of both sexes and various ages, eating a snack.

"Family fellers," Ulran explained, drawing up beside Cobrora. "Each ironwood tree takes a long time for a single family to fell, hence its costliness. In fact, there is a rapport between the ironwood tree and the craftsman and through him to the fellers. You see, the trees are not felled indiscriminately – they're cut as needed by the craftsman for specific workmanship dictated by the *feel* of the tree itself."

"I often wondered if its indestructible properties justified such expense. But, it's obvious, really." Cobrora waved briefly to the family then urged Sarolee on after the diminishing form of Courdour on the other side of the clearing.

Later, Courdour called a halt. "We'll camp here for the night."

Ulran nodded agreement, having quickly scanned the small clearing and undergrowth.

While Ulran stood warming himself in front of the roaring fire, he remarked off-handedly, "I believe we're being watched."

"Could be Garrotmen," suggested Courdour.

"No. If they belonged to the Fourth Toumen, we would never know they were there–"

"Not even you would know?" queried Cobrora with an impish grin.

"Their stealth is akin to the breeze through the undergrowth, the weeping of a forlorn leaf, Cobrora. No, I could not detect a garotter's presence unless he wished me to."

"I find it hard to believe," Cobrora declared, calmed by the casual way the two companions discussed the possibility.

"Ulran is not mistaken, lad." Courdour scowled. "I too have detected eyes other than of this forest's natural denizens. Hostile eyes..."

Back tingling unpleasantly, Cobrora edged closer to the warm fire, peering over hunched shoulders at the surrounding darkness. Red animal eyes stared back, much to Cobrora's horror.

"They're only forest-dogs – a cowardly creature, have no fear," Ulran said.

Courdour Alomar shrugged. "Tomorrow night I think our watchers may show themselves."

Nerves in shreds due to their talk and the presence of cowardly forest-dogs with gleaming red eyes, Cobrora almost wept, "How can you talk so calmly – why – why should they wait till tomorrow night?"

"We're still too close to Lornwater if they mean mischief," Ulran explained. "Besides which, that felling family is still near. No, we should be safe enough tonight – however, we'll organise watches. You, Cobrora, can have the first."

With an almighty bellow, Courdour burst out laughing. "Don't worry, city-dweller. If you hear or see *anything*, give us a nudge – though not too hard, or I might cut off your head!" He winked and Cobrora's blood ran cold.

***

On their ride the following day Cobrora shifted uneasily in the saddle, sore with riding and stiff after the first night camping outdoors.

To steer thoughts away from this discomfort Cobrora took the opportunity to converse with Ulran since the track allowed them to ride two abreast. Courdour remained in front, plunging on.

"I'm beginning to ache all over." Cobrora grinned, although not really feeling like grinning. "I was really stiff this morning!"

Courdour Alomar laughed loudly at this remark, but Cobrora didn't understand why.

"It takes a little time to adapt,' Ulran explained, "but before this quest is over I imagine you will become a good horseman. Sarolee has taken to you, anyway."

"I hope so. You know, if you questioned me as to why I'd asked to join you now, Ulran, I would be hard-pressed to explain, save that I feel drawn–"

"As do we all, in life's passage."

"Yet, also, I believe I may have grasped at this quest in the hope it would help me broaden my life's experience, prepare me for a pilgrimage to Sianlar."

"You have high ambitions, to aspire to that fane. I wish you well, when your time comes at Sianlar, Cobrora Fhord."

***

On the Fourth Dekinma they camped.

Cobrora had been leaning against a tree when suddenly face and shoulder were soaked.

"Rain–!" Then Cobrora looked around and, as Courdour Alomar laughed, realised the night sky was clear. "But–"

"You've been soaked in the sugary excreta of dahal-nasqeds – night-devils to you, boy! They're busy feeding in your tree – that's why you couldn't hear them!"

Cobrora sulked by the fire, the clothes smelling quite vile as they dried.

That night five men charged in without stealth or skill. Evidently they anticipated no strong defence. From their vantage point they could descry the entire camp in the firelight and the sheen of the moon in its last quarter: neither the old man nor the thin one would present them with any problem. But Ulran's prowess they knew well, so three of their number leapt at the sleeping form of Ulran.

But Ulran was no longer in his bedding, only some provisions in a rough human shape. The three murderers bristled, stabbed the sacks, spilling grain as they looked about the camp.

Courdour Alomar idly parried the downcutting blade as though waking from slumber, and, leaning against the tree bole he swung his shortsword in a vicious, deadly arc that severed his attacker's arm from its shoulder. He silenced the vibrating scream with a quick thrust.

Cobrora had been on watch when the attack materialised. An assailant leapt out from the darkness, blade glinting in the waning firelight. Cobrora froze. The villain's knife flashed out, stabbing viciously at the city-dweller. Miraculously, the blade shattered on contact with an ironwood effigy of Amasor.

As Cobrora Fhord sank to shaking knees thanking the white god, Courdour Alomar leapt across the flickering fire and despatched the dumbstruck villain. Then the warrior whirled round to see the three by Ulran's bedroll: one lying dead, two others hard-pressed by the scything blade of Ulran's long curved sword.

Quickly now, Ulran skewered a second assassin and with a deftly placed kick disarmed the last.

Winded, the only survivor knelt before the innman's lowered sword. Ulran stood, with his weapon's point touching the attacker's forehead.

Courdour had expected the would-be killer to whimper for mercy as he dropped to his knees; instead he simply bowed his head, offered to the victor. A mercenary, then.

"Who bought you, Mercenary?" Ulran demanded.

Courdour Alomar listened intently while Cobrora slowly and unsteadily groped to stand. Though next to the fire, Cobrora still shivered.

"Tell me, Rashen Pellore, and I will spare your life."

Rashen Pellore raised eyes with no light in them. "You know me, innman?"

"I know you."

"How?"

"It is my business to know. Now, tell me and I will let you live."

"I cannot live other than by being a mercenary," Rashen Pellore declared levelly, "and if I reveal my employer's identity I will never again be employed as a mercenary." He shrugged fatalistically. "So, as you see, it is better that you kill me now, as I would have killed you, Ulran of the Red Tellar."

"So be it," Ulran sighed. "But Badol Melomar's not worth it." And Rashen's surprised eyes widened, moments before the massive blade smoothly decapitated him.

"Oh, ye gods!" Cobrora exclaimed and lurched away.

***

Ulran knelt by the other attacker, removed a ring from the corpse's finger. "An assassin's gildring," he said, sliding it on his finger adjacent to the red ruby. "It might prove useful," he mused, looking towards the edge of the clearing where Cobrora Fhord was retching spasmodically.

He showed no emotion at observing Cobrora's reaction, but noted how annoyed Courdour Alomar was with the city-dweller. Why hadn't Cobrora sensed the danger, as a true psychic would? Was fear blanketing the ability? If so, then they now had a great problem on their hands. Yet, Ulran decided to reserve judgement. He cleaned his sword on some dry grass. Cobrora would need watching all the time.

A day and a night followed without further incident.

During the day they passed varied groups of travellers heading for the carnival city, Lornwater, but exchanged hardly a word. Cobrora's part – or rather, lack of participation – in the repulsion of the ambush had driven a wedge between the city-dweller and Courdour Alomar. Ulran was hard-pressed to keep them on forced civil terms. At the slightest thing, Courdour's temper would be vented upon the city-dweller. And, being a sensitive person by the very nature of those unreliable abilities, Cobrora was going to pieces with the eroding tension. And hothouse days and cold nights did little to relieve the situation.

Ulran, as able as any stioner in weather-lore, forewarned his companions of any forthcoming chill night or debilitating hot day. In that humid forest, it did not seem possible that a man could go thirsty, yet without Ulran's stionery Cobrora would have expired for want of water: the ambush had cost them their water-skins as well as some grain. But Courdour Alomar seemed not to care for water or food, answering Ulran with monosyllables, intent merely on keeping on the move.

So it was with hardly suppressed relief that Cobrora looked down upon the circular palisaded town that nestled in a natural hollow in the forest, giving it a stark, ghostlike appearance. The Cobalt Trail ran down cleaving through the grassy slope, under the guarded wooden gateway and led to the very centre of Soemoff.

Buildings were few. On the right of the entrance was the rich quarter, as evinced by their whitebrick dwellings and Arqitor Fane. The long town garrison abutted the main road. In the centre of the town a wagon-park stood bereft of wagons, and just before the park a toll office spanned the road. Ulran smiled, pointing it out to Cobrora.

On one side of the park were the stables, then behind these were wooden houses built in haphazard fashion to right and left, pushing against the tannery walls. Dregs of the tannery's smoke curled into the cloudless sky: business had obviously shut down for the carnival.

To the far left of the town was the large marketplace, also empty, and, nearby, storehouses, their huge wooden doors padlocked. To the far right, bordering the main road, which bent towards the cobalt mines, the Soemoff cattle pens held but five scrawny beasts not worthy of barter in Lornwater.

"We'll obtain further provisions and another mule here," Ulran informed his fellow travellers.

Courdour grunted acknowledgement; Cobrora nodded, evading all eyes, though clearly anxious to ride down into Soemoff.

At any other time the deserted town would have made Ulran or Courdour suspicious. But the townspeople had obviously left for the carnival, which was due to start in three days, on the First Sabin of Fornious – the First Quarter of the Seventh Moon.

A speck in the sky caught Ulran's attention. Scalrin, soaring high above them, sought a cloud directly over the town and vanished from sight.

On the way down the sloping road Cobrora strained to stand upright in the stirrups and could descry the crenellated walls and a solitary corner tower with embrasured windows, beyond the trees to their right; the resident noble's fortress.

They rode slowly into Soemoff, past the idle sentry at the gateway of the tall palisade. Although the last all-out war with the Kellan-Mesqa had been in 1820, Soemoff supported a small garrison for protection: the Devastators still liked to raid occasionally.

Besides the garrison there were living-quarters for the miners on the left, while the farmers and the few merchants necessary to provide Soemoff with continued life inhabited the other end of town.

The overpowering smell of the tannery reached them. The majority of the buildings were made of wood upon stone foundations, quite unlike Lornwater, thought Cobrora; the timber was not the impervious ironwood, as that cost more than common townspeople or farmers could afford.

As they approached the barracks on their right, it appeared that the only remaining residents were the three innmen; they would rake in a great deal from the itinerants heading for Lornwater; though a great deal less when they passed through on their way home, usually broke! It seemed the blacksmith, too, had decided to stay: Cobrora could see him across the gravel wagon-park, standing grime-faced at the stables' entrance, the big man's forge burning with a red glow, though his hammer and anvil were silent; he scrutinised them, doubtless speculating on the odds of ready custom.

One establishment seemed to be doing exceedingly good business, strategically situated directly opposite the barracks; Cobrora flushed hotly as a half-naked woman leant over the frail-looking wooden balcony and beckoned to join her upstairs.

"The brothel will do well." Ulran grinned. "Saurosen IV always called Soemoff a town of animals – and he wasn't referring to the market..."

"*That* impotent pig!" Cobrora spat out suddenly, then started, realising how dangerous those words were.

"So... You have some fight in you, after all!" Courdour chuckled.

"Don't worry, Cobrora, your 'treason' is safe in our company."

"Speaking of company," observed Courdour, nodding ahead.

As one, they reined-in.

Across the dirt road spread four troopers bearing the breast-plate crest of the local lord. A short distance behind, the toll office and bridge spanned the road. The garrison leader stepped forward. "Welcome to Soemoff, travellers. What business brings you through the lands of Lord Cantonera?"

Leaning forward on his pommel, its leather creaking slightly, Ulran smiled down at the soldier. And Cobrora involuntarily tensed. "We two are travelling in search of work," the innman lied and thumbed behind: "Courdour Alomar here has offered his company on the Cobalt Trail."

The garrison leader's eyes tracked to the warrior and widened perceptibly, his face draining of blood, as though some childhood horror had risen up before him.

Evidently, Courdour's fame had even seeped into these small towns. The garrison leader shakily saluted, waved his spear at his guard and the way was made clear. "You'll find board at the Gilded Crest," he said helpfully, indicating an inn on the right of the wagon-park, though doubtless neglecting to explain that he would earn a percentage for steering them there. The other two inns, Barter House and The Blue Flame, probably had similar arrangements with his comrades.

"Thank you. We'll be on our way again at first light." Gentling Versayr forward, Ulran signalled for his companions to follow.

As they passed beneath the toll bridge a man rushed to the rails and shouted down, "Stay! You have not paid your toll!"

All three looked up.

"For our safe passage through Oquar?" queried Ulran.

"Aye, traveller, that's Lord Cantonera's ruling."

"Then, here, catch your toll!" And Courdour threw up a sack.

Gingerly, the toll collector caught it.

Ulran urged Versayr to go on.

A scream from the toll-collector drew their attention and they glanced back. Face ashen, the toll-man dropped Rashen Pellore's head to the road, where it bounced and then lay still. Further back, the garrison leader stared, immobile.

"So much for your lord's protection, toll-man!" shouted Courdour Alomar, and they rode on at a brisk canter, across the crunching stones of the wagon-park.

Some time later, after they had settled into their respective quarters, a heart-rending cry sent both Courdour and Ulran grabbing for their swords and rushing to the open doorway of Cobrora's room.

Spread upon the cotton sheets of the bed were all the pouches, amulets, effigies, signs, papers and vials of Cobrora's superstition. Kneeling by the bedside, head buried in hands, Cobrora was wailing and crying.

"What ails you now?" Courdour demanded, his tone indicating he disapproved of men weeping.

Between sobs, Cobrora answered, "My – my token, my figurine – for Alasor – it's gone... stolen!"

Stepping forward, Ulran sheathed his curved sword. He knelt beside the heartbroken city-dweller. Cobrora looked as though the whole world had crumbled underfoot, eyes dark and lost. "The white lesslord of water?" queried the innman after a moment.

"Yes. All I'm left with is his antithesis – Mussor." Blood-shot eyes streamed in the candlelight. "Don't you see, this is a bad omen. Evil surviving over good–"

"Ye gods!" seethed Courdour in the doorway.

Ignoring the warrior, Ulran smiled and clapped Cobrora on the back. "Stop worrying. You probably lost it during the ambush. Why not throw Mussor away as well, then you will be balanced, neither triumphing?"

Courdour leant against the door frame and grunted.

Sobs quieting, Cobrora said, with reluctance, "I suppose I could try. If I burned it–"

"Now, try thinking ahead yourself, Cobrora," Ulran said, building a fire in the disused hearth. "Don't rely only on the gods and their omens.

You walk of your own accord. Try thinking ahead on your own too."

Dropping the effigy of Mussor into the flames, Cobrora nodded and mustered a tentative conviction in voice that was hardly felt: "I'll certainly try."

And the wood hissed and steamed but could not burn.

"Oh, no!"

***

A dismal mist hung close to the ground as dawn glimmered weakly. Now they had two mules fully provisioned with ropes, axes, blankets, shovels and food sufficient for the journey to Courdour's toran. They bid the Gilded Crest's innman farewell.

Turning down the street, they peered into the haze. Cobrora was on edge, eyes betraying lack of sleep. Of few words as they prepared, Cobrora had settled for declaring that the mist was attributable to the ill-omens amassing about them, preparing to cut them all down.

Courdour simply laughed.

Though the Crest's innman had said the mist always came down in this hollow area just before dawn when the Sormakin blew, and dissipated two orms after sunrise, Ulran decided not to wait. Once outside Soemoff's palisade, they would leave this trail and break new ground.

Scalrin still hovered as they left. Ulran was tempted to enlist the bird's help, but a more fruitful path presented itself. He called ahead: "Can you see further, Cobrora?"

Turning with a start, the city-dweller blinked as though awakening from a doze. Was this what Ulran had meant last night? *See* ahead? Stionery could not help the innman in this. "I'll – try." Cobrora gently edged Sarolee forward, past the skeptical Courdour Alomar, into the wispy curtain of moist air.

Outside the palisade's gate, the clearing and small patchwork of upward-sloping vegetable farming petered out and undergrowth thickened beneath the horses' tread. A tracery of outlying saplings warned of the beginnings of the forest.

Cobrora slowed, peering through narrowed slits, temple pounding with the necessary concentration. The esoteric faculties had never been employed at a continuous pitch for any length of time comparable with this, and the effort was seriously draining. The headache jabbed insistently, but Cobrora persisted, forgetful now of last night's ill omen, oblivious of the jangling effigies on either hip.

Distraught though Cobrora had been, it was not difficult to appreciate the calming effect of Ulran. *Perhaps I can understand a little now why*

Courdour, a fighter, behaved so painfully after the ambush: a man with fighting in his blood wouldn't easily accept another cowering from the glory and pleasure, as he would deem it. A strange man, was Courdour Alomar.

Slowly, they penetrated the woods. The strange prescience was such that Cobrora could not see shapes with eyes but rather sensed them. As a back-lashing branch almost thudded into Cobrora's face, the city-dweller ducked instinctively and realised with a pleasant shock that, whereas earlier – using eyes alone – it would have been almost impossible to see it in time to dodge.

On two occasions Cobrora called a halt and on dismounting they had discovered deep and vicious animal traps directly in their path. Weird. Unable to describe the danger precisely: it had been simply a cold, clamminess about the heart, recognised from past experience as a warning.

Their progress was slow; but eventually they reached the edge and emerged to see the woods curving to their left, rising and falling with the grassy escarpment land.

Now they rode to the manderon, the last wisps of morning mist snaking behind them, clinging to the humid woods. Cobrora looked back, and all that was visible were the tree-tops, looming out of an uncanny swathing haze.

As they left the forest behind a slight warming breeze passed over them, and their clothes – damp with dew and mist – clung coldly. But soon, under the climbing sun, their garments dried and the breeze lessened.

The cultivated land receding behind them, they were now traversing plainsland, pocked with humps of sand, patterned by the whim of winds and plains-creatures.

Always out of range of Alomar's arrows or sling-stones, small herds of fawn idly grazed, their solitary sentinels eyeing the travellers till they had passed.

Dotted about were purple plants as tall as two men, which, Ulran said, "provide a milky liquid quite palatable, though if you drink too much a reaction takes place in the stomach and bloating occurs, so severe that within two days the stomach bursts." Cobrora shuddered. "The Overlord intended man to enjoy all things – in moderation." The innman grinned, eyes flashing in amusement.

The day drew to a rapid close; a silvery sheen of the quarter-moon heralded Sufinma.

They stopped by a shale promontory that would provide shelter against the plains-winds and frost: even through summer, Cobrora knew, the plainsland was thinly blanketed with frost in the dawn.

Lashing blankets together upon poles, they anchored the tent with rocks while Cobrora lit a fire and unpacked pans and food.

Stars glimmered in the firmament and the eyes of plains-dogs shone in the sudden blackness that circled the camp. But Cobrora's mood had lightened throughout the day's journey; the headache still persisted and its cause certainly gave some concern, but the psychic efforts in the wood had provided a sense of achievement, though Courdour Alomar refrained from acknowledging this. But, stirring the stew over the smoking fire, Cobrora again pondered upon the awful headache, the like of which had never before been experienced.

***

Because mist's very nature had from time beginning been regarded as a weapon of arcane power, Por-al Row was pleased as he looked upon his stagnant pool.

The addition of herbs from the peaks of the Sonalumes had helped; he had been loath to use these, for the times of harvesting were short and only occurred every seventeen years. But King Yip-nef Dom's rising ire had demanded something be done hastily, lest even the royal alchemist and enchanter should feel the anger of the king and go the way of all his poor concubines. Which would be most annoying, drastically upsetting his long-term designs. And the small sacrifice had been worth it, for now he could scry exceedingly well, aided by the reflective qualities of the mist.

Unfortunately, having remained within Arisa's ancient bounds for so many years, he recognised neither traveller, though he was surprised to observe that a third member had joined the party.

Yip-nef Dom's face paled at sight of the newcomer, a giant of a man dressed entirely in black, a large floppy hat concealing his face.

"Is – is that Cour – Courdour Alomar?" the king queried, flabby cheeks all of a tremble.

Interest quickening, Por-al Row leaned closer, squinted. "Difficult to say, sire... Could be – though he would indeed be foolish to return to Arisa!"

Yip-nef Dom barely contained his fear and hate. Glass eye glinting blue in the reflection of the astral picture, the king added, "Courdour's toran is reputed to be somewhere in Marron Marsh, I believe."

"That could be it, sire – he's only accompanying the travellers as far as there." The alchemist scowled. "See, the bird, how it persists in flying with them." He flinched involuntarily.

"Yes, I would like to know why your mysteries desire these two men to be brought here with that bird."

So would I, so would I, thought the alchemist, but said, archly, "In time, sire, we shall learn all." He grinned, baring ill-formed teeth.

CHAPTER FOUR
ORB

"Spiders are nasty!"
– Queen Neran II of Lornwater
(Crowned 1153 – Deposed 1185)

Durin blossomed into light early and the sun soon melted the tracery of frost and warmed their bones, which felt frozen to the very marrow. Cramp spasms assailed Cobrora. Stepping forward, Courdour Alomar roughly massaged Cobrora's left leg and the pain gradually eased.

Soon afterwards they were packed and moving across plainsland. The terrain, though undulating in deep and shallow waves, sloped up towards the varteron, doubtless aiding the teen-flow from the Sonalumes. Over their right shoulders was the edge of Oquar II Forest, extending as far as the eye could see.

Save for a few flocks of birds, they saw hardly any wildlife. They travelled without a break until topping a prominent rise that commanded a view of land beyond.

The middle distance to horizon was an indistinct haze, but directly ahead Cobrora could see the plains feathering into lush grassland, with flat-topped trees dotted about. Then there was a meandering ribbon of blue crossing from dunsaron to varteron, source and destination of Saloar Teen lost to sight – until Cobrora peered through narrowed eyes, with palm shielding them.

While the scene ahead greatly affected Cobrora with its beautiful contrasts of greens and blues, it paled to insignificance when compared to the towering mountains beyond the haze, myrtle in shade, with white-pointed caps, as though great fortresses floating upon clouds. Surrounding some peaks to lend the fancy more credence were wraithlike clouds, white and solid-looking, made more substantial by the blue sky.

Pointing just above Saloar Teen, Courdour Alomar said, "Marron Marsh is there... no, you won't see it yet, even through a spyglass. In the haze... it is perpetually surrounded by a dense fog."

"But first," interjected Ulran, observing Cobrora's blanched face at mention of the marsh-fog, "we must descend to the lower plain and cross Saloar Teen."

The rugged promontory from which they descended was high and steep, and had to be negotiated with care.

Fortunately, by now, Cobrora could well manage Sarolee, though at times like this the thought occurred that perhaps the palfrey was leading and not the other way about.

And, always above and ahead, the darting shadow of Scalrin.

"How far to the teen?" Cobrora asked, nauseated with the repeated jolting of the descent.

"About two and a half days."

To combat the queasiness, Cobrora counted off the days: Fourth Durin, Sapin. First Sabin of Fornious. "Carnival Day!" the city-dweller exclaimed humourlessly.

"Seems like an omen?" Courdour Alomar said, grinning.

Cobrora shrugged, the warrior's irony wasted.

***

Crossing the high grasses during Fourth Sapin was almost carefree.

Cobrora's earlier nausea had returned and Ulran noticed. "Don't worry, it takes city-men a couple of days to get accustomed to the motion of the grasses. Hearsay has it that The Sea is like this."

Groaning in reply, Cobrora managed a nod and reddened at the sound of Courdour's laughter.

Swathing back as the horse's chest ploughed through them, the grasses hissed and slithered, wavering like some inland sea. The sun beat mercilessly, the grasses already parched; the horses sustained small fine cuts in the flanks and chests from the scything dry blades.

For a brief while Ulran called a halt and together the three unfurled blankets to use as improvised buffers for the horses, after which progress quickened, much to Cobrora's disgust as the brief stop had been a most welcome respite.

Their diet was supplemented by Courdour's archery: his arrows skewered a couple of rabbits. Another time, he used his slingshot to good effect. Cobrora felt they fared well and now looked forward to the camp-side meals.

But, to Cobrora's consternation, the mountains did not seem to get any nearer. And there was almost another day before the teen.

Already, after only seven days the city-dweller sensed a noticeable change within, feeling more physical somehow. The first couple of days were filled with suffering, wrists aching till they virtually dropped off with gripping the reins; buttocks were still bruised and red raw in places and thighs underwent agonies of cramp. But now, Cobrora thought, I sit in the saddle a great deal more confidently: it was painful at first, but I am hardening to it, sleeping soundly when not on watch, untroubled by the many night-sounds. Must be getting braver. At least I'm not in unremitting agony – more like a dull ache, I suppose. The sun's bronzed my skin too. Thank the Lords and Gods I don't possess a fair skin like those Ranmeron folk."

Though still many launmarks away, Saloar Teen exerted its influence. The air seemed clearer in the distance, cleaned by the constant freshwater spray; and here underfoot the grass was becoming greener as they closed the gap.

On four separate occasions Ulran dismounted to study hardly noticeable patches of broken grass. Once, a scuffed rock, and once he declared that the odd traces of trampled grass signified a herd of wild horses, chased by a horde of Devastators a while ago. Another time, he felt the warmth of some creature's dung, testing its consistency, and remarked: "This could be Kellan-Mesqa stock. They feed their horses a special additive to their oats. They came this way not more than five orms gone."

Cobrora's eyes described a full circle but could only see the contrasting waves of green and yellow grasses all round; and, behind them, the far promontory tapering down to the forest. As in the forest, there was the crawling sensation up the spine, as though being watched with malice.

"I've heard the Devastator hordes are gathering, preparing for another war of attrition."

"Not all the Kellan-Mesqa are as bad as the land-tillers impute, Alomar," Ulran said, recognising the fashion where the family name was first and the given birth name second.

Courdour shrugged. "I've never had cause to like or dislike them. And though I may listen to rumours I never give them any credence."

"Gossip is mightier than the sword!" quipped Cobrora.

Looking askance, Courdour Alomar rejoined, "Many a truth concealed in a jest, Cobrora Fhord."

The creasing of Courdour Alomar's mouth sent unwelcome shivers down Cobrora's spine; almost preferring the open antagonism to this new aspect of the warrior. "Indeed, Alomar," came the answer, using the warrior's chosen name. Not for the first time, Cobrora wondered at Ulran's lack of a second appellation.

"We'll just have to keep our eyes open," Ulran concluded and they rode on.

* * *

Headless upon a spit, the rabbit sent up tantalising smells as Courdour basted and turned it above the licking flames. Trickles of fat sizzled on the fire. To one side lay the animal's head and paws, the latter saved as requested by Cobrora for charms.

Camp was a happy place this evening; as Ulran remarked, "Tomorrow, we should see Saloar Teen!"

Being their first significant geographical landmark, it had held an almost hypnotic importance during the days' travelling. The next day would signal barely a seventh of the journey, but once the teen was crossed it would be a psychological victory, the first barrier overcome. Spirits were therefore high.

Ulran decided to break out the limited beer ration after they had crossed the teen.

"In moderation," Courdour said and they all laughed, Cobrora most of all.

Later, lying beside the blazing fire, Cobrora dozed fitfully and felt quite contented, fears mostly dispelled. Though the headaches had gone, their nature still caused concern: always they seemed to be accompanied by a rancid, often stagnant stench permeating nostrils.

Yes, I feel almost one of them now, Cobrora thought, eyes closed, strangely replete.

A fighter I will never be, but at least both Ulran and Courdour Alomar now tend to accept me as one of them.

I have no guilt at the deception, no guilt at all.

***

Presentiment probably alerted the city-dweller first. The immediate instinctive reaction was to open eyes and jump up, nerve-endings were so desperate in their message of alarm. But another, quite insidious and insistent stimulus had penetrated, just in time before acceding to instinct.

Ulran's urgent whispering, "Fhord – do *not* open your eyes..." repeated softly, rising in volume until it filtered beyond subconscious to conscious self, "Fhord – do not open your eyes. Don't move even a fraction. Concentrate on nothing. Be calm."

Naturally, the urgency alone impelled Cobrora's body to spurt additional adrenaline; a need to *see* what in all the gods' names was happening.

Very faintly Cobrora could feel – more sense than feel – the exiguous tracery of threads upon brow, cheeks and nose. Resist all impulse to jump up, to blink eyes open. Relax!

Instead, concentrate on mentally picturing the sensation: it was a web.

"That's better," Ulran said. "Whatever you do, do *not* open your eyes. Don't even blink." Then: "There's an orb-spider's web covering both your eyes – the spider is suspended over your right eye at the moment."

"*Light – closer!*"

"Don't spea–" Then the innman realised Cobrora had not spoken. He had snatched words from the psychic's mind. Knowing the orb-spider would not be affected by light, he grabbed a flaming brand and held it closer.

Now, with the light upon flickering eyelids, sliced by the criss-cross web of the creature's devising, Cobrora Fhord could dimly perceive shapes through the eyelids, against a flesh-redness. As concentration deepened the picture became even clearer.

The webbing was like dew, little gobs of it drooling, shining in the torchlight. The web over the right eye was taut and suspended upon it was an all-white spider, easily measuring the span of a man's hand. Beautiful in its symmetry and the detail of its hairy legs, the patient poise of its head and cruel-looking pincers, it stared down at the right eye, aware that when Fhord awoke the eye would open.

Cobrora had always thought these grassland denizens were pure fiction, created by children's storytellers for salutary nightmares. Detecting the glint of the white of the eye, the orb-spider would lunge its sharp pincers down, extracting the entire organ. It would quickly gorge the eye, storing it in its cheek pouch whilst scampering crab-wise to safety.

Apparently, they fed on unwary or ill grassland rodents and newborn calves and foals.

Cobrora's entire skin felt as though it were cringing at the horrid prospect.

Sweat seemed to saturate clothing. And would the vile thing lunge anyway, slicing through eyelid?

To compound matters, the spider possessed a dangerous, virulent sting-tail, capable of felling a man with one jab.

"It's worth a try–" Courdour Alomar too had remembered the orb-spider's eating habits and his earlier kill – the rabbit – had given him an idea: "I know these orb-spiders have the patience of the gods – but Fhord can't lie there forever." He cut out one of the rabbit's eyes.

"It's his *only* chance."

Skirting Cobrora, the warrior slowly reached out to the city-dweller's left eye with the rabbit's orb and pressed it through the web, so that it stared skywards on top of Fhord's lid.

The breaking of the web gained the orb-spider's attention and the creature's sudden movement alarmed Fhord who somehow resisted the reflex urge to blink.

Time stretched then the spider noticed the rabbit's eye.

It was over within the blinking of an eye, though Cobrora's were now incapable of that automatic act, so frozen with dread after this narrow escape.

The rabbit's eye vanished within the spider's pouch and it scurried away, leaving the delicate spoor of web in its wake from grass stalk to grass stalk.

Cobrora Fhord let out a thankful sigh and stiffly sat up. Hands shakily coming away from eyes with tacky threads, the touch sent great shivers down spine and limbs.

"A drink, I think," said Ulran and broke out the wine skin. "After that ordeal, you deserve it!" He smiled, recalling those brief alarming words from the psychic's mind, because something else had slipped through too. Your secret is safe with me, Cobrora Fhord, he thought. "You were very brave, Fhord."

Gratefully, Cobrora took a gulp then turned to Courdour. "Thank – thank you, Alomar. I couldn't think of any way at all of unseating the thing!"

Courdour Alomar crouched in front of the fire without speaking. Then he turned. "Come, let us savour the rabbit, it's cooked now."

So Cobrora Fhord learned something of the mysterious Courdour Alomar: some things did not require thanks. Saving a man's life was one of them.

Stomach feeling a little more settled after the first reaction, Cobrora sat down with Ulran and Courdour and ate heartily, though still occasionally brushing away imaginary webs from both eyes in response to an uncomfortable tingling memory.

**

In the heavy blackness of no-moon, the mountains rumbled and shook. Freak high pressure ridges had caused a sudden imbalance and now anvil-headed clouds mounted each other, swirling blue-grey against the deeper black of night sky.

Denizens of the foothills had mysteriously gleaned the atmospheric changes and sought shelter in ample time; recluses high in the mountains had their ways of knowing also, and calmly battened down their cave entrances.

With abrupt violence the storm broke.

It was as though the gods had filled a gigantic hide-gourd with half an ocean then rent the gourd open, to gush contents in one almighty deluge. The massive weight of water swept almost all before it; conifers which had clung to the lower slopes for years, loose boulders which in turn loosened others, creating a muddy avalanche as well as worsening the incredible welter of water.

And the cause, the storm, had expended itself as quickly as it had come, leaving the great torrents of water, seeking and pounding the rifts and valleys.

The water tumbled into the teens, swelled them to capacity, coursed on and on, piling a wall of water ahead of it, together with logs, weeds, dust and silt.

Tumultuous in its force, unstoppable in its raw natural power, the flash flood seemed determined to rush headlong through the land, on and on, to spend itself in one final stupendous cascade over the Varteron Edge.

Floreskand: Wings

CHAPTER FIVE
SEER

On the first day of the new moon, spill an innocent's blood; fill the 17 prepared cups; drink of one each day; thus, for 17 days you will be able to See for half an orm.
– *The Xadra of Quotamantir*

Cobrora Fhord burned intensely. Lying in the chill night, the city-dweller's body flushed uncannily yet did not awaken. This was no fever or reaction to orb-spider poison.

Courdour Alomar watched his companion toss and turn and cast aside a blanket. Even in the fire-glow, Cobrora's flush was unmistakable. And as the warrior knelt closer he saw Cobrora's cheeks and brow were inflamed in criss-cross fashion where the spider-web had lain. As though branded, he thought fancifully.

Suddenly, the campfire emitted a disconcerting shower of sparks, the wood cackled evilly and a falling branch rolled out and across the ground, into the grass.

The horses whinnied in alarm.

Courdour Alomar sprang up and started stamping out the burning grass as it leapt in a narrow trail of fire evidently in the wake of the orb-spider. Finally, he had extinguished the flames and all that was left was a thin black line.

And in the camp itself Cobrora still lay restively whilst Ulran was now sitting upright, curious. "Trouble?"

Courdour shook his head. "No, only a few stray sparks." He did not actually doubt the evidence of his own eyes. But he was loath to admit what he had seen.

"Time to shake Cobrora for his watch, anyway," suggested Ulran on glancing at the sky.

The city-dweller was mumbling something and finally, on waking, said, hazily, "Osasor! I called him but he came too late! O, Osasor!" Then Cobrora looked around and shivered. The unusual flush had gone and left a face as white as alabaster, save for faint red traces where the webs had been.

"Your watch, Cobrora."

"Hmm? Oh, thanks. I'll put more firewood on – it's even colder tonight."

Courdour Alomar settled into his bedroll and looked askance at

Cobrora. He shook his head in bewilderment and closed his eyes to rest.

***

First Sabin of Fornious was spent without rest or food for the three travellers. Ulran pressed on without regard, hoping to make the teen by nightfall. Scalrin soared above, always in the lead.

Besides the occasional and annoying facial after-tingling of the web, Cobrora again suffered incredibly vicious headaches. And accompanying them was the smell of something rotten, decayed and vile. The constant unremitting jogging of Sarolee, an empty belly, the headache and the vile stench that clogged nostrils combined to weaken Cobrora so the city-dweller couldn't help but lag behind, to Courdour Alomar's voiced chagrin.

But the agonies were real and Courdour's temper was nothing in comparison. Only an arcane ability to transcend the physical plane, albeit briefly, prevented Cobrora toppling from the horse.

The day's fast helped martial weakened faculties until now the city-dweller was in a perpetual half-reality, the inner-being warmed by half-formed shapes, indefinable but benign, of buildings of black, of people of warmth, of flames of beauty.

***

A cowhide was stretched between a ring of upright posts and filled with bubbling blood.

Por-al Row sweated not from his exertions but from fear. His liege had commanded that if blood was necessary for the enchanter to See, then blood he should have, by the bucketful.

And now the blood of Yip-nef Dom's hapless concubines gurgled unpleasantly, the stink colouring both himself and his king green.

But the lengthy incantation appeared to be having some effect, at last.

Gauzelike, a picture rose with the steam: the image shimmered, of Lornwater's Gildhouse on the first day of the carnival: the First Sabin of Fornious. But there was no laughter here. Few words penetrated through but it was evident, by reading lips and expressions, that the gildsmen were massing together, anxious to oust Saurosen IV.

King Yip-nef Dom looked worriedly at his alchemist, his good eye nervously watering. "We cannot afford a civil coup – and those gildsmen are the best organised to accomplish it, if any can."

The alchemist nodded, pleased with his experiment's results. "I agree, sire. Our pl – your plan might come to nought if the unrest is either quelled or the king overthrown."

Nose twitching at the noisome concoction, Yip-nef Dom said, "Well, what do you propose to do about it?"

"I have been looking at a certain gildsman in Lornwater. A man of dubious morality. Gildmaster Olelsang is ambitious, proud and conceited. He may serve our ends, sire."

***

First Sabin. And they could smell and hear Saloar Teen now.

Cobrora had shaken off another headache and breathed in the invigorating spray-breeze.

Ulran drew up Versayr on the rise ahead and the others reined in beside him. A short distance below swirled the teen, a good fifteen marks wide, running fast and deep.

Cobrora was unsettled by the sight and swallowed nervously at the prospect of crossing.

"Further upteen are some narrows with stepping-stones," said Ulran. "We'll ride on till dusk. The narrows should be about a half-day's ride after that."

Slightly disappointed, Cobrora gazed skywards, searching for a familiar shape that usually blotted out the sinking sun in its circling flight. But Scalrin was nowhere to be seen. A bad omen, for sure.

Later, they passed stunted trees on either side of the teen. "The dead remains of leech-trees," Ulran explained. "They were felled long ago, in the times of legend. Their leaves hung down into the teen, clogging the waters, and sent poisons down-teen to the early settlements."

Cobrora shuddered, for though blackened with age and death, the tree stumps exerted an evil, sentient presence.

A short way further up-teen Courdour Alomar grunted and dismounted.

Cobrora alighted too, pleased to rest weary limbs and eat.

After the welcome meal, closing eyes and, sensing that the next day might bring great exertion, Cobrora slept the instant head touched saddle. But after a short while exhaustion was slaked and sleep became fitful, bathed in a swamp of sweat. The loss of both lesslords of water was troubling.

When Ulran came to shake Cobrora for the next watch, the city-dweller was already awake.

In the darkness of no-moon, Cobrora watched the starlit water glistening, roiling. The tethered horses moved on the grass restlessly, snorted at any movement.

Animals tended to be aware of Cobrora long before they sensed another person's approach.

It was tempting to go across to commune with Sarolee, then, attracted by the clear night sky, the idea was dismissed.

Stars shone, forming the Pyramid there, the Ranmeron Point at the apex; and, there, a spiral of stars resembling the fluting of a taal-shell. The taals. Cobrora had read much about Taalland, of the legendary towns on stilts, but had not even seen a taal shell, only beautifully detailed drawings in the Archives. Small wonder the Archives were regarded as hallowed ground. So much history and learning within their mighty tomes.

As a youngster Cobrora had realised full psychic potential there, within the long musty lanes of books, aisle upon aisle of knowledge; as though feelers of thought actually reached out, guiding a young mind to those particular esoteric works now remembered so well.

Cobrora had read voraciously, returning daily to feast, little appreciating then how the volumes of philosophy opened the mind and un-clamped the shackles.

Then one day Cobrora had seen the Librarian stumble and fall on a stairway; only to learn later that the Librarian had indeed fallen – but a full quarter after Cobrora had seen the accident. Fortuitously, immersion in the philosophical treatises had prepared the mind for this shock: Cobrora was a psychically sensitive person, one in ten thousand.

Since then, nightly training followed, but always within the comfort of the city walls.

Now, sitting the water's edge, chewing a piece of milk-grass, the city-dweller raised closed eyes to the heavens, slowly opened them and gazed to a fixed point, higher and beyond the stars. Cross-legged, Cobrora swayed. Body temperature lowered. Shivered. Blood coursed through temples, slowed and became sluggish. Head spinning giddily, Cobrora persisted in staring at that point so far away. Swirling, blood in ears pounding, dizzying, eyes ceasing to focus, save down a dark cold tunnel, spiralling, and – Cobrora could see, yes – *see*!

Faintly, but discernible all the same, a small pin-point of light in the darkness. White in texture, soft and beckoning, enlarging painfully slowly, exasperatingly slowly as Cobrora Fhord continued to swim ever faster and sickeningly in the vortex of subliminal emotions. Cobrora's whole body felt as though it was being violently shaken apart. Then whiteness enveloped all self. Cobrora was submerged, bathed in an eerie glow, and gradually the glow took shape, jagged, leaping, cavorting. The configuration of flames, of effulgent searing fire, coloured reds and yellows and oranges.

But no scream of burning pain crossed tight-pursed lips, only a beatific smile. This was surely ecstasy, the closest yet to Osasor! Cobrora felt at peace, as though coming home at last.

PART THREE
FIRST DEKIN – THIRD DLOIN OF FORNIOUS

The Song of the Overlord – part the Third:
Each quarter of the moon is devolved
Round His own insistence, His own desire
He hath nurtured and become the five elements
Indeed, nothing existeth, that He is not
His vitality is all of life's source, itself
And He is all speech, every mouth is His own
He is all senses, listening with every ear
The sight of all eyes is He.

CHAPTER SIX
TEEN

> Like the empty sky it has no limits
> Yet it is right in this place, ever profound and clear
> When you seek to know it, you cannot see it
> You cannot take hold of it
> But you cannot avoid it –
> Death.
> – *Dialogues of Meshanel*

Dawn light shimmered in the dew-laden air. The sound of the teen spray dimly penetrated and Cobrora finally awoke, brows and hair covered with globules of dew and spray.

Then, I slept well, after all, Cobrora realised; strangely, I feel refreshed.

A dun-coloured warbler chirped its first song of the day as Cobrora rose on slightly stiff joints. Was this a foretaste of old age? Cobrora smiled, recalling the ages of the other two: a long way to go, yet! Clothes, particularly the leggings, clung to cold-pimpled flesh; knees trembled as if with ague, and all fingers were blue.

Rigorously slapping hands together and stretching toes within the hardened hide boots, Cobrora glanced back at the small camp.

A sinking feeling. Being on watch last, the fire should have been kept burning; but now it was too late, only dying embers smouldered beside the still forms of Ulran and Courdour.

Seeing the wispy ashes evoked memories of last night's dream or vision, of the close proximity of Osasor. Bodily, Cobrora tended to warm just at the thought of Osasor and thus emboldened felt capable enough to face the teen. Still ague-ridden, the city-dweller went to shake the others: Courdour was already awake.

Having un-hobbled the horses, Cobrora led them and the mules to the teen.

The air was fresh. The surrounding land emerged from the haze in the distance. The mists of Marron Marsh seemed to slice across the view at the far extremity of the grassy plain. And beyond, jagged and snow-capped, the myrtle shapes of mountains, the Sonalume Range.

Involuntarily, Cobrora rubbed hands over upper arms and clasped tight, shuddering.

The sudden appearance of a dark shape swooped above, obliterating the weak morning sun. Cobrora jerked up, startled.

"Scalrin!" shouted Ulran as he elbowed his way out of his sleeping roll. "At last!"

Eerily silent, the bird swooped and glided as though seeking human prey, then arched in a sharp turn, circling time and again, hovering as if in warning over the waters of the teen.

Ulran answered Cobrora's and Courdour Alomar's quizzical glances with a typical shrug. "He seems to be warning us – but if we're to go on we've got to cross the teen." He eyed Scalrin, said aloud, as if to the bird, "No matter what."

So while Scalrin soared and plummeted above the teen, the three travellers sat down to a cold breakfast. Courdour's scowling countenance did not particularly perturb Cobrora now as they ate: so I let the fire go out, so what? I'm only human.

Midway through the meal Cobrora questioned Ulran about the bird Scalrin: "Until now I've taken for granted your ability to understand that red tellar," Cobrora said, jerking a greasy knife skywards. "But how do you do it?"

"I don't honestly know. A gift, I suppose – similar to your own, perhaps?"

"I see – I just wondered, for I've never before heard of such a remarkable bond between man and red tellar – not even in the legends of the Kormish Warriors!"

Ulran eyed Cobrora steadily. He shrugged and stood up. "We'd best be moving out. Ready, Alomar?"

The warrior nodded. After the dishes had been washed and stowed in the packs, they mounted up and followed the teen.

As they rode on, Cobrora looked at the swirling depths and the turbid waters that violently brushed the overhanging grass tufts on the banks, acutely aware of physical limitations. "I'm no Kormish Warrior, Ulran. I'm sure I'd drown trying to cross that. Osasor's disciples don't take kindly to water."

"Next you'll be telling us we shouldn't have lost your Alasor amulet!" barked Courdour irritably.

"It would have helped," Cobrora said, flushing.

"Don't worry, Cobrora," said Ulran, lancing the warrior a disapproving look. "You'll manage the stepping-stones with Sarolee's help."

"Overlord, you know not what you do!" the warrior said enigmatically, eyeing the heavens. He shrugged, urged Borsalac to ride further ahead. "Come, then, we're wasting time," he shouted over his shoulder, and shook his head in disgust.

Cobrora and Ulran exchanged curious looks. He didn't understand at all, thought the city-dweller.

***

"I'm concerned, Por-al Row," declared Yip-nef Dom irritably, his eyelid around the glass eye watering: it had been a long day and grime now grated painfully, but his pride prevented him from removing it in front of the alchemist. Curses on that fiend, Courdour Alomar! "I want you to See – yes, I know I've run out of concubines, yes I know how scrying saps your strength and power – but we need to See!"

"Very well, sire. I shall use the bones," Por-al Row reluctantly agreed, turning back to his dog-eared books of the arcane, lest the king perceived his annoyance.

The king's peevishness had worsened of late, and he did not like it. Obviously, that she-devil was spending too much time with him, twisting him round her every whim, damn her to the ashes! But whilst the liege was in this mood he dared not say or do anything too ambitious, for the king might do something irrational.

Was it possible, he wondered, this insanity I have carefully fostered might be the ruin of me instead of the salvation? Leafing through the thick parchment xadras, muttering to himself, Por-al Row shivered within his black voluminous robes at the thought of the monster he might have unleashed.

***

At midsun they halted by a small mort-taal. Scalrin had flown out of sight up-teen. Here, the teen was no more than eight marks wide and shallow, the banks steep, with glistening smooth stepping-stones to the other side. The waters gurgled, barely covering the stones. "We'll cross here," said Ulran, dismounting.

Versayr baulked as Ulran took his bridle and stepped into the teen.

"Here, let me go first," said Courdour. "Borsalac's example should calm him."

Ulran stepped back, though puzzled at his mount's behaviour. "The air is so still," he remarked, glancing towards the haze of the Sonalumes. Not a bird stirred in the cloudless sky.

Courdour Alomar led his horse onto the flat slippery stones. The fast-flowing teen swashed against his boots, seeming to splash higher as he progressed across. The speed of the water increased as well.

Cobrora Fhord watched; a dim nagging at the back of the mind, heart cold with the loss of Alasor.

The innman followed the warrior, and though Versayr appeared reluctant they began to cross the stones.

Dismounting, Cobrora steadied Sarolee. The mules seemed unaffected; yet something had upset the horses.

Suddenly, the stillness altered. A whispering rose, became a mounting roar.

All eyes jerked up-teen.

From the direction of the uncanny roar, a haze of water-droplets reflected countless intersecting rainbows. Louder, nearer, it sounded unlike anything Cobrora had ever heard.

The teen-water was now fast-running, threatening to unbalance men and horses. Then, as Ulran barked, "Flash-flood!" it came plainly into sight.

At least two marks in height, a massive foam-flecked and murky wall of water bore down on them, waves of white overflowing each side of the teen.

And flying above the water-wall was Scalrin, great wings beating the air, and a high-pitched shriek of warning filled all their heads though the bird uttered no sound at all.

Transfixed by the incredible sight, Cobrora stared with mouth wide.

Ulran and Alomar were only three-quarters across the stepping-stones. Without a word, they both gripped their mounts tightly and swung up into their saddles. The horses whinnied, sensing the down-rushing danger, their hoofs splashing and clacking on the stones. Ruthlessly, they forced their mounts over the slippery rocks, towards the manderon bank.

Then it was upon them, deafening, and blasted into them broadside on amidst the squeals of the horses and the panicky braying of the mules.

Cobrora's feet were swept from under and Sarolee's taut reins snapped. With incredible violence the wave lifted them up and Cobrora landed upon the turf some distance away. While being lifted, Cobrora saw both companions hurled from their horses and then all vanished beneath the turbulent dark brown barrage of water. Then, mercifully, Cobrora lost consciousness.

On, the flash-flood coursed, unimpeded in its rush to the distant Varteron Edge.

***

Swept abruptly from Borsalac, Courdour Alomar sank like a stone beneath the onslaught of silt-filled water.

The flood's tremendous force dragged him bodily along the teen-bed, battered him remorselessly, threatening to expunge every last breath of air from his protesting lungs.

His senses reeled.

Blindly, the warrior struggled to attain the bank he knew to be near.

He must reach the edge! Though a dark, ancient part of his mind distantly thought, it would be ironically appropriate, death by drowning.

***

Clumps of silt and slimy weed caught in Ulran's fingers and brushed against his face but he couldn't see anything, the murk and dust churned up was impenetrable.

Swirling and gyrating at the whim of the raging wall of water, all he could do was slowly to leak air through teeth, bubbles breaking in his face or burgeoning to the stormy surface of foam. Cross-currents, whirling eddies, and pockets of violently contrasting current-surges tossed him as though he were a piece of timber. Bits of mud, chunks of wood, fingers of eye-piercing branches belaboured him continuously. Then, amidst the pell-mell, something heavy yet soft hit him on the temple: a dead vole or rabbit, he guessed.

Another raging current snatched him bodily and he turned an involuntary somersault, the breath almost bursting from his tired lungs. In the same instant he realised his left leg was tangled in some weeds.

Doubled-up, bubbles seeping out of his mouth at an alarming rate, he wrestled the leg free. Now his chest strained to breaking point.

Must surface!

His lungs felt on fire, muscle-ache nagging insistently, crying out for oxygen, air, air!

Yet because the teen's agitation prevented him rising at will, no sooner had he pointed to the surface than a sudden surge would tumble and twist him and thrust him down onto the muddy bottom. No longer was the teen shallow. He had no way of telling how far down-teen he had been hurled, either.

And what of the others, and the horses and mules?

Detritus, some slimy and clinging, wrapped itself around his thigh. He was set on one more attempt at surfacing but must free himself first – if only he had something more manageable than his sword.

Movement under his hand – he could feel the thing pulsing against his thigh – this was no teenweed!

Something thick, muscular...

Valuable air streamed from his tight-clamped mouth, strength ebbing unavoidably. Ulran's spanned fingers estimated the thing's girth – at least the waist-size of a woman.

The coils tightened upon his thigh and another – or possibly its opposite extremity – began winding across his abdomen.

Primeval panic threatened to assault his senses; only steely control with weakening resources enabled him to keep calm, to determine the size and power of the sinuous creature. Where earlier he had anticipated cutting free with his cumbersome sword, now these constricting coils enveloped him and made it impossible to reach the weapon.

A monstrous thumping and pounding assailed his shoulder and chest.

Reflexively, he reached out, fist clenched in retaliation.

His entire fist sank into something soft and fleshy – a mouth, its roof ridged but toothless, and a thick raspy tongue.

Before the creature could react he grabbed and pulled sharply, tapping the last dregs of his reserve strength, and the thing bucked and whipped, swirling him with it, yet he held on till finally he came away with a great length of tongue, half as wide as his forearm.

But he was done for, he knew, the creature had not relinquished its throttling hold.

And now the water and his whole body were being pounded by an eerie, thrumming vibration, his ears bombarded with the dreadful ululation that threatened to shatter his skull with its piercing intensity.

What little air that remained was squeezed out of his chest and he could feel his grip on consciousness slipping.

White spots danced in his mind's-eye, his head buzzed, he coughed once as some water seeped into his mouth.

This was the end, then, the start of a vicious cycle, coughing to clear water and in the end only admitting even more, till the lungs drowned.

***

Pummelled with debris and weighted down with his waterlogged leathers, Courdour Alomar felt his straining lungs were incapable of holding on any longer. Perversely, he had no desire to die like this; against his better judgement, he wanted to fight, to–

Abruptly, he thudded into something hard and solid, which winded him. With the sudden blow against his stomach, he let out the last of his air, clamped his mouth shut as his head giddily spun with oxygen-starvation. But his pell-mell rush down-teen had stopped. His cloak had snagged a branch or root in the bank's side on his right.

Instinctively, he clawed at it, and pulled himself up hand over hand.

Blindly, fingers feeling bloated and stubby, numbness steadily pervading him, he broke surface, and coughed and coughed as the raging flash-flood swirled round him.

He blinked open his eyes. Life-giving air surged into his lungs.

The root was sticking out from the top of the teen-bank on the manderon side, where the water-wall had gouged out the soft loam to bare a fibrous bush root.

The water-bore was far down-teen to his left now. Here, the embroiled brown water had risen to the top of the bank.

His hacking cough eased. As he pulled himself up, water gushed from him and his weapons clanged against each other.

On hands and knees, he peered around. A few bushes similar to the one that had saved him, undulating grasses: no sign of Borsalac, Ulran or Cobrora.

***

In a thrashing, spectacular mountain of white foam, they both broke the agitated surface and arched high into the air. Coughing and spluttering though he was, Ulran was quick to realise his opportunity. Calmness again prevailed; he sucked in deep gasps of air, then as his coughing died he took in hasty, continuous gulps to serve him in good stead for the coming ordeal. They plunged back under.

Immersed again in the rolling impenetrable water, bubbles swirling noisily about his ears, his thigh numb with restricted blood-supply, his measured blows, cushioned by the water, could not penetrate the constrictor; he had sustained broken skin on his knuckles as he ineffectually belaboured the anvil-shaped skull. He tried gouging out the eyes, having glimpsed their position in the little time above-water: but always his fingers jarred against coarse, hard sacs.

His replenished air was giving out quickly with the exertion.

Air again gushed over his lips; his lungs screamed for fresh vitality. Unavoidably, he breathed out and the excruciating pain lessened a little.

For a second time the gigantic constrictor whipped out of the water.

Ulran gasped for air, preparing for the shuddering dive back into the teen. Fleetingly, he felt that next time he wouldn't survive.

But the duration above-water seemed longer.

He opened his streaming eyes as he realised he was swaying. He was suspended aloft, still entwined within the constrictor's coils. And the creature was in turn clutched within the huge talons of Scalrin.

The fabled red tellar soared, talons clasping the constrictor's sinuous neck. His great beak hacked at the anvil-head, and blood of a purple hue splashed over the innman. At each successive blow, the coil about Ulran's waist slackened; and with each breath of air, his own strength returned. Now he managed to slide his sword free of its scabbard.

Like some disjointed puppet on the end of a line, Ulran danced and jerked till he ached. He stayed his sword for the moment: they were now swaying and bobbing above the ranmeron bank and when the constrictor went limp he'd be dropped either back into the teen without sufficient strength to fight the current or he'd end up on the same side he had started from.

"The other side, the manderon bank!" he croaked, already sensing the life ebb from the creature.

Scalrin must have heard and understood: as they flew lower they crossed the teen. Now Ulran sliced upwards, his sword-point sinking deep into the under-side of the constrictor's mouth. Repulsive blood streamed down the sword-runnel, over the guard and the innman's hand, arm and chest, and suddenly the grassy bank rushed up to meet him.

Fortunately, the cushioning of the constrictor's body beneath him – still loosely girt about his waist and chest – prevented any broken bones.

Lifeless, the constrictor's savaged head thudded to the earth with a dull sound, and sent up a puff of dust.

Ulran wriggled free, but was too spent to move further. He lay by the body, and a dull ache spread through him.

***

An empty expanse of teen; its level was high and brushed the very edges of the banks whilst on each side the grasses were sodden and discoloured with mud. Cobrora lay in a foul-smelling muddy pool and stared forlornly at the water.

A clink of bridle attracted attention. One of the mules was standing quite close. Cobrora groaned; then, perhaps the other was lost – with the food.

And Sarolee, what of her?

Again, images seared the mind, of Alomar and Ulran being swept under the gigantic wave.

Ill-omens spoke truly, then. Cobrora shivered. Dusk was creeping across the land.

Cautiously, the city-dweller stood up, aware that the mule was still skittish, and whispered, "Don't fret, now." A pace at a time, Cobrora neared the mule; it backed away, but less distance each time.

Finally, the coaxing worked: a quick lunge and the reins were grabbed. After a few moments of calming talk and stroking, the mule was hobbled; it carried some blankets, spare poniards and cooking pans, but no food.

Casting about, Cobrora located brushwood some distance from the spray and built a fire. The tinderbox was dry in its pouch. Cobrora shivered, as clothes needed drying out, too.

As the mule fed, Cobrora whispered, "I hope they see the fire." If, the chilling thought came: if they had survived.

***

Courdour Alomar stripped off his clothes and wrung them out, aware how the night-frost would freeze them and him like a board.

Try as he might, he couldn't so easily relinquish his hold on life.

Once dressed again, he decided to head up-teen.

Somewhere, plains-dogs howled.

And night was coming.

***

Slowly, Ulran regained his feet as dusk settled over the land.

Scalrin was sill perched on his kill, casting a pair of yellow eyes at the innman. Ulran felt the chill of the night seep into him as he walked over to the red tellar. He knelt before the white sekor on Scalrin's throat and closed his eyes, communed briefly.

The tie was transitory, or so it seemed, yet now the great bird flicked his wings, and rose majestically into the night sky.

If the others were to be found, Scalrin would locate them.

Circulation painfully restored, Ulran followed Scalrin at a jogging trot.

At first he was troubled by the ugly welts that criss-crossed his chest and the dull throb of his shoulder bruise which was now the size of a melon.

But as he loped up-teen, the tatters of his trousers slapping at his knees, his red-raw waist chafing, he lapsed into no-mindedness, and ignored the spreading ache.

***

Eyes wide, staring fearfully about, Cobrora was too nervous to risk sleeping. A horrible snarl and scuffling came from the impenetrable darkness, frightening the mule on the edge of the firelight.

Unaccustomed to a sword, Cobrora's hand was clammy, the hilt slippery, while pacing up and down past the flickering fire, occasionally stoking the flames with more brushwood. Earlier, the thought had occurred that eyes other than those of companions might spot this fire. But now the city-dweller was becoming reckless: better to die at the hands of some warlike horde than endure much more of this nerve racking solitude!

Must keep busy, Cobrora decided and collected wood, and built four more fires, roughly in a line with the camp, about three marks apart from each other. Then, taking a flaming brand from the first fire, Cobrora lit them all. Making sure they stayed alight would help to keep moving and alert, anyway.

Another coughing snarl from the same direction – and Cobrora edged closer to the nearest fire.

Then, a sudden swishing of grass, swept aside at full gallop, sent heart hammering and hand tightening on sword.

With startling suddenness, Sarolee burst into the firelight, lathered in sweat and eyes rolling with fright.

Relief surged through Cobrora, though it was tempered with caution. By the sounds on the edges of the surrounding darkness, wildcats had chased her.

Despite her panic and fear, Sarolee recognised Cobrora. Once she was unsaddled and wiped down, Cobrora let her graze by the mule, near the fires.

Cobrora no longer felt alone.

The teen shimmered with the firelight along its side. It swirled, mocking, the level already dropping.

A stark picture of the teen entirely drained forced itself into Cobrora's mind: bodies twisted grotesquely, bloated and half-submerged in the slime-bed. Cobrora shuddered and resumed the rounds of the fires, hugging the cloak tight for warmth and reassurance.

***

Strident and close by, the long shriek of a horse stopped Courdour in his tracks. The chill night mushroomed breath in white wisps from his panting mouth. About his eyebrows and shoulders was a layer of rime-frost.

Instinct told him to hurry, for he recognised the cry. But caution advised otherwise. Sword in hand, he edged away from the teen bank, and headed towards Borsalac's whinny.

Starlight dimly illuminated the scene, sufficient for him to see Borsalac backing away. Rearing on his hind-legs, the horse's flailing hoofs thudded fatally into a furry shape that darted upwards.

About the trodden-flat grass lay the corpses of four plains-dogs; another five of the pack surrounded the horse, his withers streaked with blood.

As he neared, Courdour's night-sight perceived the throb of veins in Borsalac's head, the whites of eyes bright and fear-ridden. The white gnashing teeth of the wild dogs and their barking snarls sent the horse into further fits of panic, circling and panting, whinnying at every sound or movement. Borsalac would know that, in the final analysis, he would become yet another kill.

Then, as Courdour watched, planning his strategy and loosening his stiffened shoulder, a change came over his horse. Borsalac halted, sniffed the air, and his demeanour alerted the plains-dogs at the same instant.

Master- and man-scent perceived by Borsalac and the dogs at the same time. The five snarling and snapping dogs swerved away from the horse's deadly hoofs, now intent on Courdour Alomar, a man afoot – easy prey to the pack!

Before the pack leader reached him, Courdour had swiftly checked the immediate fighting-ground – fairly even grassland, without stones or other obstacles. And now he crouched – ready.

The leader leapt, the pack close on its heels. A blur of grey; slavering jaws wide and vicious; eyes red; left-hand brow scuffed bloodily and raw, courtesy of Borsalac, fur foul-smelling: the impressions leapt at Courdour as swiftly as the plains-dog.

In one smooth movement the warrior side-stepped, passing the sword to his left hand, and swept downwards as the foiled animal gnashed at thin air and tried turning in mid-flight. The sword-blade thudded into the arched spine, its downward motion briefly arrested, then Courdour completed the down-cut and severed the wild dog in two. Before the sundered animal fell to the ground, Courdour had passed his sword back into his right hand, ready to meet the other four.

But Borsalac had not been idle. As the four plains-dogs halted abruptly, whimpering and now snarling half-heartedly at the sight of their defeated leader, Borsalac's great hoofs thudded down and crushed the life from the dog furthest from Courdour.

The warrior leapt forward, sword circling, and the leader's blood flew from the blade. The three plains-dogs, completely demoralised, ran to right and left, whimpering with their bushy tails between their legs.

Courdour thrust his sword into the grass, where it stood upright, quivering. He embraced the neck and head of his faithful Borsalac and laughed.

His horse squeaked his affection and snorted.

"You accounted for yourself well, my friend."

Later, he found only thin surface scratches on Borsalac's withers and on one side of his neck. The saddlebags, blankets and other equipment were quit damp but otherwise intact. He withdrew a small pouch of thick mucous-like ointment, which he spread on his horse's wounds. It clearly stung, but the trusting animal did not shy away.

***

Without feeling, Ulran loped along the side of the teen. Infrequently, he emerged from no-mind, each time with more effort, his mind wishing to salve his body; but he must continue his search for a trace of the others, though his eyes had to strain to detect any clue in the poor starlight.

At a rather sharp bend in the teen the racing torrent had evidently over-flowed and battered the banks, upturned the soil. Here, Ulran stopped, detecting some kind of movement at the water's edge.

At this point the rows of leech-tree stumps jutted blackly along the teen's side; one had been violently uprooted by the water-wall's force, another was askew, roots sticking up against the dark sky. A muffled snorting sound issued from behind the farthest tree-stump, by the water. *Versayr?*

As Ulran crossed grass and upturned soil and stone, he glimpsed the shape of a horse's head between two stumps.

The stallion showed up clearly now, black against the grey of teen.

For a moment Ulran wondered why Versayr had not climbed up the crumbled bank, for it was shallow enough to negotiate; but then he spotted the bared roots of a leech-tree stump, reaching out. Needle-thin roots were entwined about the animal's neck and legs. Already Ulran thought he could detect discoloration around the roots, where the tree sucked the animal's blood.

Withdrawing his sword, he jumped onto the muddy bank, slid down and hurled himself at the nearest root, slashing with all his might.

Versayr had seen him on the bank but hardly reacted, so drained was the animal.

Leeches had tasted of Ulran's blood before; the roots, however, sucked blood in a different manner to the jungle and swamp worms. They did not merely stick to the victim's flesh; they dug in, pressing tighter with every ingestion of blood.

But the sword, glinting dully in the starlight, was more than a match for the terrible roots. One after another was slashed, until the innman was covered in rancid lime-green sap that stung slightly.

Having hacked himself clear, Ulran splashed through chest-deep water and severed all the roots wrapped about his horse.

No sooner was Versayr free than he leaned against the teen's current and plodded towards the bank. Haltingly, he climbed the muddy surface and stood dripping wet, too worn out even to shake his soaking mane.

Ulran waded to join him, but stopped as he caught sight of a familiar if forlorn shape – a wet floppy felt hat – hanging on a root.

He smiled: the warrior might not be too far away, then.

But what of Scalrin? If Courdour Alomar was near, the red tellar would have returned with news by now.

He wrung out the hat and tucked it in his waistband. Then he joined Versayr and examined the wicked black-and-blue welts. His own forearms were discoloured too; it would pass.

He turned away, walking Versayr up-teen.

***

Cobrora Fhord jerked awake, the preceding day's nightmare agonisingly fresh. Dying embers crackled and caved in upon themselves and thin streamers of smoke wisped into the dawn air.

Cold and cramped, Cobrora ignored these bodily complaints and looked around, quickly, fearfully, but Sarolee and the mule were nearby, still hobbled, now contentedly chewing grass. Then, whatever it was that had been out there making those horrible noises last night, it had gone.

Shaking the damp dew-laden blankets, Cobrora knelt by the accursed teen and soaked face and hands, the icy coldness shocking the city-dweller fully awake.

As Cobrora stood, the effigies jingled derisively from their belt.

Better search the surrounding area at once. Besides, there's no food for breaking fast, even if my stomach felt inclined. Stomach rumbling in disagreement, Cobrora saddled Sarolee and, leaving the mule, blankets and the few pieces of equipment, rode the palfrey inland, determining to wend a zigzag trail down-teen, searching as they went.

From here, the land to the dunsaron stretched quite flat, so that Cobrora was able to glimpse the vague shape of Funderem Forest's treetops some 200 launmarks distant, peering over the horizon – tall trees of mystery. At least I can be thankful I wasn't cast alone within *their* shadowy confines, Cobrora mused.

A short time after setting out, Cobrora came upon the mutilated remains of the food mule. Paw marks of at least three wildcats circled the carcass. Not satisfied with the food in the packbags, they had torn the mule apart, leaving little for the carrion.

Black shapes of crows flew out of the cave-like ribs, hovered above as Cobrora rode closer, stomach heaving emptily. Thank the gods I hadn't broken my fast!

Flesh-eating voles scampered away into the longer grass; flies buzzed and assembled. Sun-glint showed an orb-spider's web above an empty eye-socket.

Slowly, Cobrora dismounted. Sarolee shied away, nostrils aquiver with the odour of death. After hobbling her, Cobrora neared the carcass, and gingerly unstrapped the blanket and pack-bags containing medicaments of inedible form, a shovel, and a second quiver of Courdour's arrows.

Cobrora would return these to the camp, then resume the search.

***

Courdour Alomar pulled in Borsalac on the edge of the teen opposite Cobrora's camp at the precise moment that the city-dweller returned. The warrior grinned, for Cobrora was staring down, letting Sarolee take them back to the camp. Courdour cupped his hands and shouted across the roiling water, "Cheer up, for your gods' sake, if not mine!"

Cobrora hurried Sarolee to the teen's edge. "Courdour, you old devil! Where've you been? I've been worried sick!"

"Oh, what womanly consternation knits your brow, youngster," chided the warrior, enjoying himself immensely, unwilling to admit that he was pleased to see the superstitious city-dweller.

"But... Ulran – where –?"

As if in answer, Scalrin swooped down and landed on the bank near Courdour.

"I think he'll be on his way." The warrior smiled.

"We've lost our food! And wildcats killed one of the mules!"

"No matter – I still have my bow – and I see you've got a spare quiver of arrows. We won't starve!"

"But how will I get across?"

Courdour held up a hand. "Simple, boy, just simple. But stay there, till we learn of Ulran – if he's on your side of the teen, we might as well wait."

* * *

Versayr had recovered his strength during the night and Ulran had ridden on, with the dark shape of Scalrin guiding him in the dawn sky. Now, the midsun warmed his back, lent him new vitality. He came upon Courdour shouting across the teen.

Ulran simply handed over the floppy hat. Courdour Alomar grinned.

Though joking at the city dweller's expense, Courdour had not been idle; he had unravelled thread from a blanket. He now fired an arrow across the teen and it sank into the turf at Cobrora's feet. Attached to its flight, the thread. "Pull with care, Fhord!" he called.

It took time and patience. Courdour sat astride Borsalac and paid out the thread, and then the rope attached to it. Its weight brought it close to the frothing water – one wavelet would be enough to snap the tenuous link of thread and rope.

Cobrora sat astride Sarolee and pulled in the coils of thread and then rope, mumbling to the white gods; this time it seemed they answered, for at last the rope was across, grasped in both hands.

"Right, boy, you know what to do," the warrior urged and, in an aside to Ulran, "I briefed him while waiting for you."

Ulran nodded, not thinking it strange that Courdour should have known he too would have survived and found his way back. The innman watched with interest.

The scabbard was passed through the bridles of Sarolee and the mule, and tied securely there, so that the scabbard formed a kind of yoke between the two animals. Now, Cobrora secured the end of the rope that spanned the teen to the scabbard's centre. As an added precaution, though not instructed by Courdour, the city-dweller decided to fasten the reins of each animal together as well.

Having collected all the equipment and evenly distributed it between the two animals, Cobrora gently walked them forward to the teen-bank, holding the scabbard which jogged at chin-height and sloped to the left as the shorter mule was by that side.

At the edge, Cobrora hesitated. Against better judgement, the effigies were in the pack-bags and the city-dweller felt immeasurably vulnerable. All that was left were prayers. Invocations tripped from trembling lips.

"Go on, boy!" chided Courdour not without impatience.

Whether the slight had been intentional or not, it served its purpose. Goaded, Cobrora urged the animals into the turgid water.

There was a high-pitched whinny from Sarolee on the right.

The icy coldness sent teeth chattering. The sun was past zenith now, but had not warmed the fast-flowing waters that coursed from the snows of the Sonalume range. Cobrora's heart leapt and fluttered at the very powerful force of the current, tugging at thighs and torso.

Spray clogged nostrils and Cobrora, suspended between the two animals, was soon drenched.

Shakily whistling out of tune to the two animals, Cobrora tentatively eased them forward, feet chilled and hardly capable of feeling their way across the submerged stepping stones. In an act of preservation more than an offer of guidance, Cobrora desperately clasped the scabbard that joined the two horses.

With reluctance, Sarolee and the mule, whites of eyes showing behind their blinkers, stepped through the teen. Courdour Alomar had had the forethought to suggest improvised blinkers, sensibly restricting the violent view about them and thus reduce their excitability. Could have done with some myself, Cobrora thought.

All the while, Ulran and Courdour – both mounted to provide more purchase – pulled the rope towards them, steadying Cobrora who was now wading up to neck height.

After about a mark or two of unsteady, tense moments between the two animals, Cobrora's arms ached, growing weaker while gripping the lifeline and the scabbard. Had I been an accomplished horseman, or so Alomar said, I could have ridden Sarolee across, leading the mule behind. No chance!

Fortunately, Sarolee had swum teens before and was now coping well, her attitude helping the mule. It was only the abnormally swift running current that had alarmed them.

"Not much further!" Ulran called encouragingly and Cobrora could detect the beginnings of weariness in the innman's voice. To a less perceptive person the change would not be noticeable, such was Ulran's incredible control, a will-power that never ceased to amaze.

When Cobrora's knees thumped into the firmness of the opposite bank the city-dweller was surprised. Almost automatically, feet stumbled up the muddy edge and Cobrora fell, arms on fire, chest heaving spasmodically, legs numb.

Ulran handed the rope to Courdour, jumped from Versayr and slid down the bank. He helped the horse and mule up, talking gently, and led them onto firm ground, where, blinker-free again, they shook themselves dry and grazed.

"Your clothes need drying out, lad," Courdour Alomar said.

"No, the sun will do that." Cobrora trembled, as with ague.

Ulran leaned close. "How are you feeling?"

Feeling like a survivor from Below, Cobrora felt like responding, my whole body seems to rebel, disgusted with the constant abuse heaped upon it! Sensation slowly stung back to lower limbs. "All right. I think." Cobrora's head shook, as if to deny those brave words and re-focused eyes. Then the city-dweller's stomach rumbled loudly.

"I'll forage for some food." Courdour Alomar grinned.

It was well past midsun already. "No," Cobrora said, "hadn't we better go on? We've lost almost two days crossing this accursed teen!" Body-ache and hunger berated Cobrora for being a fool even to suggest it. "You could hunt ahead, perhaps?"

"Aye, why not?"

"Then, let us ride on, even if slowly," said Ulran, helping Cobrora up, careful not to show he was impressed with the city-dweller's attitude. "At least we will be covering ground."

With more help Cobrora mounted Sarolee; they trotted beside Ulran.

Courdour rode ahead, soon out of sight in a depression, scouring the land for small game.

As they travelled, the sun dried their clothes and eased Cobrora's aches.

The day was nearly done when Courdour Alomar rode back with the carcass of a small gazelle slung over his horse.

"We've ridden enough for today," said Ulran and they made camp.

After the meal, Courdour insisted on treating Ulran's wounds with some ointments he procured from a concealed pouch. "Their efficacy has been vouched for more years than I can remember – though, alas, you can't obtain the haemoleaf in Floreskand."

"Then – how –?"

The warrior coldly eyed Cobrora. "When you've aged, youngster, you'll know better than to ask such questions."

On completing his ministrations he gave a small portion of the haemoleaf to Ulran and Cobrora. "I have a feeling we may need to use it again, before we're done with this quest."

They were pleased to share the only surviving skin of wine that Ulran broke out from the meagre provisions. All three toasted the First Sidin of Fornious – a day none would forget, "Least of all you, boy, eh?" said Courdour and laughed.

As much to change the course of the conversation than anything else, Ulran turned to Cobrora. "Back at camp yesterday you again referred to Kormish Warriors." The innman looked into the flames. Rumours about him had persisted for many years; but he was continually on the alert lest he should by some foible or accident give credence to such fanciful whispers. "What do you know of them?"

A summing look flickered in Cobrora's brown eyes; the city-dweller shrugged dismissively. "Only what fable tells me – though I have a feeling you could enlighten me – if you had a mind to."

"Riddles, you persist in speaking in puzzles!" remonstrated Courdour.

Cobrora turned. "Have no fear, Courdour Alomar, I don't pretend to believe all the tales of Kormish Warriors! I'm not entirely as simple and childish in years as you make me!"

Ulran released an amused bark.

"I know they're far from being invulnerable."

"Aye, they're not that," Courdour conceded with a scowl.

"You've known one, then?" darted Cobrora as Ulran leaned forward, attentive.

"Two, I think – though it is often hard to know one when you see one." Courdour Alomar eyed Ulran curiously, as though seeking corroboration. But finding none, he went on, "And I saw both die. Deaths that not even I would envy – no, in no way would I choose their manner of going, albeit they had no choice in the matter! Mind you, attractive..." At this point Courdour lapsed into silence. Then: "Must be getting old, rambling now, you see," he mumbled almost to himself and, as if amused at that idea, he burst out laughing.

As Ulran settled back to give the warrior's cryptic disclosure some thought, Cobrora was quick to see a chance at retaliation: "And you accuse me of speaking in riddles!"

CHAPTER SEVEN
PRESENTIMENT

"Fast through the land approaches the foe!"
Scarce could he falter the tidings of sorrow
And when the sun sank on the Valley of Saronvale,
He turned his back on her shallow grave of shale.
– Romantic ballad: *Fiel of Erejhur*

For the next three days they rode manderon and come First Durinma they sighted firelight some distance ahead.

Ulran and Courdour were reluctant to make their party's presence known to whosoever might be abroad. But, after Cobrora's surprisingly vehement and convincing argument, they agreed that it would be advisable to identify the camp and its occupants. Though they had discovered no sign of any Devastator horde this side of Saloar Teen, it was well known that this area was one of their favourite raiding grounds, as evinced by the very few plainsland housesteads that still survived here.

Ulran suspected Cobrora's keenness stemmed from anxiety; for all the commendable control over rank superstition and fear of the outdoors, Cobrora still betrayed signs of disturbance when in the company of Courdour and him.

He had tried curbing Courdour's acid tongue. But it was difficult, for if the rumours about him were true, he'd had more cause to be short-tempered with youngsters like Cobrora and even himself! For his own grandfather had told tales of the peregrinations of one Courdour Alomar and even then he had been Legend. It was possible that Courdour came from a close-knit family who inter-bred, continuing the line of legend, one inheriting the other's looks and mien. But although he knew very little to be impossible either in Floreskand or beyond, he doubted if that could explain the myth that surrounded the figure of Courdour Alomar. If he didn't know any better, he'd say the warrior was a renegade Korm! But that too seemed impossible: the Overlord wouldn't permit one of His own prime movers such free-roaming leeway. Yes, indeed, Cobrora must be very eager for the company of more normal mortals.

With the horses hobbled, the three stealthily skirted the camp in the darkness. Courdour veered left, Ulran right, and Cobrora brought up the rear, not being versed – as Ulran put it – in the art of no-noise.

Remains of two fires quite close to each other smouldered with wisps of thin smoke curling upwards. A little silvery illumination was offered by the beginnings of the first quarter.

Now the shapes of four wagons loomed out of the blackness, dark brown smoke hovering about their gutted superstructure.

Distinctively fletched arrows stuck out at all angles from the bodies strewn about. Severed limbs and heads gruesomely indicated that the Devastators were abroad.

While Courdour clung to cover with a brace of arrows ready to loose, Ulran stepped among the reeking carnage. Judging from the tacky consistency of the blood and the horse-droppings, he estimated the horde had left just over four orms gone.

Through slit eyes Ulran scoured the dimly lit place, crouched low and still: the only sounds were those of the settling embers, the creaking of fire-ravaged wood. But he could be patient.

From days of old, he knew the Devastators: any unproven warrior could volunteer to remain behind after the raid in the hope of taking fresh travellers by surprise. A trial of manhood, one that Ulran had frowned upon.

Slowly, continuing to search the shadowy places, he raised fingers to lips and uttered a low-pitched night-warbler's cry that told Cobrora to stand stock still. For he had detected the faintest of movements. It could be a survivor. Though he had never known the Devastators leave even one.

If it was indeed a novice out for manhood, he was very good. Even now he had no real idea where the youth was hiding: only the slimmest inkling of – there! Quite young, then, he thought. The waiting was beginning to tell; now he could detect the Devastator's desperate attempts to regulate panicky breathing. He managed it, too, but not before Ulran had identified his whereabouts. Second wagon in, to the left of the fire.

With no sound Ulran trod across the dusty earth, stepping over corpses that resembled porcupines, and approached the wagon. The burnt wood glinted jet black in the slice of silvery moon; the wooden sides, reinforced with ironwood struts, had only partly burned, leaving the thick wooden bars intact. From these hung the roasted corpses of what had been men, chained to the struts.

He was glad he had warned Cobrora to stay back. On his way across he had located the huddled shape, behind an iron chest. It was fortunate for the Devastator that the floorboards were of ironwood too. Carefully, he levered himself up onto the backboard and the whole frame creaked under his weight. He peered about the interior, inwardly sickened at the stench of incinerated flesh.

By his own personal code he must wait for the Devastator to act first; how the warrior acted would decide his own reaction. Purposefully, then, Ulran turned his back on the huddled figure in the shadows, though not without a warning tingle that danced his suddenly exposed spine.

He pivoted round as the youngster shrieked the horde's battle- and death-cry. His hide-clad forearm swung round, glancing off the thrust short-sword and the blade passed harmlessly. In the same instant Ulran saw that it was a young girl, her dark eyes and faultless skin corrupted with hate and blood-lust. The dirk left his belt and severed her jugular and was dry in its scabbard within the span of time it takes for a heart to beat – or to cease beating.

Gently, he caught the falling body and nodded, pleased, as the hate and venom vanished from the adolescent features: a serene peacefulness washed over her countenance. It was done, then.

He straightened up and whistled for Courdour Alomar to join him: the place would now be safe. Warrior-status was earned in solitude; there would be no others.

As Courdour stepped into the open, bow still drawn, Ulran glanced about him. The encampment probably comprised tannery freelancers. The far left wagon was a heap of ashes – obviously the bark had burned well.

When he had first suspected them of being tanners, he had wondered why they were so far off the track for the immense oak forests of Forshnorer. For that was the only authorised tannery forest for the next ten years – much to the chagrin of Forshnorer's tree-house inhabitants. But now, seeing these poor wretches shackled, it was obvious.

The wagons had diverted to rendezvous with some illegal merchant caravan. It was common knowledge that slave labour was cheaper and less tedious to use in tannery operations. All he knew for certain was that these slaves had not left Lornwater in these wagons. The sentinels at the gates checked all covered conveyances: there were laws against overcrowding slaves and their hygiene was strictly monitored too. Small headway, indeed, those laws. The slave trade was so deeply entrenched – harking from Tarakanda – that it would take more than his strong sword-arm to free them all. Money talked too well.

Jumping to the ground, he saw Courdour kneeling by some dying ashes. In their midst was a severed head. He knew of only one horde that relished such treatment of human beings. He stooped and withdrew an arrow from a corpse, examined its flight. Nearby, a fallen sword with its special metalmark confirmed his thoughts. "The Baronculer horde!" he shouted across to Courdour.

"After all these years – they're still unchanged."

"It has always been their way; perhaps it always will be." Ulran shrugged. "There's nothing here for us. I see no point in bringing Cobrora –whose stomach's not that strong at the best of times–"

"That's true enough!" Courdour stepped closer, conspiratorially, and shouldered his bow. "Tell me, why did you bring him along in the first place?"

Ulran was not one to hesitate, especially after his training and his daily self-reappraisal; but now he hesitated. And then said, "It wasn't for the want of company, Courdour Alomar." He left it at that. Much as he admired the old warrior, he would not betray Cobrora's trust in him nor countenance Courdour's continual ill-temper towards the city-dweller. His tone tended to convey this.

Courdour simply shrugged, apparently content with the evasive answer.

***

Easily noticeable signs of the departing Baronculer horde showed them moving away from the Marron Marsh route. Ulran kept his report brief when Cobrora showered him with questions. "The Devastators massacred an itinerant tannery group. At least four orms ago they headed varteron. We'll be safe tonight."

It was well into the latter part of First Sapin when they topped a rise that overlooked a solitary housestead; it nestled in a shallow gully directly in their path. To one side was a small grove of mulberry bushes, though the soil hereabouts was not conducive to producing high-quality silk.

"We'll be cautious," declared Ulran. "I'll go down first."

"No," countered Courdour. "I'll go. I think I know this place. Friendly enough folk..." He lanced a sharp look at Cobrora.

Friend. Obviously, that was Cobrora's lack, Ulran realised. Courdour's earlier question niggled: no-one really knew why Cobrora had volunteered for the journey – Cobrora included, though the city-dweller had seemed somewhat more replete with a sense of purpose the night before the abortive teen crossing. Still, friendship was clearly something Cobrora longed for and felt acutely: a need to belong. And for someone of such sheltered upbringing and insular city-life, to aspire to friendship with the like of Courdour Alomar was pure wishful thinking.

He liked Cobrora for the laudable perseverance shown and was even amused at the superstitious antics, but as to regarding the city-dweller as a true friend, no, Cobrora just couldn't qualify. True, friendship wasn't something won or even passed as if in a qualifying examination: it happened. Then, no friendship had blossomed between them.

How strange we are, he thought, at our first meeting at The Inn I knew and Courdour knew that we would be more than friends – without any thought or effort on our part. And yet poor Cobrora, who tries desperately to win Alomar's favour, is friendless.

But Ulran believed Cobrora was necessary for the trek to Arisa: so he determined to intercede should Courdour bait the youngster further. Perhaps they could not be friends in any real sense, but they could afford each other mutual respect at least. And, having guessed Cobrora's secret, Ulran greatly respected the city-dweller and with a wry grin wondered when Alomar would find out.

Courdour emerged from the wooden housestead accompanied by two women and three men. His grin was broad and his moustache curled in the slight valley breeze.

Ulran and Cobrora gently urged their horses down the slope with the mule trailing behind them on a tight rein.

"Bashen Corl, the head of the housestead," said Courdour, slapping the back of a sheepishly grinning grey little man. "He always makes a weary traveller welcome!"

Bashen Corl's palms were coarse and his forearms were iron-hard sinews as he shook hands with all three travellers in turn. Then he introduced his family. "Yoan, my wife," was a red-haired woman of ranmeron stock, pale in complexion and shapeless with child, though the gentle smile that revealed buck-teeth was truly welcoming. "My son, Dyr and his wife, Neran." Both could have been brother and sister, dark of hair and eyes, tanned of skin and docile, mute in the company of strangers. "And my son, Slane."

Ulran hastily introduced himself and Cobrora and they shook hands with the whole household.

Slane's hand was fair, small and warm within Cobrora's. He was wan, taking after his mother, but there the resemblance ended: his blue eyes sparkled with the life of a fountain, his fine muscular figure hugged the ochre breeches and his flaxen hair streaked with black set him completely apart from the others. Cobrora stammered when being introduced and it was only Courdour Alomar's caustic cackle that brought any semblance of reality back and Cobrora abruptly let go of Slane's hand.

Politely accepting Corl's offer of food, Ulran, in return, unpacked the remains of the last skin of wine from their provisions plus a few delicacies from his own bag, which the Bashen family would never have tasted during their normally frugal daily repast.

"I'll chop logs for you in the morning," offered Courdour, now seated comfortably in a broad high wing-backed wooden chair in front of a roaring log fire.

Corl murmured his thanks and offered round his pouch of grass-weed, a sweet delicate blend of plains-grass that smoked delightfully.

Courdour, already prepared by previous visits to the housestead, fished out his ironwood pipe and scooped some of the blend into its bowl. "Where's – Cobrora – got – to?" he asked idly, holding a lighted taper to the mixture and puffing.

Knowing full well where Cobrora was, Ulran shrugged. It seemed the revelation was imminent, he thought.

"I think," Corl grinned, "she took a liking to Slane – she's helping with the dishes."

The warrior almost choked on the smoke mushrooming from the bowl. "*She?*"

Ulran explained. "Cobrora's been disguised as a young man since she came into the Red Tellar. She knew from her reading in the city library that women don't go adventuring. She concealed her feminine aspects very well."

"By the gods, that's cheating. Deceitful! Typical of a woman, though. You can't trust them!" Courdour Alomar seemed to calm down and added, "When did you find out?"

"After the orb-spider attack. Until, then, I hadn't any idea. She was good."

"Then why didn't you tell me?"

"It wasn't my secret to divulge. But since Corl saw through her straight away..."

Corl grinned. "I couldn't mistake the look that passed between them. Slane recognised the woman in her as well, I warrant."

***

While the three men talked round the fire, Yoan sat out of earshot with her small contribution to the land's silk production, sewing a garment.

The scene presented to Cobrora Fhord through the serving hatch as she dried dishes looked like a typical family get-together. Yet the weird and powerful aura about Ulran and Courdour could not be completely dispelled even in these homely surroundings.

She turned back to the dishes and smiled to herself. The secret was out – and Ulran had already guessed. Well, it was for the best, after all. She didn't like deceit. She hadn't felt so at ease since the journey began – in fact, she'd never felt like this before. She blushed, recalling how Dyr and his spouse had excused themselves after the meal to retire.

Now she accidentally brushed her hand against Slane's – smooth, wet and soapy, and she didn't draw it away. Her heart pounding, she raised her eyes.

Faintly, as though issuing from another world, laughter and raised voices could be heard as Courdour recounted a few tales to Bashen Corl's amusement.

Instinctively, or perhaps because she had studied Ulran for over a quarter already, she attempted hiding her true feelings. "They're talk – talking about war – battles – that's not me, I abhor violence–"

"Me too. I'm a land-worker, not a fighter!" He chuckled. "They're mentioning women, also," he added, a mischievous smile playing on his lips.

She flushed. "I've – I've never done those things that the warrior talks of –" Why did she say that? Normally, she would skirt round the subject of passion and love. She was an outsider even in the city, respected for her intellect but not really liked or loved.

His hand gripped hers tenderly and she felt a strange warm current suffuse her being at his touch.

"I'm sorry, I was teasing – shouldn't have."

The smile she offered could forgive him anything. The dishes seemed forgotten, in the other-world.

"You're no warrior – but why should you be?" he said in recompense.

"I've proved that well enough already!" she said bitterly.

"What happened to make you hate yourself so?"

She faltered, only a moment. "Do you believe in the gods, Slane?"

He smiled and her heart somersaulted. She caused that smile!

"Only the good ones," he said.

Coldly, objectively, she looked down at her waistband clogged with effigies of good and bad, white and black, to be accorded affection or anger according to their lights. "I'm afraid my faith's not as great as yours."

As he lifted her chin she saw pain in his eyes. "Why forsake respect in yourself, Fhord?" he asked and the halting inflection seemed to be from his very heart.

Again, those mesmerising eyes, so questing, searching out the truth. And the truth was obvious to her now, though there seemed little she could do to right matters. She had inwardly felt more and more inferior in the presence of Ulran and Courdour as the journey progressed.

Her belief in the amulets and other superstitious trinkets hadn't impressed Courdour at all: that warrior believed only in the might of his sword-arm! And whilst Ulran had been kind and considerate beyond any normal man's patience, she had of late intuitively detected a subtle hint of resignation in the innman, as though both were suffering her stoically, grudgingly.

Again and again, she asked herself the same question: in that case, then, why did they let her come along or even stay? And what would their attitude have been if they had known she was deceiving them?

The words rushed out, telling Slane all her inmost fears, some of which hadn't properly formed until now, and she left little unsaid.

Her chest visibly expanded as she related her efforts in the mist-shrouded Oquar II Forest, acting as the group's eyes when the famed red tellar could not.

Slane seemed to share in her low moments, and now he enjoyed her evident pride. Impulsively, he leaned over and kissed her.

It began as an impetuous, joyful kiss, but that first touch was enough to change everything for them; the kiss lingered and their hearts were soon hammering together.

"Slane!" Yoan's strident voice sliced them apart. "What are you two doing in there?"

It was Slane's turn to blush; he gathered the dried dishes together. "Just finishing!" he called.

Evading his eyes, Fhord helped to stack the crockery away.

Then they were walking into the room, bathed in a light that to them existed far and beyond the paltry luminescence of the log-flames.

Silence and mocking or curious eyes met them: but neither felt any cause for embarrassment now.

***

Bashen Corl had obligingly cleared out the lean-to fixed at the back of the house. It was dusty and looked disused, awaiting the autumn when crops would be stockpiled for the winter. Now the stone storage cubicles were bare save for cobwebs. To one side was a large box containing trays of brush and silkworms.

The three travellers agreed to keep watch in turns, just in case a wandering montar of Devastators came by.

For what seemed like ages Cobrora couldn't sleep then, mental exhaustion overtaking her, she dozed fitfully, her dreaming moments filled with a weird ancient city, once regal and splendid, now cold and drab. And then the city would be bathed in a funereal pyre of suffocating smoke, as though the earth had gaped wide beneath the city's foundations.

Turning restlessly, she was unable to wake up, trapped by the

Floreskand: Wings

haunting images. And in the flames she could see herself, smiling. A man was with her; for a while his features were indistinct: then, as if a shroud had been pulled away, she saw him – Slane. But their flesh wasn't burning, nor peeling off and bubbling. No, they were whole, happily bathing in the blaze as though it were but a waterfall.

She had no way of knowing in her dream, but she believed the tongues of fire were friends, like Slane – of Osasor's ilk.

When she finally woke she was lathered in sweat and Ulran was waiting for her to take her turn at lookout.

Shivering uncontrollably in the cold morning air outside, she wrapped her cloak about herself and paced round the lean-to and the house.

Towards the end of her first circuit she noticed an oblong of light on the ground: one of the ground-floor windows was still lit up, its blackout curtain drawn back.

She jerked her head up at the brow over which they'd come, its shape dimly silhouetted against the lesser darkness of the night sky. Plains-dogs howled far off.

Her heart beating in anxiety, she rushed to the window. Like killer-moths, the Devastators would be attracted to the light.

She cleared her throat noisily outside the window, and was about to tap a warning on the wooden shutters – for the family could ill-afford glass – when Slane's head poked out.

"Hello, Fhord," he said tenderly.

At the sight of him her heart lifted and her anxiety trebled. She grimaced. "The light–! The Devastators might see it, investigate."

"Oh, I forgot." Leaning upon the sill, he kissed her.

Utterly disarmed, she couldn't withstand him. A delicate fragrance wafted to her nostrils and unconsciously she dropped her sword – so ineffectual in any event in her custody – and sat upon the window ledge beside him. Without a second thought she folded her arms around his firm strong body clothed in a flannel night-robe.

Gently, he pulled away, placing a finger to her lips. "Come in," he whispered, a nervous tremble in his voice. "I'll blow out the light."

Fhord needed no further urging: to be with him was all she asked of the gods; the morning chill was forgotten in his presence, and he too seemed not to feel it.

She was glad of the shadows, the room only faintly illuminated by the thin scythe of silver moon-glow.

The pulse and heartbeat within her body quickened and she felt so inept and tongue-tied: she had never lain with a man before. She sat upon the edge of the bed, hands feeling the luxurious softness of the duck-down mattress. It seemed years since she'd had a decent bed.

He stood close, silhouetted in the window-frame, the contours of his body clearly distinguishable beneath the robe.

She swallowed, unsure of her threshing emotions as she saw his garment lifted above his head and discarded.

As she stood there, expectant, she blushed and felt a deep-seated anger burning in her stomach: she was utterly helpless! She didn't know what to do!

He stepped a pace closer and she could hear his breathing.

The thing to do was to undress, she told herself stupidly; from the book *Elements and Mechanics of Conjoining* by Lehun Dess she knew the cold physical aspects of lovemaking, but this was different. Knees quaking, conscious of the effigies and amulets jingling at her belt, she slipped out of her jacket and lowered it to the floor.

Slane moved closer still, just out of reach.

Hands trembling now, she removed her belt of charms. She was surprised at how fully his sex was responding: she stepped out of the hide-breeches.

At last she too stood naked, conscious of her body-fragrance, his nearness and of his strained member. She should feel stupid, she thought, yet it seemed quite natural.

Her hands rested upon his bare shoulders, cool and gentle, and her heart hammered as his sex brushed her curling bush of hair; and then their movements ceased to be tentative and inhibited. Instinct embraced them.

The warm and vibrant touch of her body against his was devastating. She felt herself quickening, aglow, soaring to hitherto untapped heights. Yet the ecstasy was short-lived and her emotions tumbled and it was all over too soon, before she could fully savour it.

Later, Slane tenderly stroked her cheek as she laid her head upon his rising chest. "It's supposed to be like that," he whispered understandingly. "I'm like you, Fhord – it's my first time. My sister told me, I'm supposed to endure the same frustration you are right now."

"It's natural? This let-down feeling? It was so wonderful and then…"

"It gets better next time, I'm told."

"You gave me so much pleasure and I want to return that to you." She recalled the poem by Laan Gibb, *What is love?* "Love is the gift that is lost too soon." She felt utterly lost, empty, and defeated: she couldn't even perform like a woman, Lehun Dess be damned!

"Yes," he answered, a croak in his voice. "The gift of love is in the heart – no matter what failings the body has, my dearest Fhord."

She embraced him.

As they caressed each other, he said, "Tell me a story from your Archives, Fhord. I love to listen to stories."

She smiled, feeling she was on sure ground now, and began her little tale which she called "Works wonders":

*

"What urge?" the boy asked.

"Thau-mat-urge," old An-sep repeated, his parchment face creasing in amusement as he leaned over the rough-hewn palace garden wall. "A worker of wonders."

"So you're a miracle-man, a – a magician, is that it?" the child observed brightly. "Like Por-al Row in the *Annals of Floreskand*?"

A frown summoned up a strange, almost other-worldly throaty sound. "Well, sort of, only I'm a little more consistent with my spells." The lad shrank away slightly, biting his lower lip. "But I follow the Path of Light, unlike poor Por."

This hasty exposal tended to mollify the boy. Inevitably, he demanded, "Do me a spell, then, old mage, if I'm to believe you!" His tone was imperious, as it should be, An-sep supposed: the boy's blood was royal, after all. Still, the thaumaturge wondered why he bothered: no amount of patient guidance helped. Once the royal children tasted power, their best intentions went to Oblivion.

At that moment An-sep espied on the other side of the wall the boy's gravid mother, Queen Marosa strolling between the aisles of sekors, flora of the Overlord.

Perhaps it amounted to sacrilege, but he fancied that the sacred flowers' beauty paled beside that of the queen.

She was gracefully adorned in a gold brocade maternity gown, her plaited dark hair trailing behind.

There were no attendants in evidence.

She had always been a raven-haired beauty, with shimmering cobalt-blue eyes. But now even at this distance An-sep could detect disquiet in her face: sleep-deprived eyes and a down-turned mouth implied she sorely missed her Lord whose almost obsessed quest for peace in Floreskand had sent him on a mission to neighbouring Goldalese.

"Well?" demanded the prince, glaring.

An-sep shrugged away his concern for the vulnerable-looking woman. Might as well keep the child happy, he'd be ruler soon enough! Intoning words of Quotamontir, he flourished his hands aloft and two white doves materialised, flicking their wings as if to shrug off the after-effects of their astral journey.

The boy was suitably impressed.

Warning tremors surged in An-sep's temple.

Without thought to the consequences, he scaled the wall and landed in a flurry of robes on royal greensward; the prince exclaimed in alarm, for any commoner who so much as bent these blades of grass would be rent by sword-blades: this was the Law.

But An-sep's impulse was beyond man-made edict.

Queen Marosa cried out and sank to her knees.

Dragging the boy with him, An-sep ran over the divine flowerbed.

He knelt obeisance and then gently lowered her to the grass. A gnarled cool finger on her head uncreased the brow and the pain seemed to flow out of her.

Her boy prince was trembling, eyes starting at sight of the baby emerging into the world.

It was not a difficult birth; the baby cried with healthy gusto.

The young prince cried too, as he cradled his new brother and held him to his mother's smiling lips.

"Thank you," she whispered.

"By your leave," An-sep stood, bowed and walked the way he had come.

And in his wake the flowers and grass so recently trampled upon now resumed their natural posture as if he had never trespassed.

"Now that's a miracle, Thaumaturge!" the prince shouted, drying his eyes.

"No, young prince," An-sep called back, "the real miracle is the life you hold in your arms."

*

Slane dug Cobrora Fhord playfully in the ribs. "Ah, that was lovely – poor Por, indeed!"

She winced and then sensed his spent member growing as she noticed her nipples hardening to his touch. "I must admit I've never known any neighbour's birth be easy – it's obviously a man's tale!"

"No," he said, kissing her breasts, "I think I understand it now. It wasn't difficult because An-sep eased all the pain."

"That's right, dear Slane," Fhord whispered.

As he and his confidence grew, he entered her. "Never heard of Queen Marosa, though."

"No, I made it all up."

"Well, it was – is – lovely. I'll remember old An-sep as long as I live, darling Fhord."

This time, there were no disappointments.

***

She must have lain there for some time. Obviously, the awkward position, lying upon his chest, had aroused her. But no, it had been some form of presentiment.

A threat, she felt sure, though the form it would take remained a mystery.

***

The bones had never lied before. "But him!" snarled Por-al Row. How in all Arion could that weed of a man be a threat to his designs on Yip-nef Dom? The king's bitch, he could fear her, yes, and that bird. But him? And yet the bones had never lied.

For the last five solid orms he had sweated and strained, losing much weight and power in the effort.

And now he had detected indications regarding the future. A nebulous future, by no means incontrovertible. But the never-to-be-repeated spell had provided an answer.

He hoped it would prove sufficient, for were he to tackle the spell again he wouldn't survive to see the results.

So, fire was the answer: the bones had been plain enough there!

Por-al Row wiped sweat from his puckered brow and praise to Honsor tripped over his foam-flecked lips.

***

Cobrora Fhord sat up in bed, turned back the covers. Slane smiled contentedly in sleep.

Carefully, she stood and padded to the window.

Dawn was rising quickly today, she thought, as she descried the horizon lightening with a red hue, faster and faster, illuminating the plains beyond to the dunsaron.

Some nagging feeling ordered her senses without her volition. Mechanically, she dressed, hardly moving her eyes from the lightening sky and plainsland.

She glanced back once: Slane continued to sleep and she had no wish to disturb him.

Instinctively, she believed that the danger threatened Courdour and Ulran. No reason, just a feeling.

Fully clothed again, she stepped out of the window, retrieved her fallen sword and ran round the building towards the lean-to.

A cursory glance before entering the lean-to disclosed the land all lit up with an eerie red-and-yellow glow, quite unlike any sunrise she'd ever seen. Yet – she blinked to make sure – yes, the horizon to the dunsaron had now darkened again. As if some celestial body of light were streaking across the land in their direction.

She barged in and shook Ulran awake without ceremony, her whole body and mind rebelling at the sight she had just witnessed. It wasn't natural, surely.

To her surprise Courdour was awake and fully clothed, studying the rafters.

As Ulran unquestioningly thrust his feet into tough hide boots, Fhord said, "I fear some wizardry – an attack on us!"

"Wizardry?" queried Courdour derisively. "You came barging in here – disturbing my reverie – and for what?"

Ulran shot a warning look at the warrior. "What signs, Fhord?" he asked levelly.

The use of the first-name was not lost on her. "Light – fire - streaking across the land – it isn't natural–"

The blast and explosion shook the lean-to and the rafters groaned, metal pins squeaked free and splinters showered all of them. The silkworm cages burst open onto the floor.

"Get out!" Ulran shouted, shoving Fhord to the door. "It's an attack!"

Courdour Alomar was close on their heels, the whinnying of the horses shrill in their ears.

They got out barely in time.

Tears streamed down Fhord's face as she stared, clamped in Ulran's firm embrace. "It was a fireball, just a freak, not an attack. It hit the main house," he said. "They didn't stand a chance."

The rest of the house was a raging inferno and the flames rapidly spread to the collapsed lean-to.

Starkly lit, the group stood well back from the incredible heat.

"Let me go," Fhord wailed, "let me at least try to help them!"

"It's not only the fire," Alomar growled. "You've got smoke to contend with – and you're not kith of *that* lesslord!"

Sobbing uncontrollably, she lowered to her knees, fists pounding the dirt in anguished futility.

Ulran tried telling her that Slane wouldn't have suffered greatly. The entire family had been wiped out in an instant. But his words seemed quite inadequate consolation.

All she could say, over and over again, was "But who – who – who could've unleashed a weapon of the very demons of Below?"

***

Second Sabin's daylight showed the sad remains, merely a few charred uprights of ironwood, a blackened stone tower where the hearth had stood.

Floreskand: Wings

There was nothing to bury, the heat had been so intense.

Fortunately for them, the paddock where the horses and mule spent the night had been far enough away to survive unscathed, though even in the new day the horses took some calming even with all Ulran's remarkable gifts.

As they rode across the charred grass that led dunsaronwards, Courdour Alomar leaned on his pommel. "Don't read any more into last night than you ought, Cobrora Fhord," he said sternly. "It was simply a fireball – a rare enough phenomenon, true – but natural enough. Do you understand – natural, not supernatural?"

Wordlessly, Fhord nodded.

Courdour persisted. "You young folk must learn to take knocks like this, you know. I mourn their loss too; I knew the whole family for a long time. By the gods, if you'd lived my span, you'd know! I'm telling you – I've seen fireballs before. It's an accident of nature – nothing to do with your silly gods!"

"Alomar!" Ulran warned.

The warrior shrugged, pulled his floppy black hat over his eyes. "She'll learn." He sighed and rode on ahead.

***

Pale and trembling, Por-al Row stared, bemused, at the dimming picture. He would have liked to believe it was through his own influence, but he knew neither his power nor his spells were that strong. No alchemist living would have achieved that!

Still, he couldn't help but wonder at the startling coincidence. The fireball had almost claimed the youth, as the bones had revealed.

He felt sure that fire was the city-dweller's nemesis.

He scowled. If Yip-nef Dom had been here to see it, he would have claimed credit for the fireball's appearance! The fool, knowing no better, would have believed him and been impressed. What an opportunity to curry favour, to beat the king's she-cat at her own treacherous game! But it was no use thinking of what might have been, he scolded himself. Also, he had to face facts: apart from the grossly vague predictions through the bones, there was no way to view the future.

Por-al Row sighed. If only the Old Ways of the Sonalume Angkorites hadn't been lost all those years ago!

***

Two days from the Bashen housestead's burned husk, on the Second Dekin of Fornious, they came again upon Saloar Teen and rode along its bank for two days.

Over this period Fhord remained morose and uncommunicative.

Courdour supplemented their diet with his hunting prowess, his arrows and sling-stones claiming buck, rabbit and the occasional fowl.

At times Fhord found the warrior's vitriolic tongue unbearable and fretted, unable to sleep. She was aware of a gradual decline in her general fitness, and her appetite had diminished to the point of virtual fasting. No urging from Ulran seemed to persuade her to eat. Although aware that her secret was revealed now, she didn't care. It no longer mattered. Even if they didn't want a woman to accompany them, they wouldn't leave her behind; they'd come too far now to send her back. She rode with them but to all intents and purposes was not of their company any more.

To compound the feelings of loss and inadequacy that she experienced, Ulran's matchless stionery kept them sheltered and dry when clouds burst and the winds howled. She appreciated Ulran's efforts to keep things as smooth as possible between her and Courdour, but she was beginning to feel that perhaps the warrior's opinion was correct, that Cobrora Fhord, psychic and city-dweller, had no right to be on this trek.

She eyed her amulets with rheumy eyes. What good were they? Her hands trembled, and she was tempted to throw the trinkets away. She had tackled Courdour with the loss of the effigy and the near-tragedy at the teen. But the warrior remained unconvinced that the two incidents were connected. Their argument had grown so heated that she had feared they would come to blows; she'd almost welcomed it! But Ulran's calming intervention prevented that.

She didn't particularly care, she'd become quite reckless of late.

Time and again, as she cast modesty aside and took off her shirt to wash herself in the teen, she would imbibe the scent of Slane left on the garment and she would fight to keep back the tears. Thoughts of Slane invaded her conscious moments repeatedly and were brutally obliterated with a dusting of black, anonymous ash.

***

All this time, Scalrin hadn't landed once, forever gliding and soaring, sometimes jostling for sky with a few audacious plovers or forktails. To Ulran, Scalrin always seemed the epitome of logic. Yet, for mortal man, such implicit reliance on logic was dangerous: instinct and intuitive practice had saved him on countless occasions where strict application of logic would have doomed him. He wondered too about the running feud between his companions. Now Cobrora Fhord was definitely becoming a liability. And, for all his age, sagacity and renown, Alomar was a cantankerous old devil at times!

***

Courdour Alomar's thoughts on Fhord had mellowed since they had rejoined the teen. At the sad remains of the Bashen housestead, he had not fully appreciated how deep the girl's feelings for the Slane lad had been. Unbidden, painfully clear memories of Jaryar invaded his mind. Indirectly, it was because of her that he was perpetually wandering, seeking the Navel.

The warrior involuntarily sighed; yes, he understood the strength and implacable nature of love. Perhaps he had been over-harsh with Fhord because of Jaryar, not wanting her to suffer as he himself had. But the girl irritated him immensely – because of her youth? Or perhaps because of her mortality? How young, he thought suddenly, how young was I when that fateful day occurred?

Too much time had passed; he forgot; but he was probably no more than Cobrora Fhord's age. He shook himself savagely; so long since he had dwelled upon his past, particularly that agonising portion. Feeling sorry for yourself won't help you find the Navel, he thought.

They spotted no recent signs of the Devastators and on the Second Dloin they struck manderon, away from the curving teen, with the miasma of the marsh on their horizon, no more than a day's hard ride distant.

CHAPTER EIGHT
NEBULOUS

A fortress, precipice-enfolded
In a gash of the wind-lashed Sentinel Mountains.
— The Lay of Lorgen

At first light they reached Marron Marsh. Grey-green wisps eddied above the long damp grasses and reeds. Fhord grasped for her amulets; but there was no god of marshes. The horses sensed something uncanny about the place as well; as they approached, the marsh-cloud looming ever larger, the animals shied and the travellers had great difficulty calming them.

Even Versayr proved troublesome and excitable. Ulran called ahead to Courdour: "You really live in that muck?" There was no incredulity in his voice, no surprise: he just could not find the idea normal.

"Aye. Toran Nebulous is in its centre. Well-guarded, don't you think?"

Behind them, birds whistled and sang, the breeze rustled the grass, the air smelled fresh and was clear. But as they reined in at the brim of the Marsh, not a sound carried from that place. They could glimpse but fleetingly a little distance within the swirling murk. Unpleasant prickling traced Fhord's spine.

"Let's get on, then, I'm eager to be home!" Courdour disparagingly eyed the city-dweller. And so saying he pushed Borsalac deeper into the mists, hoofs squelching and splashing in the bog-like ground. "Follow me closely else you'll be dragged from sight and human ken!" he bellowed over his shoulder and laughed.

And his laughter echoed, seeming to bounce from the grey banks of mist.

In an effort at keeping Cobrora's spirits up, Ulran asked, "Do you know of the Marsh's history, Fhord?"

"Not really." She shook her head, eyes wide as she scoured the briefly visible patches of marshland. "Only that the battle of 1227 lasted a full two quarters. Oh, and the combined hordes of the Devastators were eventually beaten by the Lornwater forces. But wasn't it a Khamharic victory?"

"Yes; many men lost their lives on both sides. And since that time the marsh, as you obviously know, has been given a wide detour by all." He noticed Fhord shudder. "Did you sense something then?"

"Yes, a cold clamminess, but not of fear. Believe me, I know the feeling of fear well, and this was quite unlike anything I've experienced before."

"I don't want to alarm you, but since the battle repeated sightings of the dead warriors have been made. The walking dead... Could you–"

"–sense the dead spirits? Possibly, Ulran. It isn't an area I would have normally ventured into. But..." She closed her eyes and relaxed to the swaying of Sarolee.

Tentatively, she opened her mind. There was indeed a presence, yet it always backed away as they neared it. No, she was mistaken. There were many, countless separate sensations, hovering, trying to close in yet always mysteriously repelled.

Sweat beaded her brow.

She paled to an almost alabaster hue. "The ghosts – if that's what they are – they're unhealthy, mean us harm, I warrant they do." But the uncertainty was plain in her voice.

Courdour overheard. "Afraid of a little legend and rumour, Fhord?" he chuckled.

Ulran answered for her. "She mentally located a number of ghosts. She suspects they're harmful and I believe her."

The warrior raised an eyebrow, as though copying Ulran. "Interesting, very interesting. So the will o' the wisps have some form after all, is that it?"

Fhord nodded, still reeling at the thought of Ulran not only backing her but also believing in her. "Yes. Their presence fills the air all around us – and yet – yet at a certain distance they back off, as though afraid."

"Afraid?" Courdour grinned.

Ulran turned to Fhord. "I think Courdour Alomar is suffering from a little mortal pride. You see, he is also known in legend as the Deathless One. Is that not so, Alomar?"

"Aye, you have me sitting transparent before you. I imagine the spirits you speak of are leery of me – though the gods know why!"

Suddenly, without warning, the warrior reared his mount. "What – do you see that?" And he pointed ahead through a brief gap in the curtain of mist. "What do you make of it, eh?"

As the thing vanished behind a thick screen of mist, Fhord rubbed her eyes. "It looked like a tree – upside down!"

"Quite so, youngster, quite so. And I know every part of this marsh and there are no such trees here!"

"Then perhaps we had better investigate?" Ulran suggested, slightly amused at Courdour's discomposure.

"We had better!" Alomar hurried Borsalac and the splashes quickly diminished as he melted within the surrounding mist.

"Come on, Fhord," urged Ulran, "we can't risk getting lost here – my stionery won't be of any use and your mental eyes will hardly penetrate the interfering spirits, I shouldn't wonder!"

It was a short though nerve-racking ride.

Courdour had dismounted and stood calf high in the muddy brown bog. He cupped his hands and called upwards into the strange tree: "Come out, show yourself!"

Truly, Fhord had never seen the like before. It resembled the roots of the tree family, all dark brown and gnarled, misshapen, twisting in all directions. And from these grotesque branches hung slimy green lianas and now, vaguely visible, she spotted a small, rather cramped wooden dwelling deep within the midst of the weird branch network.

***

Some of the branches had inverted their quest for sun and air and had turned down into the mire, thickening into secondary trunks. It was obvious why the branches had twisted and bent upon themselves: they would constantly be reaching for the few instants of sunlight that managed to filter through the enveloping mist, forever straining for a different beam of sunlight, a different break in the murk.

And now someone emerged from the shack, clothed in sackcloth that was burred and holed in many places, smeared liberally with patches of mud. The man's face was little better: lined and pallid, somehow lifeless, the long white beard and eyebrows streaked with stunning silver threads of hair, the man presented a most unusual sight. His hair, matted and black, contrasted with his apparent age.

Eyes of flashing mischievous agate looked out upon the three travellers. "I have waited for your coming," was all he said, the words croaking like a tree-frog yet quite distinguishable.

Taken aback, Courdour blurted, "But how came you here? To my knowledge this tree wasn't here when last I–"

"You forget, Courdour Alomar: your sense of time is wanting, alas."

"Never mind my lapses of memory, never mind how you came here, then," said the warrior with impatience. "Who are you?"

"A friend. But our friendship is not destined to blossom just yet. I wished only to make an introduction. In time – in time, Alomar – we shall meet again. It is just possible I shall assist you with your quest for the Navel."

At this disclosure Courdour splashed forward, reaching up, "How–? Tell me, old man, tell me!"

Then he was suddenly staring at mist clouds. Alarmed, he thrust his arm forward where the tree bole had stood, but there was no solid resistance. He peered and stepped forward, but the tree, dwelling and the old man had vanished.

Fhord was disturbed to see the consternation on Courdour's face. Until now the warrior had been above all things, it seemed, disdainful of mortal feeling and foibles. But, at mention of this "Navel", whatever it was, he became a trembling wreck of a man.

Kneeling in the mire, Courdour stared emptily into the swathing mist and cried, "Come back, old man, tell me, please! Tell me!"

Slowly, Ulran dismounted and splashed over to the stricken warrior. He laid a hand on Courdour's shoulder. "Be easy, Alomar. Remember what the old man said – he'll be meeting you again, at a time of his choosing. Then you will learn, perhaps, all you need to know."

Gravely, Courdour nodded and, using Ulran's arm for support, raised himself. "Yes, yes, you are quite right, my friend." He turned, almost self-consciously, to face the unbelieving stare of Fhord. "I have good cause to be affected, young woman," he said. "Soon, I think, I shall relate some of my sorry tale – then, yes, then you will realise how little your suffering is in comparison with mine."

Wordlessly, Fhord nodded, uncomprehending, but sure that within the mind and breast of Courdour Alomar was locked some strange and astounding secret, some pain of immeasurable agony. But she could bide her time until the warrior saw fit.

"Enough of this!" barked Courdour. "Let us get on to my toran!"

***

First to appear were the battlements, irregularly poking through the mist ahead. As the travellers neared, the mist thinned and afforded Fhord a better view.

The toran was really a castle, although small by any standards, filling hardly more than a square launmark. Their horses stepped onto firmer ground, an island. Now Toran Nebulous stood before them in all its mysterious splendour.

The island's sloping banks provided a suitable scarp and running round the island some way up was the first defensive wall of greystone; every ten marks along this was situated a square crenellated turret. Fhord half imagined curious eyes looked down upon them from the narrow dark archer's holes.

Directly ahead was an earth ramp, the mud dried and compacted, which led to a double tower over the toran-gate.

On either side of the ramp was a stone revetment – its smoothness dangerously angled – making any sally on the barbican impossible. Fhord looked above the barbican, at the armorial bearings of Courdour – a black and white sekor, or so it seemed. She was startled by the sight and kept looking back as the heavy iron-shod oak gates closed behind them.

Their horses came to a halt in a small, quite confined outer ward, the ground unevenly paved. Here, the phenomenon of the The Lake's Inn seemed repeated for her, with the weeds and grass – which asserted their presence in cracks and joins – disappearing disconcertingly when looked upon directly.

Towering above ahead was the rest of the hill, garbed in more dark greystone blocks, these walls likewise turreted at regular intervals. Some of the walls merged with the central building or donjon. From this hold buttresses and towers protruded in haphazard fashion, some interspersed with merlons and crenels of irregular shape and positioning. Loopholes and small arching windows betrayed no presence of inhabitants. Even the gate, she recalled with misgivings, had not opened with the apparent aid of man's hand.

As Courdour halted before some stone steps that zigzagged up to another gate and defensive tower in the curtain wall, Fhord looked at the weirdly darkening sky.

The mist didn't trespass over the castle's walls at all.

The sky above was normal if ominously filled with storm clouds.

Ulran followed her gaze. "Yes, I thought a storm was brewing before we entered the mist. Yon marsh-warblers cried it plain enough before we had even neared the marsh."

"We'll leave the horses here – they'll be tended for in good time," said Courdour. He dismounted and climbed the first few steps, breathed in deeply. "It's good to be home!" He must have given the old man in the marsh a thought, for he shook his head, murmured, "Wouldn't have thought I'd been away that long, though..." He shrugged. "Follow me, please."

Dust lay ahead on the stone steps.

Again doors opened without hint of servitors at work.

They passed through the archway, beneath the dark machicolations: dried tar and pitch still clung to their sides.

Courdour waved his hand airily. "Regard yourselves as my honoured guests."

To left and right below them was the inner ward, paved just like the outer. They now stood upon an arching stone-built bridge that opened into the donjon.

Floreskand: Wings

The last door opened and then resoundingly shut behind them.

Before them was a tiled hall. Armoured pieces and swords and other battle accoutrements adorned the walls. Everywhere seemed deep within the clutches of cobwebs, though only glimpsed and not seen: here, Fhord realised, there was no mistaking the fact that Courdour Alomar's demesne had fallen into disuse.

Abruptly, a shape appeared out of the shadows.

"Laorge!" exclaimed the warrior and both servant and master briefly embraced. Courdour winked. "Could you find apartments for my two guests? And," he grinned, "arrange some decent food. We're travel-weary and in want of some sustenance!"

The nervous Laorge nodded and shuffled towards a wide arched entrance. "In here, my lord?" He opened the tall double doors.

The place was a long hall, a dining table in the centre, the interior again appearing thick with dust and spiders' webs, except when viewed directly. Light peeped through narrow loopholes and it looked quite uninviting to Fhord. She had suddenly lost her appetite.

"Yes, clean it up as best you can, Laorge. How's Wral, your good lady?" Courdour enquired, rising on the first stair.

"As normal, my lord. Tired and always eating!"

"Good, good! Change isn't always good for people!" He turned to Ulran and Fhord. "Laorge will find you suitable accommodation. I'll show you around the toran then we'll eat."

Both nodded.

"Then, let us say, in half an orm, meet me on the dunsaron battlements. Laorge will show you the way."

He turned and with the aid of the balustrade strode up the creaking stairs. Half-glimpsed dust fell on either side of the treads and then he was gone.

***

Dressed in woollen garments to ward off the draughts which she sensed rather than felt, Fhord tested the mattress; it felt incredibly yielding.

And, unlike the rest of the castle, this room she had been allocated was spotlessly clean and lavishly adorned with cheval-glass, gilt-edged furniture and chests; and she felt sure the shagunblend lamp-holders set in the draped walls were of solid silver.

There was a slight mustiness of misuse, but not unpleasant. Sekor pomanders hung in the oak cupboards and their fragrance helped dispel the odour.

From the glass-filled window in the casemate on either side of the bed she could look out across the rolling clouds of mist and see the

Sonalumes. Below stretched the sheer toran walls down to the grassy mound on which the donjon was built.

Still no-one was about in the inner ward nor on the curtain walls. But why use sentries when the mist and legend would provide ample protection? If they had not had Courdour to lead them, she certainly would not have ventured even a step into the marsh!

The heavy wooden door opened, creaking on rusted iron hinges.

Startled, she pivoted round, her grey-wool robe swirling. While the floorboards had creaked on her own entry they did not announce any presence – and yet she saw Ulran standing in the doorway. "You startled me–"

"Sorry." Ulran smiled. "Habit. If you're ready, let's find Laorge and seek out our host."

Fhord inspected the hinges and they were neither rusted nor lacking in oil. "Yes, of course."

True to his word, Courdour Alomar was waiting for them on the walkway of the dunsaron battlements, his whole frame concealed beneath a myrtle-coloured cloak. "Ah, my guests! What do you think of the view?" He swept his hand to encompass the panorama laid out before them.

These battlements were the highest of the toran, subject to strong gusts. Bracing against the wind, Fhord looked around. The view from her bedchamber was nothing in comparison.

From here was spread the plainsland, the silver shimmer of Salaor Teen, and vague on that horizon the forests of Oquar II.

To the dunsaron, Sonalume Mountains, to the varteron, a smudge on the horizon that must be Goldalese, and just below it the tip of Altohey and to the manderon of Ulran's natal city was Astle, both volcanoes smouldering, thin brown-black smoke curling upwards.

And manderonwards, their goal, the Twin Peaks – Soveram Torne and Soveram Marle.

Short of the mountains and volcanoes, this vantage point must assuredly be the tallest. She was dizzy at the thought and marvelled at the incredible structure.

It seemed there was yet a long, long way to travel just to the Soveram peaks.

In spite of an unreasonable distaste of the man, Fhord hoped Courdour Alomar would consider accompanying them; until now, the warrior had only "toyed" with the idea.

Immediately above and casting its shadow on them, the black storm cloud gathered, unaffected by the winds.

Floreskand: Wings

This high up, overseeing so much of Floreskand, she should have felt like a powerful lord or even a god. But in truth she felt insecure, conscious of her slight size, minuscule in comparison with the rest of the universe and the creations of nature. Why, Scalrin, for example, was immense, obviously a bird designed for giants or gods.

She peered up and, yes, there was the red tellar, appearing from behind the storm cloud.

"He won't lose us, have no fear," Ulran assured her.

The innman eyed the scene. "Quite impressive – a view any king would envy, I'm sure," he remarked. "But tell me, why is it that though the marsh can be seen from a distance, the toran and these battlements in particular cannot?"

Courdour grinned. "I was wondering if you'd notice! It's a trick of the mist, I believe. One of my retainers has been attempting to analyse the mist's properties for over forty years now. If you'll come this way I'll show you his little chamber."

He ushered them through a small doorway that required them to duck. "But he's no nearer the solution," Courdour went on, his voice echoing as he led them down a narrow spiral stone stair.

Cages of glo-moths eerily illumined the staircase; obviously shagunblend fumes would have been too overpowering in such a restricted area.

They came upon a broad landing with a wider stair running further down and a doorway abutting onto the landing.

"In here," Courdour said, and opened the door.

The chamber was musty and various odours met them like an invisible barrier. Shadows abounded. The air seemed thick with a faint purple haze.

"Meet Cas-sun Eron." Courdour waved an arm vaguely at a wizened bent old man struggling to rise from a bench littered with glass bowls of every hue and all in some degree of fomentation.

"No, no, don't rise, Eron," said Courdour solicitously. "Carry on with what you were doing, please." He eyed his guests. "He has also been employed on another puzzle for me, oh, it's quite a time now, I think–"

"Seventy years, m'lord – and my father before me, as well, for almost five score."

"Yes, yes, of course," Courdour interrupted. "I'll doubtless explain further over our meal later, but now, if you'll excuse us Eron, we must be away as I wish to show them the rest of the toran."

At the point of shutting the door after them, Courdour faltered as the ageing retainer looked up. "Welcome home, m'lord," said Eron.

As they descended the stairs, Fhord asked, "How long has this toran been here? I've heard legend, of course, and that credits the place as being built at the beginning of time!"

"I built – er, it was built the year following the battle."

"Over eight hundred years old, then?"

"Something like that, I suppose. Dates and time I found tedious... now I don't bother with such trifles."

As they penetrated deeper, the walls seemed to glisten wetly with mildew and the cobwebs reappeared and thickened; Courdour Alomar brushed them aside carelessly.

Fhord's initial foreboding on entering Toran Nebulous returned with mind-numbing force.

"I have something here which I know you, Ulran, will be surprised to see." Courdour Alomar stopped at last outside what appeared to be a dungeon, a small barred window set in a door. A rusted key was in the lock and after a few moments' effort Courdour turned it.

The click of the barrels connecting echoed. Somewhere Fhord detected a drip-drip-drip.

The door was flung open by their host and he stepped back.

Within, it was pitch black.

Then, imperceptibly at first, the darkness receded, and a vague light-source originated from the cell's centre.

Fhord looked up: some kind of movement above – and in the shadows she could see there was no ceiling to the cell: storm clouds scudded across stars.

Now the light tended to pulse: she felt a little weak at the knees and fearfully looked towards Ulran by her side in the doorway. The innman also had sensed something and though he didn't show it Fhord believed he too was affected by the ever brightening mesmerising pulsations of light.

At length the cell lightened sufficiently and they beheld a black and white sekor.

An aura surrounded it as the large octagonal petals slowly opened.

Seeing this, Fhord reeled with disbelief and would have fallen to the earth cell floor, but Ulran caught her in time.

The innman turned to their host: "I didn't know such a sekor existed, Alomar. Myth, only in myth has the black-white been whispered about. I think we'd better leave, before it drains Fhord's life-force completely."

Courdour nodded and made to shut the door while Ulran backed out with the unconscious Fhord. "You know the sekor was draining you, then?"

"Yes, it's a sensation I've had to experience before now. There are ways and means of achieving a balance, though, which I'm afraid Fhord will never master. These special sekors of the gods must have life, but only in measured doses, else they will extinguish their hosts and die themselves. But this is the first time I've experienced the sensation from a black-white."

As they ascended another set of stairs, Courdour said, "In some way I'm sure that sekor has the answer I'm seeking. As Daqsekor in His magnanimity placed me in this limbo it seems fitting that His flower should–"

"But the Overlord's sekor is white," countered Ulran.

"Aye, but each god has his own coloured sekor and all gods are answerable to Daqsekor in the final analysis, are they not?"

"Except Nikkonslor and his minions."

The warrior scowled. "Gods? I was only stating a generalisation, pointing to the irony – I don't believe in them, I'm above all that!"

"Don't tempt the Overlord too greatly, my friend. I know His mercy's tempered with untold agonies: but at least He deigns to bestow mercy occasionally!"

"Mercy? You call this – this life an act of a benign god?"

"Rumours and guesses are all I know of you, Courdour Alomar. Either cease speaking in riddles, as Fhord here would say, or quieten your irritable mewling. If you require sympathy or help, then tell us."

The warrior swung open a door and Ulran carried the slowly reviving Fhord through into the dining hall.

"Well, I had planned to relate some of my tale," confessed Courdour Alomar. He eyed Fhord suspiciously.

"She'll stay and listen as well," said Ulran coldly, brooking no argument.

"Aye, why not? Maybe then she'll appreciate my bad humour!"

"Perhaps she will."

At that instant the dinner gong echoed throughout the toran and, outside, the storm broke.

CHAPTER NINE
JARYAR

*In life we meet strangers,
in death we meet friends.
– The Tanlin,* 139.6

As the succulent warm flesh of duckling melted in her mouth, Fhord once again studied the transformed dining hall.

How Laorge and other retainers had accomplished it she was at a loss to fathom. Surely, she was seeing things?

The ironwood and oak walls and doors were polished to a degree that cast reflections, lightening the place in addition to the wall-sconces of shagunblend and other, more aromatic lamps. The floor was terracotta and spotless, the beams above without smoke-blemish or cobweb. In the central hearth roared a log-fire, warming the place. Colourful arrases adorned some walls.

And the table fare was so varied and delicious!

Courdour Alomar removed a bone from his mouth and picked at his teeth with the point of his knife. "Do you like the duck, Fhord?" he enquired.

"Yes, it's melting in my mouth! Your cook must be greatly gifted."

"Oh, yes, he is – but the duck helped. You see, before the battle this marsh used to be famous for its duck."

"And since?"

"You'll be lucky to catch even one over a period of fifty quarters!"

Fhord leaned back, replete for the moment. The golden coloured brandy from the long-dead city of Kclenand had mellowed her, sorrow at Slane's loss temporarily receding as did her usual reticence. "Sounds like you've got a story there," she said, grinning.

"I daresay the tale would be of interest, yes, I daresay it would." Their host swallowed more brandy, refilled his silver goblet. "But I think it is about time I related some of my past." He leaned forward, brows beetling, eyes threatening and black. "Understand me now, what I am to tell you must not go beyond these walls."

Nodding, Fhord looked at Ulran opposite.

The innman had not moved; though she thought she detected an acknowledging glint in his eyes.

"Right. Here, refill your goblets first. It may take a while in the telling." Courdour Alomar chuckled. "Aye, it took a while in the living of it, as well!"

*

His travels with his father had trodden the mercenaries' trail ever since the loss of Alomar's mother in a horrific raid on their housestead. But now young Alomar was becoming travel-weary and desired to settle down, recalling the warmth and security he had enjoyed in his parents' home.

Becoming lost in a tremendous quarter-long storm, they had accidentally crossed the Tanalume Mountains and – near starvation and suffering from exposure – they had collapsed upon soft juicy turf at the foothills.

When Alomar awoke, his mouth was parched, his thick swollen tongue extended and almost choking him.

Dizzily, he crawled under the high treacherous sun to his father.

But his father was no more: where he had lain was only an incomplete skeleton, the flesh pared from most of the bones. He wanted to cry bitterly and lie down and die; but he seemed devoid of moisture and had no strength even for sorrow, and some instinctive force within him would not let him renounce his life without a struggle.

Only as he stood unsteadily did he realise the carrion birds had tasted of him as well; his left thigh was a fleshy mess, blood blackened round the deep gashes, and there, the knee bone shone whitely in a couple of places.

The sight turned his stomach and on incredibly weak legs he collapsed.

Yet he felt no pain; he was beyond feeling, it seemed. He was sure that his life was ebbing fast. The last chasm to cross was near. Then the Overlord would claim him as He claimed all mortals who had completed their allotted span on His world.

"*He'll never walk again, if he lives...*"

The words swam round in his unconscious time and again.

Eventually he opened his eyes.

But the sight was not of carrion birds pecking at his limbs, nor of the endless grassland, nor of the sheer Tanalume Mountains.

He was in a room built of wood. It seemed to benefit from the ministrations of a woman; clean curtains covered the single window; on one side stood a pot of strange globular flowers; the cool sheets of his bed smelled fresh.

He elbowed himself up and the shooting agony of his nightmare exploded in his brain.

His legs, they were on fire!

Sweat of panic gushed out of his pores as he heaved himself up and out of the bed.

His head swam giddily, but he inwardly quietened, seeing his legs were there, though heavily bandaged.

The floor was of highly polished wood, he remembered thinking as it came up to meet him.

"You're coming out of the fever," said a soothing voice. *"Hold on to my hand when the pain gets too much."*

Later, he was dimly aware of having lain for a long time, of having been spoon-fed like a baby, of having cried in his sleeping hours. He had seen only this same room through hazy eyes, as though he had spent all his life within these four walls. Smells occasionally evoked other memories, sometimes unbearable remembrances, of his loved ones being eaten alive and him incapable of preventing it.

Then, all of a sudden, the past and the present came into sharp focus and he hauled himself up in bed.

A girl was sitting at the foot of the bed, studying him, concern in her wide green eyes that were framed within a long trailing cluster of chestnut-brown hair.

She took in a sharp breath between full red lips and seemed to be holding herself back, anxious to reach forward and help him raise himself.

As he winced with the continual pain, her eyes showed compassion. She bit her lips but didn't move.

At last he was able to lean against the bed's headrest. "Where–?" He found his voice was deeper, croaked.

Tongue wetting cracked lips, he began again, "Begetter? My father?"

Her eyes clouded over and he remembered.

After a while, he asked, "Where am I?"

A fleeting smile then she was serious, concerned again. "In Fullantran, near Janoven," she said simply.

He had never heard of these places. "What's that?" he queried, hearing for the first time a lapping sound. His nose twitched as a strange smell wafted through the open window.

"The sea – you can probably smell the brine. It's quite choppy at the moment."

Alomar shook his head. "I'm afraid I don't understand. Everything about you and this place seems alien to me – yet you speak my tongue!"

The girl rose and came closer. "We have one god, like you, if your speaking-dreams are true – the Overlord. It was He who created us and gave us all the same language in His infinite wisdom." She described the sign of the Overlord in the air in front of her with a fingertip.

But Alomar just growled, dissatisfied with her explanation. "Religion is for the weak!" he snapped. "What god could sanction the horrible death of my father, tell me that? Was that a merciful act?" He looked down at his sheet-covered legs. "Was it His infinite wisdom that made me a cripple?"

At this the girl stepped back, shocked. "Then, you know?" She trembled.

"Aye, I don't recall much in my delirium, but I well remember that – I'll not walk again!" But the reality of such a prospect had not hit him fully yet; he was still a little groggy. "But tell me, how long have I been here?"

"Four moons." She bowed her head and blushed.

He was aghast. "So long?" Then he realised his youthful bluster had hurt her; she was evading his eyes.

He said, tenderly, "Please look up. You have eyes to behold, not to be cast onto mere floorboards!"

She faltered.

"Please."

As she looked at him, she said, "I understand how you feel, Alomar– I–"

He smiled, patted the bed covers at his side. As she came over to sit there, he grinned. "You have me at a disadvantage. What is your name?"

"You spoke your name in your dreams. My name is Jaryar."

"And you've nursed me all these moons?"

"My mother and father did most," she hastened to explain. "But they're busy people – we have a large family to keep fed and clothed – so I've sat with you most of the time since you were brought in."

Only now, as he grew accustomed to her natural beauty, did he observe that she was in need of sleep, the skin below her eyes a faint purple. Finally, he asked, "My father's body?"

"You were found crawling into the village outside Janoven. It was some days before your ramblings made sense to anyone, then they sent an expedition and brought your father's remains back. He was interred in our cemetery, oh, over three moons ago–"

"Can I visit the grave?"

"When you're well enough, yes," she said unsteadily. She cast a furtive glance to the far corner in shadow.

There stood a chair with what appeared to be wheels on either side of it.

"The haemoleaf has worked well on you – your strength's returning rapidly; soon I'll wheel you outside and it won't be long before we can visit your father's resting place."

"Wheel me?" Realisation was seeping into him. Never to walk, to run, to ride – condemned to a sedentary existence in a wheelchair contraption! "I'll not–"

"Plenty of people have these chairs in Fullantran," she interposed. "We've had many accidents at sea where mastheads have fallen on our sailors."

He shook his head, hands to ears, and grimaced. "I won't listen! I don't know what mastheads or sailors are – and I don't care! Those contraptions may suit them, but you'll never get me in one!"

And he grabbed at a carafe of water by his side and flung it into the corner. It smashed into fragments and splashed the wooden walls, hangings and chair.

"Oh, no!" Close to tears, Jaryar jumped up and rushed to collect the shards of glass. "My mother's best–"

"I'll not be wheeled in any chair!" Alomar cut in harshly and flung off the sheets. At sight of his unbandaged legs, mottled, covered in ugly bedsores and suppurating blisters, he nearly retched and the strength seemed to desert his frame.

Only with the greatest effort of will-power was he able to swing those ugly limbs round and rest his bare feet on the fur bedside mat. "I'll walk, do you hear?" he yelled.

Jaryar suddenly saw he meant every word and rushed forward, discarding the broken glass. "No! Alomar, please!"

But she was too late: he had put his weight on his legs and they immediately buckled under him.

With a tremendous crash, he hit the floorboards.

She was by his side an instant later, cradling his bruised and sweat beaded head in her lap. Tears were in her eyes and she was sobbing: "Why, Overlord, why?"

He looked up through a numbing haze. "I must learn to walk again, Jaryar," he croaked. "Please help me."

Her heart was surely breaking. She burst into a racking flood of tears.

Over the last four moons she had grown to identify with this young man and his implacable will to live. Now, as he called for her aid she could not refuse him. The cleansing tears washed away any surface hurt his earlier outbursts may have unwittingly inflicted.

She held him close to her and knew that for this man she could refuse him nought. From the moment he had been carried into her life, she was a part of him. "Yes," she sobbed. "Yes, I'll help you walk, Alomar."

To begin with they moved his bed beneath the window so he could look out upon what he termed the Salt-taal and they called *the sea*. So near to the breakers crashing upon the shores in white-flecked agitation, so unlike the moon-led ripples of the taals he knew. And, further up the coast, the grey-green rock of Janoven, quite unlike any citadel he had ever seen. Apparently, all the walls sloped against the threat of a flood, though the last sea encroachment had not been in living memory.

He learned a great deal about the fishing community of Fullantran and though drawn to the majesty of the Janoven edifice, he preferred to watch the fishermen readying their nets and vessels alongside the scintillating semicircle of the breakwater. Jaryar said they had used shells to build the mole and the same type of shells also served them in their boatbuilding.

She spent many orms by his bedside, telling him of the village history, of her childhood.

It took what seemed to Alomar endless moons for him to progress from the bed to the reviled wheelchair. Until this time, Jaryar had walked him across the room daily, to prevent his limbs atrophying altogether.

As she helped him into the wheelchair, he joked about it and remarked on her mother's water-jug.

Jaryar smiled, as the memories flooded back. "It was a little like you, Alomar – a vessel capable of being emptied or filled. And when you broke it, it was as though I was picking up the broken pieces of you."

And for the first time she wheeled him out into the bright village, where the sun made their eyes water.

Most of the time he liked to be wheeled along the top of the mole; wooden walkways had been nailed into the top surface of the shell-constructed arm. Here, the salt-breeze was strongest and he could catch the flavour of fresh-caught fish, the glint of sun on mollusc-festooned boats.

At length he progressed to crutches and finally to a walking stick as one leg had been slightly less severely damaged.

So finally he got his wish and Jaryar took him to sea one fine day in a small pleasure-boat, the breeze cracking into the canvas sail. As he had never been in a seaboat before, he felt both awkward and a little afraid, but his long familiarity with the craft by the mole lessened the fear and soon he was able to enjoy the exhilarating experience.

Jaryar was an accomplished handler and though the hull was formed with numerous shells, the boat cleaved through the waves with the greatest of ease.

Because Renjhoriskand's dwarf trees were unsuitable for large construction, only small boats were built using the wood for the craft's skeleton only; then countless large shells were nailed together and to the ribs, the inside of the boat was then covered with a thick layer of othenal which caked hard and water-resistant when dried. Reeds were then spread on the othenal and twined to form seats. The sail-mast went through the bottom of the hull and acted as a stabiliser, hence the additional need for the mole as the boats could not normally be beached.

As they joined a small fishing fleet with Janoven just on the horizon he watched the fishermen circle their combined nets, drawing them in closer and closer, and then set sail for the village: their craft were incapable of holding the mighty weight of so many fish. They followed the procession with its catch of silver-glistening fish, expectant, for tonight there would be a beach-feast.

He dimly recalled those nightmarish moments at the foot of the Tanalumes and was thankful he had not succumbed to the wish to die.

This was what life was all about: to breathe in the heady fragrance of the Salt-taal, the fresh winds and spindrift, to hold this sweet woman's hand.

In the intervening moons Jaryar had grown into full womanhood and, imperceptibly almost, he felt a change in attitude towards her. Whenever she could not be with him for some pressing reason – and the reason had to be very pressing indeed – he felt lost, as though his right arm had been amputated. The joy of life waned in her absence; but for his reasoning that she would be back soon, he would have lapsed into a profound melancholia. She was with him so much, her soft caring voice in his ears so often, he lived and breathed Jaryar.

Their regular visits to the graveside of his father transformed abruptly from a sombre pilgrimage to something special, to be anticipated, as the Ramous flowers budded and the warm sun beat upon them. For here, in the home of death, they found a reason for living, yet they never voiced it.

Then the day came that he no longer needed any support at all. He had lately been unable to sleep, knowing that the true test was approaching. And he had asked himself night after night, would Jaryar still feel for him when he could walk unaided? Or would the bond snap between them? Was his disability the only thing that really kept them close? However irrational he told himself such thoughts were, they persisted.

Solemnly, he laid the walking stick upon his father's grave, stood up straight and stepped back.

"You've done it!" exclaimed Jaryar, eyes alight.

For many many moons Jaryar had willed this to happen. This was the culmination of all the tears of frustration, the pain of failure, the soaring sensation of hope and faith reborn from defeat.

He held her hand, gripped it tight. "Not without your help, my love," he said. And they kissed.

For so long she seemed to have sensed his innermost reasoning: not until he considered himself completely whole again would he commit himself; she intuitively knew that his feelings ran as deep as her own. In that she could not be mistaken; especially not now, as their first kiss lingered.

Alomar's doubts sailed away on the breeze. They were as one and would always be so.

Shortly after their marriage, with the dowry, they moved into Janoven.

The oceanic island born from the great deeps rose one dawn without warning. The size of the landmass was incredible; the Janoven inhabitants could hardly believe their eyes.

Steam gushed, smoke billowed high into the sky and the surrounding sea boiled and bubbled. And still the island rose higher and higher, an immense hunchback of basalt rock, red-hot lava spraying out of its hollow cone.

A few people appreciated the imminent danger and tried evacuating the city, but the spectacle drew so many crowds the roads out were soon blocked with wagons and villagers.

Alomar himself had been working high up in the citadel's armoury when the island emerged; he had a spectacular view. Then, he realised that the water level was agitated and rising.

The steaming hot water was spreading towards Fullantran – and today Jaryar habitually went to the village to buy fish. Surely, the fisherfolk, well versed in the ways of the sea, would recognise the danger and seek high ground?

But he could not leave it to chance. He discarded his tools and hurried down the high winding steps.

The island continued to rise and then exploded, showering the area with white-hot stones and boulders; but, worse, the eruption created a tidal wave of boiling water.

And the wave came on and on and overwhelmed the entire fishing village. On the wave rushed, climbing high up the banks, flooding the outlying hamlets of Janoven.

Finally, the waves crashed violently against the city's defensive walls. Though all the gates had been closed, water still seeped under and some splashed over the walls with the first pounding, and scalded spectators.

Then the wave's force veered around the city's sloping revetments and created a quagmire moat.

Alomar came upon the city gates just after they slammed shut. One of the gate-men fell into the seeping water and screamed and screamed as he was boiled like a wildfowl.

Only instinct for survival prevented Alomar from threshing through the water and opening the gates.

"Jaryar!" Scrambling to the battlements, he clutched onto a feeble hope, that she might somehow have avoided the wave and the island's spewing vomit from Below.

From the curtain wall of the city, among hundreds of others held in thrall, he watched as the fateful island settled and slowly sank until only about one-third remained above the surface, brooding almost, mocking them all.

It took some days for the water to cool and drain away.

He found her and she was not like he had remembered.

Physically and mentally numb, he returned to the sad remains of the cemetery, the place of so much happiness shared, and there he interred her amidst tears that no amount of will-power could quench.

There was nothing left in life for him; that he knew as surely as he stood there, face crumpling while he looked upon her grave alongside his father's. There, too, wedged in the cracked tombstone of his father, a little rotten now, his walking stick.

The legs that she had helped to save trembled and he collapsed to his knees, painfully hitting the stone flags.

He left the place of mourning only as the moon shone its silver cold luminescence full upon the grave. He walked away in a dream.

Alomar was still in a dream when he purchased certain potions mostly used for god-worship. He mixed the vile concoction and swallowed the entire thick and glutinous liquid.

A full bottle of inferior wine washed it down.

After that, everything took on a nightmare quality. He had no regrets about taking his own life. He suffered no pain, for which he was glad. It seemed until this point in time when he was forsaking even time itself that he had always borne some form of pain, some terrible loss.

Enough! Die and be salved.

But then things were not quite right. He knew not what the Overlord looked like, but he knew one thing: the Overlord refused to see him!

But without seeing the Overlord, there was no death – only a timeless limbo.

He lay upon the quartz-tiled floor, paralysed with the effects of the potion and stared up at the ornate ceiling of the empty shell that had been their home. The patterns of the ceiling swam before his eyes, foggy and swathing, lowering green and white, sickly of hue. Everything seemed to coalesce into a vaguely human shape, the facial features shimmering but never discernible, save for the black maw of a mouth.

And then the mouth opened and closed and spoke in a thunderous, deafening basso profundo:

"*You have deigned to come too soon, Courdour Alomar! You come to a god you deny! Daqsekor is greatly displeased for you were not summoned! In consequence of your temerity, the Overlord believes your fate should be never to rest eternal! Think, Courdour Alomar. Dwell upon this, a fate that would condemn you to an eternal wandering!*"

Unable to move, incapable of even batting an eyelid, Alomar lay there and his whole inner being seemed to writhe and jerk in anguish at the horrifying prospect of being denied the oblivion of death.

"However," the Overlord's messenger went on, "*Daqsekor, in His infinite wisdom and mercy, has decided to give you one last chance. There is one place upon this world where the living and the dead, gods and demons, human and non-human co-exist together. One place, alone. If you, Courdour Alomar, can find this place, then you shall be admitted to the Overlord's domain. If not, then you will continue to live, to exist until the end of time itself! This place you should seek is the Navel of the World.*" And as suddenly and as strangely as it appeared, the apparition faded and was gone. Slowly, painfully, Alomar's limbs contracted in violent spasms. Face contorted in incredible agony, he raised himself and staggered, vomit rising in rebellion against the vile potion he had swallowed.

Cursed! Condemned to an everlasting life with no respite, to live a loveless existence, never to join Jaryar in the Grove of the Overlord.

In one shattering impulse, he grabbed his sword from its scabbard and whirled it above his head, brought it down and across his offered throat. No man could live with his jugular vein emptying life's blood from the body. He would defy the Overlord; he would–

The sword slashed into his throat, cutting painfully, but it broke. As the snapped blade fell to the floor, he eyed himself in a mirror. All he had sustained was a superficial cut, a flesh wound, and a great deal of pain.

Over the years to come he realised his folly in trying to inflict a mortal wound on himself. Something always went wrong, saving him.

All kinds of pain.

All he could do, then, was roam the land in the hope of finding the

Navel of the World. And in his constant search, he could live an adventurous life in the hope that another sword might cut him down, extinguish his immortal flame.

*

Fhord lowered her goblet and stared at their host. "Then – you're immortal?"

"Aye, lass – now you know why I regard you as but a youngster! All who walk this world now are but babes compared with my age!" The warrior leaned back and laughed bitterly.

Fhord froze. "Your throat –?"

"No scar, eh? Alas, the Overlord is too kind to me. My body can repair itself – after many years – and of those I have plenty!"

"And you still seek the Navel?" Ulran asked quietly.

"Oh, I've grown to live with this curse!" He chuckled at his choice of words. "But that one hope keeps me sane, that one day I shall find this place and rejoin Jaryar." Sombrely, he lowered his gaze. "I only hope I realise I've found it when I get there."

"And you think that that–" Fhord hesitated, the memories of the cellar starkly imprinted on her mind, "– that sekor, it will help you in some way?"

The immortal shrugged. "I have no way of knowing, but deep in my bones, yes, I believe it will help me, somehow. When it is ready."

"So, what will you do now, Alomar?" asked Ulran.

A grin. "What else? I'll join you to Arisa! My life is destined to lead where happenstance directs. Fate brought you into my company. There must be some Grand Design in our journey to Arisa and I trust my quest will be connected. Like Cobrora Fhord, here, I too feel *drawn* to join your quest. So, yes, I'll leave with you first light tomorrow."

Floreskand: Wings

CHAPTER TEN
BLIGHTED

They depart when we hate to lose them.
– *Dialogues of Meshanel*

When Courdour Alomar descended the stone stairs into the ward on the following day, Fhord, astride the patient Sarolee, involuntarily let out a gasp, so imposing was the immortal warrior's presence.

Contrary to Ulran, Courdour believed in using armour in combat. Each man to his own, she thought, but she wondered how the warrior managed, weighed down as he was. Surely, it was better to be unhampered?

Courdour had discarded his distinctive traveller's trappings and now stood at the foot of the stairs, completely attired in accoutrements of war. Over his hide shirt and leggings hung strips of ironwood strung together to form his breastplate; similar armour protected his pelvis and thighs; whilst his arms and shins were covered with lacquered wood plates. A dull grey mail-shirt guarded his genitals and mail gloves and hood protected his hands and throat.

In contrast, he still wore his floppy black hat and in the crook of his arm held a burnished gold helmet – which appeared as old as the rest of the equipment – its crest gone, only a plinth remaining. His shield – oval with a few holes through which he could jab at his opponent – was scarred and dented, and hung from his shoulder. A large two-handed broadsword with nicks in the blade was slung across his back.

To complete his stock of weaponry, a short-sword and poniard were strapped to his wide leather belt.

"You seem well enough equipped to take on the entire Kellan-Mesqa hordes," Ulran remarked.

A shrug and his armour rattled. "Aye, but it's tried and tested and has never failed me!" He held up his short-sword amidst further clinking and rattling. "The gear is so old its like is no longer made. But then, in those far gone days, things were made to last."

Ponderously, he mounted his black Borsalac and swung the stallion around. "Enough talk – let's make tracks!"

So, Fhord mused, despite taking them into his confidence, Courdour's attitude and abrupt manner had not improved. But at least she could appreciate the causes. She still pined the loss of Slane, but now that she shared a similar loss to Courdour, she felt she too could rise above the pain of sorrow.

The spirits of the marsh still attempted infiltrating their ranks but were mysteriously repelled. Here, too, was cause for Eron to study.

They negotiated the manderon side of Marron Marsh, with Courdour leading the way.

It had been an uncanny feeling as they left the silent Toran Nebulous behind. Fhord glanced back after a few paces to see it no more. But the prospect of adventure ahead emboldened her.

On emerging into brilliant daylight, Fhord breathed a sigh of relief. Their horses and mule briskly trod the firm turf of plainsland. The grasses were moist after last night's storm, yet the Castle grounds had remained dry.

"We should make good time now," said Ulran.

Scalrin, like some good omen, flew above them, sometimes a little ahead, sometimes trailing, and the bird's presence certainly tended to calm any fears Fhord harboured.

But she still clung to her amulets.

When they came upon Kellan-Mesqa tracks, she tried pitching her mind ahead, in the frail hope of contacting other minds, other movement. But her attempt was doomed.

It was precisely at this moment that a terrible screeching deafened them all.

As one, they peered up.

Scalrin was in trouble.

As if from nowhere, a large flock of hawks appeared. The great bird was surrounded by the darting, screeching grey-brown bodies and flapping dark wings.

Scalrin weaved and bit, talons clawing at those foolish enough to come too close, but numbers would eventually tell: the great bird was outnumbered by about fifty to one.

Fhord's heart lurched as one reckless hawk dived from on high, thudding home, arrow-like, into Scalrin's wing.

Red feathers scattered and the great bird's beak opened in a silent scream of agony.

Other hawks saw their chance and closed in, about ten at once.

Amazingly, Scalrin beat them off, only sustaining two further jabs at his back.

But the onlookers could see that the red tellar was losing and would soon be vanquished. The brave creature's retaliatory moves were already slower and laboured.

Scalrin must have appreciated the hopelessness of his predicament, for he suddenly stopped, plummeted earthwards toward Ulran and his companions.

At the innman's instructions, Courdour Alomar was prepared for this eventuality and unlatched his bow and arrow from the saddle. He loosed five arrows in the space of a heartbeat and five attackers, closest on Scalrin's tail, dropped to earth, dead or, screeching, mortally wounded.

Fearlessly, the remainder flew after the now escaping red tellar, as Scalrin had taken advantage of the respite afforded by the warrior's arrows. He was winging close to the plainsland, massive red wings beating, the wind-rush of his movement bending the grasses beneath him.

Soon the red tellar was out of sight. The screeching hawks speeding after him also vanished, their noise lingering for a few moments.

The sudden onset of contrasting silence made Scalrin's departure all the more eerie.

All three travellers kept their thoughts to themselves.

At length, Ulran spoke. "He'll be back." His voice held unshakeable confidence.

Fhord couldn't help but wonder if the innman might be mistaken. With all her being, she hoped not. More than all her charms, Scalrin, she felt, was their good luck. With the Overlord's bird in their company, how could they come to harm? But now...

"Aye, he'll be back, I warrant," Courdour echoed. The bird's absence affected them all. "But where in all Below did those hawks spring from?" He dismounted and studied a dead hawk, with an arrow skewering its chest. On its left leg was a small gold band. "They're hunting hawks, Ulran."

"I thought they must be."

"You mean, that attack was deliberate?" Fhord trembled at the thought.

"It seems that way," replied Ulran. "But I know of no Kellan-Mesqa horde that uses hawks for hunting."

"What if it isn't the Devastators this time?" asked Fhord, approaching panic.

"Then we have other, well-concealed enemies, Fhord. And until they show themselves, we must just bide our time – and beware!"

Astride the now jumpy Sarolee, Fhord suddenly felt very vulnerable in the middle of this expanse of grass and scrub.

***

Later, Fhord called across to Ulran, "Have the Kellan-Mesqa ever crossed swords with Kormish Warriors, do you know?"

Ulran grinned. "You appear remarkably interested in them. Why?"

"Well, as you'll recall, I always wanted to make that pilgrimage to Sianlar and, well, I'd heard rumours about The Drop – that if people spent too much time there, they went insane. I just wondered, how the pilgrims fare, for Sianlar is close to the Varteron Edge..."

"Go on."

"It just seems to me, perhaps the Kormish Warriors have something to do with the acromania rumour. Otherwise, quite a few of those pilgrims might have diverted to The Drop, and even attempted scaling down it out of curiosity. But few would risk the madness."

Ulran shrugged. Fhord's imagination certainly did her credit.

"And the camp fires people have seen in the jungles at the bottom of The Drop – green-yellow, I think, someone said. Obviously, some people live there, perhaps the Insane Ones."

"That seems like a piece of quite valid reasoning." He couldn't mention the firefly trees without explaining. "When you do go on your pilgrimage – perhaps after we've finished whatever we have to do in Arion – you will embark on the road to Sianlar. Then, you could test your theories. I'm afraid I cannot give you an answer. The pilgrimage is a private affair, for each individual, and as such must be kept sanctified within oneself. So, you see, I am bound not to say anything. Though, I might add, you're quite right about people keeping clear of The Drop; that, I saw, clearly. And, obviously, the insanity rumour had much to do with it."

"Then, is it true Kormish Warriors have infiltrated into every strata of Floreskandian life?"

Ulran laughed. "You're asking the wrong man, Fhord. Honestly, the way you go on, you'd think I was the country's accredited expert on Kormish Warriors!"

The city-dweller sighed. "I was just curious to learn–"

"No harm in learning, Fhord. But, alas, I can't give you answers I don't know, now, can I?"

"No, I suppose not."

***

They bivouacked beside a small copse of plains-trees in the brightening light of the moon. After eating two well-cooked voles, they sat around the low fire.

Fhord once again mentioned the Kellan-Mesqa: "I know you're not an expert, Ulran," she began, "but you seemed to evade my earlier question about–"

"Crossing swords with the Kormish Warriors?"

"Yes, seeing as you were a captive once."

The innman grinned, lifting his hand. "You have it wrong, Fhord. But, to answer your question first – there are no known recorded cases of such confrontations. But in the Kellan-Mesqa folklore, mention is often made of the hordes fighting with and against the fabled warriors. Does that answer your –?"

The tree snake had moved so stealthily in the foliage of an adjacent plains-wood, that even Ulran had not detected any sound until too late.

Its huge sinuous weight fell across his shoulders and draped into his lap and down his chest.

Fhord let out an involuntary gasp and cringed.

Courdour withdrew his short-sword but a censoring look from Ulran stayed the immortal's hand.

The innman sat, cross-legged, his body crying out in panic, impelling his legs to run, for his hands to thrash out at the alien thing draped about him. But his mind was in complete control. He recognised the tree snake for what it was: "Bane-viper," he whispered, unmoving, unblinking.

Though his pulse raced and sweat soaked his brow already, he was succeeding in shallowing his breathing, calming his nerves and primordial fears.

"If it bites me," he said, addressing Fhord, "you must catch it, use the fluids inside its eye-sacs mixed with salt and some pounded herbs in my saddle-pouch – the grey-green dust."

Afraid to move, Fhord nodded very slightly. Then, frantic at the realisation that they must catch the bane-viper she began to tremble and looked sharply at Courdour for support and guidance.

"Can we kill the thing before extracting the fluid?" asked Courdour.

"Yes – but it must be extracted within a dacorm, by all accounts."

As they talked, the tree snake slithered only a little across Ulran's broad cloaked shoulders. It was possible that the cloak might absorb the venom completely. "I suggest you prepare the other parts of the anti-venin now – just in case," he said levelly.

Slowly, noiselessly, Fhord rose and edged back towards the saddles and bedding.

Courdour Alomar made to follow, but his armour – which he purposefully left on even at night in case of an attack – chinked and rattled at the slightest movement. He froze immediately.

Ulran whispered: "They have no ears but detect sounds or movements by vibrations."

The immortal's look implied *Are you sure?*

"I'm risking my life on it, Alomar."

The immortal turned, nodded and went after Fhord. But his foot came down upon a thin layer of dried dust over a weasel-hole and the giant warrior tripped.

The weight of his armour carried him noisily forward a few paces then he righted himself and swore, his ankle slightly twisted.

He cast a hasty glance at Ulran and froze again: the snake had obviously been disturbed by the footfalls. It sank its gaping mouth into the innman's right arm and seemed loath to let go. Incredibly, Ulran sat unmoved, staring directly ahead.

Courdour raced forward, unsheathing his sword. "Fhord, bring that stuff! Quick, lass!" He ran on till he came to an abrupt halt before the still tableau of man and snake.

Decapitation was the only way, but how could he accomplish it without hitting Ulran?

Yet, to hesitate brought the innman closer to complete paralysis, coma and death.

He swerved round, indecisive for the first time in countless years.

Fhord was racing across the dusty ground, avoiding the pot-holes and in her arms were bundles of salt and other potions from Ulran's pack.

Bracing himself, Courdour kicked at the bane-viper, first on its glistening green back. But that had no effect. Then he kicked even more viciously at the base of its triangular skull. The response was instantaneous and frightening.

The creature darted round, so sharply that it snapped one fang, leaving it imbedded in Ulran's forearm.

Venom and blood left a thin spray as the snake darted from Ulran up at Courdour, straight for his unprotected face.

No shield: he raised his sword arm protectively and the first attack blunted upon his lacquered wood-plates.

The bane-viper hit the ground, zigzagged incredibly fast, and suddenly leapt out again, like a spear.

But this time Courdour was prepared and side-stepped, bringing his sword sweeping down upon its back as the thing passed in mid-air.

Little resistance, a dull thwack, some crunching cartilage, and the bane-viper dropped to the ground, head falling some distance from the mindless body.

Fhord gaped as the headless body writhed and swerved and covered the ground in red and green outpourings in its nervous death-throes.

"Now!" Courdour discarded his sword, grabbed up the severed head.

The reptilian eyes blinked twice before going an opaque white. He withdrew his poniard and pierced the eye-sac beneath the staring eye.

Fhord was by his side, a terracotta bowl offered, and the sac-fluid dribbled in. Courdour repeated the same technique on the other sac and then threw the head into the tall grass. Her stomach threatening to disgorge, Fhord busily mixed the ingredients.

Courdour Alomar knelt by the innman, studied his eyes: they were not as deep a brown as before. Sweat lathered the innman's face. A pulse in his forehead indicated sluggishness – but, he reminded himself, that would be Ulran's doing: reducing the blood-flow by whatever arcane means he had at his disposal would at least slow down the movement of venom within his system. The sheer control of the man: still sitting cross-legged; immobile.

The immortal glanced down at Ulran's forearm. Using a cloth and his poniard he extracted the fang and washed the wound thoroughly.

At that moment Fhord came up with the sickly-looking thick paste.

But Ulran had neglected to explain how the anti-venin as he called it should be administered.

And time was of the essence. "We'll try more than one way, Fhord."

"Right. Alomar..."

Alomar spread the paste liberally on the open wound, pressing it deep within the cut he'd made. "Right, you bandage that up quickly while I treat him elsewhere."

The city-dweller looked puzzled but did as she was bid.

Alomar shuffled across to the innman's other side and having heated his knife in the fire he cut into the flesh of Ulran's upper arm near the muscle. Fhord was about to protest when the immortal silenced her with a scowl and began applying more of the unguent to the fresh wound.

It was a messy process, packing the mixture in with sticky blood gushing over the wound, but at last he had packed it well and stemmed the blood-flow. By the time he had done this, Fhord was finished on the other arm and took over the bandaging of this one. Alomar was then free to roll the remains of the anti-venin into a small mushy ball and drop it into Ulran's mouth. "It should dissolve in time – it may help, may not."

Then, their efforts completed, for better or worse, they stepped back.

"We can but wait now," said Alomar.

Unable to take her eyes off the statuesque innman, Fhord nodded and a lump came to her throat.

That night, lying in her bedroll or whilst on watch, Fhord prayed very fervently indeed to all her white gods: "Please don't let Ulran die!"

It was as though the animal kingdom bore them a grudge. "The animals we've encountered – they are as lethal as any assassin!" she railed aloud.

Alomar must have heard. "Man has no especial right to walk this world with impunity, Fhord. I think Ulran would agree – we're one with the animals and the earth we tread on. That's all."

For the next two days they remained in the camp and Ulran continued to sit cross-legged, unmoving.

Repeatedly, they checked his breathing, so shallow, and his heartbeat, so slow, and kept him warmly wrapped in blankets during the night and well aired in the reinvigorating sun of the days.

The ground about the innman had taken on a sort of crystalline appearance with the outpourings of sweat, the moisture having dried in sunlight, leaving only the salt content.

The third night was half-gone when Fhord took over from Alomar as lookout.

"Nothing untoward," the immortal reported and lowered himself into his blankets. He cast a look at the sitting figure of Ulran, blanket-swathed, and shook his head. "It's uncanny," was all he said, and then pulled down his hat's brim to rest his eyes.

Over the last couple of days Fhord had not slept much, worry about Ulran constantly gnawing at her, until now she was drowsy and close to exhaustion.

She fell into a deep dreamless sleep, leaving the camp unguarded and vulnerable.

***

Alomar heard their approach, but by the time he had raised himself with the cumbrous weight of his armour, he was surrounded by a ring of spears.

His first angry reaction was to seek out Fhord.

The city-dweller lay by the dull embers of the fire, one hand stroking a bloody patch at the base of her skull. The attack had been soundless.

Then he thought of Ulran, wondering what the Kellan-Mesqa would make of the innman's immobility.

But Ulran wasn't there – only a heap of blankets.

"Where is the third member of your party?" asked one of the Kellan-Mesqa who sported a rush helmet.

Fhord shook her head and shrugged. The Devastator was speaking in the Common Tongue but his accent made it difficult to understand.

"What third member?" Alomar asked.

A Devastator with a bear-hide headband eyed the old warrior. "You cross our path dressed for war, old man. What is your purpose here?" He paused, strode over to the immortal. "Tell me, before I, Wolderiq, decide on your fate."

"These plains are free. I've trodden them for many more years than you've seen Nikkonslor's Eye. We but pass through, intent on reaching the Sonalumes."

"You lie! Now tell me, where is the third–?"

His query was answered: Ulran leaped to the ground immediately in front of the apparent leader. The branch above rustled and was still.

Alomar was as surprised as the Devastator who stepped back in amazement.

Fhord breathed a sigh of relief.

The innman assessed Wolderiq. Talk would be of little use; he was obviously a man of action. "I challenge your ability to lead!" Ulran spoke in their language and was faintly amused by their reaction.

"You are a Furdhar, you have no right to challenge."

"If you are afraid, I will fight one who is not. One who is worthy to lead."

The Devastators round Ulran put up their spears. Wolderiq had been challenged according to tradition, so whoever the Furdhar was he at least knew their ways. The men relaxed slightly to watch the verbal play before the actual fight. A few took bets on who would lose face by attacking first.

"Furdhar! I, Wolderiq the bear slayer, will make you beg for your life!" A bear slayer was held in high esteem in most hordes but not in Ulran's eyes.

"How many bears have you killed?"

"Two," Wolderiq said proudly.

"You will have to be careful next time. The cubs' mother could be around."

Fhord could not understand what was being said but things appeared to be working out, for the onlookers were laughing at Ulran's remarks.

"Furdhar! You will be glad to crawl into the dung heap you call home when I have beaten you and torn out your vile tongue."

"Be careful, bear slayer. I am not a cub. But to give you a chance I will fight only with one hand."

Wolderiq's face grew bright red.

"What's the matter? Are the odds still too much for you?" Ulran had him hooked. The Devastator was on the verge of exploding. He sent home the final barb. "I will turn my back." Ulran began to turn, adding, "Even a Nameless warrior would have the–"

Wolderiq's scream of fury pierced Fhord's nerves as the bear slayer leaped at Ulran's back.

The innman continued his turn, brushed aside the attack and sent the Devastator rolling across the fire.

"Did you trip?" Ulran asked innocently.

Wolderiq rushed again and the innman side-stepped at the last possible instant.

Six times the Devastator rushed and each time his opponent seemed to disappear. "Stand still and fight, Furdhar!"

Which was exactly what Ulran did the next time.

Wolderiq, in his anger, left his guard open when he rushed in. Ulran's foot came up and hit the Devastator three times before it touched the ground again.

The challenge was over.

Fhord's sigh of relief was choked off in mid-stream as another Devastator jumped in front of Ulran and levelled his spear at the innman. Fhord began a prayer to Osasor but that too was interrupted by a voice crying out from the darkness, "Hold!"

The Devastators froze and Ulran smiled. Out of the gloom stepped another group of Kellan-Mesqa and they were led by a man with a birthmark on his forehead.

"Solendoral!" exclaimed the innman, clasping the Devastator's arms.

The gathered Kellan-Mesqa were taken aback and a couple were all set to let loose their throwing spears when Solendoral said, "Ulran? Could it be? Why, you have altered so much."

"It is many years."

At this point Alomar interrupted. "You know this Devastator?"

"Aye, we are adoptive brothers. This group is a montar of the Hansenand tribe."

"Alas," interjected Solendoral, "this is almost all that is left of the Hansenand. I can count the numbers of other montars on one hand. Times have grown grim since you left us, Ulran." Solendoral stood as tall as the innman, but more lean and sinewy. His long narrow face did not smile.

Solendoral eyed Wolderiq; a couple of his men were helping him to his feet. "I watched your challenge, Ulran. I have never seen anyone fight in such a manner."

"As I said. It is many years and many experiences since we parted."

"It is good to see you recovered," interrupted Alomar, "But why did you not warn us of the Kellan-Mesqa approach?"

"There was no–" Ulran was interrupted by the sound of jeering.

Wolderiq, the bear slayer, was a broken man. He had lost face – beaten by a Furdhar. He was now a serf, little better than a slave. Ulran stopped the baiting. "What is happening here?" he asked. The warriors fell silent. "Who are you to ridicule a bear slayer?" No one answered.

The innman strode up to Wolderiq and spoke for all to hear. "I give you my life."

Fhord was confused by these events but later after setting up camp Alomar explained that Ulran had given Wolderiq his face back by giving him the highest honour available – that of entrusting his life into the Devastator's hands.

"Which reminds me, Ulran," said Alomar, "when did you come out of your trance?"

"Just after the forward scout had seen us."

Solendoral looked puzzled. "Trance, brother?"

"Yes."

"He was bitten," supplied Fhord, nursing her head. "By a bane-viper. Three days ago."

The Devastator stepped back a pace, eyes widening almost in awe. "And you still live?" he said, echoing his men's thoughts.

"During years of study I learned much about the body, Solendoral. After that, I studied the mind. The trance situation is essential to the process of removing the snake's poison. It is not unlike your own abilities or those of your Tangakols."

"We must talk more of such matters."

Ulran smiled. "I would like to – but we must get to Arisa."

"We are heading manderon also," countered Solendoral. "We go to a Giving Feast."

"Then we shall travel together," declared the innman.

At this, Solendoral and his men grinned, content to travel with their leader's brother and these two strange travellers.

Clasping a bare arm round Ulran's shoulders, Solendoral patted the innman's chest. "Where's your armour?" He slapped his own lightweight lacquered wood platelets covering chest and thighs and then nodded at Alomar's.

"I find it too constricting. You saw how Alomar had difficulty in rising."

"So that is the fabled Courdour Alomar?"

"Indeed. It is fortunate your men had him pinned down before he could rise or wield his broadsword."

"I believe you!" Solendoral paused, called some instructions to one of his men.

Shortly afterwards, six wagons trundled into camp with the rest of the montar.

There were about fifty Devastators, all busily erecting tents and transferring lighted fuel from their ironwood fire-wagon for the camp-fires. Of that number, about two-fifths were women.

Both Alomar and Fhord, Ulran was pleased to see, mixed with the Kellan-Mesqa and pitched in to help the formation of the camp. Fhord had certainly picked up the guttural tongue with astonishing speed; possibly her psychic ability had helped in some way. He looked around again. A mere thirty men. And, according to Solendoral, the other Hansenand montars numbered just as few. Ulran's eyes glazed with remembrance.

"You must tell me all you've done since you left us, Ulran."

But he didn't hear, for his mind was deep in the past.

*

With great stealth at the coming of night, innman Conofrack Jasebours and his wife Elar, together with their third child Loring in a bundle of blankets, sneaked out of the siege-ridden city of Goldalese.

Loring remembered little, though the twinkle of countless camp-fires surrounding the city stayed imprinted on his mind. The city was due to fall to the forces of Lornwater and his father believed life under the conquerors was so unbearable that they must flee.

This decision created a rift in their family, for Loring's brother Aska and sister Usa – both over twenty years old – were determined to stay.

But Jasebours was as adamant: so they risked all to head to the ranmeron, ironically in the direction of the enemy city.

For almost three moons they walked and stumbled; they received rest and paid for food at the numerous housesteads dotted on the plainslands.

They feared the soldiers of Lornwater more than the Devastators.

But one day, as Nikkonslor, in a typical fit of jealousy, blotted out Jahdemor's azure sky from the eyes of mortals, their encampment was brutally attacked.

The Lornwater mercenaries, returning from the ransacking of Goldalese, had spotted the small camp fire and, ever-eager for fresh booty, encircled the camp. When they saw there were only two adults to contend with, they sprang into the clearing.

Jasebours put up a good fight, slaying one mercenary and wounding two others. There were six more, however: too many. Knowing the odds were hopeless, he fought with unequalled savagery, giving Elar time to melt into a breach in the attackers' ranks.

Reluctantly, tears streaming, Elar ran into the long grass with young Loring in her arms.

On the edge of a copse, Jasebours fought until sheer weight of numbers downed him, swords slashing his legs, muscles and tendons. On his knees, he fought in his own blood – until he was disarmed and dispatched with no less than five swords piercing his brave heart.

Blood-lust was rife among the surviving four mercenaries as their wounded comrades died at their own hands: fewer shares for the pickings.

They ransacked the camp and, angered at the lack of decent loot, they recalled the fleeing woman.

Confident that she wouldn't have run far, they charged through the long grass in her wake.

The clouds of Nikkonslor wisped away at an inopportune time, revealing Elar's blue dress partly concealed amidst a large cluster of yellow flowers.

A sunbeam betrayed her.

She screamed as the mercenaries loped through the grass, their swords dripping her husband's blood upon the flowers. Before she could rise from her hiding place with Loring, they were upon her. Two pinned her down, ignoring her pleading shrieks.

She called for Loring to run away.

Another ripped off her clothing while the fourth held the boy at bay with difficulty.

They each took their pleasure until Elar ceased screaming and lay staring wide-eyed and inert. Her child was racked with terrible sobs.

Then the boy's captor kneeled forward with an arrow entering his left ear and emerging from his right.

The present molester died more slowly, an arrow piercing each of his buttocks, and a third sank into his back instants later.

The other two let go of Elar only to run into the arms of ten Kellan-Mesqa.

Loring ran to his mother but she didn't respond though quite alive.

He knelt and sobbed on her breast as the Devastators dealt rough justice to the two surviving mercenaries. Once emasculated, they were let loose to stagger across the plains naked. If they did not die from loss of blood, they would succumb to exposure.

Tenderly, the Kellan-Mesqa warriors wrapped Elar in furs and carried her on a hide stretcher. The largest of them carried Loring who had fallen into a sleep of exhaustion.

In truth, Loring should have been irreparably affected by his experience. But the Hansenand Kellan-Mesqa at that time were led by a leader of great kindness and sagacity: against all advice, he kept the child away from his mother for a full year. Elar was well cared for but quite insane.

After the year, Loring was able to sleep most nights without screaming in nightmare. He was told about his mother, how she was deteriorating; immediately, he offered to help her, and became her right hand. She was exasperating at times but he was determined to help as much as he could.

Almost another year passed for them, then she gradually improved and began speaking lucidly where before there had been no speech. As advised, he did not betray his own identity as her son; it was felt that remembering him would pitch her back into her catatonic state.

Elar died during a battle between the Hansenand and the Baronculer hordes. The Hansenand won at great cost. But the enemy was broken; after that, peace prospered.

Loring ran away shortly after committing his mother to her last resting place. He was caught suffering from exposure two days later and was punished by being kept in the women's tents for two solid quarters.

Many more times did he run away in the ensuing moons, but as he matured and made friends with the young men of the horde, he ran away less and less, and finally settled.

But by then he was stuck with his name, Ulran – Runaway.

They had been idyllic days and nights, sleeping in the open beneath the vault of stars, camping in their thousands on the rolling grassy slopes of the plains. Colours and furs dotted the slopes, pennons from lances furled in the summer breeze.

The Hansenand became the most feared and respected horde of Kellan-Mesqa.

Their leader had eradicated the lust for blood and raiding within the horde itself and hoped to affect the other hordes similarly by their example.

But intrigues existed, of which he was unaware.

A boy then, Solendoral had overheard some plotters discussing the proposed poisoning of their leader and he had rushed out into the night to find Ulran and ask his advice.

The orphan of Goldalese had been as shocked as Solendoral.

Alas, being youngsters, they were not able to obtain an audience with their leader.

When they approached Solendoral the Elder, he guffawed and said smugly that no such thing could happen to the Hansenand's leader. They were a mighty horde with enemies, true, but the enemies were weak and divided.

Two nights later, unearthly screams issued from the leader's tent, as though the very devils of the Underworld had rampaged upon the earth.

Guards rushed in.

All was chaos: upon the floor writhed their leader, face the colour of his purple robe; he coughed up his insides in vain. His death was the beginning of the end for the horde's monopoly of power.

Fewer and fewer hordes paid geld to them; the raids upon housesteads increased and, finally, when a montar of Hansenand attempted saving a housestead, they were branded as surely as the true culprits.

Thereafter, all hordes were again maligned by every city; trading fell off and caravans were strengthened with outriders employed to hunt down small montars and kill them for per capita payment.

Their decline was gradual. The Kellan-Mesqa measured time by counting the days their leaders ruled over them. A legacy from the older days when the Kellan-Mesqa had lived like the Furdhars in their own countries before Hewwa's Revenge.

If a man became leader and possessed the name of a previous leader, he must change his name for the Kellan-Mesqa calendar's sake. So the decline of the Hansenand stretched over many leader-days, or almost thirty city-dwellers' years.

And Ulran only saw the first seven years following the great leader's murder.

He had witnessed the writing on the wall, clearer than most. His boyhood friend Solendoral had seen it too but fervently hoped he could once again make the Hansenand a great people, if chosen.

Ulran hoped so too, just as ardently, but he felt drawn to finish with this nomadic life. He must seek out new horizons.

He was inexplicably attracted to Lornwater, where Queen Neran IV reigned; she was said to be fair and honest, quite unlike her predecessor who had warred for pleasure and sacked Goldalese.

Ulran's leave-taking was sad but there were no regrets on either side. Men now, they understood each had to go his own way, make his own mark as he saw fit, as the Book of the Living decreed.

***

Ulran and Solendoral stood in front of a blazing log fire at the door of his round hide-and-wood flat-roofed tent. His eyes looked glazed, recalling the vast numbers in the camps of old. "Days too far gone ever to be recalled, Solendoral."

"Our world is changing."

"Change is good for all of us. Floreskand's history has been one of stagnation for too long."

"Aye, that I can vouch for," added Alomar. "I've seen more than most." He chuckled. "A thousand years seem to pass–" He faltered, eyeing Solendoral and his strange looks.

Fhord smiled and delved into the bowl of vegetable stew and buckballs.

"So we shall be together, Solendoral, you and your people, at least as far as the mountains?"

"Yes. We have much to speak on."

***

Two days later while traversing a burnt area of grassland, Solendoral called a halt to their movement. He turned to Ulran. "Blighted," he said savagely.

Curious, the innman said, "In what manner?"

"A great bird – a red tellar – we saw it being chased by hawks – and it was suffering from countless wounds." He shuddered at the memory.

His brown eyes, slanted and wary, saddened. "I ordered my men to shoot down as many attackers as possible. Ever mindful of the Overlord, you see," he said, tapping his birthmark, the one thing he had always avoided mentioning to Ulran. "But there were too many. My men's marksmanship was good, see–" He pointed to the skeletons of birds strewn around the burnt-out patch.

Fhord was out of ear-shot but Alomar was listening intently beside the innman. Neither showed the anxiety they felt.

Fighting down his inmost fears, Ulran asked equably, "And what became of this red tellar?"

"Downed with two birds clawing at each wing and another with its beak at his throat." He swerved in his high saddle, hand on pommel. "We were there when the bird came down." He pointed to a knoll. "I can hear the thud even now. We covered but half the distance to here when a sudden bright burst of flame broke out."

Solendoral pointed to the scorched grass. "That was all that remained, of pursued and pursuers..."

Floreskand: Wings

PART FOUR
THIRD SUFIN OF FORNIOUS - FOURTH DURIN OF DAROUS

The Song of the Overlord – Part the Fourth:
Of everything, He is the potentiality
He is one with all perception and sensation
He made Love and Strife aforetime and evermore
Prevail in each turn of life's rich cycle
Where the feeble senses of man fail
He doth dominate with gentle firmness
His will and inclination are with all
With His own acts through others, satisfied is He.

CHAPTER ELEVEN
TRIAL

*Respect and co-operation are in all things the law of life;
jealousy and avarice the law of death.*
  – Tangakol Tract

The day after the discovery of the blighted grass, they were attacked by a roving montar of Baronculer. Their five wagons and fire-wagon afforded some protection but the attack had been well planned, the Devastators waiting for them to arrive in a narrow hollow in the land, easy prey to the Baronculer arrows.

Neither horde knew or showed fear, nor was it evident in the eyes of Alomar or Ulran. But Fhord, still badly shaken at learning the fate of Scalrin – their good augur from the Overlord – was barely capable of wielding sword and shield.

Ulran seemed to be everywhere, unhampered by any cumbersome armour. He fought so swiftly, turning and pivoting, as though he possessed a third eye in the back of his skull. On two separate occasions he saved Solendoral's life.

And the Hansenand were glad that Courdour Alomar was present and on their side. Seeming slow and ponderous, he was more than enough to be reckoned with – any Baronculer horseman foolish enough to battle with him ended up in the Vale of the Overlord with cleft skull and often a cleft torso as well. The immortal's sword rang clamorously and dripped redly, flashing to and fro, the mighty arm endowing it with preternatural power.

During a slight lull – as the attackers regrouped for another mounted sally with freshly-honed spears – Alomar again heard the distinctive sound of the innman's weapon. Where had he heard that before? Their eyes met over a fresh corpse. Together they signalled, as if kin, and both grinned.

The second Baronculer charge broke into shreds. Crippled and wounded were left sprawled as the surviving fifteen or so fled.

Victory cries followed them, taunting.

And over all billowed the smoke from the fire-wagon.

But Solendoral, staunching a wounded thigh, soon brought them back to sober thoughts. For they had lost three, one of them Wolderiq, and a woman. This great montar of the Hansenand horde was now reduced to forty-six. And only four of the women were of child-bearing age. The girl-children would not reach puberty for another three years.

Beneath the waning of the full moon and highlighted by the lambent camp fires, Solendoral explained. "You know, yourself, Ulran, we Hansenand have always been of good stock, respecting life and belongings of all men. We have remained pure of blood, also. And this is where we are weakest."

"Inter-breeding can produce weak people," observed Cobrora Fhord to everyone's surprise. She went on pedantically: "If you recall the history of Carlash. Yes, the intermarriage of the royal house. After eight generations, what did the queen produce? Weak, half-rabid children, prone to the vacillations of the moonlight, incapable of ruling themselves let alone a kingdom!"

Courdour Alomar grunted, poked a stick in the fire. "The bookworm has a good point. You're in danger of extinction, Solendoral. You and your people must accept changes in your ancient laws – or perish. I've known of some housesteads..." He paused and Ulran wondered if the immortal was perhaps thinking back a good eight generations himself. "They kept to themselves, became powerful in the immediate area and thrived, the family growing. But eventually, the interbreeding told, the offspring were more and more aberrant. The more brats they had, the worse they became. That housestead is now a ruin – yes, I'm talking about Ivasr knoll."

The eyes of those Kellan-Mesqa present widened. All had heard tales of that ghostly hulk of a building upon the grassy knoll, the timbers long-returned to the earth, only the stone-pieces and the countless shrines to the interred remaining. Some said that on a night of full moon voices could be heard there.

Lines furrowed Solendoral's brow, evidence enough that Fhord's and Alomar's arguments were wrestling with the leader's conscience. "But since Hewwa's Revenge we've always kept our marriages within the tribes – exchanging blood only at Giving Feasts."

"Then, when you were counted in thousands and Giving Feasts were often, it did not matter," Ulran said. "But now, your numbers are so small you'll suffer. You'll become extinct while the others – the Baronculer and Selveleaf – will become stronger and more plentiful than the Hansenand. Because they won't baulk at mating with outsiders, with ranmeron slaves or captives. You know, yourself, Brother, no matter how beloved of the horde I was, I would never have been allowed a spouse within your montar. The laws and the Elders forbade it." Ulran sighed. "It may be too late already, but I advise you to seek new paths. A great people don't resist change: they remodel it to their liking, to their advantage. You," he rose, waved his arms to encompass the small encampment, "the Hansenand must do this – or cease to be."

Next day they skirted the Halas housestead; it stood in a similar hollow to the Bashen's.

The sight revived memories for Fhord.

Yet there was no real comparison. The Bashen's miraculously had been ill-fortified, and manned suicidally by but three men and two women, while the Halas place was twice the area, with stone revetments, the building raised on barrows of earth, built with stone and wood – a small fortress. Even the tilled fields had watch-towers overseeing them.

The last occasion Alomar had been there, he remarked, he counted no less than four families living together, numbering something like twenty men and twelve women. Enough to hold off any small raiding montar of war-hungry Devastators.

But they would not be visiting any housestead, whether or not he had personal experience of the owners. The Hansenand were Kellan-Mesqa and all Devastators, peace-loving and war-hungry alike, were hated and feared.

Trying to forget the unbidden memories of Slane, Fhord drew Sarolee alongside Versayr and asked, "Ulran, I'm troubled by Scalrin's uncanny death."

"Wait, Fhord, please," replied the innman. "Firstly, we do not know for certain that the bird Solendoral saw was Scalrin." Fhord was about to remonstrate when Ulran raised a peremptory hand. "How can we know – there was no trace. But, should your fears be realised, and Scalrin was killed – though how, in what manner, and by whom, we couldn't even begin to guess – then, we have nothing to fear. No, it is whosoever destroyed Scalrin who must be filled with dread. Yes, fear of the Overlord's wrath."

"I suppose you're right." Fhord shook her head, forced a smile. "I – I've never seen a man fight as you do, Ulran – with such faith, conviction – and so incredibly fast!"

"If you're convinced I'm not a Kormish Warrior, then next you'll be saying I'm a member of the Sardan sect!"

"I think not – my brother belongs to that secret society and though he is a mystic of great importance and possesses many strange faculties, he could never be compared with you in any way."

"And now you amaze me, Fhord. Here you are extolling the remarkable virtues of your brother, praising me in a way tantamount to hero-worship, and yet you mention nothing of your own psychic abilities."

"I was led to believe a person should be god-fearing and modest."

"And you are – especially god-fearing!" They both laughed. "But tell me, haven't you received any further images? Had you no premonition about the Baronculer or Scalrin?"

A troubled look flashed in her eyes. "No, and that concerns me. At times unchosen by me my powers have been strange, outstripping any achievements I'd have thought possible, and yet at other times I feel even worse than ungifted mortals. My mind and visions clouded, things obscured." She shuddered, lifted the little talisman to mountains, Sursor. "Sometimes, I wonder what the gods wish of me, as though they were merely toying with me – and mankind in general."

"Your headaches–"

"You knew? How could you?"

"You bore the pain well, but your twisted visage betrayed your fortitude." Ulran shrugged as if to say, *No matter, I knew.* "Have they left you?"

"But recently, yes – I'm glad to say!"

***

Over the next few days their journey was uneventful. Fhord learned a great deal about the Devastators from a young warrior called Rakcra. He explained that the Kellan-Mesqa were the oldest race in the world, in that they could trace their lineage back to before Hewwa's Revenge.

Many thousands of years ago in Orthqoma, a land bordered on all sides by mighty oceans, lived the Hewand, which comprised six great nations: Hansenand, the fair people; Baronculer, the swift; Tramaloma, the tranquil; Aquileja, the tree lovers; Mussoreal, the searchers; and Selveleaf, the silent.

The nations lived in peace and harmony with each other but as they prospered they began to neglect Hewwa, the Earth Mother, who had given them the bountiful land that was the source of their wealth. At that time, unknown to the Hewand, there was another land, which later became known as Orthmesqa – the Badland – which was copying their folly and also turning away from Hewwa – who they called Aror. It was at this time that the Earth Mother planned her revenge.

In Orthmesqa the crops mysteriously began to fail. Slowly, over the next few years, more crops failed until starvation affected everyone. It was then decided to abandon the land and take to the sea; thousands of huge ships were constructed and, apart from a handful of Aror devotees, the population put to sea.

They lived off the sea for many years whilst they searched for a new land.

When they finally came to Orthqoma only half their number remained.

On sighting the Orthmesqa ships, the Hewand realised they could not allow them to land for their crops too had begun to fail. War was inevitable.

Although the six nations of the Hewand outnumbered the people from Orthmesqa, they lacked their ferocity and the Hewand were swiftly defeated.

Shortly after the defeat of the poor and now war-ravaged Orthqoma, Hewwa unleashed the final part of her revenge.

The Earth shook, mountains crumbled, the oceans swept over the land and the people perished – all, save for a handful of faithful believers. "When the Earth stopped moving it became what you see today," Rakcra explained, "and that handful of survivors are now the six tribes of the Kellan-Mesqa."

***

Gradually, the grasslands sloped to the manderon. Nights, quite chill on their trek so far, now closed in with bitter coldness.

Each night, the Hansenand bivouacked, building roughly twenty-five fires, partly to give warmth, but also to keep prowling plains-dogs at bay.

Apparently, Fhord learned, the Hansenand fire-wagon must burn continuously, should they require a sacrificial fire. And as they feared no-one, they worried not at all about the smoke being seen for great distances. As the fire was always with them, they took advantage of it when making camp – but not to the detriment of their own fire-making ability.

The further they travelled, the wilder and more inhospitable the land became. Gently undulating pastureland gave way to dense bracken, which proved difficult to negotiate in parts where thickets had conspired to obliterate even the rough tracks left by wild horses.

Following Ulran's advice, Fhord dismounted daily for roughly two orms prior to bivouacking and walked alongside Sarolee. In this way her legs and stamina should improve for the mountains.

The Sonalumes drew ever nearer, now a matter of days away, their peaks seeming to be continually cloaked in dense grey clouds.

At times Fhord jogged along with Rakcra.

Alomar was surprised to discover that the majority of the warriors looked up to Fhord as a kind of precocious sage employed by the mighty Ulran! This disclosure quite unsettled the city-dweller.

Fhord and Rakcra became constant companions, each learning of the other's way of life. There was nothing sexual in their relationship, as Rakcra was happily linked with a young woman called Woura. Like everyone else in the tribe, Woura was intrigued by the city woman who accompanied the two warriors, and she harboured no feelings of jealousy.

During one evening, after eating, Rakcra and Fhord lounged by the nearest camp fire and recounted some of their childhood, the similarity of their growing pains surprising both. In so many ways they were different, almost alien – yet in basic feelings, they were much the same, and this never ceased to amaze them. It was towards the end of one of these whispered discussions that Fhord confided in the young Devastator.

"I wish in a way I'd been brought up in the wild, nomadic way of life like you."

"I enjoy my way of life – but yours sounds as interesting to me – I see no reason to envy me."

"Oh," Fhord smiled, serious, "I don't envy you in any sense – it's well, I think I would have been different – less open to – to – ridicule," she ended lamely.

"Ridicule – you?"

"The Travellers' Sage, is that it? You're surprised?"

"Yes."

"I have gifts, of course – though often they're more a curse... But, I'm thinking back, my brother was too old to understand or help – as far as I can remember, I have been bullied and laughed at for my bookishness. In a way, I suppose this made me introverted – I had to become psychic – it was my only outlet."

"Had to? I don't follow..."

"Everyone – or so I believe – has latent psychic abilities. But only the sensitive or introverted people seem to grasp hold of them. But I wonder, often, what real good it does me. I cannot accurately read the future – or another person's mind, even. I have little direct control over the ability, in fact. That's why I call it a curse. But to be a physical person – like yourself and your Devastator friends – that is useful, of some practical use in this most practical of worlds."

"But there is a place for psychics such as yourself. Floreskand would be a dull land if we were all alike."

"True. As I've travelled with Ulran and Alomar, I have wondered if perhaps my feelings – the inadequacy, the bullying history–"

"– and your yen for a physical life?"

"Yes – perhaps this has something to do with me leaving Lornwater – apart from the..." She hesitated. No, she could not betray Ulran's trust. "Apart from the attraction of travelling with someone as renowned as Ulran, of course!"

Every morning, before they broke camp, Ulran trained men not on watch or carrying out duties. Fhord – and Rakcra, when he could – joined in and by the end of a quarter Fhord could actually feel an improvement: she was suppler and could move faster. But the exercise which most interested her was the breathing control: here, she proved a keen and adept pupil.

Alomar showed some pleasure at Fhord's continued progress and determination, though – naturally – not to the degree of giving open praise. But the simple absence of dissent from Alomar gave Fhord the will to persist.

Into their second quarter together, Fhord joined Rakcra outriding on the left wing of the forward van. Both carried fur cloaks rolled up and tied to the rear of their saddles.

A great bank of silvery cloud mass loomed ahead, casting a shadow upon the grassland ahead.

"Looks like a thunderstorm," observed Rakcra.

"It seems to be moving in our direction."

Sun shone brilliantly everywhere except where they were going. Darkness spanned the horizon; there was no way round it. The sight alone cast an indefinable fear into Fhord's heart. Knowing that she was being premature and foolish, she nevertheless delved into her side-pouch and withdrew the storm-idols, and prayers traipsed over her lips. In the past, from the safety of her shuttered windows, she had peered through the wooden slats at the startling flashes of forked lightning, hurled down by the jealous Nikkonslor. But she had never actually weathered such a storm in the open. Yes, she realised, she was afraid. Greatly so.

Rakcra reined in his whinnying horse. "Stay as outrider, Fhord, while I seek Solendoral and find out what he plans to do." He squinted to manderon. "There's no shelter anywhere – we may have to ride on through it, hoping for the best."

He swung his mount round and galloped down the crest into a small vale where the main body of the Hansenand montar rode, oblivious of the encroaching anvil-clouds.

Musty, dry breezes gusted through Sarolee's mane. An unhealthy taste filled the air, oppressive. Her palfrey baulked a couple of times but Fhord kept her cantering up and across the sloping bracken. Occasionally, she glanced back over her shoulder, anxious for word from Rakcra or Solendoral.

At last a rider and horse hurried towards her, the man's fur cloak billowing in the warm breeze. Fhord was almost wheezing on the close air now as she saw it was Alomar.

"We're to quicken the pace, lass. Solendoral says these summer hail storms can be deadly. If we stop moving, we're lost!"

Not for the first time on this expedition, Fhord's heart sank. "Hail? In summer?"

"Freak weather hereabouts. Some say this is Nikkonslor's peeving-ground. But I reckon it's something to do with the weird cluster of mountains – the Sonalumes don't seem to obey the natural laws as our so-called experts predict them. Give me a tried and tested stioner any time!"

Fhord led her horse down the slope, joining the van with Alomar. "Did Ulran–?"

"Yes – predicted it last night, he did – hence his advice this morn to carry fur cloaks. But what else can we do? There was no shelter at camp, and we've come across none since, either. Some of these slopes may shield part of the effects – if the hail falls slantwise. But if it comes down straight, then what?" Alomar grinned, his moustache long and unruly now.

Fhord nodded and released her fur cloak, put it over her shoulders.

"Close up!" came the shout from behind.

Neither Fhord nor Alomar lessened their pace but after a time the rest of the montar, complete with trundling fire- and equipment-wagons, closed up to their rear.

"Keep together!" shouted Solendoral as the horde began to ascend the shallow ridge directly in their path.

Ahead, flat unrelieved ground of hedge and thicket with grass interspersed. Hardly a tree in sight, not a boulder cluster to be seen.

"Keep it tight!"

And so they rode full into the fury of the storm.

The prospect was daunting as Fhord – still one of the front riders – entered into the deep shadow. The surrounding air-temperature abruptly dropped. The sun's light and warmth were suddenly obliterated. She looked warily upwards and all was black, a great rolling mass of cloud, seething slowly on hidden winds.

Then the torrential hail fell. Alomar's words had readied her for it, but no preparation could have shown her what it would be like to experience.

Each hailstone must have been the size of an eyeball. As Alomar had feared, the hail sluiced straight down, pounding upon their heads and shoulders and the backs of their necks. Horses whinnied continually and the great pounding persisted, reverberating through their bony frames, almost tearing the clothes from their backs.

At least Ulran's stionery had forewarned them. Upon entering the black shadow they all donned heavy protective cloaks and, if no helmets were to hand, hoods.

The canvas roofs of the wagons boomed like massive drums, echoing thunder rolls from afar. The fire-wagon hissed and steamed and black smoke billowed around it.

Bruised and slightly stunned by the storm's vehemence, Fhord shoved a young Devastator by her side: "Use your shield over your head!" she shouted, pointing to others who had already done so. The rataplan of hail on wood and steel and canvas heightened. Some hide shields were rent with the hail's force, but others held.

Head down, Fhord rode on without a shield, riding blindly, her mind numb and unable to *See* ahead. Vision was impaired to fractions of marks as the hail fell in thick sheets.

Many times Sarolee was jolted as another rider blindly led his horse off course. As for navigation, it was no real problem. The Hansenand, like all other hordes of the Kellan-Mesqa, had instinctive directional sense and would continue manderon.

A shriek, from a woman just in front, momentarily halted Fhord. She realised that if she tarried, someone would collide with her from behind. But she couldn't leave the woman to be trodden underfoot or perhaps drown.

Bruised and weak from the constant pummelling, she gasped for air as the hail broke into water and drenched her to the skin. She gripped the reins tighter and peered through slit eyes, bracing herself against the storm's terrible oppressive fist.

As she concentrated, she found she could perceive that little bit further through the slashing sheet of hail.

Ahead, on a hard piece of ground – a small island midst the mud – where the hailstones bounced off with staccato sounds, she detected a slight movement, the patch of red – possibly a dress.

With almost manic force, Fhord tore at the reins, brought Sarolee round slightly and headed the short distance to the patch of red.

Now the shape was distinct. But there was no movement. It was a girl-child, lying prone. All about her were puddles, splashing. *By the–* she held back, biting on an imprecation. The child was probably dead already, drowned if not crushed under the horse-hoofs.

She reined in beside the still, pathetic figure, peered behind and could picture nobody about to collide. But she would have to be quick.

Against her better judgement, she dismounted and, whilst restraining Sarolee with one hand, she reached down and grabbed at the belt of the girl's dress.

Sarolee chose that moment to buck as a stark tongue of lightning flashed overhead, ephemerally illuminating the scene.

Puddles of mud glared whitely and a deep gash of red appeared on the girl's temple as Fhord pulled her over. Mud covered her eyes, nose and mouth, but she noticed the child's small pigeon-chest rose irregularly.

Again, Sarolee whinnied and heaved against her rein, jerking Fhord. The cloth belt of the dress snapped and for a brief moment she feared she had lost sight of the girl and would never find her again, her efforts wasted. And time was mounting against them. Above the roar of the storm she could hear the trundle of wagons, getting close.

"Steady, girl," said a calming voice and Fhord swung round.

Ulran, astride Versayr, was stroking Sarolee. "Quickly, Fhord, while I calm your horse!"

Amazed that the innman's voice could carry above the storm's din, Fhord needed no urging. She immediately loped across the squelching mess to the girl.

Her chest still heaved.

Fhord thrust an arm under the girl's back and legs. Stooping under the weight, she wheeled round, only in time to avoid the heavy hoofs of wagon horses and their groaning load.

Fhord stumbled as the fire-wagon passed no more than a hand-span away, hissing and belching smoke and steam like some infernal monster from Below.

She reached Sarolee a little breathless, but nowhere nearly as exhausted as she'd have thought. Her knees trembled, felt weak.

"Throw her over your pommel!"

Fhord hesitated, anxious not to be too rough.

"Quick, Fhord – no time for niceties, the other wagons will be here any–"

The groaning and creaking were close enough to hear even above the storm's noise. With an almighty heave Fhord slung the girl over her pommel and leapt into the saddle after her.

Ulran threw her the reins and together they galloped forward, just in front of a pair of wagons.

The wagon-loads were becoming heavier and heavier as leakage poured into them. Inside, the women were bailing frantically to lighten the burden for the already beaten and exhausted horses, but everything was so sodden and weighty they must have felt they were fighting a losing battle. And all knew that to stop now in this quagmire would be fatal.

"Keep moving!" barked Solendoral, his port-wine birthmark livid in a ghostly flash of lightning. His brow furrowed. That lightning had exposed a couple of men on foot to his right, off the track of gouged mud and puddles. He brought his horse round and was at that moment joined by Alomar.

"Trouble?" queried the immortal warrior.

"Join me!" Solendoral shouted.

Thunder cracked, hail bounced off the ground, wagons creaked and horses and people shrieked and called.

They were almost upon the two before they knew it.

It was an argument, two Devastators fighting with bloodied fists, no horses in sight.

Solendoral recognised them immediately. "Rakcra! Etor!"

Their leader's voice penetrated even above the din. Both simultaneously broke their hold and backed off. Defiance shone in their eyes, but there too was respect for Solendoral.

"You've lost your horses, I see!" barked Solendoral. As Rakcra made to speak, he added, "No, not now! You, Etor, up behind Courdour Alomar – quickly, man! Rakcra, here–" And he offered his arm and the youth leapt up behind his leader. "Later, we will hear both sides. But not now!" And both doubly laden horses rode on with the now retreating rearguard of Hansenand.

The storm seemed to go on for all eternity then finally a glimpse of light could be seen ahead, dreamlike in its quality. Yellow-white, completely framed by darkness, it was like viewing the Sonalume Mountains through gauze.

Wisps of steam rose and meandered. Fhord heard the song of a bird. Prisms of light dazzlingly refracted on drops of moisture in the air. Bright green grass beckoned, still, soft. Thick beams of godly light slanted through the last shreds of black-grey clouds at the rear of the ranmeron-marching anvil-heads.

"We're through!"

Such was the cry of relief as each member of the party passed into the sunlight again.

As Fhord emerged, with the girl moaning half-consciously, she looked back upon an uncanny sight.

It looked as though the Hansenand were riding out of some hideous black tunnel. The sky ranmeronwards as far as she could see was the same silvery mass she'd discerned earlier, yet close by the black feathered into brown-grey and grey and thinned into circling moving wisps, forming a mysterious tunnel. The steam and gasses from the sodden ground swathed about the horses' fetlocks, creating the impression that they rode on the air itself. They appeared like an avenging army of the gods, returning after some victory over the Black.

Here, the grassland felt as though it hadn't been touched by the hail. It was soft and dry.

There was plenty of brushwood about and Solendoral declared that they would make camp here, in a slight depression, to dry out the wagons and other belongings. He ended by saying that once camp had been formed, he wished to bring Rakcra and Etor to account.

Solendoral's second-in-command had made a roll-call and fortunately everyone survived Nikkonslor's onslaught, though few escaped unbruised or unscathed. One horse had broken its leg and was slain; a few strays rode into camp shortly after the roll-call, including one belonging to the girl Fhord had rescued.

***

Fourth Dekinma of Fornious: "Three thousand six hundred and fifty-eight Solendoral. Council to the Elders called," intoned the scribe. His quill flicked and made a scratching sound over the parchment.

Behind his kneeling form stood the Hansenand's gigantic metal chest, crammed with parchment scrolls – the horde's Elder Records – now filling two wagons. As one Devastator remarked, "The records increase in proportion to the decrease of our own numbers, or so it seems." Naturally, only the most recent Records travelled with them, together with relevant Laws and Decisions, whilst the bulk of old material was sealed and buried in barrows dotted around Floreskand, their whereabouts known only to a select few.

The pungent odour of drying rain-sodden furs filled Fhord's nostrils. Six wagons formed a rough semi-circle, the depression's slight earth ridge completing the circle form. Upon the ridge were silhouetted two mounted lookouts. Tethered on lengthy grazing ropes and hobbled, the horses were secured to the other side of the wagon wheels. Women and children sat on or lounged against the wagons.

Immediately beneath the earth-ridge was placed a wooden throne, very angular in appearance, which Fhord later learned was simply constructed from four wagons' tail-gates, with the aid of some stones and leather lashing. The speedy way in which it was erected clearly showed that it had been used before.

On the right-hand side of the throne stood a white-bearded, wizened old man, the Hansenand Tangakol, and in his bony hands he held an unfurled banner embroidered with colourful yet apparently meaningless figures.

Ulran whispered in explanation: "The patterns are memory triggers to the minds of the Kellan-Mesqa legend keepers." All Kellan-Mesqa legend was transmitted mnemonically. "This is but one of many banners, its presence here at the trial to signify that the precedence of legend will judge."

Devastators gathered to right and left. Alomar stood near, as a potential witness.

Four camp fires were dotted around the centre of the circle. Darting shadows played on grim features, and lent a sinister aspect to everything and everybody.

Then Solendoral entered, robed in furs and wearing a brass helm that glittered in the firelight. In one hand he held a drawn sword, its blade damascened; in the other, a thick tome which contained all the names of his predecessors, going back before Hewwa's Revenge.

In his wake strode two men, his second-in-command and his aide. Solendoral lowered himself solemnly into his makeshift throne and nodded for the proceedings to begin.

Without looking up once, the wizened scribe moved his quill to record every order and spoken word.

Fhord later had an opportunity to study similar scrollwork and found the Records clipped and brusque, quite unlike those of the Ranmeron Empire – contained in Lornwater's Archives – which were flowery and verged on magniloquence. Of course, brevity would be their maxim since they must perforce carry their Records around with them.

Flanked by sombre guards, both Rakcra and Etor stepped into the firelit circle. Divested of armour and weapons, they stood proudly but respectfully facing Solendoral.

"Explain," commanded their leader. "Etor first."

Tall for his few years, browned with the sun and his bronze body gleaming in the light, Etor nodded and lifted a heavily bandaged hand. "This I received from Rakcra, a reward for saving his woman!" He turned scowling eyes upon his opponent and spat upon the fire in front of them: spittle sizzled. "But let me here and now, before this Council, say I love and cherish Rakcra as I would my own kin. But I ask that the ancient Law of our people be invoked against Rakcra – here, this night!"

And so saying, Etor ripped off the bandage – much of it reddened – to display a hand with three crushed fingers, blackened and lifeless.

A murmur of disapproval at the youth's histrionics could be heard. But others were sympathetic, seeing a warrior's right hand so mutilated.

At this point Ulran stepped forward. "May I inspect the hand?" he enquired of both Solendoral and Etor.

The youth looked to his leader. Solendoral nodded and Etor followed suit.

Ulran held the hand up to the firelight, studied it closely, betraying nothing. Then he let go. "After the proceedings, I will comment, if I may? For the moment, I am content."

Etor seemed to perceive an opportunity for strengthening his case and called to the innman, "See here, Ulran – would you say I have good cause to seek proper justice?"

"I'm not your judge. You have a leader."

Those words alone were enough to redden the youth's face.

Haltingly, lapsing into a formal address, Etor continued his explanation: "I was riding like the wind against the evil hail, as were we all, when I heard a faint cry for help, off the main track. Obviously, someone had strayed. It sounded like a girl. She wasn't far off, else I wouldn't have heard her. I found her horseless: Woura, of the auburn hair. I had dismounted to give her a hand up onto my own mount when Rakcra–" he pointed savagely at his opponent, "– came by and barged into my horse. The reins broke and my poor animal, startled by the blow and the terrible storm, ran off, only to be found later after we camped. I asked Rakcra to take the girl on his horse and I would jog alongside, holding a stirrup for guidance."

Etor's tone lowered and he eyed the assembled Devastators. "And what did he do, this Rakcra? He swung his battle-axe at me! Yes – his axe! I have no doubt he meant but to use the side of the blade to bruise or stun me, but even so, he was taking his jealousy too far!" He grinned, only too well aware that all assembled knew that Woura was spoken for by Rakcra. "Fortunately, my bracer deflected the downward swing, but alas the blow was not completely spent before it landed upon these poor fingers you see smashed.

"In great pain, I grabbed hold of Rakcra's leather belt and heaved him to the ground. Ever mindful of the urgency to get Woura to safety, I told her to mount up and be gone.

"Then we fought fist to fist, though I had but one and was sorely disadvantaged. And that is the true tale, Solendoral, O Leader. Etor has finished."

Fhord expressed surprise that Rakcra, whom she believed to be innocent could stand and listen to Etor without even once interrupting.

Ulran whispered, "Rakcra dare not – one interruption would lose him the trial. One of the Laws of Justice is that each party shall have unbroken say. Truth can be gleaned from lies spoken, you know."

Rakcra cleared his throat, looked upon his opponent and smiled thinly. There were some present who openly admitted that they would not have wished Rakcra to smile at them in that manner. "Much of what Etor says is true. He did find Woura unhorsed and alone, far off the beaten track. But she was not wholly aware of what was happening and easy prey to this blackguard's lusts!"

A startled intake of breath came from the women onlookers. Etor's face coloured, his lips, tight-clenched, held back retorts that would cost him the trial. "Aye, passion seethed in my mind as I saw him: anger.

How unlike a Hansenand he has always been, I believe I thought. Woura is still lying abed, recovering. But I wonder whether it is a recovery from the fall or something far worse?

"If our Laws permitted, I would ask for a postponement of judgement till she, the prime witness, was able to speak. But that is not our way – as warriors, we stand or fall by what is in our hearts and by the words our hearts have us speak. I hold no malice towards Etor. But neither do I like him. I imagine he lost control of himself for a brief time. Perhaps the evil of the storm was somehow in his veins."

Rakcra shook his head. "Yes, I hit out at him, though not with axe. I kicked his back as he leaned over Woura. As he sprawled in the mud, his horse fled, scared by a blinding tongue from Nikkonslor. I quickly dismounted and lifted Woura up into my saddle. I had barely finished securing her in the stirrups when Etor struck me from behind, using the hilt of his sword, I think. This attack was enough to startle my horse and he fled.

"Whilst he had no intention of using the sword, he used it within its sheath, hitting me repeatedly on both upper arms as I tried to close with him. In desperation, I grabbed up a stone and hurled it – and luckily for me if not for Etor, the stone hit his sword-hand and disarmed him. We then fought with fists until Solendoral and Courdour Alomar found us grappling upon the ground like wayward children."

As he ended, Rakcra lowered his head. "And that is the truth, O Solendoral. Rakcra has finished also."

Silence fell in the camp as their leader paused in thought.

Fhord's sympathies lay with Rakcra. Yet hadn't Rakcra openly admitted that he had irreparably damaged Etor's hand?

Solendoral must have been thinking along similar lines. He raised his head and called to Ulran. "Brother, do you wish to comment on the wound, which is after all the crux of the whole business?"

"Certainly." Ulran stepped forward, alongside the two opponents. "The three fingers are completely useless."

"I see." Solendoral sighed. "Then I have no option but to pronounce that our Ancient Law be obeyed. Do you, Etor, wish for three fingers, or for payment in goods and chattels?"

A broad yellow grin. "I wish for the three fingers of Rakcra's right hand, O Leader!"

"Then you shall have them," commanded Solendoral. "Prepare yourself, Rakcra."

The young man nodded solemnly and rolled up his sleeve.

A large flat stone was carried out between two men and placed down before the largest of the fires. Another Devastator came out and handed

Etor his own sword. As was the custom, he cut his own palm with the blade to prove that there was no poison upon it.

Then Rakcra knelt and placed his hand upon the stone, the three fingers extended, thumb and little finger folded back.

A silence even greater than before befell the camp. Even the lookouts tensed, only half-watching the dark plains about the natural hollow of land.

"Three only," emphasised Solendoral.

"I trust he can count." Rakcra grinned and the sword descended.

Only one finger flew off into the fire where it sizzled.

Rakcra winced and tears brimmed his eyes as he looked upon the two surviving digits. "Take your time, friend, the judgement is yours, and rightly so."

"Good to hear you say it!" snarled Etor and chopped off the other two fingers together. "Do as you wish now!" he ended and stood up, wiping the blood from his blade.

Grotesquely pale in the firelight, Rakcra struggled to his feet and staggered two paces to the fire. He lifted out a charred firebrand and placed it over his bleeding stumps.

The smell of burnt flesh soon filled the inner circle.

Fhord felt queasy, her stomach somersaulting but she kept the food down.

Etor watched, his hard eyes showing no emotion. "And let that be an end to it!" he growled, turning to walk out of the Council ring.

"Not quite!" boomed Ulran.

"You have anything to add, brother?" queried Solendoral.

"Yes. A slight bending of justice – you see, Etor here still possesses his fingers, useless though they may be. But now Rakcra does not. The balance is uneven, I would say – wouldn't you?"

For a fleeting moment a smile flashed across Solendoral's mouth. "Yes," he said, eyeing the tome in his lap. "I believe the balance must be restored. And I command that Rakcra remove the three fingers declared useless!"

Rakcra stepped forward. "I see no purpose being served by me doing this, O Leader. This could go on endlessly, were we to subject our finger-stumps to measurement, eager to get exact interpretation – why, it may not stop at fingers! One slip and it could be a hand, an arm. I accept your judgement, Leader – spare Etor's useless fingers."

Applause broke out but Solendoral raised a hand to halt it. "Be it known, my judgement stands. Etor shall lose those fingers, though by the hands of the Tangakol Ogranth. Also be it known that on record it shall be said that Rakcra was in the right and Etor in the wrong. But whether right or wrong, violence between kith and kin within the Hansenand cannot be tolerated. We are few enough without squabbling among ourselves. Fight, by all means, but for survival, not jealousy and lust! The Council is ended!"

Solendoral rose from his throne and strode out of the circle.

Later, Fhord smiled to herself. "He intended to deprive Etor of his smashed fingers anyway, didn't he?"

"I suspect so," said Alomar.

"Yes," Ulran agreed. "He is versed in the arts of medicine too. One look is enough – gangrene will set in before the camp fires are cold. And even then, Etor might be lucky to survive with an arm."

Ulran's prediction seemed true prophecy. As the days wore on, Woura recovered and confirmed most of what Rakcra had declared, though she continued to have some blank spots in her memory.

The girl Fhord had rescued suffered with a fierce chill but after three days was up and about and back to normal.

Etor was confined in the lead wagon, tossing and turning minus his three fingers, sweat saturating his bedding. Ulran used some of Alomar's herbs and reduced Etor's body temperature and, against the wishes of the victual-women, he starved the man. Already, he feared the arm would have to be cut at elbow-height. When he told Fhord of this the city-dweller was upset. "Would that mean Rakcra would have to lose his, as well?"

The innman shrugged. "Morally... it depends... Cause and effect would answer that Rakcra is responsible. But if you were a fatalist like me, then you would accept it, blaming no-one. It simply depends on Etor – should he have any lucid moments. However, in Law there is no re-trial: Solendoral declared it ended."

Twelve days after encountering the Hansenand, on the First Sabin of Darous, they came upon the foothills of Sonalume.

For the first time, Fhord could clearly see the Twin Peaks of Mount Soveram – Marle and Torne – thinly draped in wispy mauve clouds.

Looking out from the stench of the sick-wagon, Ulran said, "Not long now, Fhord – then we'll be on our own again."

Floreskand: Wings

CHAPTER TWELVE
TALUS

*And Talus, the man of iron, as he broke off
the rocks from the hard cliff, stayed them
from making their approach.*
– The Lay of Lorgen

Despite his triumph, Por-al Row still felt uneasy as he cleaned up the mess of broken vials, beakers and earthenware pots that lay shattered upon the stone slabs of the cellar floor. A foul stench filled the dark, confined space. In some way, that creature had eluded him! And it had been downed, as well.

Irritably, he found a half-spent black candle and ignited it with his tinder-box.

If Yip-nef Dom knew how his prized hunting hawks had been employed – the enchanter shuddered at the thought of his liege's wrath. Already the cells were full. He had no wish to join the inmates, though that evil little witch would doubtless love to see it.

But he felt now, more than ever, that the bird was the real threat to his designs, along with that weedy city-dweller. As yet, he did not know *why* the prophecies required the presence of the innman. As for Courdour Alomar – if that were indeed him – his presence must be accidental; but also timely, if only to slake Yip-nef Dom's thirst for revenge.

Por-al Row used the rush broom to good effect and rid the cellar of the exploded remains of his experiment if not the noisome smell.

Well, at least there was no way that they could reach Arisa before the appointed deadline. They would be too late. The Sonalumes could not be crossed in time; even if they risked going through Astrey Caron Pass. The cold was murderous. Hadn't he experienced it himself? No amount of spell-casting helped him out there, exposed to the harsh reality of the natural elements. He had shivered as much as ordinary men, to his undying shame.

He beat his chest in silence, sobs of pent-up rage shaking his crooked angular frame.

Why me, dear gods? Why must I be accursed with this mortal body, tying me down when my mind tells me I should be striving for the heights, the pinnacle of existence, unshackled by mortal coil? *Why me?*
***
Snow-clouds, tinged with pink and purple on their undersides, billowed

all around, leaving few patches of stark-blue sky visible. White and attractive, they posed a threat of which Cobrora Fhord would have preferred to remain ignorant. She was afraid. She tried thinking of her white lord, to no avail. Though upon the lower slopes before the sheer rise of the Sonalumes, she trembled as if with extreme cold.

"This is where we part, then, brother."

Solendoral took Ulran's hand. "We have thought deeply on what you and your companions have advised. With the aid of your tuition in the arts of mind-and-body, may we find the strength to tread the correct way."

Ulran nodded and dismounted. "I know Versayr will be in good hands. Till we meet again, then, brother, on the appointed day."

"And if we don't make it?" Rakcra asked, similar thoughts uppermost in Fhord's mind.

Solendoral shrugged. "You know the Hansenand – we will stay in a camp no more than one quarter. No more."

"Then we will return for our mounts in that time," said Alomar matter-of-factly. "Simple as that!" And he grinned and handed Borsalac's reins to a mounted Devastator.

Spread around them were four weighty-looking sacks of hide, crammed with cured food, rope and dry clothing.

Alomar stooped and swung his pack on his back then slipped his arms through the leather straps. "Time passes," he said.

"True, warrior." Solendoral looked again upon his half-brother. "Are you sure one man is enough?" he said, nodding at Rakcra.

Solendoral could ill-afford to lose even Rakcra from his horde, albeit temporarily, yet he was willing to pare down his montar further to help carry their load of survival gear. "Yes, enough," said Ulran. "Rakcra has proved himself able already. And, besides, he volunteered."

At that moment Fhord felt a little deprived: Rakcra seemed to be getting a great deal of attention. Paradoxically, she felt her place was being usurped by a newcomer – because he was male? That thought was uncharitable and she stamped on it.

As Rakcra lingeringly hugged Woura and bid her farewell, Fhord mentally kicked herself, being jealous of a stout-hearted friend.

Apprehensive probably, she thought.

She felt slightly naked, having accepted Alomar's advice and divested herself of the majority of idols and charms; those that she had kept were fastened to her belt. Now she too swung the pack on her back and quailed at its weight. They really did need extra men to hump their stores.

And the prospect of their next meal – up there – was disheartening.

She cast another reluctant look at the crags of the Sonalumes, all daubed in everlasting snow.

"Farewell, then, friends!"

Solendoral and his entourage rode down the slope to join the main force of the montar, straggled in a long line, the company's horses and mule being led. Solendoral waved once then turned to ride to the head of the column.

Then they moved on, the wagons jogging – creaking axles the only sound in the still cool morning air. The small caravan dwindled quickly, the flickering red of the fire-wagon in the rear.

Here, it seemed, the rays of the sun lost their power, as though a veil were cast up from the very Sonalumes themselves. A cawcaw's throaty bird-song broke the uncomfortable silence.

Ulran turned. "Let's begin – we have a long climb ahead of us."

Wordlessly, they filed up the grassy slope, ever steepening, the mountain breeze becoming cooler and cooler as they ascended. They soon found the pace best suited to all and kept to it, with Ulran leading, Alomar following, Fhord next, then Rakcra.

The absence of any shrine troubled Fhord. She slowed her pace to let Rakcra catch up and then they walked abreast for a little while.

"I'm no religious man myself,' said Rakcra, "but I too feel for such an awesome venture as this we should offer up prayers to Hewwa."

"I suppose they wouldn't put a shrine at the base of every mountain, only those routes most used by trading caravans – which I fear we won't be treading!"

"That is correct, Fhord!" barked Alomar, startling both of them. He must have noticed them lagging and had waited. "Now stop wasting valuable breath and start climbing – we want to reach the base of Saddle Mountain by nightfall!"

"You mean we've not started climbing the mountain yet?" gasped Fhord.

"No," laughed Alomar. "These slopes are but folds in the earth's crust, forged by the Earth Mother. *There* is the mountain!"

Eyes followed the immortal warrior's pointing finger.

The crest of this slope seemed about a half-launmark higher. Above this rose a grey and green sheer rock face, cleft with vertical and lateral shadows. Mist swathed above it, occluding the snows higher up.

Fhord jerked round, eyeing the adjacent peaks of the range. All the others seemed as formidable.

"Why this one – I thought we were going through Astrey Caron Pass?"

"Answers in plenty you'll have soon enough, when we camp for the night." Alomar looked up. Ulran had already attained the crest, was waving for them to come on. "Now, let's get moving. The more work you do now, the sooner you will be able to rest – for we don't stop till we reach the mountain's base – come night, rain or blizzard."

Then he strode up ahead of them and was soon out of earshot.

Shamed into silence, and their lungs now straining to breathe with the extra exertion, the pair separated. Fhord slowly gained on Rakcra.

When they reached the crest of the slope, there ahead was an almost identical slope and Ulran was near the top of that while Alomar was halfway up. "A false crest!" Fhord moaned, thoroughly disheartened.

"We must keep going, Fhord – they're gaining on us."

The grass was now coarse and straggly, broken up often with boulders jutting out from the black earth. Footing was stable for the most part, sinking into the soft soil. Tussocks provided handy purchase for climbing and the small shell-like rocks were firmly imbedded.

At one heart-stopping point a large wildfowl flew up directly in Fhord's path, the bird screeching in alarm, huge wings flapping noisily. She made a laborious detour to avoid the nest.

Presently, they came upon a tiny trickle of a stream – barely the span of a child's hand – that gurgled over shining stones. Fhord was sweating profusely despite the chill wind and knelt a couple of times to drink a palm full of water. It was beautifully clear, cool and refreshing as it passed her lips. But a short while later it hit her stomach where it seemed to lie, cold and heavy. She decided to refrain from further drinking of snow-melt.

Rakcra was still slightly weakened from the loss of his fingers but valiantly kept up, though he swayed dizzily a few times as a rogue gust of wind caught him climbing a spur of boulder instead of circumventing it.

As they neared the crest of this second slope, Fhord had few illusions. And she was not disappointed to see yet another slope ahead, though this one was even steeper and more like a scree, with only a few large patches of moss and lichen dotted about.

Back-ache had set in early on the climb but now was just part of countless dull pains. Climbing was automatic. If only she had a walking stick, she felt sure it would have helped. To stop was worse – for recommencing movement was agony and the will was weak, the body's circulation having slowed down and cooled. Better to keep moving, she told herself, though her body protested often.

For fully six orms they climbed, virtually non-stop. And, as the day wore on, the bulk of Saddle Mountain drew nearer.

Floreskand: Wings

Now Fhord had an uninterrupted view of the peak, snow-clad and ominous, slanting away. The summit glinted white, and in its centre glared the concave formation that most resembled a saddle. But the brief freak winds quickly screened the peak once more, which Fhord felt was just as well, because the prospect of climbing to the summit was too much to contend with just now. These slopes, which were minuscule by comparison, were more than enough for her.

At last both she and Rakcra reached the two leaders, halfway up the scree.

Ulran smiled fleetingly. "See that dark cleft in the rock face to the right – there?"

They nodded, catching breath, glad of the brief respite.

"We'll camp there. It should afford enough shelter against anything the mountain cares to do to us."

"Wait one moment, Ulran," said Alomar suddenly. The eyes of the group were on him as he spoke. "I've no personal knowledge of this mountain, but tales of old say this Talus Slope we're on moves if it hears a man's voice – even a whisper. I'm not one to believe in fireside superstition," he said, pointedly looking at Fhord, "but I've seen such things happen in the Tanalumes. The sound of a man's voice is versatile, and has hidden powers. I just counsel that we should tread with care and in complete silence."

"Agreed," said Ulran. "We will slacken the pace as well."

Thank the gods for that, Fhord thought.

To reach the dark cleft about a launmark to the right they had to traverse the steep slope of sharp angular rocks. They trod with the utmost care, placing little weight on the foremost foot, tested the surface for firmness, then lowered body-weight and moved the other foot forward. Painstaking work, and all the time their packs threatened to topple them down the scree.

Only once, as they stopped to gauge the going further ahead, Fhord braved a glance back.

She gasped. The view was extraordinary and unsettling.

The way they had come to the Talus Slope was clearly imprinted, like footprints in mud or sand; then the tussock slopes peeled away, steeply, to a brim and the rest of the slopes could not be seen. Over the brim, far below, the trail the Hansenand had taken veered to the varteron, towards Goldalese.

And such was the freak nature of the weather and air here that she was afforded a view of Goldalese, shimmering yellow in sunlight and haze – over five hundred launmarks, she estimated – as though floating on a cloud-surface. Mirage, possibly, she thought, having read of such phenomena. But weird, all the same. The clear air might have aided her vision, also. But she had to turn away because the surrounding scene made her too dizzy.

Occasionally, some of the scree slipped, but only a little. Enough to send hearts hammering. By the time they reached a hard basalt surface that slanted upwards in great slabs and was pocked with indentations from long ago, all four were lathered in sweat, their clothes sopping.

Ulran unfurled a length of rope and paid it out to the others then scaled the rock, using the tiniest of hand-holds in cracks.

Finally, the innman scrambled onto a relatively wide ledge. He found a suitable rock anchor for securing the rope then hauled each member of the party up, one by one. The cleft was quite sizeable, and admirably placed to shelter them through the night. There was room for two to stand abreast in the cleft and the ledge itself was wide enough for one man to stand or sit comfortably.

Dusk was creeping upon them; no moon was visible.

"This will do," said Ulran. "First, we must change into dry clothes – before we lose our entire body-heat. The night, I fear, will be very cold."

Fhord attempted to dismiss the embarrassment she felt as she undressed and put on dry clothes from her pack. The men respected her modesty, looking away, and she did the same for them as they changed.

Ulran's fears were borne out: temperature dropped dramatically as the sun went down. Wolves howled in the foothills, their cries even penetrating the high-pitched whistle of wind.

The four huddled close in the confined crack and dozed fitfully, always brought back to chill wakefulness as one of the company broke into a bout of violent shivering or the night-winds howled through some fissure or other nearby, the sound haunting and insistent.

Those who suffered most were Fhord and Rakcra. Ulran sat cross-legged and barely seemed to be breathing, but even he was often woken to help warm the others. Alomar, hunched in his armour, clinked repeatedly as his body shivered in an attempt to create more body-heat which in turn was lost.

Their first night on the mountains, and they were already suffering from mild exposure, even in dry warm clothes. All four were grateful for the loan of the Kellan-Mesqa winter-hides, fur-lined and -trimmed jackets and trousers, together with hide gloves and hoods. Ulran had urged everyone to don them on top of their dry clothes after they had eaten the cured meat. Swilling this down with a little water from the leather water-sacks, they huddled close. Alomar had some difficulty getting his hide clothes over the armour and refrained from wearing the hood.

"With the wind howling as it is," said Ulran after a restless vain attempt at sleeping, "it seems doubtful we shall get much sleep tonight."

Courdour Alomar grunted.

"I agree," said Fhord. "Why not exchange duelling stories – though I have none to relate personally, I have come by many through hearsay and reading."

"It would help pass the time," Rakcra said, teeth chattering.

"Do you recall hearing about Regloma Troglan?" Alomar asked with a grin.

"Indeed – a famous duellist – oh, about fifty years ago," supplemented Fhord, remembering the books in the Archives. She had so envied those adventurers, little dreaming she would become one.

Alomar chuckled. "If our bookworm can recall, all the champions he unseated were special–"

"No, I can't remem – wait, they held their champion-sword for less than two quarters each?"

"True enough, but no, I was thinking of their personal lives. Perhaps that was an unfair question. Of course, I'm speaking from personal experience now." He markedly ignored Rakcra's surprised gasp. "All the champions he unseated had something to lose which meant more to them than any championship – be it family, wealth, esteem in business, whatever."

"Go on," urged Fhord eagerly.

*

Courdour Alomar had entered the Lorgen's Fable inn on his way through Endawn when he thought he recognised an old acquaintance, though he was lief to think he was mistaken.

Then the man, slumped over the table in a shadowy corner, rose unsteadily and swerved, demanding another drink.

In the light now, though unshaven and wearing old and patched clothes, his black hair in disarray, the man was Reall Demorat, until but recently a champion duellist of Endawn.

Recognition did not flicker in Demorat's eyes as Alomar held him by the shoulder and guided him back to his shadowy table. The warrior ordered another bottle of wine and settled down to talk.

Strangely, after the first new goblet of wine, Demorat seemed to sober up, and recognition slowly dawned.

After their first expressions of surprise and pleasure at this coincidental meeting, Alomar asked, "By what ill fortune have you come here, Demorat?"

"Regloma!" Demorat seethed, gripping the wine bottle till his callused knuckles whitened. "I owe it all to that devil-spawn cheat!" And, shakily, he poured another goblet full to the brim.

Demorat raged with an obsession that the present unbeaten champion duellist, Regloma Troglan, was a fraud, for he employed two henchmen to threaten any champion or contender listed to fight Regloma. The threat was basic enough: lose the fight if you wanted to see your family without disfigurement or death.

Despite the amount of wine Demorat imbibed, Alomar tended to believe his friend; such chicanery was typical for the city of Endawn. "But you weren't married – nor even involved with any–"

"My body – they threatened to cremate me!"

Of course, now Alomar remembered. Demorat belonged to a rare sect who staunchly believed that they must be interred after death; to be burned to ashes meant that the soul would dissipate and wander aimlessly for evermore. He had to admire Regloma's men, they had chosen the only chink in Demorat's personal armour. What was a duelling championship title compared with eternal oblivion?

After a while it became evident that Demorat wished to leave, though now almost incoherent. Alomar gathered that the hostel where Demorat slept shut its doors shortly; and the streets of Endawn were not safe after mid-moon had passed.

Alomar paid for the wine and, with his right arm round Demorat's back supporting him, Demorat's limp arm round the warrior's neck, and taking the main weight on his right shoulder, Alomar guided his drunken companion out into the dark alleyway.

Demorat vaguely indicated they should move to the right.

They had not gone far when Alomar's sixth sense detected movement in the shadows. He stopped, propped Demorat up against the rough-stone wall, and withdrew his sword as the four attackers stepped out of the darkness.

Alomar was hard put to it to keep all four at bay, but presently one of his assailants erred in his judgement and the warrior's sword ensured that no more errors of judgement would be committed by that man.

Demorat seemed to realise his life was at risk, and, though drunk as he was, he reached for his sword: with his trusty blade in his grip, he tended to sober a little, and clashed swords with one of the remaining three.

Alomar shattered the sword of another attacker and as its blade fell with a loud ring to the cobbles, the two other assailants faltered then backed off, and soon took to their heels.

Aware of the silence at his side, Alomar turned: Demorat was crouched against the wall, his back to Alomar. The other assassin lay dead; but a knife protruded from Demorat's side.

To withdraw the blade now might mean a slow death, life-blood oozing away; Alomar gripped the handle and with a tremendous jerk he snapped it at the hilt, leaving only the blade slightly protruding. Gently lifting Demorat to his feet, Alomar adopted the same carrying method as he had earlier before the attack.

When the two distinct thuds sounded Alomar pitched forward with Demorat, unmindful of the hard cobbles.

There he lay, unmoving though his ears were attuned to any untoward sounds from the night.

After some time had elapsed, he risked rising watchfully and slowly.

Whilst he had been fortunate, his companion had fared badly: one arrow shaft had sunk in the nape of Demorat's neck, the other in his arm roughly in the same position where it had been limply resting over Alomar's neck.

They had silenced Reall Demorat's drunken accusations for ever.

As he was in a strange city Alomar had no wish to answer questions. With regret he left the murdered champion to the street rats. He had a purpose to fulfil, however, and he would not rest until he had accomplished it or – pleasant thought! – he died in the attempt.

The latest of a long round of duels had been publicised for the next day; Regloma Troglan was billed to fight a brash young contender for his title.

As Alomar took his seat in the duelling room he wondered at the manner of leverage Regloma's men had used on this contender.

For the majority of the audience the fight was excellent – and there were plenty of thrills – especially when the lithe youngster from Lellul narrowly missed drawing the champion's blood. But to the eye of Alomar there were a few flaws in the duel. The subtleties were missed when they should have been grasped; openings remained open, to be ignored or unseen.

The warrior looked about him, studying the older, worldlier members of the audience. Strangely, there were few. It was as though the men who had once duelled stayed away by design, knowing too well the travesty of their art that would be performed this day.

All who watched were the sensation-seeking public, ever-watchful for a killing, though by tradition the challenger had the choice of first-blood or death. This aspirant from Lellul had chosen first-blood – as had all Regloma's protagonists.

At the duel's close, when the contender received a cut, lost his sword and somewhat grudgingly acknowledged defeat, Alomar tossed his poniard down into the arena.

The dagger thudded into the wood boards and the cheering subsided. His intentions were explicit enough: he challenged Regloma to a duel.

Because of the public challenge, Regloma had to accept. "Two days hence – and who, pray, shall I have the pleasure of depriving of pride?"

Alomar tendered a false name, claiming he harked from Carlash which was so far to the ranmeron few if anyone present would know the peculiarities of a Carlash native. "First blood," he declared.

That night he expected an encounter with Regloma's henchmen and he was therefore not surprised to come upon an altercation in an alleyway close to his lodgings.

The spindly silhouette of a tall man towered over a cowering figure at the end of the alley adjoining the inn.

Alomar ran up, shouted, "Stay, villain!" and his voice echoed in the narrow confines.

At that instant, the spindly fellow pivoted round, snarled something unintelligible and slashed his sword side-ways, against a knotted rope that stretched upwards. A wet-wood cage crashed down, trapping Alomar before he could jump clear. He smiled grimly. They had snared him well.

Now, each man lifted a long spear out of the heap of rubbish in the corner and advanced on him.

He felt the wet-wood and appreciated their choice: it would not be cut by axe-stroke, let alone sword; and the combined weight of the cage was too great to lift. He was trapped like a wild mountain beast.

"We want words with you, man of Carlash," said the tall one. And he jabbed the spear through the bars: Alomar dodged only to be sharply pricked from behind by the other, smaller henchman.

"Say your words, then," growled Alomar.

"Lose your duel with Regloma, friend. Or else we must perforce claim your life. If you lose, then regard the debt paid."

Yes, they had chosen well. Somehow, they had guessed aright; he would not welcome being killed as a caged animal. And, as was the custom, because he was at their mercy, his life was theirs – to claim at any time.

Alomar nodded and they both relaxed. "You leave me no choice."

He grabbed the spindly man's spearhead, ignoring the cut hand, and pulled the weapon towards him.

So surprised was the fellow, he had no opportunity to let go. Alomar pulled the man's head through the bars, jerked suddenly, and the crack of vertebrae sounded loud and awful in the night.

While the other tried stabbing with his spear mainly out of rising fear, Alomar parried with his sword and relieved the corpse of the cage keys; they were soon covered with his hand's blood, slippery and awkward to manipulate, but he finally unlocked the cage.

As he stepped out, the other spearman turned and ran down the alleyway.

Alomar picked up the fallen spear.

His throw was deadly accurate.

The same motley band of spectators was assembled.

Adjusting his bandaged hand, Alomar studied the steely eyes of the gaunt Regloma. He was a good swordsman and not to be underestimated.

After the salute, they closed and the first clash of blades sent a roar of expectation from the crowd.

Thrust and parry, attack and retreat, until sweat covered both men and the crowd as one sat on the edge of its seat. Word of the long duel had obviously passed out into the street, for many of the once-empty seats were filling.

After four orms of fierce swordplay, Alomar decided he had sufficiently worn down the wiry body of Regloma. At their next clamorous clinch, he snarled, "I killed your two henchmen, fraud!" And he whispered his real identity.

His words had immediate impact. Regloma pushed free and shakily backed off, amidst cat-calls from the crowd. Those once-smug eyes briefly reflected fear: now, he must fight in earnest.

Another clinch, and Alomar said, "I shall let you win this fight, Regloma – but any more you wish to win will be done so on your own merits... or I shall return..."

Alomar had no wish to become a champion, fighting duel after duel, as if by rote. He had needed to be footloose and uncluttered to seek the Navel. He let Regloma cut his hand and disarm him, though no one would have guessed.

He kept a wary eye on the champion, however, ready to use his poniard should betrayal enter Regloma's heart.

But Regloma accepted his defeat in victory. He was acclaimed with tumultuous cheers, the most riotous praise for any victory he had ever "achieved".

Leaving the champion to his victory circuit of the arena, Alomar caught an empty look in the man's eyes.

A bitter pill to swallow, indeed, to taste the ecstatic jubilation of the crowd, knowing it would be for the first and last time. For once tasted, it would become a drug.

*

Cobrora Fhord shivered not only with the cold. "And–?"

"And," supplied Ulran, "Regloma lost his next duel and never again won, though he travelled to all the duelling houses in Floreskand."

"The audiences of Endawn's duelling rooms once again comprised duelling men," ended Alomar.

A thoroughly miserable night, reflected Fhord as she stretched stiff legs over the edge. Dawn streamed down the crack.

Breakfast consisted of birds' eggs, which Ulran had picked on the previous day's ascent.

Then they were on their way again – though at Ulran's behest they took off the hide clothing. "At this altitude we should be warm enough – the climbing alone will cover us in sweat. If we donned these clothes now, we'd sweat moreso and weaken, our bodies losing all their vital heat."

Though no words about the expedition had been spoken, the immortal warrior now took up the rear of the company, with Ulran again leading.

"I thought we were crossing the Sonalumes through Astrey Caron Pass?" queried Fhord as Alomar passed her and Rakcra to take up his position.

"Astrey found the pass in 86 BAC: and why had no-one else done so before him? Simple – the pass is beyond these two mountain peaks we're climbing. It's guarded at the ranmeron entrance, so we're joining it half-way along."

"Two peaks?" Rakcra groaned.

Fhord fell to silence as Ulran started to scale the crack they had sheltered in. There were plenty of hand-holds but it was tiring work, and her shoulders ached before she was half-way up. The cold of the rock penetrated through the fabric of her gloves, numbing fingers. Her mind swam and she latched onto her patron white lord: she would put her faith in Osasor.

Breathless, she crawled over the lip of the crack at the top to see Ulran clambering slant-wise up a steep granite slope that led to a massive overhang.

Fhord swallowed hard and leaned down to give Rakcra a hand. The Devastator was missing those three fingers now, she realised.

Much further down, Alomar was panting heavily, his armour chinking against rock. Suspended on the warrior's pack, the shield rapped its steel boss repeatedly on stone.

The pair tried standing erect on the granite escarpment but to do so they had to twist their ankles to a dangerous degree so they settled for clambering up on all fours.

Fifteen marks up and they were beneath the great overshadowing round buttress, a steep rock wall jutting out from the mountainside.

Ulran divested himself of his pack and unravelled a length of rope. He secured the rope's end to his waist, then found suitable hand- and footholds. "Once I'm on top, I'll find some kind of anchorage and you can tie my pack to the other end and then one of you can climb up."

Fhord and Rakcra nodded.

The innman cast a quick glance down the escarpment then started to climb. It was slow work, and often he had to lower himself and find a new avenue.

To Fhord, Ulran resembled a cherese, legs and arms sprawled out, virtually slithering over the gigantic rock's outcropping surface. Ulran was approaching the topmost section, where the rock was vertical.

Alomar joined them.

Now, Ulran had to move with even greater caution, finger- and toeholds had to be deep and sure or else gravity would tug at his legs and he would be suspended by hands alone. The rope dangled from his waist. The onlookers could see the sweat streaming over the innman's features, and Fhord harboured unexpressed fears that if Ulran's hands were also sweating, then he might slip.

And sweating he was. His utmost concentration was on his breathing, keeping it shallow, and maintaining a low adrenaline-flow, as he gripped tenaciously to the hard rock. This, he knew, was the worst part. Suitable cracks in the surface were there in plenty, but holding on to them whilst upside down so high was not easy.

Fingers ached almost to numbness, as did his calf-muscles.

Slowly, surely, he moved one hand above his head, attempting to see with his aching fingers, feel a reasonable crack, whilst gripping tightly with the other hand and both feet. This time his hand held; he took the weight that his other hand had, yes... and now he slid one foot out, pressing up always, clamped tight, knowing that somewhere there had been a good hand-hold, and – finally – finding it.

Time spanned an age for each move and yet, eventually, he was gaining the rounded section. At last he was able to let his feet dangle over the outcrop, the sudden relaxation inducing a mild cramp in calf-muscles.

Then he brought a knee up, jammed it in a crevice.

After that, his strength – once ebbing – returned, and he pulled himself up the remaining two marks of the sloping rock, to a narrow shelf formed with tumbled boulders, embedded many ages past.

When he gained the shelf his hands trembled.

Finally in control again, he secured the rope to a narrow rock pinnacle and called, "The rope's fast!" His words echoed around the various nooks and crannies. "Start climbing, Fhord!"

Fhord had hoped it would be a lot easier using the rope, and it was. But, after only pulling herself up about three times her own height, her arms were weak and aching.

"Take your weight on your feet!" bawled Alomar.

Her arms became weaker and weaker as she struggled. Her confidence was flagging when Alomar held the rope steady and she was able to loop it over one foot and under the other and stand with the weight on her legs. Not a moment too soon.

"When you've got your breath back, lass, take your weight on your arms, slide your legs up the rope and take your weight on your legs again."

Presently, she did this. The rope was now sending dust particles from the outcrop above into her eyes: she kept blinking, eyes watering.

"That's it – now stretch up with your arms and pull – that's it. Keep it up – you're nearly there."

They secured all four packs to the bottom end of the rope.

When Fhord called down that she had reached the shelf, Rakcra followed. The Devastator had learned by Fhord's instruction, which was just as well as his deprived hand was next to useless. He was slower, but made it.

Alomar came last, and having rested at the buttress's base, he was quickly up and over. Once on the top of the buttress, the warrior hauled on the rope and the others aided him, and up came the packs.

Vegetation in the form of couch-grass still clustered here and there, but now it was frost-feathered – as were the rocks – on their windward sides. The tussocks occasionally gave additional useful purchase and the rime crunched underfoot.

The climb was more vertical here, but the rock face was indented and cracked enough to give ample grip.

The wind was biting-cold from the varteron, but fortunately still not too strong. Bearable – if only just.

In some places, hand-holds were scarce. Then, Ulran resorted to jamming his hand into cracks to gain a hold: "That's it, Fhord – hand-jam as you go. But take care you don't lose your gloves – else you'll have no fingers come nightfall!"

Gradually, all vegetation gave way to large rock slabs, smoothed with runnels of ice and whitened on the left with rime.

Shortly afterwards, they reached a great cluster of rocks and boulders which looked as though some god had cleanly sliced them into segments, so smooth were the cracks. "The force of nature," remarked Ulran. "The result of alternate freezing and thawing."

And just above was the snowline, yet still sporadic and only thick in parts, where it had been carried on wind-eddies.

"That's a rock chimney," explained Ulran, pointing ahead with his sword.

Above was a hole in the rock, black against the white snow. To either side of the black hole was sheer rock, feathering to right and left and creating a precarious spine that led up to the hole. "We've only one way to go – along this spine... then up that chimney..."

So saying, Ulran went first, this time on all fours and slowly.

Once the innman had reached the hole, he waited till the others had joined him. "It's just wide enough – see." The sky as a pinpoint of light at the top of the chimney. "We'll back up – I'll go first."

Again, Ulran took the rope with him and it dangled in his wake.

It was more back-breaking than anything Fhord could remember, but she persevered, hunching her back into one side of the chimney and her feet firmly against the other. Her lower back and thighs ached in agony yet on and on the rock chimney seemed to rise, then suddenly daylight burst all around him. Yet she was only half-way up.

By now Ulran had located somewhere to tie the rope and called down for them to climb using it for support. Fhord made better progress then, almost walking up the chimney's side as she rose hand over hand up the rope. The entire chimney was dotted with snow where little outcrops jutted and in other places the sun now glinted on frozen rivulets of once-thawing water.

Ulran helped her out.

She could hear the chiming of Alomar's armour as he heaved himself up, feet flat upon the chimney wall.

Eventually, all four gathered round the chimney mouth and hauled up the packs. Snow gleamed, virgin save for the infrequent bird-foot imprint, as far as they could see in all directions. And there, the summit, still a long way above!

Crisp and clinging the snow gave under their tread, but only a little. Fhord noticed that even here Ulran stepped lighter than the rest.

Shortly, they stopped to catch breath and put on their hide clothes: "The wind's getting up," Ulran remarked. "It's set at varteron now – but I reckon it might swing suddenly."

Starting again, they trudged on, and on, into the blinding glare of snow. It was easy to lose oneself, Fhord mused, if you took your eyes off the track ahead made by Ulran. How did the innman manage, though?

At last: Saddle Mountain summit. On each side, the upward sloping ends of the saddle, and ahead, the wide expanse of untrodden snow, almost circular in shape, as though filling a volcano cone. It must have measured half a launmark in diameter, sloping slightly to the manderon.

It took quite a while to cross the Saddle's seat of white and as the four stopped on the manderon side she beheld an incredible sight.

Snow-clad mountains were all around and, towering higher than the varteron pommel of the Saddle, reared Soveram Torne, ragged and beautiful.

Snow-caps slanted down from inaccessible peaks to the dunsaron and there, below them and heading in a meander to the manderon, a long hog's-back of snow led from this mountain to the one opposite, which Ulran called Glacier Peak. And now, blinking in the wind against the sun-glare on snow, Fhord could see why.

Seeming glasslike, a snake of immense width ran down the ranvarron side of the mountain, apparently terminating at the point where the hog's-back touched, falling away to each side, deep into mauve shadow, thousands of marks deep.

Fhord peered across at the Glacier Peak. In the clear air it seemed quite close, illusory. And, though the rest of the sky was clear, on the dunsaron side of the peak a trail of thin cloud eddied. A matter of moments later and a sudden violent burst of wind pounded into the company and caught Rakcra off balance and threw him into the snow. Fortunately, the gusts were short-lived.

"Let's get down before a worse squall hits us," said Ulran, lifting Rakcra to his feet.

The Devastator nodded, absently brushing off the powdery flakes.

They were all hungry, not having eaten since breaking fast at dawn. What with the exertions, they couldn't go much further, and Ulran appreciated this. He alone showed no outward signs of fatigue, but he recognised imperceptible failings in himself: he too needed food and rest.

Dusk was slinking across the skyline, spreading like an ink-blot from the dunsaron, bringing with it ponderous-looking black-and-purple clouds.

Here, they were bared to the varteron winds but, as Ulran had predicted, the gales turned, to their good fortune, and blew to the ranvarron as dusk encroached.

The slope was gradual and slippery.

In places, winds had bared pieces of rock and these helped them stop themselves careering down the mountainside as their momentum increased when slipping.

They descended in this stop-go fashion then Ulran called a halt at the brink of a sheer ice-wall drop.

The entire ice-covered rock face was glinting red in the dying sun's rays.

Ulran scanned about for somewhere to fasten a rope and tie a slipknot when Rakcra called out, "Over here, Ulran – another chimney!"

To their left, partly concealed by a fresh fall of snow, was a gaping hole in the rock.

They peered down and it was evident that the hole came out at the base of the ice-wall. "We'll try it," Ulran declared.

Alomar said he would hold the rope and follow last with it.

So the other three backed down, taking most weight on their own but using the rope as an aid and anchor should they slip.

Finally, Alomar followed without incident till about two marks from the bottom, when a section of rock gave under his weight and he tumbled feet-first down the remaining funnel to land in a muted crash upon compacted snow. He was unhurt though he cursed a few times.

"This is as good as any a place to camp," Ulran remarked and all agreed, Fhord and Rakcra grateful to stop at last, their packs off their backs no sooner than Ulran had spoken.

The feeling at first was weird, walking without a pack: Fhord tended to float forward in comparison, almost feeling light-headed.

Later, Ulran decided they would eat some of the honey-loaves the Devastators had baked beneath their camp fires.

There was more scope for survival through this night, Alomar declared, and withdrew his sword. Then he began to carve out blocks of frozen snow from the cornices behind the boulders on the slope. Rakcra helped move the blocks to the base of the chimney and Ulran and Fhord constructed a wall of the blocks as a windbreak.

As they worked, the sun seemed to set several times, because now there were layers of cloud that kept drifting in; and the sun would abruptly explode behind them, then reappear, casting the Saddle Mountain's shadow out onto an immense ridge of snow that snaked on to other peaks unnamed that were all purple and brown whilst those nearby were white and pink.

Nobody talked of duels this night.

They huddled close to conserve body-heat.

CHAPTER THIRTEEN
PRE-ORDAINED

> Weakness impairs judgement.
> – *Tangakol Tract*

First Dloin of Darous dawned with the sky filled by mares' tails, drawn out and wispy.

"Winds to mandunron," said Ulran and rolled up his blanket.

Breakfast consisted of an apple and a square of honey-loaf each.

They must have spent a warm night, Fhord realised, as her hair was barely damp, the hoar-frost having thawed. Alomar's drooping moustache looked bedraggled: the warrior and innman still shaved themselves each morn with their honed poniards.

But the intense cold and knifelike winds soon froze every breath from their mouths upon their furs and facial hair.

They descended the snow-scree, plunging legs knee-deep at times, jarring those selfsame knees repeatedly till they constantly gave way when weight was applied.

Fhord wondered how she would have fared had she tackled these mountains straight from Lornwater.

At last they came to the hog's-back, winding towards Glacier Peak, the spine of the formation about a half-mark in width.

Ulran led with Fhord, Rakcra and Alomar following in that order.

Winds battered them as they walked. Heads down, they constantly watched their feet and, blinking against the flurries of upswept snow, braced as frequent but unexpected gusts lambasted them.

And yet on they trod, never halting in case they baulked and lost balance and were pitched over the side: there was a steep slope on each side of the narrow crest, falling off to dizzying grey depths.

Snow-glare inflamed Fhord's eyes, and her lips were becoming dry and cracked with the insidious cold. She knew she must close her eyes before she was blinded and jeopardised their mission.

She only hoped her faculties were not reluctant in answering. Eyes shut, she concentrated on listening beyond her own footsteps and the haunting wind-whistle, reaching out for the crisp crunch of Ulran's footfalls. And as she did so she threw out mental feelers, and was rewarded before fear forced her to open her eyes: vaguely, she detected the bulk of the innman, just ahead.

Rakcra too was in a bad way and stumbled on two separate occasions. Before panic hurled him off the hog's-back, Alomar was there, steadying, his big hands lifting the Devastator up, urging him on.

But the incident had instilled Alomar with the feathering of alarm. "Ulran!" he called. "Ulran!" And as the innman stopped and turned, with Fhord following suit, Alomar added, "Can we rope together? It may prove safer!"

Ulran agreed whilst inwardly wondering why he had let such an elementary precaution slip his mind. Once roped together, they went on.

To make matters worse, the snow was not firm, so every footstep could precipitate a fall. Ulran slipped once, near the end of the spine, but neatly corrected his balance and went on. Nobody else felt as much as a tug on the line.

They reached a crescent shape of stagnant ice, earthy material and boulders: the dead ice at the snout of the glacier. The terminal moraine gaped where a small runnel showed. A stream of melt-water gushed down into the depths to Ulran's left.

"Keep to the right," urged the innman as they joined him.

The sun had reached zenith.

Snakelike, the glacier wound down towards them, its source firn hidden from view high up near the peak. Up each side showed irregular bands of discoloration of the lateral moraines, formed by rock debris on the glacier's surface. Down the centre, the medial moraine, over which melt-water streamed and glistened. The left-hand side was impassable, scattered with jagged ice-pinnacles and loosely packed snow that crumbled at the touch of a breeze. Across the immense breadth of the glacier too were great gaping cracks – crevasses.

Ulran hoped they could cross the glacier further up, near the source, and thus skirt the peak. He mentally shook himself: his head felt bloated, eyes puffy. They had been standing here at the snout of the glacier too long: time to move!

The right-hand side of the glacier was negotiable but proved difficult.

Twice they came upon gullies about three marks deep, which they descended then climbed the opposite side, using swords to cut foot-holds.

Wind howled intermittently; the sound whistled about their ears. Eyebrows and other facial hair were matted white by now, numbing lips and foreheads.

Heads bowed, they trudged higher till Ulran halted on the lip of an ice and rock overhang, under which the glacier had cut its ancient path. From here he swung his sword, pointing higher along the glacier's length, where it widened further up.

"Ice-fall," the innman said, sneezing. "Beyond that, I believe the glacier spreads out a bit."

Fhord thought the innman's voice sounded nasal, half-choked. Ulran seemed to blink more than usual too. A hot clammy fear clutched the base of her spine and sweat collected there, damp and uncomfortable.

At the foot of the ice-fall was a labyrinth of deep clefts and ice-pinnacles, with crevasses intersecting. Above this, the glacier steepened, like an ice-wall. A few pinnacles jutted out from this wall, casting long shadows.

Without any warning, one of these pinnacles broke away from the shoulder of the glacier and plunged down the ice-fall. Fhord was speechless. At least the size of a Lornwater mansion, the pinnacle crashed down, tearing with it huge ice-columns from the fall itself. The thunderous sound filed her with fear and awe.

Stopped in their tracks as the plumes of snow and ice-particles billowed above the ice-fall's base, they exchanged glances.

"I don't like it," murmured Alomar. "That could have set up a chain-reac–"

At that instant a shattering, tumultuous roar reached them, unmistakably coming from above, to their right.

Fhord saw billows of powdery snow in the air above the next slope.

"Avalanche!" yelled Ulran, *walking towards it.*

Fhord stumbled after him. "No – don't –!"

"We must swim through it, come on!" Ulran called over his shoulder.

Then huge powdery airborne blasts roared down onto the innman, cutting him off from sight.

Snow rode over Ulran's head. He tried swimming against the deluge, using breast-stroke, dog-paddle, anything to stay on top. Pounding filled his ears. He couldn't breathe. His eyes ached with constant buffeting and he couldn't see.

Alomar, who had been ten paces behind Ulran when the avalanche hit, was as swiftly engulfed, his world abruptly dark and cold. He reached out blindly and hit a rock, grazing his hands to no avail. He tumbled backwards, head over heels and felt the line snap. And behind him, Fhord was swamped also. The time under the black cold weight stretched to a lifetime as she tumbled upon her nightmarish descent.

Rakcra had been beside Fhord when the sight of the avalanche stunned him into immobility; he was hurled pell-mell down the track they had painstakingly made. The snow not only obliterated their tracks, but also him.

A sudden, eerie silence settled as the last remnants of the avalanche tumbled down over the hog's-back, down to the mauve depths.

Ulran was buried up to his waist. As he craned his neck round to look down the mountainside, he proceeded to use his hands to dig his way free.

Fifty marks below, Alomar was shaking snow off himself and his shield. Miraculously, his helmet was just visible a couple of paces away: the crestless dome glinted in the after-morning sunlight.

The rest of the mountain was devoid of life.

Alomar made to climb up to help free Ulran. "No!" Ulran called. "Start searching for the other two!" He scooped snow to one side. "I'll join you as soon as I can. We haven't much time – their chance of survival is halving as we speak!"

"Aye – I'll use my scabbard!"

Alomar trudged slowly down the powder-snow clad mountainside, imprinting his own tracks upon the spotless carpet. As he went, he rammed his broadsword's scabbard into the snow. He hoped to meet some kind of obstacle: hard, yet slightly yielding.

Ulran was free as Alomar yelled, "Here, down here!" The immortal warrior sank to his knees and tore at the snow with his scabbard and shield.

It was Rakcra, spread-eagled face down.

With great haste Alomar turned him over onto his back.

Ulran slid to a halt beside them.

Both had clear evidence of the avalanche's tremendous force and their own fortunate escape: one of Rakcra's legs was twisted back grotesquely, shattered in several places, the bloody protruding bone frozen. And the young Devastator's face was covered with a mask – a coating of ice. "He must have been alive when he was deposited here," Ulran observed. "See, he was breathing till his breath froze."

"Aye, poor devil – but where in the gods' name is Fhord?"

Ulran used his scabbard as well, widening their search area.

They poked through the snow, and then Ulran found her, just less than a scabbard's-length below. Fhord was almost in the foetal position, though her arms were wrapped round her face and afforded a small breathing space. She was only semi-conscious as they hauled her out and brushed the snow off. Her clothes were saturated but, surprisingly, not frozen.

Wind howled.

Ulran feared that whatever little heat and spark of life Fhord's body held would swiftly be blown away on the savage gusts now assailing them.

Dusk stalked the sky.

They heaved Fhord between them and began to trudge up the slope once more at the side of the glacier.

On their way they stopped by Rakcra. They had grown to like the young Devastator and admired his own brand of courage, but survival now dictated they forget him.

Ulran paused to cut loose Rakcra's pack and they carried it between them. Besides, another fall of snow would bury him better than they could ever manage.

They set off again and hadn't covered more than three marks with their sodden and teeth-chattering load when Ulran halted, eyes drawn to a patch of uneven shadow in the white to their right. "Hang onto her while I check." Leaving Fhord with Alomar, he loped across the intervening snow.

The avalanche had scooped up some snow-pockets to reveal the small mouth of a cave, permafrost strata glinting red in the sunset. Frozen soil, subsoil and bedrock showed like a mantle round the cave mouth.

"Quickly, let's get inside and dry her!" Ulran urged as he ran to give Alomar a hand.

After a great amount of scuffling and unfastening of packs, Ulran squeezed through on his belly. Then Alomar shoved Fhord into the opening and the innman heaved.

Alomar shoved the packs through and crawled in after them just as Ulran sparked his tinder-box.

A spill from the innman's oil-soaked wadding caught hold and the cave flickered into uncanny coruscating light.

Shadows in uneven surfaces fluctuated as he moved the light to scan the cave's confines.

They appeared to be in a circular cavern; another hole to their left seemed to tunnel deeper into the bedrock.

Whilst Alomar began unfastening Fhord's hide jacket, Ulran crawled over to the hole. He held the flaming taper into the hole and discovered it was but a small tunnel of barely a mark's length. His eyes, he fancied, were playing tricks on him.

Involuntarily, he sneezed: his fears crystallised. Angevanellian, he could do without; the last time he had suffered a relapse, almost two years ago, he had ailed terribly. Because his senses and body were so finely attuned, the presence of the dread Angevanellian had sent him awfully awry. No herbal medicaments helped alleviate it. He had to fight it unaided.

He looked into the tunnel again. "I think we're expected," he said levelly though nasally.

Alomar scrambled over Fhord and leaned on Ulran's shoulder. "Looks like a fire, all made up..." His nose twitched. "Food – I swear I can smell food, Ulran." Heated but left to cool, its aroma lingering.

"Me also." The innman squeezed through the hole. With the lambent taper held aloft in front of him, he snaked along the short tunnel and through into a larger cavernous area.

A constant drip-drip-dripping sounded somewhere, beyond taper-light.

His eyes had not deceived him.

Three seating-stones had been placed round a cluster of dry twigs, and upon each stone was an earthen bowl of broth, crammed with chopped vegetables.

He turned: they could stand, albeit with a crouch that would prove uncomfortable if prolonged. "Bring Fhord, will you?"

Ulran helped from his end and eventually they were all inside the inner cavern.

Both proceeded to undress Fhord by the glow of the now alight fire.

"You noticed how many places?"

"I know, Alomar. Either we were expected and whosoever prepared for us didn't know we would bring along Rakcra... or, they knew Rakcra would be with us, but wouldn't make it to this cave. Either way, it looks like our actions up to his point seem to have been pre-ordained."

"Fhord would like that." The immortal chuckled.

The naked city-dweller was dried off with a cloth from Ulran's pack and dressed in dry clothing. "Not a lass, but a woman," mused Alomar. "A brave woman."

All of their hide clothes were draped around the fire to dry. Steam crawled to the cave ceiling. Earlier, they had located more prepared bundles of firewood.

Both Ulran and Alomar conjectured about the destination of the other hole leading even deeper into the mountain. "I'm tempted to find out," said Ulran. "But I can't afford to be side-tracked. It could prove a shortcut, to the Astrey Caron Pass – but I'm not risking it. Of course, you could investigate if you like, Alomar – this did not begin as your quest."

Courdour Alomar shook his head of lank hair. "No, I'll stay with you. As I said at The Inn, I'm curious to learn what Yip-nef Dom did with that girl. Besides, I've noted this cave entrance by the stars – I can find it again, if my wandering brings me this way."

Ulran too had noted the entrance and was determined to return one day.

Each took a watch by the fire and kept an eye on Fhord and the two entrance holes to their cave.

The air was smoke-filled but not overwhelming: the tunnels acted as ventilation shafts.

Ulran woke to see Fhord staring at him, dark eyes shadowed, whites only showing. Her brows beetled and her forehead creased.

"What is wrong?" the innman whispered.

Alomar was by his side almost at once.

Slowly, her lips, dry and cracked, moved as with great effort: "Osasor will help me," she croaked, or rather an alien voice said through Fhord's lips. There was a mellifluous quality to it that hitherto she had lacked. "I had a vision... we will be all right."

Both onlookers exchanged glances.

Fhord's eyes blinked and then they shone. "You saved my life," she said levelly. And she shivered, despite the warmth emanating from her. She took in their surroundings with barely a glance. She didn't seem surprised. "It would seem my mountain-idol served us well, after all." She smiled, half-serious. "Rakcra perished, I take it?"

"Yes," Alomar responded. Ulran could see by the look in the immortal's eyes that he was shaken a little by the transformation of Fhord.

The city-dweller's physical and moral fibre had strengthened during their trek to the Sonalumes, but only gradually. Yet, within a few orms after scarcely cheating a frozen grave, she had steadied into a formidable woman. Something had happened to her, of that Ulran was certain.

He scanned the craggy surfaces of their cavern. Could this place be connected in some esoteric way? Unlike Alomar, he could believe in the magical nature of some idols. He studied Fhord and was unsure.

A serenity of facial muscles; a rhythmic rising and falling of her chest; a relaxed mode with which Ulran was familiar; and a steadfastness of eye that suggested a strong will and indomitable spirit. Already, bodily, Fhord had recovered from the avalanche. The shivering had stopped. But now this change had occurred.

"First Dloinma," Fhord mused. "It must be significant," she mumbled, as though to herself.

Alomar looked askance at Ulran. "We're three again," he said.

**

Their clothing was completely dry. They crawled through the tunnel into the "ante-chamber" cave.

Preceded by wisps of breath and the final smoke strands of the extinguished fire, they squeezed out into the cool dawn air.

First Sufin's dawn was crisp and windless.

"We're in luck." Alomar grinned, strapping on his pack. He scratched his stubble; neither he nor Ulran felt inclined to continue shaving.

Snow fell in a leisurely sort of way. The horrors of yesterday's avalanche seemed far removed, of another world.

To their left snaked the glacier and, beyond, silent and proud mountain peaks. To their right, the bulk of this mountain, and over its shoulder a hog's-back that meandered towards other towering peaks, stark against a bright almost colourless sky.

"But we'll still need caution," warned Ulran. "Listen."

The sound of distant rumblings – more ever-present avalanches.

Fhord thought of her friend and squinted down the mountainside, at the fresh blanket of snow, now unblemished. While in the sanctuary cavern they had each used some clothing from Rakcra's pack to manufacture cloth strips to cover their eyes, save for narrow knife-slits to see through, and in some measure this combatted the threat of snow-blindness. Any other essentials from Rakcra's pack that they might need had been shared out. She turned to the task ahead.

Roped together, sword in one hand and scabbard in the other, they trudged through the crisp clinging snow, up a zigzagging gully.

After only a few steps, the snow stuck and weighed down their feet and swords. They stopped often, to brush it free.

They climbed to the rise that was level with the summit of the ice-fall.

"If possible we'll skirt round this peak's summit," Ulran said, then coughed spasmodically.

Fhord reached out a steadying hand but the innman waved it away.

"I'll be all right," Ulran said, rubbing his forehead. *Curse you, Mirm*!

Higher up, where the glacier twisted slightly, Fhord could see it narrowed.

"Yes, that's probably where we'll cross," Ulran supplied uncannily. "We must go with great care – you see the surface glacial stream, it's treacherous." The innman's sword indicated the glint of melt-water that covered the entire glacier, trickling in wide sheets down to the brink of the ice-falls. "One slip and you could be sliding down those fissures."

Dark ominous longitudinal crevasses scarred the glacier's surface, ugly contrast to the surrounding whites, greys and blue-shadows.

Ulran led the way up the steep incline that bordered the lateral moraine. He stumbled on two occasions but the others didn't notice. He gradually gained on them and, for once, his judgement failed him. He slipped the line free and, instead of waiting for them to catch up, he determined to cross the glacier, here at the slight bend, where it was narrowest.

His head throbbed repeatedly now, and his eyes and brow felt puffed-up. He was breathing through his mouth only and the icy-cold air lanced into him as it coursed into his lungs. His body felt hot and sweat soaked his armpits, waist and neck. His legs ached: he hadn't wanted to rise at dawn, so weary did he feel; but he couldn't give in, it was not his way.

Yet a little voice in the back of his mind kept saying, *rest, rest, before you weaken*. But he ignored it: the voice of self-doubt, which he had conquered many years ago. Its reappearance now surprised him. So much training, ritual, self-appraisal and practice, and yet through a moment's weakness, all that sacrifice could be for nought.

He shook his head to clear his vision through streaming eyes and wiped his nose on a sleeve.

Wherever possible, he walked upon little upjutting rocks that were impregnated within the glacier and poked through its surface. Melt-water streamed past, so that the icy surface was doubly slippery.

Imbedded in the glacier where he crossed were bands of dark and light ice, ancient evidence of the dirt collected when the snout had been at this point many years ago.

Weakness impairs judgement; so said one of the Tangakol Tracts. He was halfway across. Unsteady upon his feet, he attempted to transfer his body-weight evenly at each step. He moved with the occasional rush of meltwater, yet the glassy surface afforded no grip.

He peered over his shoulder: Fhord had drawn level with Alomar and they were both some way further down, still climbing in his tracks.

They waved feverishly at him.

He turned and walked on. He couldn't go back now. He was annoyed with himself: he should have waited for the others and ensured a safety line was attached.

Judgement impaired, he thought, tight-lipped.

He had averted slipping onto his backpack countless times already. But, this time, he was not fast enough. His feet slid from under and he landed bruisingly hard on his pelvis and immediately slithered down the glacier on his side, unable to arrest his rapid descent.

***

"He's crossing before we're ready!" Fhord exclaimed.

Alomar looked up and stopped. "By the gods, this is too foolhardy for Ulran – rushing ahead serves no purpose." He eyed Fhord, concern flickering. "I fear he's ill, lass."

"If he slips..." Fhord left the sentence unfinished and her eyes rested on the serried ranks of jagged black crevasses that dissected sections of the glacier.

"Here, tie this rope round your waist. Unsheathe your sword. Right, and tie another line to the sword's handle – and to you, fine."

"What –?"

"We keep climbing," Alomar said, ignoring Fhord as he watched the innman's progress. "But don't move your eyes from him."

At that moment, Ulran's head turned and he looked down at them.

Fhord waved for him to come back and use a line. Even Alomar signalled. "He's halfway over now – he might as well go the rest–"

Then it happened.

Ulran slipped in the blinking of an eye and Alomar barked, "I'm your anchor, lass – dive across the ice, intercept–"

Fhord was already diving, arms outstretched. She hit the hard surface, knocking the breath out of her, but her momentum continued to move her across.

One hand gripping the sword, she slithered on chest, belly and thighs over the meltwater. She left a pink trail of blood where small imbedded stones cut into her legs.

But her momentum carried her too far across.

Ulran slithered down between her and the medial moraine.

But the innman managed to grab the rope stretched across: with the added weight, Fhord's side-ways slide jerked to a halt and they both slipped down towards a gaping crevasse barely three marks away.

Now Fhord understood Alomar's intentions and rammed the sword-blade home into the glacier ice.

Chips flew into her face and the blade came out, jolting suddenly. She quickly hauled on the line and grabbed the hilt tighter, slithering all the while on her belly, the ice-cold wetness stabbing stomach, body-core and her small cuts.

She thudded the blade into the ice – and this time it held.

Her arms were almost wrenched from their sockets with the arrested weight as Ulran jerked on the rope. Fhord twisted round a little and peered over her hunched hide shoulder. Through wet streamers of fur-hair, she glimpsed Ulran. The innman hung onto the rope with one hand, and from the waist down dangled over the crevasse edge.

Great gasps of air gushed out of Fhord as she lay there. The insidious cold began working on her.

Alomar still held the other end of the rope. He shouted across, "Ulran, haul yourself up the rope towards Fhord!"

The innman *must* be ailing, she thought, else he would normally have thought of that.

Fhord checked again, her neck becoming stiff.

Ulran had waved acknowledgement and was tugging himself up over the lip of the crevasse.

Fhord twisted round.

The left-hand side of the glacier was about a mark distant, ragged and unsightly with moraine-stain. But the moraine, almost a half-mark in width, would provide better surface grip than here. She had formulated the next move, once Ulran had reached her.

At last Ulran was alongside. He let go of the rope attached to Fhord's waist and gripped the sword-hilt. "That was quick thinking," the innman gasped.

Fear suddenly flooded into Fhord's mind. She had never seen the innman so breathless, no matter how much exertion he'd been under.

"I – I..." Fhord mentally shook herself. "I'm tied to this sword and to Alomar," she began again. "If you can put all your weight onto the sword, I'll cross to the moraine, there – if I slip, the line's not long and I should be able to grope even then."

Ulran nodded. "It's worth a try. Go, now – I'll hold the sword."

Balancing precariously, Fhord walked across, pitched at an angle because of the slope.

She made it without slipping once. As her boots crunched onto the rough and quite firm moraine, she felt sure her heart had only just begun hammering into life again.

Once she had attained the rocky edge, she wedged the line into a crevice and jammed it there with a rock torn loose from the ice. "Right, ready when you are!" she shouted.

The line draped quite loosely and enabled Ulran to hold it while he walked with a stoop. He, too, managed the crossing without further mishap.

Presently, he was beside Fhord. He released his pack and sat down on a boulder. "Can you manage on your own?" he asked.

Fhord nodded, inwardly disturbed. She then waved for Alomar to cross.

Alomar wound the rope round himself as he went, and crossed with steady, painstaking slowness. He withdrew her sword and then continued on over, still gripping the line. He slipped just before the moraine, but Fhord's hand darted out and yanked the warrior onto the firm surface.

"My unseemly haste has cost us some time," Ulran said and swung his pack on again. "I had hoped we'd get well down the other side of the mountain before the night-winds came."

Fhord wanted to say something but found herself speechless.

Alomar more or less voiced her thoughts: "Are you ailing, Ulran?"

"You're quite right, friend." The innman clapped a hand upon one of Alomar's lacquered pauldrons. "It came on me yesterday, on the hog's-back."

A thought struck Fhord. "Could it be related to my headaches?"

"That had occurred to me, but no, it's quite unrelated; anyway, your headaches haven't returned, have they?"

"No... true."

"Could be delayed reaction to the bane-viper," Alomar suggested. "A small trace in your system, perhaps."

"Perhaps. But come, Alomar, I think you should lead the way – at least till this ague passes."

And so Ulran temporarily relinquished leadership of the company and followed Alomar, with Fhord bringing up the rear.

***

Yip-nef Dom's solitary eye widened and his thick moist lips slavered. "*Lost* them, you say?"

Knees quaking beneath his black robes, Por-al Row nodded. He swallowed thickly. "It was to be expected, sire," he squeaked. "The – the Fourth, yes, the Fourth Durin I last located them, Your Excellency. Approaching the Sonalume foothills. I – they, the mountains – it's probably the mountains, Your Majesty – getting in the way, obscuring my Sight."

Yip-nef Dom agitatedly paced up and down the battlements mumbling to himself. He cast a belligerent look over his shoulder. "When will they reach the mountains?"

"I'd give them two days, three at the outside. Depends on that horde, I imagine, though." He calmed a little, guile returning to his aid. "I'm sure there must be a link between one of the travellers and those Devastators. No one city-bred could meet them and live, otherwise."

Some old Lornwater rumours niggled at the back of his mind but would not take shape.

"Sire! Sire!" called the keeper of the hawks. He dashed up the stone stairs two at a time. "Sire, your birds–!" The red-faced and breathless keeper was in tears.

"What is it – not the red tellars?" Yip-nef Dom demanded.

Por-al Row remained silent for he knew very well what troubled the damnable keeper.

Quivering before his obese king, the keeper moaned self-pityingly and pointed over the battlements.

In twos and threes, the royal hawks flew drunkenly home, many scratched and gored and not a few actually scorched. A couple were so far gone they flew directly into the battlement wall with a nauseating splat and perished.

"What – is – the – meaning – of – this?" stammered the king, levelling his evil eye upon the quailing keeper.

"I – I don't know, Your Highness! The last time I looked, they were all present and accounted for. Then – then I was called away. My wife had taken ill – some black malady that wouldn't leave her, sire. She recovered this morn – I've just returned."

Too soon, evidently, mused Por-al Row. "Negligence in the enactment of his duties, I should say, sire," offered the alchemist.

"Yes, and I think we shall show others of my entourage just what slackness in duties can entail! Guard!"

The nearest sentry hurried over the stone walkway flags, shield and spear clanking.

"Lock up the keeper for the time being. I shall hear his plea tomorrow, if I feel like it!" And he turned, dismissing prisoner and guard from his mind.

Tears welled in Yip-nef Dom's eye. "My birds, my poor birds!"

Por-al Row excused himself, ostensibly to check on an elixir, when in truth he had need to change his clothes that were so saturated with the seepage of fear.

***

A drop of a terrible distance loomed beneath the narrow ledge.

Negotiating the mantel-shelf of hard rock with patches of snow was made more difficult by the presence of their bulging packs. They could not press themselves back against the rock face, nor their faces to it, lest the packs unbalanced them and they plunged.

Progress was slow. A shuffle at a time, one foot in front of the other. Bodies three-quarters on, packs balanced above the actual ledge whilst both hands gripped and felt along the rock face.

The clothes of Fhord and Ulran had been soaked due to the glacier crossing. And Alomar now fared no better – he was saturated with sweat, because of the added weight of his armour, all of which he argued time and again he would not abandon.

The immortal warrior still led. The rope threaded through each of their belts tended to give them a false sense of security, when in truth all knew that if one fell, it was likely that all would go together.

Varteron winds sliced into their wet garments. All three shivered though, strangely, Fhord less than the others.

Even the cuts and abrasions she had sustained sliding across the glacier had begun to heal. She could barely feel any pain from them.

She still wrestled with half-formed images from her cavern sleep. But she was no longer afraid, not of the cold, the exposure, the winds, nor of the heights. She could not explain it, but she felt a strange surge of raw naked power course through her.

As yet, this power was dormant, untested, something alien to her psychic abilities. Her observations of Ulran's iron control served her in good stead. Now was not the time, so she held herself in check and mentioned her swirling thoughts to nobody.

Then they were round and onto a sloping escarpment of snow and boulders. Here, they could rest a few moments before the gradual descent into Astrey Caron Pass. Eerily, the wind died as Fhord peered around at the view.

They were higher than the top of Saddle Mountain – and the Glacier Peak's summit was still higher up. She was glad they had skirted the summit.

Just over the ranmeron shoulder of Soveram Torne, many launmarks distant, the dark stain on the countryside could be seen where the great Manderranmeron Fault ran. And, jutting through the fault, the smouldering cone of Astle, one of the four fault volcanoes.

The sky was filled with a ragged mass of cloud, scudding towards the mountains. "Bad-weather clouds," Ulran remarked and coughed, bringing green sputum to his lips.

CHAPTER FOURTEEN
ANGEVANELLIAN

The wine they drink Below
Will surely lay you low!
– Chorus of Military Ale Drinking Song

Late after-morning and nothing that resembled a pass was in sight. Fhord fleetingly wondered about the accuracy of Ulran's madurava bearings.

With Alomar still leading they descended the steep escarpment sideways, using their swords to curb momentum.

Then they suddenly came upon a gaping chasm, its icy sides reflecting the white of snow.

If it had been dusk they could easily have walked over the edge. The chasm appeared bottomless and was at least seven marks wide – too far to risk jumping.

"The sides seem to veer closer further down – it's like a great V in the mountain."

"Could be an illusion – perspective," Ulran warned. "But I agree, Alomar, it's our only chance. I'm probably the most agile here, but–"

"Yes, normally, you'd be obvious choice to go first. But now, I think I had better."

"Go?" Fhord queried.

Alomar handed the rope to Fhord in reply. "You and Ulran hang on damned tight while I climb down."

Fhord's thoughts raced to her mountain gods and she mumbled a swift prayer. "May the gods go with you, Alomar!"

"You're incorrigible!" snorted the warrior and lowered himself over the side.

To begin with, any kind of foothold was impossible. He could feel the strain on the rope. He should have taken off at least some armour before trying the descent. But now it was too late; he needed a foothold, to give his companions a respite. He withdrew his dagger and chipped away a handhold on one side of him then on the other.

Taking his weight with his arms, he swung out a little and thudded his boots into the ice, jarringly, the tremor travelling up the rope.

"Are you all right?" Fhord's shout echoed.

"Aye – just making footholds!"

Again, he swung and this time a great splinter came away and revealed rock, black and wet, but at least it was a small sturdy foothold. He rested with his weight on the one foot for a while.

Then he lowered himself further down, his entire weight again shouldered by the others.

In this manner he descended.

After some distance, little light penetrated. It was a perpetually twilit place, purple and black, and colder than he had expected. Dimly perceptible was the opposite side of the chasm. About two arms'-length, he estimated. He hoped his guess was right as he yelled up, voice echoing, "I'm jumping across – now!"

And he launched himself into the void, dagger clasped in one hand, teeth gritted, fingers of his free hand clawlike.

The crossing of the intervening space seemed to last an age, then he slammed into hard unforgiving rock.

His knife-hand shuddered with the added impact but held, which was just as well, for his left hand merely grazed the knuckles and his feet thudded home without gaining any grip.

He hung by one hand on the end of his knife and unfastened his battle-axe. He hacked below to his left side and then above, creating hand- and footholds. "I'm on the other side!" he called reassuringly.

Now the hard part began. If he slipped the rope would automatically pull him towards the side of the chasm he had just descended and he would have to begin again; small consolation – at least now there were holds to use.

Armour clanking against rock, he swung his axe repeatedly, gouging out chunks of rock and ice that rained down on his helmet and shoulders, echoing, bouncing off into oblivion. Now, he was glad of the armour.

The climb up took three times as long as the descent.

As he finally scrambled over the lip of the chasm his axe-arm felt as weak as a babe's. Ulran, he knew, would not have been fit enough.

"Packs first!" Alomar called. Icy breath of exertion floated away in clouds.

They looped the packs onto the rope and slid them across; the last to cross was Fhord's, which must have been poorly fastened because of the cold attacking her fingers. The buckle slipped open and the pack tumbled down, crashing once against the chasm wall, dully, before silence pursued it. Most of her idols were inside, but she was too exhausted to care.

Using the rope held between Alomar and Ulran, she crossed hand over hand, not daring to glance down until her feet touched crisp snow on the other side.

Finally, Ulran – the rope secured to his waist – repeated Alomar's descent and ascent and managed it with little effort on his part.

Dark of the First Sufinma shouldered its way across the sky as the trio descended the gradual slope to a kar.

All agreed they should make camp here in the hollow, the best shelter at this height they would find. As they dug into the snowy sides of the kar, the afterglow of sunset filled the varteron sky with its radiance.

But the sight was unable to lift Fhord. She had lost all but two of her charms.

***

Early on the First Durin they continued on their way, slipping and jarring down the slope to an overhang, over which Fhord and Alomar almost unintentionally glissaded and barely stopped short of the edge.

There was a virtual sheer drop to huge stone teeth a long way below, each jagged tooth of rock a good eight marks tall.

Beyond these, a thick mass of ice – an ice-sheet: a lake closed in yet with outlets for ice-melt, falling away at both sides down deep fissures that ran the length of each side of the pass.

Then, a rift valley configuration.

The ice-lake itself, Alomar reckoned, must be at least two marnmarks wide.

"Only one way through – and that's down," the warrior remarked. He turned to Fhord. "You can thank your gods we brought enough rope – we'd have been lost without it!"

For what seemed the hundredth time, he secured the rope to his waist, and the other to a nearby boulder. Then, without a word, he walked to the edge of the overhang and stepped over backwards.

Fhord's heart somersaulted as she heard a heavy double thud. Her consternation must have shown.

"He's roping down, Fhord," explained the innman. "All that's required of you is to thrust yourself out and slide your hands down the rope, gripping tight as you swing back into the rock face, landing evenly with both feet. As Alomar would say – simple."

"If you say so!"

And it wasn't too bad, she found, going next.

The initial thrust into space was frightening and the contact with the rock face was terrible, jarring her whole body, and she nearly slammed her face into the rock as well. But at the second attempt, she began to master the technique. Leaning out – against all the laws of self-preservation – she paid the rope out small lengths at a time and landed with both feet evenly. At each swing she became more confident and was surprised on reaching the bottom. But her gloves were now slit open with harsh rope burns and the cold swiftly knifed into her palms.

Ulran followed and upon reaching the ground turned and signalled to Alomar.

Two arrows were loosed in quick succession. Both hit the mark: the rope, severed near the lip of the overhang, coiled down near them.

The forest of teeth cut out a great deal of daylight and gave the place an uncanny aspect, sending forth echoes from their footfalls and accoutrements.

To their right, Ulran explained, was a narrow defile that joined this part of the pass with the ranvarron part they had avoided.

Navigating by the sun, they strove through the stone teeth all day till they reached the opening into the ice-lake.

Already it was darkening again and as nobody wished to tackle the ice-lake without benefit of daylight, they decided to wait. They camped on the edge of the gigantic teeth. "We should be in time – if all goes well," Alomar declared.

Ulran nodded and coughed spasmodically and sought a shadowy niche away from the weak silver light of the incipient first quarter.

First Durinma would be a long night.

After seeing that Fhord was settled, Alomar crossed over to Ulran. Bent against the whistling wind, his fur cloak billowed and flapped. "We'll never get a fire lit in these draughts," Alomar remarked and knelt beside the innman. "How are you feeling now?"

For all his white pallor, Ulran smiled, teeth glinting momentarily. "I'll live, Alomar, of that fact I can assure you." He winced twice then settled himself against a stone pillar, slightly more comfortable.

"I still don't see how that bane-viper could–"

Ulran's uplifted hand cut the warrior short. "It has nothing to do with the snake, friend." The innman squinted into the shadows where Fhord lay. "Is she asleep?" he asked, lowering his voice to a whisper.

"Yes, fatigue has taken her. She's done well, though."

"She has indeed, Alomar. But I don't know how she would take the information I'm about to impart."

Without a word, Alomar hunched a little closer, stone crunching slightly underfoot.

"Did you ever know of Mirmellor – Mirmellor Dhal?"

Alomar's great shaggy head nodded. "Mirm the Poisoner. Yes, I saw him once." He tensed, memory flooding his mind and body. "A small wiry man, young in age but ancient in his capacity for hate. Very few men affected me by their demeanour alone; but Mirm can be counted among them." His voice turned quizzical. "But tell me, what has he to do with your illness?"

"He was the cause of it."

The warrior's question hung in the air, unsaid. Mirm was noted for his mephitic concoctions, none of which ever failed. Hideous death, sometimes accompanied by mind-wrenching disfigurement, these were the effects of his venomous potions. "How, Ulran? If he had ill-will towards you, you'd not be here to tell me of it, that I warrant!"

"Almost correct, Alomar. It was about nine years ago–"

A chuckle passed Alomar's lips. "That was roughly when he was found dead, wasn't it? Mysterious circumstances, or so the rumours said."

"True. At that time, someone wanted to get their hands on the Red Tellar. That in itself is not unusual – you've seen evidence that the Pleasure House still covets it now. However, this – person – she hired Mirmellor to eliminate me. And of course assassination was his whole reason for existence – he thrived on it! It was during a weak moment the reasons for which aren't really relevant that my drink was administered with Angevanellian."

"What's Angevanellian?" queried Fhord, rising from the hard stony ground.

Ulran paused, eyed Alomar. The big warrior shrugged and grinned good-humouredly. "She's made of sterner stuff than when you first met her, Ulran – let her in on your secret."

Fhord came over, huddled close, rubbing her hands together. "I'm afraid I woke with a start a short while ago – I'd heard a stone crunching underfoot. I can't understand it, my senses seem to have become unusually acute," she said, bewildered, shaking her head. "I've overheard most of your tale, Ulran – I'm sorry."

"That's all right, Fhord."

"But what is Angevanellian," the psychic persisted.

"An extremely potent poison," supplied Alomar. "One drop is enough to kill a roomful of people. It comes from the poison spines of the Edalam fish found only in Solitary Taal. The Tramaloma use it on their war arrows."

"Alomar's knowledge on the subject is accurate enough," Ulran said, grinning at the immortal. "However, he did exaggerate slightly. It would have to be a small roomful."

"How did you find out in time?"

"I didn't – I drank it."

"What!" Fhord's exclamation echoed even above the continuous howling of the wind.

Alomar crouched where he was, thoughtful.

"I'm something of a connoisseur when it comes to wine," Ulran carried on, "and at the time when Mirmellor made his play I was sampling a bottle of Very Special Goldalese Aurdela, one of the best wines of my natal city. As soon as the Aurdela hit my taste buds I knew that something was wrong.

"I spat the wine out – but of course I was too late, the poison was already taking effect. All else diminished before me, my whole being centred on my actions. I managed to flush my mouth till the after-taste of the tainted wine had gone, then I forced myself to drink large quantities of water to dilute whatever I had already swallowed or taken in through the roof of my mouth. My guards told me what happened next. They burst in to find me alone, lying in a deep trance with the faintest of pulses. The trance lasted fifty-nine days altogether.

"In that time I submerged completely, drowned by my subconscious. Fortunately, my training prepared me and my body well. Whilst in that trance I ceased to be me as a man but became my body, sensitive in every pore, every cell, every organ and bone, gruelling though it was, and finally – I don't know when – I located the particle of Angevanellian. I was lucky – only one small particle had passed into my stomach and through the stomach wall into my system. I found it and isolated it. In isolating it I sacrificed an organ of my body, one of two used for the secretion of body fluids. It's now cut off completely from the rest of my body; but, what is more important, so is the Angevanellian."

Fhord sat with open mouth.

Then Alomar's large hand on the city-dweller's shoulder calmed her. "Ulran has more to say, I'm afraid," he said, seriously.

"Indeed. The trouble was, Angevanellian always remains active. The barrier I've built around it cannot stop it indefinitely – my sacrifice has only postponed the inevitable."

Now Fhord looked aghast at the innman.

Alomar's visage remained unchanged. He had lived long, long enough to have known every twisting and turning irony of Fate. Life held no surprises for him. Now, if he had had the good fortune to be poisoned, then surely his end would have come at last, his oblivion assured? He shrugged the thought aside. "How long can you hold the process at bay?"

Ulran clapped a hand on Fhord. "Don't look so alarmed. I've worked it out that I could last for a good twenty-five to thirty years from now – though this attack I'm suffering at the moment will probably knock off a few more moons."

"Let me understand you correctly, Ulran," Fhord's voice was quivering, as was her whole frame, though not with the chill wind. "You mean you're *dying*?"

"A fair interpretation. But, remember, my business constantly brings me into the path of danger. I'm fairly certain that I would never live out my allotted span of one-hundred-and-ten years. I'd wager any time that my death will be by a sword thrust, not Mirmellor's poison!" He laughed, coughing slightly.

While Fhord sat speechless, Alomar remained ruminative.

It was clear to both men that Fhord was shaken. Then, disconcertingly, as Fhord eyed them both, she began to laugh.

Alomar lanced a dark look at her. "What's the joke?"

"Don't you see?" giggled Fhord. "We are! The fine trio – what irony!" She laughed again, words pitching higher and higher. "Alomar, the immortal, something that I would like to be. Ulran, the dying man, something that Alomar would like to be. And me – sometime mystic that nobody wants to be!" Hysteria overtook her.

Alomar swiftly rendered her unconscious.

Rubbing his knuckles, he said, "I tried to do it gently."

"I know. Leave her now and let her sleep. Without dreams, I hope."

Alomar wrapped Fhord in his own blankets. "One thing I would like to know–"

"Yes?"

"What happened to Mirmellor?"

"He met with an unfortunate accident the quarter after I recovered. Nobody wishes to remember, but it seems he quite happily quaffed his most vile poison, the slowest to react upon him, and walked the Manderranmeron Fault for about fifty-nine days. When he died, even the carrion wouldn't touch him. As I said, nobody knew what could have frightened him so much for him to choose such a hideous death."

***

Spectrum colours formed a corona round the moon, uncannily outlining its bright first quarter and the shadowed side. Night-wind screeched unremittingly through the stone teeth, like some gargantuan musician whistling a madman's frenetic dance. Little sleep was had that night, the cold was so intense, the wind so cutting.

At dawn they were up, scattering the remaining embers of a quite ineffectual fire and moving stiff limbs to regain their circulation.

In the new day the ice-lake looked no less forbidding.

Alomar led, charily enough, with Ulran and Fhord following, all attached by a stout length of rope.

The watery film on the pond was quite deep and treacherous, threatening to slide their feet from under them at the slightest suggestion of imbalance. And if once they lost their balance they very probably would be pitched helter-skelter along the slippery surface all the way to the edge, to tumble over into any of the countless fissures.

The cold ice-melt soon penetrated their boots and numbed their feet; Alomar's well-clad feet fared no better.

When they were halfway across, Fhord could espy the far edge, a great tumble of ice; it went down, but how far?

At last they attained the dubious safety of the tumbled heaps of block-ice at the edge of the ice-lake. Below them stretched rough-hewn weathered ice, falling away mark after mark.

Alomar shook his head.

Ulran nodded. "No way of getting down that!"

Fhord checked either side of the valley. Climbing high on both sides, huge rift valley steps gouged out of the rock. "Then – then, we've reached an impasse – after all we've been through!" Time with these two men had changed her: she was angry rather than depressed.

The innman placed a steadying hand on her shoulder. "No – we'll use the wall steps," he said, and pointed to the four-mark deep stairs. The old sparkle had returned to his eyes. The innman again took the lead, without any comment from Courdour Alomar.

The descent took the rest of the day.

At one point Fhord feared they would be forced to sleep on a narrow mantle-shelf, exposed to the bitter elements, but shortly afterwards the going improved and they made good time. She ached in every fibre and believed her left shoulder-muscles had been pulled or at best strained when she'd lowered Alomar onto a handy shelf mid-way down to the side of an especially steep step.

But they had sought the easier route where possible, Ulran finding such chance ledges as sure-footedly as any mountain buck.

At other times they had to hand-traverse till calluses burst and sores suppurated in the ever-numbing cold.

Yet, she reminded herself again, they had accomplished it! For that alone she was content, hunched in front of a fire eating warm gruel and a chunk of honey-loaf. They passed round the frozen sack of water and sucked the ice-block.

This camp was ideally situated in a slight bend in the valley, protecting them from the funnel effect of the down-wind. They had found sheltering boulders by the thin trickle of ice-melt that streamed from the base of the tumbled ice-wall. All about them lay crisp snow, untouched till they trod over it.

Tonight, Fhord looked into the sky with a slightly lighter heart.

Halo-rings of white and red tint encircled the quarter moon, seen through a thin veil of night-cloud. Peaceful – she could hear the icicles dripping, the ice-melt gurgling, conveying the icy cold freshness of the water by its very sound. In complete contrast to the trek with the Kellan-Mesqa. But then she heard the distant warning rumbles of avalanches, and recalled the sad loss of Rakcra. Such beauty concealed menace. Yet she slept, dreamless.

They began their long trek into the pass proper on the Second Sabin of Darous. A winding, tiring trudge through snowdrifts and over icy boulders and massive slabs of rock that had long ago fallen from above.

They could not simply trudge with head down, for occasionally cornices of overhanging compacted snow jutted out, just waiting for a skull to collide against them.

By now Fhord was concerned for her fingers. If she had not been toughened-up before tackling the Sonalumes, she kept telling himself, she would not have survived so long.

"Let me see," Ulran said, pulling her into the lee of a cornice. They sat for a moment on the compact snow. "Yes, you've got problems," he said. "Your body tissues have been too long exposed to cold – see." He touched Fhord's fingers and received no response. "They're already deadened. Eventually–" He stopped, desisted from explaining that gangrene would set in, with dire results.

Ulran turned away, squinted down the valley, his nose twitching a couple of times. "The *biter* – I'd say its set is manderon... not far off, either." He jumped up, called to Alomar. "We can't fight the biter indefinitely! As soon as we find reasonable shelter, we'd best stay there!" He helped Fhord up. "Come on, shelter is what your hands need." And they moved on, pace quickening.

The innman's prediction was not wrong in any major detail. Without warning, the wind hit them, squalling down the mountains from the manderon, cold and dry, and feeling almost solid as it beat against them.

All three braced against it, leaning well forward, and their backs strained with the effort. Their breathing was stertorous, chins deep against chests.

No amount of furred clothing kept out the cutting chill.

Soon after the biter hit them, they were all cold to the marrow, and body temperatures plummeted dangerously.

After two orms of it, they had made little headway against the biter's force. Then the blizzard came down, gusting ice spicules into their faces, and covered the front of their bodies with a thick crisp coat of permafrost.

Ironically, all three felt the benefit almost immediately, for the frosted clothing became a strong barrier against the harsh freezing winds. Warmth very gradually returned to them, where it mattered most, in the body-core – the trunk.

But they could not weather the blizzard much longer, Alomar realised, and rankled inwardly at not finding a suitable shelter yet. Where was the guardian of caves now?

Then, at last, an overhang beckoned dimly through the slanting curtain of ice, hail and snow. All sound diminished in his ears as he concentrated on the place, a cleft dug deep under the overhang. Already a snowdrift had built up on the manderon side of the cleft.

"Over here!" he shouted repeatedly, waving as he ploughed heavily forward, spirits rising.

Abrupt calm and the decrease in howling noise impressed them as soon as they stumbled in.

Alomar half hauled Fhord under the overhang, and a few steps behind them staggered Ulran, his throat racked with a thick chesty cough; some phlegm bubbled on his lips and froze there.

"Must keep awake," mumbled Alomar, pummelling Fhord's thighs vigorously. As she responded and knelt without aid, Alomar unsheathed his sword. "We must build a shelter, quickly – reduce the wind-chill and draught."

The warrior hacked out slabs of frozen snow and heaved them to the slope they had climbed and placed them under the overhang. Ulran helped.

Gradually, for they were all near exhaustion after the cruelty of the biter, the snow wall grew and blocked their entrance completely. Light filtered through small niches and from above, but soon this ingress of daylight was blacked out.

The silence was incredible. They could hear each other's laboured breathing and the crackling of snow underfoot.

By now Fhord was able to assist in small measure by compacting snow into the cracks and crevices. They left a gap as far from the brunt of the winds as possible; this was their air-hole. Eventually they sat back against their man-made wall of ice and rested, jerking repeatedly as their heads sank temptingly onto their chests.

Ulran knew that not even he could stave off sleep. His throat felt inflamed, his tongue was slightly swollen and his voice cracked when he spoke. Swingeing headaches assailed him in spasms, without warning. But he knew he was on the mend.

Oddly, Fhord's situation did not deteriorate as Ulran and Alomar had feared. Eyes shut, she sat upright, facial muscles moving; she even talked, though infrequently. She seemed distant. Her demeanour was quite unlike any trance Ulran had seen or been subjected to. It was as if Fhord had become two people, one weak and suffering, the other stoical and unbowed by the travails that beset them.

When their feet, clothing and boots had been dried, wrung out or replaced by dry clothes, Alomar and Ulran agreed to take watches in turn to rest, so that they could monitor the other two and ensure that no regression or heat-loss affected them. If so, he was to wake them at once, to rejuvenate circulation.

Time lost all meaning for them but both were used to solitude and accepted it readily enough.

But the behaviour of Fhord was different, unsettling.

There was no way of knowing when the heat first increased, but Ulran, asleep, was the first to notice the change.

Subtle to begin with, but definitely a rise in temperature not attributable to their collective body-heat.

The innman slowly sat up, eyed Alomar, with a raised eyebrow.

The warrior shrugged, thumbing at Fhord. "I've just noticed, myself," whispered Alomar.

Fhord was hunched up in a shadowy corner, and all her clothes were crumpled-dry. A strange emanation or irradiation enveloped her. An orange warm glow shimmered around her entire body, slightly affecting the surrounding snow and seeming to cross towards the two companions in undulating half-visible waves of energy, sometimes glimpsed, sometimes not. But the effects could now be constantly felt. Warmth. Comforting, life-giving warmth.

Ulran stood up, his face passive but Alomar doubtless perceived his intentions. "No, Ulran – don't shake her out of it!"

"But she'll drain herself to keep us warm!" Ulran snapped, unable to conceal his concern and annoyed at his pounding head, his raw throat and the lethargy that stole over his frame.

"She knows best what she's doing. I'd say that as a psychic she has more reserves than we suspect."

"All right." Ulran nodded. "But from now on we take turns at watching her. Any increase in pallor, any sign of exposure and we knock her out of it, no matter what."

"Agreed."

Ulran had intended treating Fhord's severely frost-bitten fingers, but a close scrutiny revealed that they were on the mend already. He suspected the healing process had something to do with the heat-transmitting ability she had acquired.

That waiting cave – how long ago? – something there had transformed Fhord, something beyond mortal ken.

***

Judging by the number of times light had winked through their air-hole,

Ulran calculated this was dawn of the Second Dloin of Darous. "Time we broke out, I think." His lethargy and headache had gone.

Using knife and sword, they hacked at the air-hole, slowly enlarging it.

Outside seemed calm again, ghostly silent.

Resting for a moment, Ulran checked on Fhord.

She was a little improved. Her skin felt fever-hot and looked flushed yet she had no complaint as her eyes opened for the first time in two days.

A smile from Fhord and a nod. "Seeing the Way, at last," was all she said.

Ulran understood this, though was puzzled at her behaviour and intentions.

CHAPTER FIFTEEN
IRREA

Mud, the vesture of decay
It besmirches life, to betray.
– *Where, a Tear* by Laan Gib
(1830-1998AC)

All three felt better for the rest and the unexpected warmth. As they set out, Fhord's flush lessened and she regained her previous pallor. The gradual descent of the snow-carpeted pass was ever winding. As dusk settled they came upon a ravine.

Once through this, they were confronted by eight great acroliths, esoterically entwining with each other, detailed to the finer degree of hairs on the backs of hands and veins and the delicate patch-work of palm-grooves. The whole gleamed with icicles; and their heads and shoulders were snow-topped so that Fhord almost thought she could see goose-flesh on the naked figures.

Fhord mumbled some unintelligible prayers and then they were past them and through another narrow ravine, their departure accompanied by a faint unnatural tinkling sound.

Night had sneaked up on them whilst they stared at the statues.

They camped just outside the weird ravine.

***

On through the pass, descending, winding, the days mounted. Again they virtually carried Fhord. Despite her drained and exhausted state, she was not suffering from the cold.

Ulran's violent headaches and sore throat did not return, and he steadily improved.

After a full day's continual walking, they were grateful for a rest. But all knew that time was running out.

Twenty-two days to go. And, apart from getting through the pass and out of the Sonalumes, they had almost all of Arion to cross. And it was a hostile land into the bargain.

On the Second Sufinma they reached a tree-line where they decided on a halt. But their rest was short-lived.

Fhord spotted the movement first, though she was unaware of its significance. "The trees – they're moving."

The other two looked up. Powdery snow was in the air above the trees and, clearly visible in the moonlight, a tall pine tree stood proudly upright, moving slowly downhill towards their position.

"Avalanche!" yelled Ulran and Alomar simultaneously.

Then they were engulfed.

Fortunately, this time they were on the very edge of the snowfall and all survived, only suffering some slight bruising. Neither equipment nor weapons were lost.

Brushing himself clear of snow, Alomar grunted. "We were lucky indeed – perhaps your prayers back there helped, Fhord." He grinned. "I've seen big villages after being hit by such an avalanche as that – smashed as if by a mighty fist. Flattened."

The three of them looked on in silence as the snow rumbled and fell down the valley they were to tread.

The sound diminished, echoing.

Next day, tired with travelling all night, they came upon a narrow defile where both sides were thick with ice – a spur-hanging glacier. And within the ice were entombed bodies, the corpses of men staring wild-eyed in death. They did not linger.

As they descended, the snow broke up into patches. The stream meandered, appearing intermittently from underground. They reached a straight stretch and could see greenery ahead and below – a valley!

At this point it was decided they must rest. Fhord's legs were terribly weak.

They camped for the Second Durinma upon some couch grass by the stream. Ulran administered mashed and diluted herbs to Fhord. He could not promise her their journey was nearly over, for it wasn't. He feared her strength would give out before they reached Arisa; but the herbs just might keep her going a little longer.

The following day they came to a pass in a ridge, affording a routeway from one side to the other and here at last they attained the end of the snowline. Here, too, the tiny stream developed into a cascade, a series of small trilling waterfalls, gushing down rocky steps to the green valley a couple of hundred marks below.

It was a weird sensation, still being hemmed in yet able to see the valley a long way ahead and below.

Now they climbed down narrow ledges of granite and black rock, the same black stone that was believed to have been used for the foundations of Arisa itself.

"We must be wary of patrols from here on," remarked Alomar in a whisper. "There's an outpost near here, if I recall aright."

Shortly afterwards, their progress was halted by the formidable presence of a large brown bear in their path.

Alomar left his arrows untouched and his companions did not urge their use. Though unsaid, the thought of fresh meat made their mouths water. But they would be able to carry so little of the carcass, the rest would go to waste.

After incuriously eyeing the travellers, the bear turned and vanished behind a jumble of boulders.

That evening, they set up camp in a small cluster of trees and undergrowth.

Fhord was slightly recovered; Ulran hoped the herbs were working. At least she was able to walk unaided. The proximity of grass and trees in contrast to the bitter rugged snow-laden landscape behind them probably lifted her spirits. Fhord's determination to go on was evinced by her insistence on walking round the camp for a while. "To strengthen my legs," she said later.

They left early next day, and continued to descend the gradual slope. About mid-morning they glimpsed the outpost, carved into the rock face to their right.

A little later they evaded a patrol, though it wasn't difficult. The patrol members – all accoutred in steel and bronze, and with knapsacks untidily packed with mountain-climbing and protective clothing – were easily heard from a long way off. The soldiers of Yip-nef Dom obviously envisaged no interlopers on these mountain slopes for they joked and talked loudly and incessantly. But they were just too distant for the three to pick out any sense in the soldiers' conversation.

It was fortunate that great stealth proved unnecessary most of the time, as Fhord found it difficult to squirm along like a snake, and to crouch in bushes for any length of time sent her stomach into agonising cramps. But she persevered.

At times that day they came upon and hid behind the semblance of a dry-stone wall, many of which began nowhere special and ended as pointlessly, seemingly unfinished – as though they were thought unnecessary by some new ruler of Arisa long ago. These walls also made good resting places for the local populace of chereses and carabeetle.

On Third Sabinma they kept moving, taking advantage of the full moon. They continued to descend in a meandering fashion, encountering less rock and more grass.

Finally, they reached the end of the pass, though still a good launmark above the plain of Arion.

From the beginnings of this valley they overlooked Arion's meadowlands – an undulating panorama of temperate grassland. Such contrast to the white hell they'd been through. But other, man-like dangers were there to replace the chill of nature. It was light enough for them to observe the sheep and cattle being herded into enclosures by mere dots of farmers.

With that reassuring view before them, they set up camp.

Dawn arrived to the chorus of birds. From the camp they could see Thap Taal immediately ahead and some thirty launmarks manderon of it Olest Taal and twenty launmarks to the varteron the third Taal of the group, Irrea.

Almost equidistant from all three taals was Tritaalan, a small village surrounded by tilled and blooming fields. To left and right of the group were the lower slopes of the Sonalume Mountains. And towering high on their left, the twin peaks of Soveram Marle and the largest, Soveram Torne, which at this time of day loomed black and forbidding. The rest of the plain of Arion was indistinct in the morning haze.

For the next two days and nights they stealthily descended the lush valley and continually avoided patrols. They hid in undergrowth, often savaged by thorns, and even resorted to tree-climbing to evade discovery.

Fhord was thoroughly exhausted. What little rejuvenation the herbs had given her had dissipated, leaving her weaker than before. She was a liability and all knew it. But she had been responsible for creating the warmth when they had needed it and that alone probably saved them all. They couldn't abandon her now; she deserved more than desertion; and all this they agreed upon without a spoken word between them. Cobrora Fhord had affected them greatly.

***

On the Third Dloin of Darous three figures, crouched low, wove their way through the morning mists of the grassland and headed for Thap Taal. They made use of every piece of conceivable concealment, and yet it took them a day.

The dash was too much for Fhord. And Ulran, whilst overcoming a jabbing cramp, needed recuperation. They were forced to camp by the taal.

From here they were within earshot of some kind of festival in Tritaalan.

Torchlight endowed the night-sky around the village with an orange glow. Fences and wooden buildings showed in silhouette. The voices and music pricked their curiosity: full moon festivals were not normal in Arion.

Ulran, almost fully recovered, suggested he reconnoitre. Perhaps they could lose themselves in the festivities for a time.

Reluctantly, Alomar agreed.

At a conservative guess, it would take him a good orm to reach the village. Ulran crouched low and set out, but had not gone far when raised voices alerted him, from the direction of their concealed encampment.

Cautiously, he hastened back.

He had been out of the camp only a little while yet complete disaster had fallen in that time.

Many soldiers clustered about the camp, wielding torches and spears.

With the utmost stealth, Ulran slithered through the grass away from the searchers and looked upon the camp.

Four dead soldiers lay spread-eagled on the dusty ground, another crumpled up by the fire the soldiers had built. About six others were limping or nursing body wounds.

Ulran was surprised to see three suffering from what appeared to be burned hands and faces – which he found slightly odd since their party had not built a fire. Alomar was shackled from head to toe and his right arm dribbled black; the wound remained untreated and spilled the warrior's life-blood – not that Alomar seemed to care.

Fhord lay tethered with stout ropes and a gag in her mouth, immobile save for her defiant eyes which flashed at her captors, the whites shining in the flames. Fhord, evidently, had put up a struggle, despite her weak condition.

Ulran contemplated a rescue attempt, though not sufficiently recovered to combat so many at once. But when he overheard the sergeant-at-arms tell his men to prepare his captors for the long journey to Arisa, he decided against freeing his friends – unless they were subjected to any barbaric tortures. But he thought not; the urgency of the captain's voice, cajoling his sergeant-at-arms, indicated that Yip-nef Dom wanted the captors quickly and in one piece.

He was surprised that the soldiers seemed to have specific orders concerning his friends. Still, Ulran decided he had best make for Tritaalan under cover of dark.

Tritaalan comprised one main street and four side-roads, each edged with cottages and ware-shops. All the streets were deserted. The festivities and torchlight came from the manderon end of the village.

There, in the clearing, the village folk were dancing, drinking distilled liquor and singing to the zithering tune of a xagga.

But the innman detected something amiss. The atmosphere was not one of gaiety and seemed forced. An undercurrent of dread coloured their voices.

A great cluster of soldiers stood beyond the dancing villagers, in front of about four wooden cages, but the men themselves obscured the contents.

Stalking through deserted garden patches, over wooden fences and cesspits, he neared the revellers.

And, from this new oblique angle he could descry the contents of the four cages – red tellars.

At least ten in each cage, so cramped that they could hardly move their wings at all. However, the majestic birds of the Overlord showed no signs of distress and seemed quite unaffected by their plight or the people about them.

A small orchard curved from the dunsaron side of the village round behind the cages. This would afford him some concealment while he closed to release the poor creatures.

Quite a few of the guards were well into their cups, so he should not have too much difficulty.

Scudding clouds frequently blanketed the bright full moon and plunged the cage area into deep shadows. He would wait a little longer, till the festivities wore down.

As groups broke off in twos and threes and others slumped in a stupor, he edged his way beneath the shadowy boughs of the apple-laden trees, careful to avoid any lusting couples. The few remaining villagers seemed to have abandoned all sense of modesty now, as though their dread were driving them to desperation, to forgetfulness.

Ulran suspected they were more than a little concerned over the Wings of the Overlord being held captive in their village.

Directly opposite the cages, he could see the four remaining sentries shambling around their charges. One of the four, however, was more interested in the wench he had pressed against the cage bars. The others leered for a while then left the lovers and joined in the revelry.

A couple of villagers stumbled across Ulran's line of vision and he took the opportunity to leave his concealment and join them. He quickly clapped his arms round their shoulders and laughed with them. They barely noticed his presence, save that their unsteady gait straightened somewhat, heading directly towards the nearest cage.

Without compunction, as the three neared the lecherous sentry, Ulran slammed the two drunkards' heads together with a bone-crunching *smack!* and lunged for the soldier.

The girl froze on a scream as the soldier stood facing her, eyes staring without sensation. A red line appeared across his throat, welled up till the artery suddenly spurted, blinding her as the head toppled. She began to scream when Ulran's gentle fingers connected with a pressure point in her throat: she slumped unconscious upon the prostrate soldier. Ulran stepped over them.

Swiftly slashing the ropes that secured the doors, the innman looked about: as he had gambled, the girl's scream had drawn no attention – any revellers who might have heard would simply have shrugged their shoulders, perhaps saying how fortunate some man was this night.

Sheathing his sword, Ulran heaved at the wooden cage door and threw it in disgust into the darkness.

Crouched low, he whispered to the red tellars and received an immediate response.

To any other man the hushed, calmed flapping of giant wings as the great birds edged out through the doorway would have seemed eerie to the point of sinister.

Five birds had made their way out and all encircled the cage, eyes scouring the surrounding darkness for potential intruders. A few waddled across to the other cages, keeping to the shadows.

Tense moments passed by as two more red tellars joined their free brethren.

Unlike Scalrin, these birds were unable to communicate with him in any way. He had hoped Scalrin's ability was shared with his fellows. Now knowing this was not the case, he sensed the great bird's loss more acutely.

The sudden ear-splitting cry of the released birds momentarily numbed Ulran, seeming to pitch his nerves to screaming point. In an instant their cries had turned his body into a shivering wreck, covered in cold sweat. Instinctively, though with annoying slowness, he placed his palms over his ears, though to little effect, for the high-frequency cries were penetrating more than his ears.

And then he looked about him and saw the reason for the red tellars' shrieks. A band of about twenty soldiers – the majority appearing quite sober – was crossing the grass, encircling him and the cages.

Still with his hands over his ears, he wondered why Yip-nef Dom's men were unaffected by the screams of the birds – unless their cries were so highly pitched only a *sensitive* could hear.

It was, obviously, a warning cry for him as much as for their kind.

Well aware of the corpse to his left, he knew they might think twice about taking him prisoner. And in his present recuperative state following the effects of the now quiescent Angevanellian, he knew he could not measure up to ten men, let alone twenty.

As suddenly as they had begun, the cries of the red tellars stopped.

He backed towards the apple orchard when abruptly the cries began again – and he turned in time to see two soldiers charging him from the trees.

These he could handle: one, he dispatched with a swipe of his smoothly withdrawn sword; the other halted and tried barring his escape, playing for time.

Ulran heard the increased pace of footfalls upon the grass behind.

Feinting with a quick stab of his sword, he swept his own legs from under and rolled full into the soldier's shins. As they toppled together, Ulran's opponent screamed so horrifically that his companions stopped in their tracks.

Ulran did not dally, however, but leapt over the calfless body that threshed in its own life-blood.

"Escape!" he yelled to the birds he had freed. "Flee now!"

And he melted into the orchard and was soon lost to pursuit in the enfolding darkness.

He returned about an orm later, stealthily approaching Tritaalan from the darker dunsaron side. He stayed only long enough to ensure that the newly arrived prisoners had not suffered any further injury since he last saw them.

He overheard enough to ascertain Alomar and Fhord were not associated with the dark demon that had left a trail of slaughter in its wake.

He smiled and left for Arisa – about 140 launmarks to the varteron.

Fifteen days to go, he estimated, to the mysterious deadline.

***

As he jog-trotted through the knee-length grass, the cool night-breeze wafting through the bowl of Arion, Ulran felt more refreshed than he had ever been since scaling the Sonalumes.

He suspected the Angevanellian had seeped out as they had spent their second night on Saddle Mountain. He wished a thousand curses upon the astral spirit of Mirmellor, not for the first time, nor, he thought sanguinely, for the last.

And as he loped across the land he was overflowing with memories, of Solendoral and himself as lads, when the Kellan-Mesqa were great. At dusk, he reached Irrea Taal and waded across to the island where he hid in lush undergrowth to sleep and regain strength.

Daybreak penetrated the verdant foliage with a prism of colours and bright shafts of light. Ulran awoke as the first beams of sunlight pierced the undergrowth. An olive brown anjis newt convulsively gulped down a small nest of caddis flies near where Ulran lay quite inert.

Soundlessly, he listened. Somewhere, wildfowl coughed and croaked, then a splash, followed by many similar noises, and their flock's shadow passed over him. The silence that followed nibbled at his mind. The abrupt absence of the dawn chorus as the sun rose on this, the Third Durin of Darous, seemed unnatural.

He doubted that anyone could have followed him here. When he waded out here last night he hadn't heard any unnatural sound. This small island had offered the ideal sanctuary – unless Yip-nef Dom's men possessed more intelligence than he credited and they thought so too.

Very slowly, he raised himself and crouched on all fours, head cocked as he listened.

Still not a sound.

High above, the grey-white clouds streamed in mares'-tails, splashed against the cobalt sky. Not one bird flew over the island.

Raising himself a little at a time, he peered through a break in the vegetation, across the still metallic sheen of Irrea Taal.

At least Yip-nef Dom's men were persistent. They would have little problem tracking the swathe of grass and wheat he had left in his wake. From his slightly raised vantage point he could see the almost straight line that passed into the morning haze.

And there, emerging from that same dew, black man-shapes, seemingly spread out in a thin line, slowly moving towards the taal.

Time to –

At first he thought it was some once-dormant fumarole spitting back into life. About a half-mark in front of him, the earth bubbled, caved in on itself then coughed into the air and splashed his fur cloak.

In an instant, the spitting, bubbling eructation of mud surrounded him.

Somehow, the ground all around him had softened into mud and was now boiling, spitting gobs of the stuff everywhere.

Soon, he was spattered with the clinging muck.

He considered leaping clear – but had no idea how wide the gulf of mud was nor, for that matter, how deep it might be should he land in it.

He had the impression of a seething, boiling quagmire. But what he couldn't understand was why the piece of land he crouched on hadn't transformed as well.

The answer shook Ulran bodily.

Beneath him, the ground moved.

There was an almighty snort and moan, then he was tilted side-ways, into the seething mud.

His initial fears were unfounded, for it was barely warm. But it weighed upon him heavily, and pulled him down.

Now, he understood only too well.

With all of the island to choose from, he had by chance slept upon the back of a theakose, one of the largest of the mud creatures and now it was waking as the sun warmed the land.

It surfaced at last, without benefit of teeth or eyes. Its enormous pink jaws dripped with thick streamers of mud. Its cavernous throat could easily accommodate Ulran's head. It was a thick, broad yet sinuous creature, spurting mud and air out of two black bulbous nostrils beneath the mouth.

Ulran unsheathed his sword as he fought to stay afloat in the tugging restricting quagmire

Apart from the snorting and splashing, the creature was quiet, as he hoped it would remain. If the sound carried to Yip-nef Dom's troops, they would finish him off if this beast didn't.

Wielding the sword proved awkward.

Finally, its body buffeted into him.

He submerged an instant and blindly thrust upward with all his might and felt the resistance to the blade gradually give.

Still gripping the sword, he surfaced and gasped for air and half-choked on the slime.

The mud paled, ceased its turmoil and, slowly, before his eyes, it whitened and formed dust.

With renewed urgency, he hastened to the side of the mire, and dragged himself out, barely in time as the mud solidified into hard dusty ground without any trace whatsoever of creature or moisture.

Ulran peered once more towards the approaching soldiers, clearly visible now that the dawn mists had lifted.

Brushing off the white flakes that had so recently been clinging mud, he sheathed his sword and, crouched double, crossed the small island and entered the chill water of the taal.

They would approach slowly because of their scrutiny of the grassland.

He should be able to recapture the lost time and increase the gap between them.

Emerging from the taal, he shook himself, and then ran on with the rise of the island between him and them. His clothes weighed him down slightly, but the sun soon dried them.

It was arduous, running in a crouch. Despite being weakened by the after-effects of Mirmellor's potion and the fight with the theakose, he kept up the punishing pace.

Mind emptied, he concentrated on running and listening, and watching the horizon ahead.

***

In direct and merciless contrast to the cold of the Sonalumes, the sun beat down upon them as their cage trundled along, pulled by great oxen commandeered from Tritaalan.

It was quite a procession.

Twenty sweating armour-clad soldiers trudged through the grass, flanked by their four captains on horseback, cloaks black and still, providing shade for their owners.

Immediately behind the soldiers came the cage upon a wheeled platform with Alomar and Fhord jostled to and fro inside. Trailing them, four cages crammed full with red tellars, sinister in their collective silence.

Apart from a half-dozen soldiers on each side of the single file of wagons, the remainder brought up the rear together with one wagon for their accoutrements, provisions and booty, for they rarely ventured into the pasture-lands without exacting some toll for their ever-grateful liege.

And finally, amongst these last were a few camp followers, women of dubious virtue picked up in Tritaalan or elsewhere.

Besides the jangling of metal weapons, armour and chains, there was much laughter, barking of orders and cursing.

"Where do you think Ulran got to?" queried Fhord, trying to steady herself against the constant lurching. This proved awkward with her hands painfully tethered behind her back. Her wrists hurt, chafing against a rough wooden up-right bar.

Ropes covered Alomar's chest and pinioned his arms to his side. He wedged his shoulder between two bars and effectively stopped himself rolling over the spittle- and refuse-strewn wooden floorboards.

"He'll not risk anything just yet – though he's obviously about. Their crowing over that black devil last night proves that much. So if he's free, Fhord, he'll find a way." Alomar grinned. "You certainly burned those craven cretins!" His glinting eyes betrayed a question.

"I don't know how – I – I just felt so – so incensed, coming through that pass, the mountains, to get so near and then to be captured! It's never happened to me before." Her eyes glared whitely. She was blatantly unsettled about the incident.

"Well, you've been changing ever since that cave, surely you've realised that. And, what about that night in the mountains, when you kept us all warm?"

"I – I don't know..." Her pale lips trembled. "May the good gods give me a sign, an answer," she whispered fervently. "O, Osasor, help me, teach me!" And tears smeared her bruised cheeks.

Alomar turned his eyes away.

CHAPTER SIXTEEN
DISSENSION

Between the dark and the daylight stands the Prime City.
— Tsukcoldol Almanack

Fourth Dekinma, Ulran estimated, crawling out from an animal's burrow. The meadow-vole had tasted coarse and tough, but continuous masticating had created sufficient food juices to sustain him. He spat out the chewed meat when it yielded no more flavour, and concealed the evidence.

For the journey so far Ulran had relied upon roots and berries. He travelled only at night and reckoned he had covered about a hundred launmarks over the last two evenings. In that time, and particularly through the hiding period of daylight, he had continually evaded troops returning from their sector of the Sonalumes. Many of them transported caged red tellars.

Last night he stumbled upon a carcass, a once-magnificent red tellar torn limb from limb, discarded for carrion crow. He knelt by the corpse, surprisingly affected by it. The creature appeared to have died from a broken neck – the soldiers had required fresh meat and had not hesitated to slaughter the bird. But what puzzled Ulran was why they hadn't taken the bird with them, for there was at least another day's supply of meat on the bones. He used his knife to cut a strip of breast away. He lifted it to his lips, and the pink-grey flesh darkened until it was black and flaked away from his knife. Burnt, without the aid of flame. *The Overlord keeps whatever is His*, he mused, half in remembrance.

And now, tonight, he emerged from his vole-burrow quite close to an encampment of another group of soldiers.

The sergeant-at-arms had already deployed sentries on the edge of the camp. There could be no more than twelve in the group, he reckoned. Their captures had been few, and not, it seemed, without cost: for three red tellars they had bartered two dead and three wounded comrades, now supine in death or sprawled in moaning heaps upon the only wagon, uncomfortable fellow travellers.

The red tellars were shackled about their torsos, wings and necks to the rear of the wagon; they had to walk at the mule-drawn wagon's pace.

Any other man would have seethed with impotent anger at seeing the unkempt state of the three birds. Ulran doubted if all three would survive the final forty-odd launmarks to Arisa.

Since he was now fully recovered, he believed the odds would be more accommodating tonight.

Slowly, appraisingly, he circled the camp. Besides the sentries there were six able-bodied men, all of whom lay with their bed-rolls and saddles around the small fire, eating and joking.

Apparently the sentries had instructions not to talk to each other and looked continually outwards, into the pitch night.

Clouds obscured both stars and the last quarter.

The baying of wild dogs reached Ulran's ears and he smiled.

These soldiers were not old campaigners but raw material who had probably never ventured far from the black walls of the Prime City. He thought of Cobrora Fhord and wondered how she fared, then crept towards the nearest sentry.

Ulran attacked from the left side – a right-handed man's weakest – and before the sentry could cry out or defend himself he was lying prostrate upon blood-speckled grass.

Crouched low in the shadows, Ulran snatched up the fallen pointed helmet and unclipped the stained cloak.

After cleaning the knife on the man's jerkin, he hid the weapon in the cloak's folds.

Standing up, he scanned about him. Nothing was amiss. He would have welcomed Alomar's archery skill at this moment, but that could not be. He needed information more than arrows.

Pacing as the fallen sentry had done, he neared the guard on the varteron edge of the camp. He knew the grey accent of Arion well and said, "The night takes its time to wear thin, friend–"

The other nodded then started, eyes widening, with justification for a gleaming sword protruded from his throat, effectively blocking any cry or murmur. Ulran caught him before he fell far.

Two down...

Yet he doubted if he could maintain his disguise or element of surprise much longer. But he wanted the sentries first, otherwise they might be tempted to escape. He would risk discovery for one more, then tackle the others.

Already the red tellars had detected something, flicking their wings, chinking chains, their large beaked heads cocked, listening.

The third sentry managed to cry out before dying.

Ulran discarded helmet and cloak and ran into the midst of the others, slaying two before they could rise from their knees.

Before he joined swords with the other four, he glimpsed the last sentry standing some way off from the chained birds, staring at him.

The innman's sword played music to his ears as he slashed and carved his way through two more soldiers. Then a skilful upthrust snagged at his shirt and shallowly cut his chest: the swordsman's smile transformed into a dying grimace an instant later with Ulran's praise probably the last sound he heard.

The sixth soldier knelt before the innman and held up his sword in supplication. The innman had not relished slaughtering this man's companions and had done so only out of necessity; though had they been the same who killed the red tellar of two nights ago, he might have dwelt on their deaths longer.

"Give me information, man, or you'll die," Ulran told him equably.

"I – what – what do you want to know?"

"Slay him and I slay these birds!" called the sentry eight marks behind the kneeling soldier.

"No!" screeched the soldier. "He'll not–"

"Silence, jackal!" the sentry shouted. "Now, bold warrior, either throw down your enchanted sword or watch these birds lose their heads!"

In the flicker of firelight Ulran could see the glint of steel, the blade pointing at a red tellar's head. His quest was greater than the lives of three red tellars, of that his instinct assured him. But he couldn't condemn them.

His sword against the kneeling soldier's throat, Ulran called across: "I won't kill him as long as you keep the birds alive; if you kill them, he dies too. But I won't surrender my sword. My words might sentence the birds to death, but your actions might sentence your companion to death."

Face and body trembling, the kneeling man cried, "You don't understand, that's what he wants! He wants my wife – we hate each–"

Ulran kneed the whimpering fellow to the dusty ground and threw his long-sword across the camp and quickly ran in its wake.

So unexpected was the throw that the sentry received it full in his stomach and only managed to half-sever a bird's wing before they waddled out of his reach.

Ulran closed, disarmed him and used the man's own sword to finish him off.

The keys for the chains hung on the wagon where the wounded lay, fearfully eyeing him. "Stay where you are and you will come to no harm," he told them, then released the red tellars.

The chains clattered to the ground, the birds ruffled their feathers, flanked their wounded comrade and suddenly leapt into the night sky. No acknowledgement or mental shriek of thanks. He hadn't expected any.

Obtaining provisions for the next two days, and in addition a change of clothes, he forced the surviving soldier to his feet and the pair walked out of the camp, leaving the wounded watchers stunned.

***

Yip-nef Dom's soldier had little to tell him about the fate of all the captured red tellars, and Ulran believed him for his mode of questioning had a tendency to elicit truth and only the truth from the sturdiest of men.

King Yip-nef Dom and the enchanter Por-al Row had conjured up some diabolical scheme involving over two thousand red tellars that must be delivered to the palace alive by the First Sufin of Lamous. If Scalrin's and Fhord's portents were accurate, that left them one day to make use of the red tellars for the First Durin.

Eleven days to the deadline, then. He might not have time to await Alomar and Fhord and the chance of releasing them. His only option was to get to Arisa and locate secret brethren whom he had never met and enlist their support for his quest, the purpose of which he was still unaware.

Unable to kill for its sake alone, Ulran let the soldier go after removing the man's knee-length boots and breeches; clad only in a cotton shirt and woollen under-garments, he wouldn't travel far fast.

Utilising what remained of the night, Ulran jog-trotted towards Arisa which now appeared on his horizon, a black silhouette between the two larger silhouettes of mountains that created the Arion Gap.

Another night and he would be within the gates.

The following day dragged on as though it would never reach its dusk. He used the time to treat his slight chest-wound and taped a narrow sliver of gold leaf over the cut. He had little of the rare leaf remaining in his belt pouch, however, so he used it sparingly.

At dusk he set out, wearing the abandoned soldier's clothing over his own. He planned to arrive outside the Prime City shortly after dawn.

It was a splendid sunrise, coming over the mountains behind him to the dunsaron. Though quite high as the rays reached into the Arion Cradle the slanting reds and yellows touched upon the black rock of the solitary ancient city and lent it an evil black glow, sinister in aspect.

Yet there was no sight quite like Arisa.

Tall walls blocked off the valley entrance on either side; a massive rock stood in the centre of the Arion Gap and upon this crouched the citadel with two entrances only, one from the varteron – winding up sheer high unscaleable cliffs – and the other from the dunsaron.

He was soon mingling with soldiers and farmers, the latter on their way to the morning market. They trod a wide dirt road, a straight line towards Arisa where it would zig and zag up the rocky sides to the walled city.

It proved quite a climb in the crowds and he was sweating profusely beneath all the clothes he wore.

The black stone of the city was a bizarre contrast to the ochre of Goldalese and the grey of Lornwater. Yet it was obviously the most impervious material to use for even after two thousand and fifty years it appeared unmarked by inclement weather.

He climbed the steep winding path, jostled by bleating sheep and recalcitrant mules; the rock fell off on his right and veered on his left and blended into the structure of the city-wall itself. Ulran peered up in open admiration.

An ancient city – indeed, the oldest, for here the calendar was created. Yet now the city was allowed to fester under the ill-omened tread of Yip-nef Dom.

He passed through the tall carved stone portals of the gate. Gleaming black metal portcullis blades glinted. The soldiers on duty hardly glanced at him or the farmers and peasants. He crossed through the enclave of peddlers who set up their stalls in the great courtyard by the gate. Then he walked down a narrow street in shadow.

Almost every building's wall was a piece of ancient artwork, prized for its antiquity and beauty. But he had no eyes for beauty this day.

He turned a right angle and further down turned left and there – at the end of the street – the Sixth Gate to the palace. Guarded. A beggar-woman sat, leaning against a wall; occasionally she cast her cataract-plagued eyes up at the looming palace. Omnipresent, mocking the poor.

Idly sauntering past the palace gate and guard, Ulran eyed the adjacent houses that ran parallel with the high palace wall.

On either side climbed the mountains that formed the portals to the Gap.

He was decided. It could be done.

But first he must contact someone. He had time before the deadline. Prior to breaking into the palace, he would attempt to glean more information on Yip-nef Dom's scheme.

A good distance from the palace a shopkeeper grinned roguishly as Ulran bought an idol of Osasor for Fhord. He would have preferred Alasor, but that was the only idol on the stall. "Your craftsmanship does you credit, friend," Ulran observed, paying.

As the change crossed hands, Ulran's little finger brushed against the merchant's inside wrist, index finger jabbing lightly.

The merchant's response was immediate, his eyes widening, his throat constricting. "If you'd care to view my other work, you might find more to your liking... soldier." He indicated a beaded curtain hanging in a doorway.

"If you've anything else of this quality, I might be interested," Ulran replied.

The merchant showed him through the curtain and called, "Sapella, tend the stall, will you?"

The beaded curtain led onto a landing with stairs that descended into shadow. The gloomy room below was illumined by light-beams from the one narrow barred window set in the far wall, level with the cobbled road outside. As people passed, wisps of dust floated through.

Eyes now accustomed to the shadow, Ulran could make out a wooden table; a broad wooden bed with dishevelled blankets; a chest of drawers beneath the high window, with a porcelain basin of water and a jug inlaid with Reresmond vermicular work; a bear rug by the empty hearth; four wooden chairs; and a few idols. The ceiling rafters were partly concealed with cobwebs.

"Go down, my friend – I'll be right with you," said the merchant, following him.

Wary, despite the exchange of keywords and the secret touch signal, Ulran descended the stairs, removing his stolen helm as he did so.

The stone stairs puffed underfoot with thick dust, doubtless blown in from the street.

"My name is Grayatta Essalar. Please sit, while I get you refreshment."

Ulran sat at the table, placed his helmet gently on the knotted wood. "You live humbly," he observed. He unbuckled his sword; it clattered on the table top.

"It is better, less likely to draw attention..." Essalar grinned, giving the innman a pewter mug of beer; "Though I think there are exceptions such as the innman of the Red Tellar."

Ulran nodded, sipped the lukewarm drink: it had a bitter taste not to his liking but he swallowed it nevertheless. "Yours is the first smile I've seen on the lips of a resident of Arisa," he said seriously. "All the people seem so grey and lifeless, save for the itinerants, visiting farmers and rare minstrels."

Essalar sighed. "The malaise is biting deep, I'm afraid." He sat opposite, face grim.

In the shaft of light, he appeared to be a young man of perhaps forty years, with alert closely set blue eyes. His chin's stubble was blue, and his black hair held a blue sheen to it. His clothes were frayed at their cuffs and collar, but his leather belt and short-sword looked well-cared-for. "I'll not pretend that we've ever been a happy, carefree people in Arisa; we've a reputation for being dark and immutable, as the rocks on which our city is built.

"But the longer Yip-nef Dom's reign lasts, the blacker does his realm seem. There are whispers in every dark corner now where once there were but few."

"It is much the same in Lornwater, Essalar. Times seem to be changing for our cities – hopefully for the better. Though, sadly, revolt does not always result in the best answer."

Essalar shook his head, sipped his beer. Froth bordered his upper lip and the back of his hand wiped it clear. "There can be no revolt here, for Yip-nef Dom still rules with an iron hand of fear and retribution. His cells are crammed full, the master torturer is overworked, and the corpse caravans to the Manderranmeron Fault are proving too costly.

"Some younger ones have escaped over the varteron cliffs and others have been killed in the attempt." Essalar shrugged. "But most just sit and wait and hope. Hope Yip-nef Dom's time will come soon."

"What of his successor, Yip-dor Fla?"

"Imprisoned. He might disagree with me, but I believe he is fortunate – Dom's still scared of Fla's supporters. He knows as long as Fla lives as a hostage to the future, they will contain their revolution. But should Fla die, then Dom feels insurrection might wrest his throne from him."

"Have you any more friends of like mind who can be trusted? I need information and help if I am to get into Yip-nef's palace."

Anxiety showed in Essalar's eyes. "You are here because of the red tellars?"

"Yes."

"I wondered what brought you – I thought perhaps, but, no–"

"Our lives are shaped in mysterious ways, Essalar. There may be a hidden connection between us." Ulran leaned forward conspiratorially. "Now, have you associates you – we – can trust?"

"There are six of us, though we have not met in–"

"And you can get them here this evening?"

Essalar nodded. "It will be done."

"Good." Ulran drained his mug, shook his head. "No thank you, one flagon is sufficient. I am expecting some friends shortly, prisoners of Yip-nef Dom's men. They were apprehended outside Tritaalan. I would like to engineer their escape, preferably before breaking into the palace."

"There could be reprisals."

Ulran pursed his lips. "Then, I must see to their escape with great subtlety."

"What of the red tellars?"

"I was hoping you could enlighten me. Have any been brought into the city?"

"Indeed, well over a thousand. To begin with, they brought them under the concealment of darkness in cages covered with canvas. But of late they have been coming in at all times of day and night. The people are, naturally, becoming very nervous."

"Yet still they do nothing – well, perhaps they need an incentive, a lead. Could your group of six rally the populace round you, do you think?"

"I could not vouch for it, innman. The folk are fickle – and bloodshed has not occurred within our walls for a long–"

"What of the torture chambers, the corpse caravans?" Ulran enquired ironically.

Essalar laughed nervously. "Death always happens to someone else!"

"So, nobody knows why the red tellars are being captured and brought here?"

"Alas, no – though there are plenty fearfully curious!"

***

With nine days to the deadline, Ulran lay beneath the stairs of Essalar's house and again pictured the entrance gate to the palace, stone by stone.

A tap on the shop door alerted Essalar. His wife, Sapella, sat up in bed with a gasp, sheet drawn up to her pursed lips.

"It is only our friends – listen, the knock..." Essalar clambered out of bed, donned a fur-skin coat and tied the belt as he ascended the stairs.

Ulran had detected the footfalls of more than three men outside the front door. He was instantly ready, emerging from the dark confines under the stairs with sword in hand. He offered Essalar's wife a reassuring smile.

Hair unkempt, she sat wide-eyed, unmoving, knees drawn up under the bedclothes.

Politics are for men! He wondered which Lornwater orator had said that. Perhaps the affairs of men might be better handled by women. He turned as the door onto the landing opened; the reed curtain swished.

"It's all right, they're friends," whispered Essalar, coming down ahead of the newcomers.

There were four. "Bindar's unable to get away and Shadron was arrested last night. Someone betrayed him, we feel sure."

After brief introductions, they sat around the table while Essalar broke out the mugs and a jug of beer.

They all sipped thirstily, save Ulran who drank his sparingly. Out of the corner of his eye he noticed Sapella had turned her back to these co-conspirators and, judging by her shallow breathing, was fast asleep.

The four were distressed about Ulran's proposed plans; unwise, most unwise, they said. Retribution would be swift and bloody. Just for two friends – a whole city would suffer.

Ulran refrained from arguing, intent on doing what must be done with or without aid. He had called them together more to judge the calibre and psychology of the faction opposed to Yip-nef Dom.

Now he could appreciate how Yip-nef held sway so successfully.

Eventually, the talk swung round to Lornwater, as news of rebellion had been brought by roumers. This was the first Ulran had heard, and for a moment feared for his son. No, Ranell would cope, no matter what. Still, the implications made by the group were blatant: Ulran should first be concerned with his own city's fate.

And, besides, what matter over a few birds?

At this, Essalar jumped up, sword half-drawn.

Ulran quietened them all down. "We need not fight amongst ourselves – unless there are enemies within," he said evenly, eyeing each in turn. His meaning was made clear and they all resumed their seats, moderately mollified. "All I ask is that you think over what I have *requested* of you men. Let me know tomorrow night."

After the group had left, each with a thoughtful crease upon his brow, Ulran wished Essalar a worry-free sleep and curled up beneath the stairs.

But, as he had feared, sleep would not touch his lids. He lay and stared up at the underside of wooden treads, the complex interwoven cobwebs, the angles of dark shadow. As he lay unmoving, deep in thought, a spider emerged from a dark corner and began its upside-down walk along the wooden beams. With the greatest of ease he could crush it; and, for the same reason, he did not.

Contrary to all his own teaching to Ranell, he was disturbed, torn in two. He had known distress many times, most particularly after the tragic loss of Ellorn, but he had steeled himself against its devouring nature, and he would again, now, but each time this inner battle cost him dearly, in mental effort which could be ill-spared at present.

In a way, it was a similar battle he continually waged against the Angevanellian; the actuality of his mortality had always been with him, but lately it had impinged upon his consciousness more than before.

He might not survive this quest, and what then of Ranell? He was resigned to die one day. But for the product of Ellorn's and his own loins to die too, leaving nothing but a barren Inn. He had hoped that Lorar, daughter of the master goldsmith would make Ranell a good wife.

He cursed his morbid introspection. Another sign of his approaching old age – or death? His faith in Ranell should tell him quite plainly: his son could now fend for himself. Was he involved in the Lornwater rebellion? He felt certain that the answer to these questions was *Yes*. If Ranell had been wounded or slain, he believed he would have experienced something.

If he came out of this, Ulran decided, he would visit Sianlar again.

He was slightly shaken, for this was the first occasion that his immutable faith had wavered in the slightest.

Did it have something to do with the capture of the red tellars? How did the Overlord allow His beautiful birds to be so ill-treated without offering any defence or retaliation?

Ulran smiled, lapsing into a light slumber. The Overlord indeed worked in mysterious ways.

***

For the entire day he remained beneath the stairs, only coming out briefly to stretch his legs, relieve himself and eat, at which times Sapella kept watch on the landing above. He ill-liked this fugitive existence, but it was necessary to his plans.

As Sufinma fell upon the city, both of his protectors sighed with relief. Essalar bolted the shop door and joined them. "They should be here soon, I think."

The candle had reached low and sputtered before a pre-arranged knock shook them out of drowsiness. Ulran was instantly awake, hand on sword-hilt.

The group consisted of five this night and the newcomer was introduced. Bindar was a tall, broad-shouldered red-haired man who stood out from the crowd; for this clandestine existence he seemed far too conspicuous. Ulran observed him closely for he recognised a kindred spirit.

"We agree to what you ask," said Bindar. "If I could have dragged myself away from my beer-hall last night, I promise you none of that unpleasantness would have occurred." He looked scornfully at his companions.

"It is forgotten already," said Ulran. "I believe we could stand a good chance of releasing Yip-dor Fla, and using him to rally the populace."

All nodded agreement, hope burning in their eyes. "But," protested Elmar, "he is heavily guarded – and – and we have no information as to his health or state of mind."

"If what Essalar says rings true, which I believe, he will be alive and only slightly damaged. His mind? I don't know. I cannot speak for a stranger. Cells do fearful things to men sometimes..."

"What will it cost?"

"If my plan works, perhaps thirty men. I would estimate losing five at most; with luck, none."

His co-conspirators looked at each other with approval yet concern in their eyes.

He had won them over. "Now, for the plan... I want–"

Ulran's plan crumbled irretrievably at that instant for a sudden deafening crash sounded from upstairs.

"The door!" exclaimed Essalar as rending and groaning wood suddenly screamed and slammed violently.

Sapella woke with a start.

They rose as one, hands releasing swords from scabbards, metal glinting in the candle-light.

Three guards barged the flimsy inner door and their onrush propelled them with door into the banister; they flew over it to land upon the table with a clamorous clatter. All three soldiers unwillingly spread their blood upon the table.

Sapella screamed as she huddled in the corner of the room, bedclothes pulled taut.

But there were more: three rushed down the stairs whilst another leapt over the shattered banister, shield protecting his legs; he landed heavily and the table overturned at a touch from Ulran. Bindar silenced the soldier as the other three waded in, steel clanging.

Two others were on the landing; one of them had fitted an arrow to his short-bow. Ulran's sword ran through his attacker; he whirled round and his poniard flashed from his fingers and settled up to its hilt in the bowman's forehead.

Four more joined the trembling soldier upon the landing; but there were no bows between them.

Ulran backed away as the troops slowly descended the stairs, wide eyes taking in their slain comrades.

Only one of Essalar's companions had sustained an injury, a flesh wound on his thigh.

Ulran backed till his legs brushed against the bedclothes. "Stand up, Sapella," he urged but she simply mumbled hysterically. "Stand up, woman, now!" he commanded.

Hearing the bed creak, he guessed she had finally done his bidding.

A soldier charged him with a halberd; Ulran parried, twirled his sword and abruptly sliced downwards, severing the pike from its staff. As the soldier stood dumbfounded, Ulran sank his blade into the man's chest.

Then he lifted Sapella up in his free arm and met another attacker. Essalar's wife went limp and he found her easier to carry. "Is there another way out of here?" he demanded, annoyed with himself for not checking before.

"Yes – behind the bed – a tunnel!"

Parrying and killing another assailant amidst the clanging and thrusting of the mêlée, Ulran kicked viciously at the wooden bed and pushed it free of the stone wall. There was a good-sized square hole: black, draped in cobwebs, unused. Escape.

Overturning the bed onto its side, he used it to shield the presence of the opening.

Then Ulran called to Bindar: "Send one of your men out first!"

Before Bindar could respond, the nearest man dodged a glancing blow and fell to his knees in front of the exit: Ulran decapitated him without compunction. "Our traitor!" he called back, and kicked the corpse to one side.

He lowered Sapella to the floor, pushed her on her back inside the tunnel, and followed on his hands and knees.

If the gods whom Fhord so devoutly worshipped were kind, there would be nobody at the other end – if there was an end.

Ulran heard someone gasping behind him but kept on crawling. He grazed his knees and shoulders and bruised his forehead as, with difficulty, he pushed Sapella through pieces of rubble and shale.

"Bindar's holding them off," said Essalar from behind; "he's too broad to get in here, he said."

Faint greyness appeared up ahead, enlarging.

At last, they emerged in a garden amid sweet-smelling ferns, bushes and trees.

Shouts and whistles came from down the street, beyond a sculpted wall that bordered this garden.

"Reinforcements, I fear," Ulran observed and helped Essalar out.

Night-breeze stung his grazed knees.

Only two others followed.

Sapella groaned, regaining her wits. "Essalar," Ulran nodded towards her. The merchant knelt by his wife, told her what had happened.

"Is there anywhere we can hide before daylight betrays us?"

"If Elmar – the one you slew – was the traitor, then all our names will be in Por-al Row's hands. We'll be unable to use our warehouses, barns, shops or homes. As for our families–"

"Elmar attempted making his escape first, before Bindar told anyone to move. Only a man who had betrayed us would try that, for fear of being killed by his employers 'by accident'. There's little trust between this type."

"Then, we must split up, fend for ourselves." Essalar shrugged apologetically.

"First, we can see to our two friends here. We might be able to help their families. If only Bindar can hold them off long enough," Ulran ended, though he had no fears for Bindar for during the fight he had seen the sword he was using.

***

The Fourth Durin: seven days to go, Alomar realised, shoving his own food between Fhord's cracked dry lips. The mush was poor fare, but the immortal had not eaten for two days, in an attempt at keeping up Fhord's failing strength. His own hunger pangs were almost continuous now, but he had starved before and he would doubtless do so again. His right arm was worsening, the suppuration having dried beneath the merciless sun, the great gash blackened at the edges. He wafted at the hovering black flies.

As he forced the mush onto Fhord's swollen tongue, Alomar idly wondered if he would die of gangrene. The pain, surely, could not be worse than the Janoven poison potion so many years ago. Yet memories of pain are fleeting; the body and mind conveniently forgets. He smiled at the thought of incipient death. He would not surrender himself to the Great Leveller just yet.

Whilst Fhord lived, he must care for her and perhaps fight for her. If need be, he might have to die for her. No less a sacrifice had she given up to the gods as they shivered in those snow-filled mountains.

As they jogged along at a bruising yet frustratingly slow pace, he watched the Sonalumes diminish gradually, purple in the haze.

"Four days at least," observed a straw-chewing soldier to his watchful companion as he re-tied Alomar's hands after the meagre meal.

Four days would be in time, then. Though Courdour Alomar wondered if either of them would be alive to see the forbidding entrance to Arisa, let alone escape and resolve the mystery of the captive red tellars.

PART FIVE
FOURTH SAPIN OF DAROUS - FIRST DURIN OF LAMOUS

The Song of the Overlord – Part the Final:
Unto the sinful and vicious, He be evil
But unto the good, beneficent be He.
The light of life is cold
The light of death is hot.
For what is to die but to stand naked in the wind
And melt with fervour in the sun?
Build me more stately mansions for my soul
Sayeth He, let each new fane be nobler than the last.
He is the First Cause, the Prime Origin
All the Basic Essence is He.
Irreducible, munificent, knowledge all, is He
For He is the one, the only, the Overlord!

CHAPTER SEVENTEEN
PALACE

Ominous in its beauty!
– Anonymous

Down cobbled streets, up winding alleyways, and over numerous bridges, the five of them had wended their way towards the homes of the two nameless helpers caught in the trap at Essalar's. Thankfully, they had been in time to alert their wives and children, hastily pack their more valuable belongings and join Essalar and Sapella at the varteron gate.

Ulran determined to tackle the palace alone, leaving Essalar and his two friends to take their families out next morning when the gates opened for the few honoured merchantmen from Goldalese.

It was risky, but the only way they had of escaping the city-fortress.

But Essalar insisted on joining the innman and his argument was sound enough: Ulran had not been within the city before; he needed someone versed in its peculiarities.

Reluctantly, the innman agreed, much to Sapella's distress. Ulran promised he would try to see that no harm befell her husband and then the pair left, to melt into the shadows.

The once-great city of Arisa was now shabby and over-populated and over-built. Only the artistry of the builders and the single coloration of rock preserved any sense of form, so that instead of looking unplanned and ramshackle, the city presented itself as an awesome maze of houses and bridges. The roads and alleys formed shadowy caverns and tunnels. Besides interconnecting buildings of all shapes and sizes, there were a surprising number of buildings under ground, gouged out of the very bedrock.

Through fear of a coup, the king had long ago banned all weapons after dusk; and his deadly henchmen patrolled the streets to ensure the decree was observed, often dallying to force some unfortunate woman to please them.

Shortly after leaving Sapella and the others, Essalar and Ulran rounded a corner to discover one such watchman forcing his unwanted attentions on a mature woman who loudly said all she wanted was to return home after visiting a friend.

The mêlée at Essalar's house could not carry to this side of the city, and as they both set upon the watchman and silenced him, Ulran wondered how Bindar the red-head had fared: if alive, he would surely be a captive, suffering what indignities at their hands?

With the dead watchman over his shoulder, Ulran thanked the woman for offering them succour for the night, but refused.

Deep inside an alley, he divested the corpse of his garments and changed for the second time, becoming a watchman in rather tight-fitting clothes. "Essalar, go back to that woman's house, apologise for my behaviour and ask to stay the night – no, I'll join you shortly, after I've scouted around. Now, go, I won't be long."

Bindar, surprisingly, had escaped, through a combination of sheer audacity, swordsmanship, the cowardliness of some soldiers and the stupidity of others.

Keeping to the side-streets by Essalar's house, Ulran overheard the groans and moans of searching troops.

Apparently, Bindar had killed so many and piled the corpses of others in the only doorway so that nobody else could break through for quite a while. He must have used the time to advantage, wielding the many fallen swords as picks and shovels. He hacked a hole in the wall under the street. The shop adjacent possessed a cellar – only the wall separating the two places. With all the shouts, mortally wounded cries, and clamour of swords on the doorway, his digging went unnoticed and he broke through, crossed the cellar and forced the door. He left the house next door while the soldiers tugged and heaved at their dead comrades piled high in the doorway.

Smiling to himself, Ulran retraced his steps to the woman's house situated beneath a road-bridge of black stone, the entrance perpetually in shadow.

He knocked the pre-arranged signal and Essalar answered.

Once inside, Ulran divested himself of the uncomfortable watchman's plaid cloak. "You'll be pleased to know, Bindar escaped," the innman said. As the merchant's eyes lit up, Ulran went on, "Where will he run to, do you think?"

"His beer-hall, possibly – in Ram Street. But not for long, perhaps only to get money, a few things, clothes..." The merchantman stood in the hallway, thinking aloud. "But I should think he would head for the city wells – yes, the wells... I remember him telling me not long ago, they were an ideal place to hide. All you needed was some cured meat, a few vegetables. You've got all the water you'd ever want."

"Can you take me there tonight?"

Essalar nodded. "We'd be safe there. This woman, she's risked enough already."

They accepted some provisions she could ill-afford to spare but forced on them; then they took their leave.

Once more they melted into the shadows. Ulran again wore the watchman's cloak.

Soundlessly, they walked the streets and clung to the walls of cold drab stone.

Before leaving the house, Essalar explained that the wells had been tunnelled deep through the rock. The pavements they now trod were two hundred marks above the plain of Arion and the wells penetrated another hundred marks below the plain. But once the water had been located, the wells had strangely filled so that the water stayed roughly two-thirds up the well; which still left a hundred-mark haul for the water-carriers. "And today, even, memories fail as to the reasons for it, but at regular intervals down each well a small indentation has been cut – big enough to comfortably accommodate four men at a time."

"Survey tunnels, I imagine," Ulran suggested.

"Possibly. Anyway, I believe Bindar will have made for one of those ledges."

They leaned over the rim of the fifth well they'd tried and looked down. Ulran could not see anything: it was too dark. Essalar tossed a pebble down, but instead of a splash Ulran heard a dull thwack as though the stone had hit some sailcloth.

"He leaves a few supplies on the ledge, just in case. A cautious one, is Bindar." Essalar threw two more pebbles, in quick measured succession and a light showed to the left as a blanket was pulled back. "The blanket covers the shelf-opening. Keeps a small lamp to warm himself and to see by, as well."

Bindar crouched some ten marks below, seen dimly in the purple light. Essalar called down and explained Ulran's presence and their need for a hiding-place; his echoes died and Bindar replied succinctly: "Come, quickly!"

The descent to the ledge was simple enough, utilising the bucket ropes. As they went lower, Ulran felt the temperature gradually decrease, reminding him of the Sonalumes.

Their reunion and congratulations were brief. Bindar quickly secured the blanket again, blotting out the irregular circle at the top, which appeared from here no bigger than the brim of Alomar's floppy hat.

Soon, they settled down, though ever conscious of the damp atmosphere, the dripping walls, and the chill on their backs.

In hushed voices they discussed Bindar's intention of staying down the well for at least two days. Ulran agreed, but insisted he himself must penetrate the palace tomorrow night, Fourth Durinma.

"No-one knows Yip-nef Dom's plans, but I daresay he'll be rid of the red tellars in a like manner to his concubines," Bindar said in answer to Ulran's question. "Why'd he have them killed? They bore him no fruit. He little realised he might be at fault. Some say he might use the royal prerogative."

Bindar's suggestion rang a bell for Ulran; he wondered what Alomar would have to say about that.

Eventually, Bindar agreed to join Ulran and Essalar the following evening.

Before dawn they removed the blanket and extinguished the lamp.

The rest of the day passed slowly for all three on the cramped ledge. The monotony was broken by the infrequent raising and lowering of the water-buckets, being occasionally splashed, and the angelic singing of some young girl.

***

"A courier, sire!"

The parchment scroll was brief and badly written but its meaning was clear. A smile played on the king's lips. Slowly, he turned, talked to someone concealed behind a beaded curtain; beyond this was the splashing of bathwater: "Good news, my dear."

"Hmm?"

"News, my pet – from that captain – oh, Dab-su I think he's called. They've captured two strangers just outside Tritaalan and they're bringing them in!"

"Oh."

"Yes, my thoughts precisely. Where is the other one – or has he perished on the mountains, I wonder?"

He screwed up the parchment awkwardly and flung it across the fur-carpeted room, brushed aside the beads and the sight that befell him washed away the quivering redness of his features. "You're exquisite, you really are!"

***

Emerging at dusk, they stretched aching limbs with care, lest cramp assail them. The small square where these eight wells were situated was completely deserted, unbathed by street lanterns. Towards the latter part of the day Bindar had suggested they pay a visit on a man of his acquaintance whose profession was somewhat dubious.

Fahurar Grie opened the door a crack in answer to Bindar's carefully spaced knock.

"Let us in, my friend, before one of Yip-nef's watchers sees us!"

Fahurar glimpsed the swords beneath his visitors' robes and let them in. He hastily shut the door after them.

"Explanations later, fr–"

But Fahurar was not listening; he stared wide-eyed at Ulran's ring-hand. Open mouthed he looked up at the innman. Now, for the first time, both Bindar and Essalar noticed the ring taken from the corpse in Oquar II Forest.

Ulran refrained from enlightening them that he was not a member of the assassin's gild.

"No, no matter, Bindar," breathed Fahurar, "if you have a friend in this illustrious gild, then I shall be only too happy to supply any need you require." He swallowed and shook hands with the innman and Essalar as introductions were made.

"We spent last night down the fifth well," Bindar explained.

"Yes, I thought you might have done something like that – the entire city has been thirsting for your blood!"

Bindar looked shaken. "Why?"

"You obviously haven't heard, no – you couldn't have. Por-al Row has taken ten children into custody–"

"Not – not reprisals, surely not?"

Fahurar shrugged. "He issued an ultimatum not four orms gone. A child will die at sunrise and one more each orm thereafter unless you, Bindar, give yourself up." Fahurar looked puzzled. "What now surprises me is that they must know of your presence, Ulran, yet they never mentioned you in their statement."

"Too many people have heard of the Red Tellar's innman, that's why," suggested Essalar.

Ulran rubbed his aquiline nose abstractedly. "This is but another example of their warped minds. They won't worry about what people think of them when they slaughter innocent children, yet they are concerned for what folk might say or do if someone of, say, outside influence is killed. It doesn't make sense – and I'm not that influential to justify such back-handed compliments!"

"Yip-nef's over the edge, I fear," Fahurar said morosely. "Gelstrab – you may remember him, Essalar – the cutpurse, he was caught this afternoon. They cut off his hands, both of them, just like that! Cutpurses have always thrived in Arisa, it's been an honourable calling. But now I'm afraid to thieve anything," he ended.

***

Por-al Row was terribly upset. Yip-nef Dom had insisted that he was not on any account to be disturbed in his royal chambers for the rest of the evening. That had been over a day ago! And still he was closeted with that hell-cat, Iayen.

And he felt he had good cause to worry, for already she was usurping his place. Soon... by the gods, if she were regent! By his own carefully worded suggestions, Por-al Row had incited anger and hate for the royal concubines to overwhelm the king. Each and every one had been done to death, some serving a useful purpose in the casting of arcane spells.

But still Iayen twisted the king round her little finger!

He had tried telling Yip-nef Dom about the intruder, Ulran by name, being in the city – according to that traitor, Elmar. But he had been sent away with a flea in his ear. So when the trap snapped shut abortively, he had refrained from informing his liege. If Iayen had known of that, what capital she'd have made of it! No – he would decide. But had he done the right thing? He had nothing against the silly little brats, but they must be used.

Once they had this Bindar fellow, they would extract information out of him, one way or another. The torturer was tired of breaking weaklings; Bindar would be ideal material. He licked his lips. Yes, even such a felon as Bindar would not stand idly by and let innocent children die.

But what had been in that message the king received yesterday?

O Iayen, damn your accursed evil eye!

***

"I've got the rope you wanted," said Fahurar, "and two associates of mine have broken into the rooms. Nobody is aware. Are you sure that's all you require?"

"That will do, thank you, friend," Ulran said. "Let's go."

The three men took a lengthy and devious route to the houses overlooking the Sixth Gate of the palace. This route entailed crossing the spans of three small stone bridges in succession and it was while they were upon the second that they were spotted, merely by chance.

Ulran's sword and the rope around his shoulder were well concealed beneath the watchman's cloak. Though they had borrowed a hat to hide Bindar's distinctive red hair, the ruse had not worked; a freak gust of wind blew the hat off and the platoon nearby shouted in alarm and recognition.

"Essalar – over the bridge. Back to Fahurar, quickly now!"

The merchantman made to protest but Bindar urged him. "You've a family, man – look to them! We can handle these!"

Nodding reluctantly, Essalar vaulted the bridge wall and plummeted the four marks to the cobbled road below. He landed without serious hurt and his foot-falls died away.

Then the soldiers were upon them.

Ulran dealt unceremoniously with the foremost two and pitched their dead bodies over the parapet.

Bindar suffered a severe cut to his left arm but served up death in return.

But the hue-and-cry was up now.

Soldiers had been combing the city since Fourth Sufinma and had only been waiting for an opportunity to avenge their butchered comrades.

From all directions they came, or so it seemed. But back the way they had come was still free; Bindar immediately noticed: "Ulran, go back, lie low tonight," he shouted and killed another soldier.

Four more charged the red-head and met with lightning-like thrusts from Bindar's legs and sword. "Go, Ulran, go!" he urged at the top of his voice.

Ulran stood, on the slope of the bridge, uncharacteristically hesitant.

"Save the red tellars, Warrior!" said Bindar. His blows clashed and baulked the onrushing troops.

Ulran saluted with his sword, turned and fled down the winding alleyways. He found a shadowed alley of refuse buzzing with flies and avoided the soldiers who were all converging on the three bridges.

Bindar would be overwhelmed, numbers would tell in the end. The innman shook himself and wove his circuitous way back to Fahurar's abode.

To flee was the action of a wise man, he told himself; but the taste of it still rankled. He may be called Runaway, but since those days he had never run from a fight. Yip-nef Dom would assuredly pay for the loss of a good man like Bindar. And there were others, too. He wondered how many more, before –

He was becoming morose, he realised.

Apart from explaining that Essalar had hidden in the city, Fahurar had not spoken a word.

Now Ulran said, "Can you tell your men I'll go tomorrow night?" His lips held in a determined slit. "Without fail."

***

Alomar, stiff and cramped in the cold night, asked Captain Dab-su Hruma if he would release one of his hands so he might better keep his companion Fhord alive.

The captain, appreciating his king's acid tongue and vitriolic heart, agreed. "Aye, I don't want a valuable captive dying on me."

Alomar's right arm, now numb and discoloured, was lashed to an upright bar but his left was freed.

***

The palace wall was simply that, a wall, without ramparts or sentries. But its construction was distinctive. Gargoyles were placed at frequent intervals and in between the top of the wall that comprised snaking masonry, carved in loving detail by some long dead stonemason. How evil the black effigies look in the silver sheen of moonlight, mused Ulran. For a long time he studied the stretch of wall opposite the window.

Within the room Ulran occupied, Fahurar's two associates stood, guarding the door to the half-landing. Downstairs, two more guarded the front door, and two others were at the rear.

The owners of the building were presently guests of Fahurar. Briefly, Ulran had spoken to the old couple, assuring them that he meant no harm but desired access to the palace.

It was obvious that they realised he was involved with Bindar, for they looked afraid, doubtless thinking of the ten children.

Bindar, miraculously, had been taken alive, though only just. By all accounts he was seriously wounded, but still lived. Word had quickly spread that Bindar was held, though obviously Por-al Row had hopes to keep the fact secret, thereby strengthening the populace's fear. Ulran knew well enough, in fear was weakness. Por-al Row had learned the axiom well. But whispers had transformed into vociferous mobs demanding the release of the ten children.

Without a word, the children were all released, unharmed.

Tears and gratitude greeted them, yet another psychological move on Por-al Row's part, the innman realised. If the next time ever occurred, the people would trust the enchanter's sense of decency and fairness, two attributes which Ulran doubted Por-al Row really possessed.

The street was some ten marks below. Ulran reckoned the distance was no more than eight marks from window to palace wall.

He leaned forward, peered down the street: the sentry at the Sixth Gate twelve marks to his left was disinterestedly pacing up and down.

Ulran left the room with his rope and ascended the stairs.

From the roof-top he could look down upon the street far below and the wall. Beyond the wall was the courtyard with the black shapes of a tower and the palace indistinct but ominous.

He looped the rope into a slip-noose and, gathering plenty in one hand, he cast out and down.

As luck would have it he was successful with the first throw. The noose draped over a grinning gargoyle.

He tugged, tightening the rope about the stone beast's neck. Then he gathered up the loose end and dangled it in front of the open window below. One of his accomplices stretched out and caught the rope.

He descended the stairs and re-entered the room. Once the rope was securely tied to a door-frame, he nodded to the two men and climbed onto the sill.

Hand over hand he crossed ten marks above the silent street.

He then soundlessly scrambled atop the gargoyle and stayed there, legs wrapped around the figure.

Withdrawing the knife that Fahurar had procured, he severed the rope and it fell away, against the wall of the building opposite. One of his accomplices slowly pulled the rope up. They would then close the window, lock the house and leave with the rope, thereby safe-guarding the old couple.

Ulran replaced the knife in his belt. For a moment he paused. Still garbed in watchman's cloak and helm, he crouched over the gargoyle.

A moving moonbeam of the last quarter lit up the courtyard for a brief instant before a scudding cloud returned it to formless shadows. Yet in that time he took in the dimly lit stone arcades running along the courtyard walls to right and left.

In the centre of the courtyard stood a tall tower with wooden benches on the side farthest from him. These benches climbed in tiers and faced the black tower.

To his right was the Sixth Gate and barbican where sentries paced.

Behind the benches rose the solid mass of the palace itself, each side of its central balcony draped with hangings. At each corner of the palace, black against the lesser dark of night sky, circular towers with their pointed spires.

The drop was about eight marks as he hung by his hands. He landed with a mute thud, and looked about him, in particular at the barbican: but the two sentries were busy conferring, their backs to him.

He determined to attempt an entrance using the arcade doorways. One of them would surely have access to the palace.

But the Fourth Sapinma of Darous was a fateful night for the innman.

In his fleeting appraisal of the courtyard in the transient moonlight he had omitted to descry two figures, young soldiers playing dice on the flagstones of the right-hand shagunblend-lit arcade. The innman had been too intent on the sentries to note any movements to his right.

Only now, as he stepped a pace forward from the wall's penumbra did he hear a whispered imprecation. The arcade was pillared but not walled; he was in plain view should they look up.

Ulran stood stock still, debating whether he could afford to rush the pair. His decision was taken from him when one of the gamblers stood up in anger and threw the dice into the courtyard. At the same moment he saw Ulran.

The innman crossed the intervening three marks in as many bounds, sword drawn. His left leg flashed out, foot crashing fatally into his discoverer's chest.

The second gambler backed off and, stumbling, yelled out before he too died.

At that time the two sentries noticed the commotion and ran forward, while a third – whom Ulran had not seen earlier – hastened into the left-hand arcade and beat loudly upon a small gong.

From various doors along the right-hand arcade soldiers rushed out, hastily donning sword-belts and helmets.

The two sentries approached warily, for word of the innman's prowess had gone before him.

His faithful sword sang and within a short time the dead lay strewn about his wheeling frame. He scythed with the blade, lanced out with lethal limbs and fought his way towards the barbican, the only possible way out.

But the guards continued to pour into the courtyard. Many now held back, awaiting an opening that never seemed to occur.

Orm after orm Ulran fought, never seeming to tire, never wavering in his resolve.

At last he felt his back thud into the hardwood doors. Swivelling and pivoting, killing as he did so, he glanced at the bolts.

He swerved, parried, slashed to right and left, while his free hand felt behind him and tugged at the heavy bolt.

Most men would have needed two hands to shoot the bolt, but with a loud metallic clang it opened. There were two more: one level with his waist, the other at ankle-height. Dangerously awkward.

Yet still he kept his enemies at bay, his sword clangouring endlessly, until the whole courtyard seemed filled with the ringing sound of steel upon steel.

He was hard-pressed to keep slashing out, dissuading the foremost soldiers from pressing too close. Now he could not employ his deadly feet, only his sword and free fist. If the press of men continued to come on relentlessly, he would surely be flattened against the door panels.

Again, he repeated his earlier manoeuvre and released the waist-high bolt. But as he did so, he was a fraction too slow in parrying a battle-axe on his left. The hilt crashed against his skull and toppled his helmet resoundingly onto the courtyard flags.

Head exploding, he slashed upwards, parting the axe-head from handle.

But he could no longer see clearly. Everything and everybody swam before his eyes.

Oddly, he wondered if Alomar would have relished his end this way.

Floreskand: Wings

CHAPTER EIGHTEEN
IAYEN

By this vow, I will most horribly revenge!
– *The Lay of Lorgen*

Yip-nef Dom's obese white body rose from the countersunk bath. Sekor-petals clung to his dripping frame. "I'll join you later, my dear," he said to the diminutive Iayen who sat with her back to him.

She didn't answer, but Yip-nef Dom hardly noticed, for his attention centred upon the quivering figure of Por-al Row outside the bead curtains.

Flinging a robe about his corpulent flesh, the king padded wetly across the mosaic tiles, brushed the curtain aside and scowled at the alchemist.

The king's sudden entrance and the snaking swish of the beaded curtains caught the alchemist unawares. He jumped and stumbled back a pace, lean sharp-nailed hands going to his mouth. "Sire!" he expostulated, "I greatly regret disturbing your – your ablutions – I–"

Yip-nef Dom snarled, "You'll regret it, Por-al Row, if it is not of utmost importance, of that I can assure you!" And he shook himself in barely concealed anger, droplets of scented water scattering from his lank thinning hair.

"It's an intruder, sire – in the courtyard at this very moment!"

"So? Surely the palace guard can handle *one* man! Is that all?"

"No, sire, oh no, you don't under – er, you see, he has been fighting off the guards for fully four orms now."

Yip-nef's fleshy pale mouth dropped open. "F – four *orms*?"

The alchemist nodded. "I haven't been able to get a good look at him through the fighting, sire, but I believe he may be a hired assassin. Whispers passed back by the guards, at any rate, indicate..."

Visibly shaken at this disclosure, the king shuffled to the right, fumbled for a high-backed chair and, slumping into it, he let the robe fall from his shoulders to reveal obscene fatty breasts sparsely patterned with grey hair. "A member of the assassin's gild, you say?"

Por-al Row nodded. He regained his composure at sight of his liege's confidence beginning to fall apart. "There seems no doubt, my lord."

Eyes looking up at the alchemist – one watery and beseeching, the other lifeless and cold – the king said, "But – but if he – he – if he fails, won't they – I mean, won't they send someone else and keep on, until –

until…?"

Gravely, Por-al Row nodded. "If the gild has accepted a covenant for your er, demise, my liege, they will, as you say, bend their collective will to the covenant's, er, successful conclusion..."

"Conclusion... That's what I'll be – *concluded*!"

Scowling, the king abruptly jumped up. "Then I must double my guard." He swung the curtain back, turned, "When I've changed, I want to see this assassin – preferably alive, if you can manage *that* without bungling, Enchanter!"

The king disappeared behind the curtain, leaving the alchemist stunned and speechless.

Por-al Row bit his lip and twisted his cloak in his hands. This peremptory change in Yip-nef Dom was Iayen's doing, he was sure. My scheme! he thought furiously. My idea entirely, and now, near its successful completion, she steps in to control him, instead of me! Damn her a thousand times!

Savagely, his flushed face contorted, he swerved round and hastened through the glittering apartments. Past the tall studded doors and surprised sentries, his sandalled feet slapping and echoing, he hurried towards the royal balcony.

***

Two simultaneous sword thrusts sank into the innman as he stumbled forward with his consciousness already fading. He but dimly experienced the pain as the blades cut into him.

His knees thudded hard upon the stone flags and he toppled forward, close to his dented helmet.

At least three more swords and as many axes were raised aloft to slice into him to avenge the many dead and maimed littering the courtyard.

"Stop! Stop at once, I command you! *Stop!*"

Though breathless and wheezing, by some incredible surge of desperation, Por-al Row had run almost full force onto the royal balcony and yelled at the top of his voice.

His screeching commands rebounded from the courtyard walls and arcades.

And, because of the urgency of his voice, he had the desired effect, save for one young man too quick to halt his downward plunge. The mace crashed wickedly against the innman's right shoulder but evinced no answering cry of pain, only a muffled grunt as Ulran slid full onto his stomach.

"Leave him, let him live!" called Por-al Row as the assembled guards gazed up at him half in surprise, half in anger at being robbed of their sport and revenge.

Trembling, the alchemist was barely able to control the pitch of his voice. He was well aware how finely the intruder's life balanced upon the thread of loyalty on the one hand and blood-lust on the other. "The king wants to see this assassin before the man dies!" he explained.

As he leaned forward, the tendons in his neck stretched. "Our liege promises that you may deal with the intruder after he has been forced to talk!" he lied. "I'm now sending down guards to put the assassin in his cell, to await the king's displeasure!" he concluded and thrust a finger at the two dumbstruck sentries by the doorway he had moments before entered.

"Go!" he snapped, "and make sure he lives!"

He forced himself to stand and watch, with his shaking knees threatening at any moment to collapse under him.

It seemed an age for the two sentries to drag the bleeding figure across the body-strewn courtyard and towards the cell doors set in the arcade below on the right.

Aware of the suspicious eyes of the battle-weary guards, he shouted down, "Guard him well! If he dies, be assured, the king's wrath will know no bounds!" And, imperiously, he turned and strode off the balcony into the spacious salon adorned with gold-painted furniture, brocade drapes and wild-bear skins.

With shaking hands Por-al Row stopped by a carved chest of drawers and opened a side-cupboard, withdrew a bottle of green liquid. Spilling some of this, he poured it down his throat, chin glistening wetly before he had drained it.

Slowly, his nerves came under control again.

***

Consciousness of a kind returned. Pain seemed to wash over him in waves, threshing against him, centring upon his head and descending to his torso and then his anguished extremities.

This he must conquer first, Ulran realised, trying to assemble cohesive thought after the timeless immersion in some horrible black pit.

Eyes shut, he forced his protesting body to lie supine and managed to convey messages to arms and hands that seemed apart from him to rest upon his forehead.

Slowly he lessened his breathing, moderated his rising and falling diaphragm, ignoring the objections his poor body made.

Ignore, ignore, and ignore. Calm, calm, calm. Assess, assess, and assess.

It took him longer than at any other time, but eventually he was in deep enough to survey the damage, which was severe.

The left-hand side of his skull was covered in blood, the majority having congealed since he entered his trance-state. The gash measured about a hand's-width, but the skull bone itself was only slightly cracked and had not been chipped or displaced.

Bruises were spreading and already encompassed almost the entire left side of his face, and beneath both eyes. Reasoning was not impaired, nor, he felt, would his reactions be, if he could but rest a short while and rebuild on the mauling he had taken. But this too relied upon the state of the rest of him, which he now began to explore, sending out mental sensory feelers, testing, probing, until he had discovered the full extent of the injuries.

One sword thrust had pierced his side, exiting at his back, barely missing vital organs; the second blade had doubtless been a thrust from the side, for it had dug into his torso beneath his stomach-muscle and exited above his navel, a clean thrust severing muscle fibre alone.

His right shoulder-muscle had been pulped but not beyond painful use. A bone had been chipped, also.

Considerable bruising, especially on his hands, showed where some guards had kicked and stamped on him whilst hidden from Por-al Row's view.

His appraisal completed, he slowly slithered out of his trance-state. But he continued to employ a part of his mind to blanket the surging spasms of pain from his damaged body.

Moving his throbbing head as little as possible, he sat up then pivoted, eyes attempting to penetrate the darkness of the cell. He stood up, and straw swished under him. Alone, even without the company of rats.

By touch, he began painstakingly measuring the cell.

The stairs numbered five, down which he had been thrown. Beneath these was a half-empty wooden bucket of stagnant water and another bucket brimful with excreta, flies buzzing contentedly.

The walls, once he had paced them out, each measured no more than three marks. The only ventilation was through the crack between solid door and door-frame: the place stank. He had no need to jump to test the ceiling's height; it forced him to bend as he walked.

Stooping, he crossed to the corner farthest from the rank-smelling steps and picked up the straw, smelled it, tested its texture.

Soft in places and not yet stale; the absence of vermin helped. It seemed they either replaced the straw frequently or previous prisoners had not wandered further than the steps; of course, unspeakable tortures might have rendered the straw beneath the previous occupant worthless, necessitating renewal; but why bother with even this modicum of "comfort"?

Using choice pieces of the straw, he stanched the wounds in his abdomen, shoulder and head. With powders from his inner tunic soaked in phlegm, he daubed the medicinal paste on his head and other wounds, and secured it there with a few pieces of gold-leaf and strips of his outer tunic.

If they left him alone long enough, the healing properties of the haemoleaf and gold would work. If...

***

Two orms after their previous meeting, while sunrise had been a full orm gone, Yip-nef Dom now strode into the gold salon ahead of his alchemist. He left in his wake an aromatic sekor-scent which quite nauseated Por-al Row. The odour too keenly reminded Por-al Row of Iayen, the witch!

The king stood for some time on the royal balcony, looking beyond the tower in the courtyard's centre. His visage crinkled in consternation as he watched the gaily caparisoned chariots enlisted for want of sufficient carts for their macabre role of funeral wagons. He had already given strict orders that the guards' bodies were to be incinerated that evening, to join the corpse caravans to the Manderranmeron Fault. So many, slain by *one* man!

When the king turned to break the long uneasy silence Por-al Row feared for his life, seeing in his liege's eye no sanity whatsoever, only a fiery redness.

"This one man has been subdued yet still lives?" Yip-nef's voice was icy cold, threatening.

"Yes, my lord. In – in the arcade cell."

"Is he hurt – wounded at all?"

Por-al Row swallowed, nodded. "Yes, they cut him down before I got – got to him – but he lives, sire."

"Good. I say *good* for your sake, Por-al Row. Now, tell me, can you guarantee me complete safety for these next six days? Will I live to see the First Durin of Lamous, eh?" His odd eyes had not left Por-al Row once, nor had he blinked.

Quickly, the alchemist nodded again. "I will see to it, sire. I'll treble the guards on the palace rooms, corridors–"

The king sighed, looked at the painted and sculpted ceiling. "I don't wish to know the details, man! Just make sure you guard me well, for if you should fail before my time comes on the First Durin, I pray the gods will let me linger long enough to silence *you!*"

And with that he stepped forward and brushed past his alchemist.

Then, at the door, he turned, making the enchanter start. "See to it the assassin is brought to my royal chamber after we have eaten!"

"Yes, sire."

"Oh, and... alchemist–"

"Sire?"

"Ensure he is guarded well!"

***

Mid-sun of First Sabin was overcast. A freak storm cloud drenched the stronghold city. Rain gushed without warning. Rivulets coursed down the cobbled streets, created treacherous cascades over the many steps and, from the soaking vantage points of the dozens of bridges, the road below them seemed like raging torrents.

Only those who had no option but to be out in the rain could be seen, scurrying under drenched cloaks from wall to wall, feet splashing upon the gleaming black stone.

As they dragged Ulran out of the cell, the overcast day seemed little contrast to the dim light of his cell.

Rain pattered loudly from the pillars and paving stones of the arcade.

His five captors bustled him roughly towards a double doorway at the end of the arcade, just forward of the soaked wooden seats beneath the royal balcony.

The courtyard glistened black and the solitary central tower loomed dark and windowless in front of swirling ominous blue-black clouds as the storm slowly passed over Arisa, heading for the plains of Floreskand.

***

Thoroughly soaked, chilled to the marrow, Alomar wrapped his hide cloak round Fhord's shoulders. He squinted through the wet cage bars and eyed the winking sun which attempted to force a few reluctant rays around the side of the retreating storm-cloud.

The troops had fared no better and were drenched and miserable.

But there was no point in stopping: the brush and timber was as wet as they were so they couldn't make a fire. Besides, Captain Dab-su Hruma had already sent a courier on the fleetest mount to inform Yip-nef Dom of their imminent arrival.

No later than the First Dekinma, he had said in the parchment. That would still leave the king four clear days before his mystical deadline. Ample time to use the captured red tellars; and more than adequate time to question his two prize prisoners.

Presently, mid-sun boldly showed and warmed them and steam began rising from the strange cavalcade.

The birds of the Overlord appeared the most bedraggled in that caravan and not for the first time Alomar wondered why they were being captured in such vast numbers. Yip-nef Dom had gone to insane lengths, it seemed.

The numbers of birds captured must be in the hundreds, if not thousands, judging by the soldiers' talk. And now Dab-su Hruma's caravan was joining up with two others, from the ranvarron and dunranron, and both hauled behind them no less than twenty large cages crammed with the same stonily silent red tellars.

More than before, the immortal warrior realised the time was approaching the deadline. He smiled grimly, forefinger and thumb absently curling his drying moustache.

Was this part of the Overlord's design, gathering all the elements together, converging on the First City, the black Arisa? But, more important, was it at all conceivable that he, Courdour Alomar, might find a clue to his long quest?

He shrugged and then removed the city-dweller's leggings and wrung them out.

***

The royal chamber also served as Yip-nef Dom's bedchamber. Fifteen marks by ten, its walls lined with ivory pillars that spanned up to a domed ceiling inlaid with gold and twinkling jewels, it always affected anyone on first sight. Smaltglass tiles upon the floor added to the scintillating splendour.

In the centre of the room stood a vast circular bed complete with flounced canopy and gleaming silver ornamental posts. Spread untidily upon the floor around the bed were seven silver trays with the remains of a large meal.

A short distance from the bed was a crack along the ceiling: this provided the king with much amusement. "I do not want to show you to this assassin, my dear – not just yet." He stood up, eyeing the ceiling crack as he scratched his hairy belly.

With her back to him, Iayen lay on her belly, naked little buttocks shining like porcelain, plainly languorous in after-love. "It would amuse me, though, to see him."

Stepping into his silken pantaloons, he grinned. "You shall, my dear, you shall." He strode across the room and pulled down on a thick sash sewn with threads of red, green and gold.

Presently, the ceiling crack registered a slight movement and an opaque film – a curtain – descended, shimmering in the coruscating light. When it was lowered completely, it blocked off the bed and the rest of the room.

"Now, then, can you see me clearly?"

"Yes," she giggled, and he heard the zithering sound of the silk bedclothes.

Perhaps he had time to –

"Sire, the prisoner is outside," intoned the door sentry on entering.

Damn!

Tying the sash about his flowing black-trimmed red robe, he ordered, "Bring in my seat. Get a move on!" He clapped his hands sharply.

In no time at all he was comfortably ensconced upon the lightweight throne at the right-hand end of the shimmering curtain and diagonally facing the double doors, his feet resting on a pile of cushions. Rings now adorned all his fingers; as a concession to Iayen he always removed them before –

"The prisoner, sire!"

Clash of accoutrements, some panting and squelching of sodden footwear then the group entered: five soldiers and three guards together with the assassin in the centre and the door sentry to one side.

"Stay there!" barked Yip-nef Dom imperiously, raising his bejewelled hand.

The group halted about eight marks from the throne cushions.

Yip-nef leaned forward, squinted. There was something familiar about this man, he thought, the hollow beating of unease in his chest. But it was difficult to see what he looked like, for even the soldiers looked unkempt after their soaking in the freak storm. Already, puddles had gathered at their feet.

And the assassin was certainly in a poor state. In the unnatural light of the royal chamber, Yip-nef could clearly see the gleam of dried blood on his head, shoulders and belly, and the clothes had been rent and slashed in many places. Strangely, straw and pieces of cloth appeared to be serving as makeshift bandages.

"What medication has he had?" Yip-nef enquired coldly, guessing the answer.

"None, sire – the scum murdered twenty-f–"

"*Silence!*" Yip-nef stood, kicked aside the cushions and his bare bejewelled feet padded with clacking sounds upon the smaltglass. "What manner of man wounded as he," he mused aloud, "manages to treat himself, I wonder?"

"Sire?" A puzzled look on the spokesman of the soldiers.

"What proof have you that he is an assassin, man?"

Roughly, one of the guards grabbed the innman's unresisting arm and shook the ring fingers in front of the king. Both the red ruby and the gildring shone.

Studying the ring-hand which now showed the beginnings of contusions, another flicker of recognition agitated the back of Yip-nef

Dom's mind. But it concerned the red ruby, not the assassin's ring.

He paled. "Let me see his face, quickly, man!"

Savagely, and with much pleasure, two soldiers from behind grabbed Ulran's disordered hair and heaved, jerking his head back.

He showed no sign of pain though the gash in his skull broke and blood gleamed freshly again.

The king stepped back a pace, aghast.

"You – in Por-al Row's visions!"

Head still held back, Ulran looked down at Yip-nef Dom, eyes narrowed. Sweat glistened on him as the pain from his opened skull wound jabbed insistently. He knew of Por-al Row and his alleged power. Now he thought he understood the headaches Fhord had suffered. He remained silent, studying the king who no longer appeared imperious and defiant but rather ashen and afraid.

"The innman! You're the innman!"

Through gritted teeth, the innman growled, "Yes, Yip-nef Dom, I am Ulran of the Red Tellar."

At mention of his name and the association with the Red Tellar, he felt the grip of the soldiers slacken a little. The whole city was afraid of the consequences of capturing the Overlord's birds, but still they feared their king more.

Pacing up and down now, eyes afire, mumbling incoherently to himself, Yip-nef Dom presented a fearful picture to his soldiers.

Ulran only observed a man see-sawing with insanity.

"Yes, yes, now *I* have it! Ulran – the runaway from the Kellan-Mesqa!" He barked aloud, an uncanny unnatural laugh. "Yes, that explains your friendship with the Hansenand!" And again he mumbled to himself, still striding up and down, his red robe flapping.

Suddenly, Yip-nef Dom sprang forward. The back of his hand swiped outwards, robe-cuff cracking.

Royal rings thudded into Ulran's left cheek, scored viciously, and the king skipped away, chuckling merrily, sucking the blood from the large ring-stone.

Raw and incisive, the anguish tore at Ulran's skull, threatening to lift the roof off his head. But outwardly, he showed no emotion at all. In the fogginess while he combated the new hurt, he could discern a tinkling sound, of childish giggling, and for a moment he wondered if perhaps Yip-nef had finally stepped over the rim into absolute insanity. If so, his life was as good as forfeit.

But as he came fully to his senses again he realised the giggling came from behind the shimmering wall – or rather, curtain – on their left. A girlish giggle. Sadistic. But who?

"A foretaste of what you can expect from my men, innman," chuckled the king, "when I finally return you to their tender mercies."

Unsettlingly, the king had regained his composure and sat back upon his throne. "It's a pity you are the incorruptible innman of the Red Tellar, my poor man," he went on in his sickly-sweet voice. "Anyone else, and I would have offered a pact. Tell me all you know about Lornwater's defences for your life."

He shook his head, pouting lips now red with Ulran's blood. "But no, you wouldn't turn against your adoptive city, the city that killed your family and ransacked your home! You're too *loyal*!" And he sneered as though addressing some filthy insect.

But Ulran was unmoved, though he found it difficult to maintain his position as wave after wave of punishing pain swept over him.

"Yes, Ulran, your beautiful Lornwater is raising column upon column of smoke, and destruction ploughs through the streets. My scryer sees all!" His real eye widened, glinting devilishly. "Looting, rape, fire and death! Your precious inn is under siege! Lornwater's civil war is working *my* way!"

Again Ulran spoke between clenched teeth, his voice surprisingly level. "An opportune time for you to attack, is that it?"

"Of course! I remember the last war between Lornwater and the manderon cities well – in 2009, but this will be the most savage, the worst by far. Yes, the war to end all wars for Floreskand. And *we shall win*!"

At that moment Por-al Row entered.

Recognition was instant: "Ulran," he breathed, suddenly trembling.

The innman's guards moved uneasily.

Suspicion tinged the king's narrowed eye. "How do you know his name, alchemist?"

Walking around the soldiers and the innman, Por-al Row replied, "The pieces fell into place almost immediately. I hadn't seen his visage clearly in my spells, and I had not seen him fight until last night in the courtyard. Only one man of Lornwater who is also an innman could fight in that manner. Once I recognised him as the innman and not an anonymous assassin, sire, it had to be Ulran of the Red Tellar."

"Very logical – and, doubtless, honest." Abruptly, Yip-nef swerved round, spat out, "Make the prisoner kneel!"

Ulran was forced to his knees. His head was still held painfully back, but his grim mouth remained firm.

"What are we to do with this illustrious innman, then, Por-al Row?"

Mind racing, the alchemist shrugged. "He'll never join us, I fear."

Clearly, the king knew nothing of the fight at the merchant's house, nor of the child-hostages or the capture of Bindar; for it had been through the traitor Elmar that he had learned of Ulran, including his name. "But perhaps, coerced, he could impart a great deal." And he rubbed his emaciated hands together, the corner of his mouth curving.

"I had in mind something of the sort, Enchanter. But I feel he is still far too stubborn to bend easily, without breaking him beyond use. No, I think we have time to bide, to soften him a trifle more, hmm?" And he cocked his head towards the shimmering curtain.

Yip-nef's back-handed blow caught the innman partially unawares, slapping into his right cheek. The guards grunted in pleasure. He felt a warm trickle from the corner of his mouth. His cheek stung, felt raw.

"May I compliment Por-al Row on his *seeing* powers?" the innman said. "Yet he hides the truth from you all, I see."

Por-al Row had been about to step forward to listen to the innman's praise when the last words penetrated and his face altered, paled.

"You are all destined to die on the fateful morning."

Yip-nef Dom looked up, startled by the innman's lack of forcefulness, his complete resignation to the pain he must be enduring and to the prophecy he uttered. "Is this the truth, Enchanter?"

"No, sire! No, of course not! He tries to divide us, sow seeds of doubt with his pernicious lies!"

Ulran chuckled grimly but said nothing.

The alchemist crouched in front of Ulran, though not too close. He scowled. "You lie, innman. In five days' time your precious birds will be slaughtered, every one! And it might be a good idea to slaughter you with them!" He spat.

Unmoved by the alchemist's spittle drooling down his cut cheek, Ulran said, equably, "Why kill the birds, why bring the Overlord's wrath upon you and your people?" Judging by the grip of his captors, he believed his words had troubled the guards.

"Why?" The king laughed as Por-al Row stood up. "In time, innman, in time you will learn!" Yip-nef kicked out, full into the innman's chest, but the blow was weak, the foot fleshy and unaimed.

"Take him back to his cell! I want him starving and thirsting! Do not harm him further, let hunger and thirst do their work! Now, go!"

***

Dusk was feathering the sky, darkening the cobalt-blue as Ulran was pushed and dragged along the now dry arcade and back to his cell.

He was flung down the stairs but managed to land on his feet, butting against the far wall.

He smiled thinly. So they desired that he fast. Then fast he would, on his own terms.

Calmly sitting cross-legged upon the straw in the far corner, he began to meditate upon the thin crack of light beneath the cell door.

***

"These precautions, they're going ahead well?"

"Yes, my liege," responded the enchanter, proudly looking around the enormous room.

The royal shrine salon measured thirty marks by eighteen, its teak-beamed ceiling twelve marks above and adorned with tall idols of every conceivable god, each hanging from a noose.

Along each wall, roughly two marks from the ceiling, was a single row of arched smaltglass windows, each measuring two marks across and divided by an ornate black-stone pillar.

Every vestige of other shrines, idols and the lesslords had been removed in preparation for the Rite of First Durin.

At the far end of the salon stood a marble dais – the royal platform – with three steps round its circumference. Behind the dais were four doorways, each with different coloured damask curtains, presently drawn back for the craftsmen and metal-smiths to pass through unhampered.

The only other doorway was the double entrance where they now stood.

Workmen filed back and forth. Woodcutters and metal-smiths busily constructed massive scaffolding and pulleys. Shavings littered the marble tiled floor. Two braziers puffed up smoke, glowing red-hot as smiths worked their metal.

"It will be ready in time?" It did not seem possible that the Rite's preparations could result from anything so disorganised.

"We require a full day before the rite, sire – yes, it will be ready."

And Por-al Row grinned. For although Iayen had a hold over the king, Yip-nef still wanted the promise the rite offered, and the promise meant more to him than any caresses the she-devil could provide. And once it proved successful, why, then Yip-nef Dom would discard her, for he would be seeking to sate himself on the world, not a mere witch-girl!

***

Ulran was in deep. Body inert. Breathing undetectable. He sat as though one dead. But in this state his body could begin its formidable task. Healing. Releasing the pain.

He was no-mind – save for one tiny piece of his subconscious that remained on the alert for any intruders into his cell or trance. For his excessive vulnerability had to be safeguarded, even at the cost of a valuable contribution of mind.

He sat and healed. Slowly.

***

True to his word, Dab-su Hruma led his caravan through the portals of Arisa on the First Dekinma of Lamous. His steel-grey eyes saddened for no cheering crowds came out to welcome his men, save for a few loot-hungry harlots. No praise for his captures, either.

His beloved city was afraid, as were his men.

He remembered with pride his return from other battles, when he had been a young soldier like these men he now led. Then, times had been different. He turned in his high saddle and looked at the caged prisoners. What glorious fighters we have become! he thought with deep and hurtful irony.

***

Alomar sat eyeing the city as it closed about them, black and forbidding, familiar to his ancient eyes. His memories of loosing that fateful arrow seemed of but a few years. He wondered how long it had been.

His companion lay asleep, a great deal thinner than before, but possessed of a wiriness of frame that belied her inner-strength, for Fhord's stubbornness to live had truly surprised the immortal warrior. She may cry occasionally, plead with her useless gods at times, but she was still a brave woman. And that was compliment enough from Courdour Alomar.

And what of Ulran? Two days back they had encountered some straggling soldiers still searching for the innman but to no avail. But was Ulran's track cold, as were his pared bones? In this land, even the innman might not have survived.

Morbid again, warrior? he thought with annoyance.

Growling, he spat into the street.

Fhord slept on.

***

The bird-cages were left at the side wall of the palace building. Above, the ropes and pulley dangled, the vicious hook waiting for another full cage. Of necessity, the stones of the palace wall had been removed, providing an adequate gap to accommodate the cages as they swung inwards. From there they would come to rest upon the broad landing and be wheeled through the double doors, into the royal shrine salon.

Captain Dab-su Hruma sighed, led his caravan round to the courtyard entrance-gate, and dismounted. Turning, he addressed his men. "Go gently with our prisoners, men – and bring them up after me. And guard them well!"

He entered a side entrance and walked without pride up the steep winding stairs, his sword, buckles and armour clanking and echoing as he ascended.

***

Inwardly, Ulran was shocked at his companions' appearance, though he realised to them he must seem just as bad. He hoped they felt as capable as he, eager to take advantage of any laxness in their guards.

At hearing of Dab-su Hruma's arrival, the king had ordered that Ulran be brought up into the preparation salon that adjoined the royal chamber. Here, kings of Arisa were dressed in all their finery for the state occasions.

But now the place was neglected and gaudy: Yip-nef Dom had no intention of wasting time with pomp and ceremony in his new reign following the rite. He had added that the innman be brought in chains.

So Ulran stood, inwardly refreshed from his meditations, with faculties at acute pitch because of his enforced fast. The chains that secured his wrists, neck and ankles hung limp, as if weightless beads on him. His immediate concern was for the welfare of his companions.

Neither Alomar nor Fhord recognised him at first. The innman studied them.

Hair was matted and unkempt, their clothes filthy and stained. Alomar's fiery eyes still retained their glint of ironic amusement but his pallor was unnaturally pale, tinged with blue; his right arm which hung useless could account for that, for it looked hopelessly swollen, discoloured grey, almost black. Fhord stood only with Alomar's support and she appeared to have grown thinner to the point of emaciation, her clothes hanging loosely. Fhord's eyes stared darkly, unseeing, out of white skull-flesh that appeared pasty and rough.

Then, as Alomar's steadily roaming eyes came to the innman his lips curled in an amused grin. "You made it, then?" was all he said.

With a chink of chains, Ulran nodded.

"Silence in my presence!" screamed the king. He was visibly trembling, unable to remove his stare from Courdour Alomar. "Bring the old one here, at once!" he commanded, voice breaking at the end of his order.

Alomar looked as though he debated the viability of felling his three guards and attacking Yip-nef Dom. But then he shrugged inimitably and looked up, unwavering.

"Kneel, dog!" Yip-nef demanded.

Captain Dab-su stepped back nearer the doorway as the guards forced the warrior down on one knee.

"After fifteen years, to finally have you at my mercy!" The king chuckled and spat in Alomar's face.

Alomar received the insult without blinking, his eyes dark and staring.

***

"You insolent–" the king coughed on more spittle, stepped back. After a racking coughing bout, he flung out his arms. "Away with him, take him away! I can't stand the sight of the swine! To the Tower of Ash with him!"

Dragged back to his feet, this time Alomar resisted and said, "Yip-nef! Before I go, tell me one thing."

The king held his head to one side, perplexed. He indicated to the guard to let the warrior have his say. "What?"

"What became of the baby and her mother, Yip-nef? Tell me that!"

Laughing on the verge of hysteria, the king snapped the slim chain about his neck and swung the glass pendant in front of Alomar's face.

Within the glass was a grey-green eye.

"I dropped her, Courdour, just as your arrow ruined my eye!" Pointing to his glass orb, he said, "So I took one of hers in payment!"

And he laughed even louder. At that moment a door to their right opened and a girl of no more than sixteen years entered, wearing a diaphanous dress bordered with gold lace.

As she neared, her young face came into full focus.

Half of her visage was horribly deformed, squashed upwards, save for the intelligent shining eye which studied the assembled men. Her other eye had been plucked from the unmarred side of her face, leaving a black pit which compounded her misbegotten lopsided appearance.

"That's her – my heir!" cackled Yip-nef Dom. "Iayen, named after her mother who died down the mines!"

The lopsided face changed subtly, evilly, and Alomar realised she was smiling dotingly at her accursed father. Fifteen years... It hadn't seemed that long ago.

"Your arrow did more than deprive me of an eye, Courdour Alomar," said the king, returning to a more sober mien. "It twisted her heart into hate, a hate more vile than mine."

He stepped back, sat upon one of two armchairs. He patted the other to his left. "When I hand over my *enlarged* kingdom to her, she will have no qualms about murdering Yip-dor Fla or anyone else!"

Iayen sat beside her father. She leaned over him and her dress folds fell from her small rounded shoulder, baring a young girl's pert breast. Cupping her hand to Yip-nef's ear, she whispered and giggled. Ulran recognised the malefic sound.

Yip-nef Dom's response was immediate.

He stood abruptly, one eye staring, head thrown back as he laughed aloud. "I have news for you all, my friends!" he said. "My royal prerogative has produced an heir of my own loins! Iayen is to have my child!"

An unsettled murmur arose from the soldiers there. But the three prisoners remained unmoved, fully aware that whilst incest was acceptable for royalty and for the gods, in the case of these two it was despicable and somehow obscene.

"Now," said the king, still standing, "take Courdour Alomar to the Tower of–"

"No, wait, please," came the soft voice of Iayen. Her jewelled hand rested on her father's.

She stood beside him, smiling crookedly. "Why not cut away his eyelids first, then he can savour every instant of his own death?"

King Yip-nef Dom chuckled then said, "Do as she says – remove his eyelids!"

And they took Alomar away.

CHAPTER NINETEEN
ASH

From Man to Ash to Fault.
— Creed of the Disbelievers

It was late into First Dekinma when Yip-nef Dom ordered Fhord and Ulran to be placed in separate cells.

Dab-su Hruma had excused himself earlier, claiming he was tired after the journey whereas in truth he was sickened by his king's behaviour. He left with his mind reeling. His hands groped against the stone walls of the winding staircase, his belief in his captaincy shattered. But what could he, one man, do?

His loyal men still awaited him, many dozing in the saddle. He shrugged off his depression and mounted up. "Come, men, I'll buy you all a well-deserved drink!"

And they rode out of the courtyard, hoofs clattering upon paving stones. The sound bounced from the narrow black streets.

In drink there was forgetfulness.

***

Fhord lay comatose and groaning, aware she was alone without the presence or comfort of Alomar. Her slow awakening was agonising and she was on the verge of tears.

How different this situation was compared with the glowing hopes she secretly harboured when she volunteered to accompany Ulran.

One by one the disappointments and privations had mounted, each atop the other, and now she lay, stinking in her own waste, bruised and wraithlike, her belly continually rumbling for sustenance. Yet she did not cry, though the temptation was great.

Her cell possessed a small barred window in the door and through this streamed the red glint of First Sidin's dawn.

And with the dawn was hope.

She wondered if that was a saying of Alomar's.

During their journey through Arion the immortal warrior had spoken often, and many times his meaning had been lost on her, but the comfort given had helped. More than comfort, though, she now realised.

She pressed herself against the dry wall and rose upon thin shaky legs.

Alomar had unknowingly instilled into her a sense of purpose, an iron unshakeable will that seemed to bolster her up even in this, her darkest time.

Half-remembered sense impressions came to her of last night. Yip-nef Dom's laughter, but not his face; Iayen's crooked visage swam before her, smiling wickedly; and Alomar, standing unbowed.

Panic welled in her – Ulran! Then she recalled the beaten shackled figure, so unlike the lordly innman, yet he too was unbowed.

She paced her cell, ordering her senses to ignore the hunger pangs. And all the while she tried tidying up her torn clothes.

Constantly she had to cast out of the back of her mind the day's prospect, for she was under no illusions that torture might be a good expedient for Yip-nef Dom, though she couldn't imagine what they could want to know.

In the cell next door but one, Ulran sat cross-legged again and controlled his breathing rhythm. Today, he knew, he would require all his reserves. And still the secret of the red tellars' proposed slaughter eluded him.

But the innman would get his answer soon. The soldiers came for them both and they were taken up to Yip-nef Dom's preparation salon.

Fhord felt near collapse with the combined weight of her chains but seeing Ulran and hearing his "Are you all right, Fhord?" made her bear the burden without complaint. She managed a nod in response.

Today, Yip-nef Dom and Iayen were ready for them.

Hooks and pulleys had been fixed to the ceiling beams during the night.

Now their wrist chains were hooked up and they were slowly raised, to dangle about a half-mark from the floor, ankle chains just above the tiles.

Ignoring the agonising pain in his shoulder, the innman cast a look at Fhord without betraying his concern.

Her face had paled even more and her mouth trembled slightly as she tried keeping it clamped shut against the cries of anguish she so wanted to utter.

"What do you want from us?" queried the innman.

Both Yip-nef Dom and Iayen were dressed alike in yellow flowing robes that trailed on the dais, jangling gold bracelets on their wrists. On their heads, at a jaunty angle, sat crowns of studded gems, Iayen's making her lopsided features all the more bizarre.

Without a word, Iayen walked up to the edge of the dais, her face level with Fhord's, and grabbed one of her arms and swung her round. Iayen was surprisingly strong for a young girl.

Chains clanged against each other. The ceiling beam creaked.

"Tell us, innman, what we want to know!" Iayen seethed and turned to face Ulran, ignoring the hapless Fhord whose eyes wavered with nausea.

Abruptly, Iayen turned, reached out, both hands clamping onto Fhord's shirt. She pulled down, ripping the garment to reveal Fhord's breasts, then cupped one in a hand, her pointed nails digging in and drawing blood. She purred, "Or you know who will suffer..."

Yip-nef Dom stood on one side, podgy fingers stroking his flushed cheeks. A she-devil incarnate, this had been of her devising last night, shortly after their debauched celebration of the conception. "Use the weak one against the innman," Iayen had advised. He tried adjusting his robes to conceal the arousal caused by Iayen's actions.

"What do you want from us?" repeated the innman.

"The red tellar–"

"Which one, you've got hundreds here?"

"Two thousand and fifty, to be precise," Iayen answered, arms now akimbo, single eye flashing defiantly. She licked Fhord's blood from her fingernails. "The red tellar that accompanied you, Ulran. Why did it lead you here? And by what means did you communicate with it?"

"No red tellar led us here," he replied. "We saw one a few–"

Iayen's double-fisted blow hit him full between the legs, and with the weight of chains he was unable to take any avoiding action.

The pain was slight compared to the rest of his body, but he was surprised at her strength. For a frail-looking young girl, she hit hard.

"Do not treat us like the fools you are!" she said, crossing back to Fhord.

This time she grabbed the city-dweller's belt and pulled downwards, until Fhord screamed, her wrists almost wrenched out of the iron cuffs.

"All right, stop!" barked Ulran. "I'll tell you whatever you want to know." There was no anger or defeat in his level voice.

"Good!" And she tugged at Fhord once more, forcing another cry from the city-dweller.

Then she left Fhord alone to her pain.

Standing in front of Ulran, Iayen said, "Go on, innman. Speak."

"The bird *was* leading us. Don't ask me why it came to the roof of my inn, I can't answer you that. It landed, carrying tied around its leg a parchment message."

Looking down at her then across at Yip-nef Dom, he believed they did not doubt him as he went on, "The message was brief. All it said was, 'Come to Arisa, quickly. Hundreds of the Overlord's birds are being captured by the king.' That was all."

The king and his daughter exchanged glances.

"Who could have betrayed us, father?"

Yip-nef Dom shrugged.

"Por-al Row, perhaps?" she suggested.

"No, why would he do that, since the scheme's of his devising? It doesn't make sense!"

A cunning look came into Iayen's eye. "You recall your hunting hawks?"

He nodded, looking askance at her, their two dangling prisoners momentarily forgotten.

"It seems strange, does it not," she said, "that your late lamented keeper's wife went down with a black fever shortly before the hawks disappeared."

Ulran interrupted. "That would explain the hunting hawks that set upon our guiding red tellar."

Iayen looked up, bangles jangling. "What happened to it – the red tellar?"

"Killed, after a grisly fight." He had no intention of going into detail.

Yip-nef Dom signalled for his daughter to join him and they both walked to the opposite end of the dais. Hand in hand, they whispered together.

Ulran looked across at Fhord.

The city-dweller was drenched in sweat, her clothes torn, shirt in tatters round her waist, baring a lean belly and bruised and cut breasts. Fhord smiled fleetingly, as though to say, "I will endure."

Ulran nodded, proud of her, and resumed his study of their enemies.

Four guards stood by the door, the others having been dismissed. Even the king, it seemed, did not wish to have too many witnesses to his incestuous relations and his open brutality.

The pair returned. "Your disclosures could be false, we find," said Yip-nef. "However, we shall look into the matter of the hawks."

"In the meantime," Iayen said, "we desire to know why you felt it necessary to come here in a hopeless bid to rescue a few birds."

"In my time as landlord of the Red Tellar I have studied the Overlord's birds," Ulran replied. "Their numbers are rare enough. I saw no point in senseless killing. So I determined to find out why they were being killed."

"But the parchment message mentioned no killing."

She was quick and astute, he realised. Never having been a man of falsehood, he had made a simple mistake. But his brain functioned as fast as hers: "Hundreds of birds are not captured to fill the cages of a zoo," he said scornfully. "Too many and you lose your public's interest."

"True," said Iayen, ruminatively. "So you assumed they would be killed?"

"Yes."

Again he beheld the travesty of a smile upon her crooked lips. "You intend us to believe you travelled all this way, crossing the Sonalumes and braving Astrey Caron Pass, on the basis of an *assumption*?" She shook her head, now studying her bangles, idly toying with them.

"Yes." Then he remembered Alomar, who might soon get his dearest wish – death. "That is correct. But I was intent on coming to Arisa by the established routes – until I met Courdour Alomar."

His friend's name alone affected both of his inquisitors.

He went on. "He mentioned the incident of finding you as a babe and his parting arrow. As I was travelling to Arisa and he was simply out for adventure, he decided to join me. But he insisted we approach Arisa from the dunsaron, bearing in mind his last visit. That is all."

Iayen nodded, turned, and pointed at Fhord. "And how does she fit into your company, innman?"

At this juncture Fhord answered before Ulran could formulate a suitable reply. "I'm a dreamer," she said weakly. "As you can see, I'm no adventurer." An ironic laugh passed her lips. "I talked Ulran into taking me with him. You see, I hadn't strayed outside the walls of Lornwater before. I wanted to broaden my horizons!"

Well done, Fhord. "That's what she told me," said Ulran. "I welcomed company. And we had no sense of urgency about the journey, either."

"I see..." She faced her father again. He nodded. "If you wish, father, though I see no reason to waste any further time on them."

King Yip-nef Dom grinned. "My dear, Trulan will squeeze a little useful information from them, I'm sure. Any information can only be an asset to our attack on Lornwater, don't you agree?"

"Yes, but–"

"*But* nothing, darling Iayen. I like my enemies to know the lengths to which my own cunning and skill go. It makes their suffering under Trulan all the more excruciating, knowing that all their endeavours have been wasted. A bitter pill to swallow, my dear, when you're pleading to be put to death."

Fingering the shackles about Fhord's ankles, Iayen said in a deep whisper, "Yes. I like that." Iayen pushed all her weight against Fhord and stepped back. Fhord swung pendulum-like, to-and-fro, yet this time she must have been anticipating Iayen's move for she didn't yell out though her face was suffused red with the effort of will-power to deny the little bitch that satisfaction.

"So!" Iayen exclaimed and ran across to Ulran.

The innman too was prepared. Her flurry of blows at his groin and thighs diminished after the first vicious onslaught, for her slight muscles weakened quickly.

Finally, she swung him as well, his wrists chafing on iron cuffs, but he would not give her the pleasure of even the movement of his facial muscles.

Round and round, dizzying, swirling, agonies shooting through his shoulder-wound, his head throbbing, his abdomen aching dully, his groin numb. And round and round, seemingly without end, the ceiling gyrating, rocking.

Then an abrupt alarming cessation, though his head still spun wildly, his body still.

"Hear me well, innman, and think on my words as you break under the skills of Trulan!"

Dimly he was aware of Fhord still swinging, the chains rattling, the wooden ceiling-beam groaning. What was Iayen saying? He must listen, concentrate.

"The sacrifice of your precious red tellars is necessary, innman," Iayen explained quietly, her transformation quite unsettling. Was the mad streak hereditary?

"Por-al Row has concocted certain arcane ingredients which must be mixed with the blood of freshly slain red tellars, and the mixture must be accomplished precisely at mid-moon of the First Durinma of Lamous, which is as you know the sixth night of the new moon – astrologically significant indeed!" She paused but received no response from the innman.

Ulran had guessed as much. But why?

"The potion will make my father invulnerable and with the same number of red tellars as the year – two thousand and fifty – there will be enough to administer to all his loyal soldiers. And Yip-nef Dom's invincible army will then ride on Lornwater, with their king in the lead!"

***

Edu-seren Grippore was one of Arisa's most accomplished surgeons and took great care when slicing off Alomar's eyelids. He was surprised and pleased to see that his patient possessed an iron control, sufficient not to blink, so that he did not have to use his local nerve anaesthetic, a derivative of the saur plant.

Eventually, he stepped back to admire his skill.

Blood filled the warrior's eyes, making the whites a rheumy pink.

As he left his patient with the king's enchanter, he thought it was most irregular to perform such surgery, particularly upon a naked man tethered securely in a chair. But the payment of two sphands seemed enough to stay any qualms of conscience.

Por-al Row studied the warrior intently. He had not mind-probed for almost six years, not since he made a disastrous mistake with one of his king's favourite concubines. The trauma reverted her to a child of four; and he had been badly shaken by the experience, barely escaping with his own mind intact.

But he had to know more about these men. The visions he had seen were too inconclusive, relying on his own interpretative ability. He felt in his bones that in some way these men could still endanger all his plans.

He placed his long thin fingers to his own temples and concentrated fully on Alomar's face, a stoic bearded visage with uncanny light-blue eyes beneath bushy brows.

It was a gradual process, more difficult to begin with, as he had to focus upon the blood-washed eyes, the life-fluid obstructing the man's inner eye.

Then his mind reeled, as though a massive hammer had crashed against his skull!

Steadying himself, Por-al Row shook his head and shakily began all over again.

Sweat soaked him before he reached the margin. This time he withstood the mental belabouring, yet gleaned nothing but flashing impressions, incidents, incredible action and violence, until his mind was over-flooded with information. There was too much, these thought-pictures could not conceivably come from one man's lifetime of experience!

Por-al Row sank back, baffled, and his head throbbed uncomfortably.

Many of the impressions remained with him, so forceful had they been.

"You will be left alone this night, Courdour Alomar, to contemplate upon the morning. Tomorrow you shall have an audience. Tomorrow you will learn how this Tower of Ash will destroy you!"

The alchemist left the circular room.

Blood spattered Alomar's chest and streamed down the sides of his face from his severed lids.

He had already established that the chair was bolted to the floor and a had attempted forcing the thick lashing of leather but there was no give at all.

As the alchemist said, there was nothing for it but to brood on his coming death in the morning. And, oddly, as much as he looked forward to joining Jaryar, he perversely wished to disappoint his enemies.

To die in battle, that he would not baulk at: but this, this he would resist, for resistance was in his nature as much as Jaryar was in his heart's-blood.

***

Por-al Row descended the winding stairs at the back of the circular Tower of Ash that stood in the centre of the courtyard. His head still throbbed from his experience with Courdour Alomar, but he would try the other two as well – *if* that she-devil had left them alive!

He entered just as Iayen was relating the purpose of his own diabolical scheme, as though it was of her own devising. He reddened and stepped forward, ignoring the presence of the guards.

He grasped the swinging form of the unconscious Fhord. "Sire," he said.

Iayen swerved round, only now aware of him.

"Yes, Por-al Row?" said the king.

"I would like to mind-probe these two, Your Majesty."

"What of Courdour Alomar?" Iayen asked before her father could reply.

"He is a mass of confusing and conflicting impressions – he isn't possible!" Por-al Row opened his hands, shrugged and turned away from Iayen. "Sire, I'm sure we may find out something of use to us."

"Try it, then, Por-al. But Iayen and I shall stay to watch."

This he had not anticipated. For after his experience with the warrior he was dubious about his ability. It was as though they were both scheming to trick him. Trap me into showing my limitations! As if I've ever claimed to be perfect!

He stepped forward, approaching Ulran first while Iayen clicked her fingers and sent a guard away.

As Por-al Row stared into the innman's forehead and concentrated he was outwardly aware of a bucket of water being brought in and thrown up at the dangling woman. Then he met something. Yes, he was getting somewhere. A mental contact.

But all he could perceive was an illimitable void, a state of no-mindedness which sent his own thoughts scurrying round and round as though in a vortex of air, lost without any reference points, and he had to make a dangerous conscious effort to break away, and found himself gasping and swaying drunkenly between the dangling bodies of Ulran and Fhord.

The witch-girl's giggling made him flush with anger.

He shook himself and faced the wet features of Fhord. Por-al Row was still surprised to find that Fhord was a woman. His scrying hadn't revealed that, only that this person represented some danger to him and his scheme. The woman's eyes rolled: she was not suffering from a nightmare but reality.

"Look at me, woman," Por-al Row whispered, and Fhord, curious and still hazy, looked.

Their eyes met. The mesmerising gaze of Por-al Row held, clamped onto those dark brown orbs. Because Fhord was still unsure of her predicament, the enchanter found an easy quick opening and glimpsed some knowledge of a red tellar actually communicating with someone – a man.

Then nothing, more like a white-stone wall, yet a burning orange glow emanated from behind it, quite unlike Ulran's no-mindedness. So! The woman, for all her apparent weakness and exhaustion, possessed a formidable mind!

Hastily, Por-al Row explained to the king what he had gleaned.

He was pleased to see that his reference to the red tellar communicating with someone had disturbed them both – even the imperturbable she-devil Iayen! "I believe my mind-probing could cut deep into this woman, if she were first softened by Trulan."

"I agree," the king said. He exchanged a look with his daughter and she nodded. "Send them both back to their cells," Yip-nef ordered. "Trulan can begin his work on them tomorrow. We still have three days to learn anything of interest before First Durin."

"And they pose no threat to us, anyway," added Iayen. "So if they should take longer to break, no matter."

"Yes, but–"

"No *buts*, Por-al," snapped the king. "You do not *but* Iayen! Now go and see to the preparations for the rite!"

***

Shortly after breaking their night's fast while the royal couple were still abed with the meal's remains discarded untidily on the fur rugs, Trulan the torturer was permitted to enter.

He was a gigantic bull of a man, almost two marks tall, his girth capable of equalling that of two men. Muscles bulged from his neck and arms, as his torso was traditionally bare. Doubtless his thighs were as well-proportioned beneath the grey-wool breeches he wore which were tucked into calf-length leather boots. He was shaved completely on his right side only, again a tradition perpetuated by master torturers.

Iayen appraised him. Her thin tongue contemplatively licked her scarred lips. The big man felt her eyes upon him and stood uncomfortably awaiting the king's command.

"Have you seen the prisoners, Trulan?" Yip-nef Dom enquired as Iayen helped him shrug into a silk dressing gown.

The torturer bowed, muscles rippling. "Yes, sire, I believe we would be wasting our time with the one in the Tower – also the other – the–"

"The innman?" interjected Iayen, her eye caressing him.

"Yes... him. I would recommend concentrating completely on the woman. She looks easy to break."

"You may then begin on her, Trulan. Her name is Cobrora Fhord."

"Thank you, sire. I shall begin at once." He smiled, revealing a mouthful of broken teeth.

Later, Yip-nef Dom – humming contentedly to himself with Iayen by his side – welcomed the surgeon, Edu-seren Grippore. "Por-al Row, my alchemist, tells me you performed a masterly piece of surgery, my dear doctor."

Head bowed and talking to the tiled floor, Edu-seren falteringly said, "I have tried to please, Your Majesty. I'm only sorry to disappoint you today, but I think–"

"*Disappoint*, Doctor?" The king's tone had altered frighteningly.

Trembling visibly, Edu-seren said, "Yes, sire. My patient, the man Courdour. Really, to use his eyes effectively he needs another day's rest."

Disconcertingly, the king laughed. "Another day's rest, you say?"

"I've just returned from my morning inspection. Sire, he – his blood hasn't fully congealed. I think it has something to do with his wound. I think his right arm could do with treatment, it's–"

"His arm?" said Iayen, her single eye wide.

Still the doctor did not look up, nor had he done so since entering the royal presence.

Silence grew between them, making the old man uncomfortable; he so wanted to look up, but surely common folk did not face royalty eye to eye.

Then the great double doors opened on rumbling hinges and a roumer hastened in, his clothes dusty from a long ride. "Your Highness, news of Lornwater!" In his mud-stained hand he gripped a thick scroll of parchment.

Yip-nef Dom leaned forward, said, "Excuse me one moment, Doctor." He stepped down from the dais and brushed past Edu-seren. "Good or bad, man? Tell me!"

It was succinct, bare of the gory detail he wanted to hear. Nevertheless, the news was good. Civil war was in full spate, the palace of Saurosen IV was under heavy siege while pockets of his force still fought outside the New City. Fire raged and people were fleeing the city in droves. The nearest townships were brimful with refugees and the pall of smoke could be seen for launmarks around.

Iayen joined him and read the parchment over his shoulder. She sighed with annoyance. "You want a city, dearest, not a heap of rubble. What conqueror's prize is a burned-out shell?"

At her forthright appreciation his countenance soured. He flung the scroll back at the messenger. "Damn you, man, how long did you take getting here?"

Though taken aback and fumbling with the scroll, the rider replied steadily enough: "Ten days, sire – without rest."

"Good," said Iayen, impressed. "Then you have earned a rest now, messenger." And she delved into her waist purse and tossed him a sphand, which he caught adroitly, eyes like saucers at sight of such wealth.

Having dismissed him, Iayen said, "With our invulnerable army, dearest, you could be in Lornwater by the Third Dekin of Lamous, welcomed as a *saviour*!"

Ignoring the doctor's presence, Yip-nef smiled. "Yes, I will be saving them from themselves. It fits so beautifully, Iayen! They'll believe it, too."

Again the door opened, and the city crier entered, panic etched on his porcine face. "Sire, I have distressing news!"

"Out with it, Crier!"

"Five influential merchants have gone missing, Your Highness! Watchmen investigations have revealed that they were involved with the man Grayatta Essalar who escaped your trap on–"

"*My* trap?"

"The raid on Grayatta Essalar's house, sire – when that fellow Bindar killed all those poor soldiers then escaped himself. On the Fourth Sufinma of Darous, sire."

So. Por-al Row had some answering to do, Yip-nef thought, exchanging a knowing glance with Iayen. "Go on, Crier – these five merchants were involved with this Bindar fellow, you say?"

"No, sire – Bindar's in your cells, exchanged for those ten children." This time Yip-nef remained quiet. "Grayatta. But the most distressing news, sire, is that Dab-su Hruma, your third-captain has disappeared."

"Dab –?" Then he remembered: the captain who brought in Courdour and Fhord. "What signs, Crier?"

"Foul play is not suspected," the crier ended sotto voce, seemingly aware of the implications of this disclosure.

"Then he has gone missing of his own free will?" queried Iayen, surprise arching an eyebrow.

Dumbly, the crier nodded.

"All right, you are dismissed!" snapped the king ungraciously. He turned to see the now quailing doctor still facing the empty thrones, his head bowed as before. "You may leave, Doctor – your patient has his extra day for healing! Now go!"

In ill-humour, Yip-nef stamped towards his throne. "Iayen, my love, ring for the first-captain, will you?"

When he arrived the first-captain was ordered to instigate an immediate search of every house and shop, within and without the palace walls. Dab-su must be found, dead or alive.

And when the first-captain had hurried to do his king's bidding, Yip-nef Dom growled, "Iayen, it is time I paid another visit on my dear cousin." He rose, descended the dais steps. "Are you coming?"

She shook her head. "No. I would perhaps lose control and rid you of him for good."

He sighed. "Sometimes I wish I were more like you, my daughter. But this dread in me won't let Yip-dor Fla be murdered whilst I am king."

Iayen nodded, as though saying, "So be it."

***

Guards dragged Ulran and Fhord in chains through the echoing black-stone corridors beneath the royal courtyard. They passed a small torture chamber illumined by smouldering red coals. Within, upon a blood-spattered rack, lay the spread-eagled body of Bindar, his red hair cropped and baring a bruised skull, his impressive body stretched and drawn.

Though hurried on, Ulran detected the faintest vibration of a powerful heart, fighting for continued life. *For me, Bindar had come to this.* Yet both knew there was no obligation on either, implied or otherwise. If the roles of circumstance had been reversed, Ulran would have done the same.

"I'll return to that stubborn one later, after I've broken you, little woman!" Trulan the torturer said and chuckled as he waited for them at the doorway of the lower chamber.

Trulan led the way. They descended well-worn steps into an infernal place lit with red torches that lent the cavernous chamber a hellish hue. Trulan said, cheerfully, almost conversationally, "This lower chamber has a nice atmosphere, don't you think? An aroma all its own!"

The stench of decaying carcasses rose to meet them. Fhord retched on a strained and empty stomach and bitter bile moistened her lips. Now they could discern various metal contraptions standing in the centre of the chamber, and upon the walls hung hideous-looking pincers, knives and prongs. "Tools of my trade, you see – each one with a special purpose – to extract truth!"

Chains still jangling, they were led across to the far wall, opposite the staircase of stone. Here, the sentries snapped more shackles on them, firmly securing both Ulran and Fhord to ringbolts in the rough-hewn wall.

"Yes, this is all necessary, you see," said Trulan, "to get the subject into the right frame of mind."

Ulran was unimpressed by Trulan's antics. The torturer's performance so far showed him plainly to be an adept of Lornwater's own torture training school, whose sessions Ulran had often watched, studying the psychology behind torture and also the minds of the men eager to become master torturers.

Trulan walked over to a large spit supported above a long wide brazier of smouldering coke. "This is my favourite." His biceps bulged as he manipulated the enormous bellows to produce gusts of flame and a deeper reddening of the coke.

"I can see you are unimpressed, innman," he went on, his back to them. "But as far as I'm concerned you are at the moment merely a spectator. I have my eye solely on your Cobrora Fhord here." He turned in time to see Fhord edge away as far as her chains would allow. Trulan grinned. "Yes, this is all for you, young woman!"

***

Yip-dor Fla stumbled drunkenly across the confined cell, his mouth dribbling blood. As he cannonaded into the cell wall, his cousin's high-pitched laughter rang in his ears.

"Your cousin has an heir budding in Iayen's belly, Fla! How do you like that, eh?" Yip-nef walked forward, heaved Yip-dor Fla to his feet and struck him repeatedly with his vicious, damaging ringed hand.

If Yip-nef Dom had been brave enough to enter the cell alone, Fla would have fought back. But a long time ago he had learned to his cost: the two armed guards had beaten him insensible with their spear-hafts the one time he had retaliated against Yip-nef. But he would not let his spirit succumb as easily as his body. "Your days," he mumbled defiantly, spitting out a tooth, "are numbered – First Durinma will be your time of reckoning, Dom, not mine!"

He paid dearly for his defiance, but short of some insane mistake he would survive, he thought and blacked out.

***

Fhord felt strangely quiescent and had done so ever since they shackled her to the broad ironwood beam that served as a spit. She lay on her back, with the rotary spit between herself and the brazier fire.

A whole orm had passed since the guards left and still Trulan was having some difficulty with the fire. He forced the bellows repeatedly down, but all he managed was a few stray sparks and gusts of choking black smoke.

She smelled completely of charcoal, and coughed almost continually. Sweat poured from her, not from fear, but with the warmth from below. Surprisingly, she thought, the torturer had refrained from stripping her completely and had only torn off the remains of her shirt, baring her torso.

"Can't understand it," murmured Trulan, huffing and puffing over the bellows. Then, in an aside to her, he said, almost reassuringly, "Don't worry, Fhord, I'll have you roasting nicely in no time. I'm doing my best."

Then, at last, flames erupted. A deepening red, the crackling of fuel-gases. "Ah, that's better." He flung the leather bellows to the floor where they loudly slapped down. "Yes, warmer already, are we? Good, good."

To her own surprise Fhord began objectively studying the torturer's psychology. It was as though the man only lived to inflict pain yet talked and talked to his victims to convince them that he really meant no harm, he couldn't help himself. The thought, perversely, amused her and she smiled thinly.

Strangely disconcerted at sight of her smile, Trulan said, softly, "One rotation at a time. Slowly does it."

The beam began to move. Slowly.

Fhord rotated side-ways to her left, slipped a little as she went round but the chains caught her with a jolt. She lay stretched out above the burning coke and could feel her face and chest flush red with the heat waves wafting upwards.

Then she was moving, rotating, thankfully away from the intense heat, completing full circle. She sighed with relief as she slumped back onto the ironwood beam.

Her body suddenly broke out in beads of sweat that lathered her, some dribbling off and into the fire with harsh hissing sounds.

"We'll take it gently, you see. Get you accustomed to it, so you'll begin to expect it before it actually comes. You see my meaning?"

Talk, talk, and talk. Rotate, rotate... Warmer, warmer... Hotter, hotter... Over and over again.

When Fhord had first entered the lower chamber she had sensed an evil presence, though she had not been surprised. But now she felt she could actually identify the entity here. It was as though the whole chamber were permeated with the aura of Honsor, black lord of fire. One of the strongest, most evil lesslords in existence. She felt weak at the thought alone.

After each rotation and the singeing of her leggings and hair she could almost feel her little remaining strength of will and body dribbling off with the out-pouring of sweat. As if the resultant hissing was Honsor's demonic laughter.

Though at least four marks away, Ulran could feel the heat from the brazier beneath Fhord. He marvelled that she had suffered so much without even a murmur. But she could not take much more, surely? Ulran tested the strength of his chains; but the ringbolts were secured fast. Yet still he heaved. His aching body cried out in protest – and was ignored.

Fhord's mouth curved in a grim stubborn smile as she faced the terrible heat once more. Again, she looked into the red-hot coals through slit eyes that streamed with tears and sweat.

"You're doing well, Cobrora Fhord." Trulan rubbed his hands as he left her suspended over the fire a little longer than before. "You have my compliments. Yes, you've done well – so far," he ended ominously.

And still Fhord smiled grimly as the skin of her face blistered and the smell of singed hair and clothes filled her nostrils, stronger than charcoal and all else.

The smell of Honsor.

***

While they watched the preparations for the rite begin to take shape out of the former chaos, Yip-nef Dom said, "You're sure the potion will work, Por-al Row?"

Seething within himself, the alchemist nodded. *After the way he has treated me recently, he still comes begging reassurances! By the gods, if only my powers hadn't waned of late with all the demands he has made on me! Then I would brew something appropriate for that she-devil!* "Yes, sire, it won't be long before you are invincible – Lord of Floreskand!"

"And you say the after-morning has been set aside to view Courdour's demise?"

"Indeed, sire. But now, if you will excuse me, I must descend to the lower chamber to probe the mind of Cobrora again. I think she should be just about ready!"

The alchemist backed out of the salon, bowing.

Iayen appeared from behind a curtained doorway at the rear of the dais. "Why didn't you question him further on the man Bindar, and the merchant Grayatta, father?"

"Oh," shrugged Yip-nef, "he works for me now for fear of you. But he still believes he has my trust even if you possess my heart. As long as he believes that, he can prove useful – at least until the rite. Afterwards, well..." And he shrugged expressively. "But were I to begin asking him too many awkward questions, he might learn to distrust my intentions. And he could be a dangerous opponent, Iayen."

"Then have him slain."

The king smiled. "That's your answer for everything, my sweet. But whilst he is useful, he must live. After the rite, you may deal with him as you see fit."

She smiled.

He had a twinkle in his eye. "And I would like to watch!"

***

Trulan hummed to himself and stoked the fire and said over and over, "Give in, Fhord, you can't last!"

Ignoring the torturer, Por-al Row concentrated on probing Cobrora's mind. He was somewhat disturbed to see she had withstood the fire for so long.

"Three orms," said Trulan, as though proud of his victim's achievement.

A blank white wall, with that orange glow, as before; a barrier that showed no sign of a breach whatsoever. Not without a tinge of envy, he wondered how could such a weak specimen withstand so much?

"I'll return later, Trulan. If she feels like talking in the meantime, send word to me. Do you understand?"

Trulan nodded and contentedly rotated the human spit again, Por-al Row forgotten.

As the alchemist departed he cast a baleful look at the innman who was ineffectually straining at the wall-chains. He shook his head, face burning. At least Courdour Alomar's death will cheer me up, he thought.

***

After-morning sun beamed upon the royal courtyard. A scattering of nobles had arrived early and occupied the foremost seats facing the clear-glass front of the Tower of Ash. The tower stood ten marks tall and showed through the glass to be almost two-thirds full with ash. Wooden poles criss-crossed about a mark above the surface of ash. The top of the tower was boarded up.

A fanfare warned of the imminent arrival of the royal party and entourage.

All those present hastily stood as Yip-nef Dom, hand in hand with Iayen, stepped forward onto the balcony above the wooden benches. They sat and the nobles followed their lead.

The king was already drooling. And Courdour Alomar had not been brought out yet. "After so long," he whispered feelingly, "revenge at last!" His solitary eye flashed in the sunlight. And, solicitously, his daughter laid her hand on his.

Revenge today, the historic rite tomorrow! All's well with the world – and damn Fla to ashes!

***

Fhord suffered. Scorching-hot branding irons pressed down hard upon her abdomen and breasts, burning into blisters. The body-suppuration sizzled. And still she fought back cries of anguish.

Honsor hovered. She could feel the foul presence close by, as though salivating with anticipation, to burn up this meagre offering.

Ulran had lapsed into a semi-trance and mustered hidden subconscious reserves. He knew full well that if he exerted such reserves for any lengthy period he would later be as weak and as helpless as a babe. But he must attempt saving poor Fhord, before she was too far gone. He gouged and rubbed a link of chain against the mortar surrounding the stone-block where one of the ringbolts was attached.

***

Within the Tower of Ash, Alomar stood in the centre of the round room, two marks in front of the chair in which he had spent the previous day. His wounded arm had not deteriorated further. The doctor's ministrations might even have saved it – for what, though?

In a tempting bundle to one side lay his lacquered armour-plating, complete with leggings, cuirass and chainmail, sword, shield and helmet. But as six spears completely surrounded him, he shrugged. Tempting his accoutrements might be, but he could resist that kind of enticement! He wondered at the small weights about his waist.

Without warning, the floor beneath him gave way and he fell a distance of about three marks onto a criss-crossing of round wooden poles.

Lidless eyes wide, he quickly appreciated he was in full view of an audience below, all pointing at him, laughing and talking.

The trapdoor above slammed shut before he could stand and attempt jumping up.

He now understood why the tower had been so named. Black ash showed below through the gaps between the poles.

Abruptly, one of the poles moved and was pulled out.

He understood at once. So, a dance of death!

The audience mostly stood now, waving fists and cheering, many of the women as bad as their men.

As another pole was retracted and another, he saw Yip-nef and Iayen laughing together. But no anger crossed the immortal warrior's face; he was too intent on guessing which pole would next be pulled from under him.

One slip and he would speedily sink into the ash, aided by the weights round his waist.

Another pole was removed and he skipped back. The loss of his lids was annoying. He had to keep wiping away the salty stinging sweat and yet concentrate on the poles as well.

It appeared they were being retracted purely at random.

Yip-nef Dom vacated his throne and jumped up and down by the balcony baluster, wishing the warrior would slip.

Iayen too was smiling, her misshapen features hideous in the bright clear light of day.

Suddenly, a cheer went up from the audience below.

Yet another pole was removed and Courdour Alomar jumped to safety, tottered and almost lost his balance.

Righting himself barely in time, he skipped away onto another pole as the one beneath his feet rolled and moved, swiftly withdrawn.

"Not long now!" Yip-nef said, spitting as he spoke. "Look, Iayen! There can't be more than six poles left!"

"Yes, dearest, he is too big to balance on only one – it won't be long now!" She drew beside him, encircled his waist with her thin arm, arousing him. "Afterwards, we must celebrate your triumph, father!"

"Yes, yes, my love – but look, look, he *nearly* went then!"

***

Sensation had left Fhord but recently, bewilderingly. Her senses had suddenly attenuated, rising to a peak she had never known. It was as if she were no longer physical, as though the threshing, lancing pain were other than her own.

A threshold, as if she had stepped into a different chamber, somewhere without the presence of Honsor.

Could it be delusion? Delusion before death?

Her eyes still recorded images, but the lower chamber had altered, seemed brighter.

The walls shone white and shimmered. And at the centre of all this whiteness she vaguely discerned a white shape on white. An inchoate symbol formed, shaping itself on the apparently reed-paper-thin walls.

As the symbol changed, gleaming with incredible effulgence, she saw flames of white. Fire. White-fire – Osasor!

***

Against all odds, Alomar had managed to balance upon the depleting number of poles. Now, the immortal warrior remained perched upon the final pole. But his efforts were inevitably doomed to failure, and finally this too was retracted.

Though unable to hear the almighty cheer that went up from the audience, he caught sight of them, mouths gaping, eyes starting, fists in the air.

Then he fell into the ash.

Choking clouds blanked out his view of the death-hungry crowd. Yet even with the small weights about his waist, Alomar was determined to deny them their pleasure for as long as he was able.

No sooner did he hit into the ash than he began to dog-paddle in an effort at keeping his head above the choking stuff. This proved difficult for his right arm was weak, swollen and almost lifeless, but it moved if stiffly.

He managed to remain with his chin just above the surface of ash, his eyes watering as grains grated against the lid scars. But he continued to paddle, fighting the weights, ignoring all else.

The day had been long. The audience had not appreciated the passing time as they watched till they grew hoarse.

Dusk approached.

The crowds gesticulated and hissed and booed as twilight fell.

Alomar smiled grimly, pleased at their annoyance.

And he continued to paddle, creating choking gusts of ash-cloud that stung his streaming eyes.

Though his thoughts repeatedly returned to Jaryar, he knew this time she would understand. Perhaps he would succumb to the choking dust and sink in time, but as long as he was able, he would fight it, and cheat them all of their sport.

If die he must, it would be with honour.

CHAPTER TWENTY
RITE

> The gong sounds the orm of rites unholy
> And stirring the creatures of Below
> Evil rears and stalks the lonely
> Frightened people with nowhere to go.
> – *Night* from
> *The Collected Works of Nasalmn Feider* (1216-1257)

Outside the palace walls, the noise of the king's blood-lusting guests drew crowds of the curious and the morbid. The Tower of Ash was held in great awe – it contained countless rebels and visionaries who transgressed against the accursed Por-al Row. Ash was so much a part of their minds – everyone was incinerated on dying, without exception. Ashes were regularly transported to the Manderranmeron Fault and dumped – save for the honoured few. Kings and those of the royal lineage had their ashes interred in the cellar vaults of the palace. Traitors and rebels had their ash left within the tower.

Gradually, as the evening's shadows deepened, the crowds dispersed. But a few remained.

"Whoever they've got in there is keeping them in suspense!" said a stooped old man in an entranceway.

"'Tis the warrior – Courdour Alomar."

"The one who loosed the arrow?"

"The same. This time Yip-nef and Iayen – curse her to ashes! – have gone too far. Legend has caught up with them, old man, at last!"

"What ails you?" queried the old man. "You sound treasonously disenchanted with yon two royals!"

"Aye, I'm more than disenchanted, friend – I'm sick unto death. When I think of all those years – wasted, ruined now. You see before you an empty man, broken in spirit, afraid to–"

"Afraid? Never, not you! But listen, this Courdour fellow still has them going hoarse! What I'd give to see it! No, friend – if you dare speak out – aye, even in shadows – you're a braver man than most of Arisa can boast."

"But I've turned my back on–"

"If you lead, they'll follow, you know."

For the first time in a long while, a lively light shone in Dab-su Hruma's eyes.

***

In the darkness of First Sufinma the courtyard was silent, illuminated by shagunblend torches in sconces upon the palace walls.

The benches were deserted save for the figures of Yip-nef Dom and his daughter. Both huddled close and involuntarily shivered as they watched the indistinct bobbing head of Courdour Alomar.

The warrior continued to dog-paddle in the mushrooming clouds of ash.

As the beginnings of the first quarter cast its silver light upon the scene, Yip-nef Dom rose and shuddered with subdued anger.

His daughter joined him as they strode down the benches and out through the wrought-iron gate, entering the palace through a side-door. Above, a cage of red tellars swung on its pulley, abandoned for the night.

"Tomorrow..." the king murmured, dejected. "Tomorrow, I shall become legend!"

***

As the royal couple left the courtyard, Fhord's mind reached out and ignored the pains and the sickening stench of her own roasting body.

She was heartened by her so-white vision.

Her smile at seeing white-fire remained fixed.

It pleased her to see that her inquisitor appeared sorely troubled.

***

King Yip-nef Dom rose early. Having dressed himself quickly, he hurried through his apartments to the royal balcony. Through here the First Durin's sunlight streamed.

A fresh day, a momentous day, he thought, shaking off the dejection of last night. He only regretted he had been unable to see Courdour's last moments of life –

His single eye stared and his fleshy face paled as he leaned over the balcony. *No, it isn't possible!*

Yet Courdour Alomar was still there, ponderously paddling amidst the clouds of ash. The warrior was even grinning down at a few watchers in the courtyard who were calling him names and cursing over their lost wagers.

Burned out torches issued intermittent purple wisps of smoke across the scene.

At that moment Por-al Row approached the king. "Excuse me, sire, but the time nears..."

Shocked by the alchemist's soundless approach, the king swung round. "Eh – what? Time, time for what?" The spectacle of the Tower of Ash had sent his brain scurrying madly. Then slowly he comprehended. "Oh, the sacrifice! Already, Enchanter? But the rite isn't until tonight."

Por-al Row put on a pained expression. "If you will recall, sire, I warned you that your own personal preparations would take some time. We must begin early, to accomplish all you desire this eve."

"Damn your–" Yip-nef bit back on his words. "Very well, but let me join you in an orm's time, in the shrine salon. In the meantime, I shall be closeted with my daughter." He sighed. "It is a pity you cannot project Courdour's death into the salon. I would have liked to see..."

Sudden cries of delight from outside interrupted.

Heart hammering, Yip-nef hastened to the balcony.

Courdour Alomar finally sank beneath the surface of ash, close up against the glass so that they could see most of his naked figure and, surprisingly, he had folded his arms. He remained visible against the glass walls as he sank, his face impassive, as though resigned, without any fear or panic etched there.

The king, Por-al Row, the audience – all of them watched enthralled as the warrior slid down against the glass walls without protest. Then he slithered back, into the depths of the ash, out of sight.

Whispers wafted up. No man had ever accepted suffocation in this manner – none! Usually victims had screamed and cried, ineptly attempting to struggle but only succeeding in pushing themselves down faster.

Troubled, Yip-nef Dom turned on his heel and left the salon. In a way, Courdour's final gesture of defiance had robbed him of the sweetness of revenge. But at least the man was dead! Soon his ashes would be part of those already there.

As he left, the trapdoor above the ash opened and the soldiers threw down the immortal warrior's accoutrements for the gear was too weighty and ancient for any Arisan to wear or wield. They sank quickly without trace.

***

Strength from Fhord knew not where filled her being. She was apart. As though floating above, she saw herself stretched out upon the ironwood spit, turning and sizzling as her earthly body scorched and blistered, reddening horribly.

And the torturer of Honsor bent to the handle, turning, turning, and talking all the time with words that melded into one long half-muted chant.

She could see herself still, apart, as the fire-ravaged figure that was Cobrora Fhord strained at the metal shackles which had gradually become red- then white-hot.

Suddenly the chains broke away and she sat up amidst an abrupt cavorting of flame. But these were not tongues from the torturer's brazier: these flames seemed to sprout from the very air itself, licking towards the dark ceiling of the chamber.

Darkness no longer existed in the low chamber. Darting white flames flecked with the faintest tinge of blue sought out the smallest corner. Blinding bright.

Ulran had seen something to fell his stoical calm.

The torturer stepped back, hands covering his sweat- and smoke-streaked face.

But their eyes no longer remained on the sitting figure of Fhord. Now they looked upon the intrusive white flames themselves.

"A battle 'tween Honsor and Osasor!" screamed the torturer in tremulous realisation. He stumbled back towards the wall near Ulran.

Fhord staggered off the rack, landed upon the stone flags amidst a spray of upset charcoal from the brazier. She was burnt and ragged. Her flesh sizzled as she walked jerkily, her hue red – as red as the sunset. And one eye would not open, damaged by a multitude of wicked sparks.

Yet on she walked, amidst the flashing shadows by the dancing flames.

While behind, just beyond the forsaken brazier, flames of white and brown-black spat and gyrated in tumultuous silence. Their very movement shook the entire chamber.

Trulan ineffectually tried shielding himself from the incredible heat that emanated from the battle and the approaching figure of Fhord.

Ulran strained again at his shackles.

The scorched city-dweller diverted her inexorable tread, and moved towards the innman. At sight of her, Ulran involuntarily flinched. Fhord lurched towards him, the stink of her burnt flesh clogging the innman's nostrils.

Bones were now visible in parts. Bubbling body-fat was on her shoulders, drooling down her burned-red and branded breasts. It was as though Fhord was being burned up alive from *within*!

Then she was upon him.

The stench was asphyxiating. Smouldering hands fell upon Ulran's chains. Nails had gone; the bones of her hands glinted red as they snatched hold of the chains near the ringbolts.

Transfixed, Ulran watched as the chains in her grip whitened and snapped as if they were only brittle reeds.

Trulan jerked out of his immobility and shock. His captives were attempting to escape, no matter by what hideous means. He rushed forward, snarling loudly, and snatched up a halberd from the wall.

Fhord dropped the broken chains and turned unsteadily. Flames now began to sprout from her neck and engulfed her entire head. Ulran found the sound and smell overwhelming. It was uncanny but while Fhord burned and sizzled, she still retained her basic appearance.

Suddenly unsure, Trulan stopped with his halberd pointed in front of him. But the torturer was lost, his mind no longer his own. Fhord's now blind dark coals of eyes drew him unwillingly.

Hands suddenly limp upon the weapon, Trulan lowered it as he approached Fhord. There was little struggle of will, for Trulan's mind was not capable of this form of contest.

As Ulran stepped away free from the wall, short lengths of red-hot chain hanging from each wrist, he noticed for the first time that, despite the flames, no smoke filled the chamber. Only raw fire, an intense conflagration that seemed without surcease.

Ulran watched as he had never seen the like before; he was filled with a morbid fascination and buoyant admiration for his travelling companion, the quiet psychic woman. As he watched he rubbed his arms, relaxed his body in degrees and slaked off the weariness of his earlier attempt at calling up reserves.

Finally Trulan walked into Fhord's out-stretched flaming arms.

They fell together, embraced, and upset the burning charcoal brazier. The fire's contents spread across the floor. The coals bounced and burst into fresh red flames, a kind of phosphorescent incandescence that briefly blinded the innman.

In an almighty roar and explosion the walls behind the fallen brazier shook and trembled.

Ulran felt the slabs beneath him quake convulsively. But his eyes were upon Fhord and the torturer in her embrace. They lay upon the coal-covered floor. Each seemed to melt into the other, burning into a black and red dust.

Words from the *Book of Concealed Mystery* forced themselves upon him: "I dare as well defend the great Osasor, refuted by men of sagacity, since my heart dwells in fires which thirstily I drink, and feels no pain."

Ulran made for the stairs and then hesitated at the bottom for one final farewell to Fhord. Rising from the black and red dust was a white incandescence, a shimmering thin spiral; this dazzling white light quickly coalesced into an opaque beam that pierced the torture chamber's blackened ceiling. Moments later, Ulran shielded his eyes as sparks filled the place and a fissure appeared in the stone roof. Then the white light was gone, plunging the room into silence and darkness.

Until that instant, Ulran had felt Fhord's powerful presence, but now she had departed.

***

A number of guards were attracted to the few flames and puffs of smoke that issued from the doorway under the arcade. But they were tardy in their estimation of the fire's seriousness.

The charge-sergeant detailed a man to fetch a water cart. In the meantime, he advised the others to use the water in the nearby horse-troughs and watch the area and raise the alarm only if the fire looked like getting out of hand.

The nobles on the benches in front of the ash tower dispersed, absently noting the small puffs of smoke in the arcade area. The soldiers could handle that.

Many of the nobles who lingered chatted about the warrior who had surprised them all and only but recently smothered.

Others remained behind to toy with their women, the sight of Courdour Alomar's death having aroused them.

Tomorrow the warrior would be ashes, adding to the tower itself. Life's transience impinged upon a few wise enough to associate Courdour's death with their own life; but what use philosophising, when –

The tower's glass front cracked, pierced by a sword, and abruptly burst outwards with a muted yet ominous sound, drawing all eyes in alarm.

Glass and ash showered the foremost nobles and women. Then they espied in the midst of the massive wave of billowing ash a familiar shape; the figure of Courdour Alomar, streaked in black, fully garbed in lacquered ironwood armour, sword and shield in his hands, teeth and whites of eyes gleaming, his laughing mouth pink-red.

Panic should have impelled them to run, but they were stunned, incapable of believing their own eyes. They presented pitifully easy targets for Alomar's slashing sword and he showed no mercy.

He ran down from the benches where lay at least twelve fresh corpses, and his black imprints traced his steps. He ploughed towards the horse-trough, immersed his head and swished it around, shook his head and sneezed, twice: "Damn! That damned ash!" His eyes streamed, producing white rivulets upon blackened cheeks.

By now the four soldiers studying the puffs of smoke at the dungeon entrance had shaken themselves out of their stunned torpor. They turned as one. And died almost as one.

Alomar's thought was of the torture chamber and, oddly, he was gravely concerned for Fhord. If they had killed her, after all they had been through –!

He kicked down the door and stepped onto the stone landing.

Thick smoke engulfed him, made him cough.

A couple of guards below at the first level were fighting the smoke with blankets, while trying to quell the shrieking prisoners who clung to the rows of cell-bars. Upon seeing him through the swathing smoke, however, the guards and even some prisoners backed away as though he were some apparition from Below.

Without pausing, Alomar jumped down the stairs and slew the two guards. He yelled to the prisoners: "I'll release you on my return!"

Coughing on the smoke, he jumped to another broad landing that overlooked the low chamber.

He prepared to meet an upcoming charge from a single man but stayed his sword in time. "Ulran!" he shouted, hoarse. He sneezed again, cursing the ash.

At that moment, as the innman drew alongside him and they clasped hands, the chamber below rumbled.

The black roof collapsed at the far end, directly upon the ashes, all that remained of the mortal body of Cobrora Fhord and her torturer.

Alomar's eyes quizzed Ulran as they both turned and climbed the stairs, choking on the smoke.

Ulran shook his head.

Alomar nodded, that was all. Later, if they survived, he would spare a thought for Fhord; but not now.

They snatched torches from the wall-sconces and hurried along the echoing passage, shadows flashing. Ulran lagged a little and conserved himself – his side ached.

Finally, in answer to Ulran's directions, Alomar swerved to the right, grabbed a battle-axe from the wall and ran into a small chamber where Bindar lay.

Ulran followed him through.

"Ulran, friend, you've come!" Bindar smiled weakly, stretching his chains.

Alomar's axe crashed down, shattering the offered metal links.

Then Bindar was free, though unsteady on his feet.

Alomar thrust the battle-axe into the freed man's hand as Ulran said, "Follow us up, Bindar. We cannot tarry now, we're making for Yip-nef Dom! Free the prisoners after we've left. The city's outbreak begins now!"

Weary eyes abruptly lightened with a fierce fire. Bindar nodded and followed their flickering torches up the smoke-laden steps.

Another two guards had come down from the courtyard, wet cloths round their faces. As they emerged out of the wall of smoke ahead, Ulran ran forward and swung his chains at their legs. Both fell heavily to the stone steps and Alomar swiftly despatched them to the Fields of the

Overlord, though not without some envy.

Shouts and screams reached them, coming from the cells. "They're down there, Bindar – good luck!"

The red-head veered right, down a gloomy smoke-filled corridor, smashing his battle-axe resoundingly against the locks of the cells. For all his ill-treatment and wounded arm, Bindar's strength was up to the task.

With shouts of joy, the emaciated prisoners surged out of the cells.

Ulran followed Alomar up the steps, his wounds slowing him; fortunately, they had not broken open afresh. For he felt sure that if he lost more life-blood, his strength would drain away with it.

At the door's entrance – within the shadows of the arcade – Ulran and Alomar discarded the torches and halted to survey the scene in the courtyard.

The arcade further down on the left-hand side had collapsed, revealing a gaping black hole, with flames and smoke sprouting up as though out of the Pit itself. Soldiers had formed a water-bucket chain, though they could not see the end of it as the billows of smoke obscured most of the courtyard. Above this smokescreen rose the Tower of Ash and the wooden benches with the sprawled figures of the slain spectators.

Alomar and Ulran crossed the heaps of ash in front of the tower, and their boots made cracking noises upon the shattered glass. But nobody paid any attention.

Dangling on either side of the royal balcony were richly embroidered pennants, yellow on black. And slung over the topmost benches on poles was an awning.

Unnoticed, the pair climbed the benches and leaped over the bodies.

Almost without pausing, Alomar swung round and offered his cupped hands as a foot-rest.

Ulran placed his right foot neatly in the immortal's hands and Alomar lifted him with a loud grunt.

Summoning up his strength, the innman sprang upwards, reached out and caught hold of the awning with both bruised hands. He gripped, held tight. The material partially ripped under his weight – as did his abdominal wound.

As he swung suspended – pain lancing – he arched his back and kicked his legs up and over, knees hitting *smack!* onto the taut canvas. And it held.

For a brief moment he rested and checked the seepage of blood – slight. Then, from here, he bounced over and grabbed hold of a dangling pennant. After testing the strain he hauled himself up, feet against the black-stone wall, hand over hand, his damaged shoulder throbbing. Then he reached out and his fingers wrapped round a carved baluster.

In an instant he was up and over the balcony, though breathless.

The salon was deserted. From here, the courtyard appeared in complete pandemonium, swathes of smoke obscuring vast areas.

Below, Alomar waited patiently, unnoticed by the scurrying soldiers with slopping buckets of water.

Slightly recovered, Ulran tore down the heavy brocade drapes, used Alomar's knife to slice them into strips and quickly tied them together and to the baluster. The immortal warrior was too heavy to copy Ulran's athletic feat, so they had decided on this method. Ulran threw the brocade rope over then ran to the salon's doorway.

A guard hurried up the stairs and gaped stupidly at the bedraggled and bloody sight the innman presented. He fell dead back down the stairs, one at a time.

Grunting and sneezing, Alomar clambered over the balcony.

"Where to now?" queried the innman.

"Down – next floor. I'd wager he's got the birds in the shrine salon."

They both cast one last look over their shoulders, through the balcony opening. The sun was setting, the sky already dark.

Running from room to room unchallenged, they came upon the stairs.

As they descended through choking fumes that wafted upwards – the staircase seemed to act as a funnel for the smoke – the half-landing materialised where two guards stood and coughed spasmodically. Ulran took them completely by surprise; the chains on his wrists whipped out at their heads. Helmets flew off and the men tumbled over the banister rail, screeching.

Ulran and Alomar hurried down the rest of the stairs and came out on a wide and not too smoky landing with closed double doors. "This is it." As Alomar tried the handle he sneezed twice. "Locked! Bolted for the ceremony, I warrant!"

The immortal backed up then charged the door with his left shoulder.

Something beyond splintered and cracked. The door gave a little.

They could hear shouts near the panelling on the other side.

"Again," Alomar said and rammed full into the door with a resounding *crash*!

***

The doors swung open wide, wobbling on their hinges, and Alomar stumbled in.

Only Ulran's swift upsweeping snake of chain averted the warrior's decapitation by a soldier to the right. As the chain wrapped around the axe, Ulran hauled it out of the man's hand and Alomar sank his sword home.

Everything froze into an unreal tableau as Alomar crashed the doors open. Both seasoned fighters immediately took in the complete scene.

An array of about five hundred inter-connecting large terracotta bowls stood in a semi-circle around the dais. They were supported on scaffolding that placed them roughly two marks high. The area under the bowls themselves was scaffold-free, and upon the floor beneath were trays of sand.

One man, presumably the royal tester, stood naked underneath one of the bowls and a red liquid trickled from its underside upon his head and shoulders. As Alomar burst in, the tester was busy lathering the liquid onto his chest while Por-al Row's invocation echoed:

"Come, children of Bridansor and preside over the operation of this day. Come, Incomprehensible Nikkonslor with all your might, haste to my assistance and be propitious to my undertakings, be kind and refuse me not your Powerful Aid–"

Yip-nef Dom sat upon the dais to one side of the alchemist. He only wore a colourful bathrobe, awaiting the results on the tester.

Above the bowls, suspended from the rafters, were tethered red tellars, eight to a cage. And above the tester's bowl lay the body of a red tellar, its life-blood spilling down into the bowl.

The remaining birds watched, restless, silent, their reflections appearing mauve in the high glass windows that surrounded the salon.

Upon suspended wooden platforms beside the cages were soldiers, each armed with a long slim spear to slash the birds' throats.

Diminutive in the gigantic salon, Iayen stood by her father's side.

Soldiers numbered about twenty on each side of the salon, armed with pike, sword and shield. Though judging by the number of bowls, the chosen initiates for invulnerability would be close at hand, to stand under the showers of blood.

"Slay them!" shrieked Por-al Row.

But as twenty or so soldiers began to charge, Yip-nef Dom barked, "No! Hold!"

As they stopped in their tracks, the king said, "Wait! Let us see how the tester fares!" He turned to Por-al Row. "Is his initiation finished, Enchanter?"

A croak: "Yes, sire – it'll work – he's invulnerable."

"Good." He signalled to the sergeant-at-arms at the front of the group of soldiers: "Give him your sword, Sergeant."

Alomar signalled to Ulran, *this is my fight.*

Another volunteer stepped down, dropped his cloak and stood under a bowl, his tall, stocky and powerfully muscled naked body glistening with some arcane preparatory solution. And another red tellar's throat was cut.

"Continue with your invocation, Por-al Row, while we watch Courdour Alomar face *your* invulnerable warrior!"

"Yes, sire."

The tester didn't seem too confident, standing naked before the armoured Alomar, his borrowed sword held without enthusiasm.

Sword in his left hand, Alomar lunged forward.

Instinctively, the tester parried and the metal clanged.

Once the battle was joined, the tester proved himself an able opponent, giving no ground. His body shone with a coppery sheen.

Still finding breathing difficult, Alomar sweated and couldn't blink the salty moisture away. He had often tested himself with his left hand, but he would never be a good sinister swordsman, however long he lived! But he could match this opponent blow for blow, at least.

They skirted the trellis-work of scaffolding.

Alomar parried and sliced, feinted and jabbed, and missed, but a wooden upright shattered, the bowl above toppling to smash into pieces to one side of them.

An opening, and Alomar seized it, sliced down at the tester's chest – and the sword clanged as if against a metal bell!

Heartened by this exhibition of invulnerability, the tester grew reckless, pressed in his attack, and Alomar backed against another upright.

Yelling in triumph, the tester slashed at Alomar's armour.

But Alomar side-stepped and jumped up, slid his sword into the tester's wide open shouting mouth, pushing in and down with all his might.

The tester stared, disbelieving and then gagged. Suddenly, blood spurted up the sword's length, and vomit: and the coppery patina on his body cracked and flaked away.

External, not internal invulnerability, mused Alomar as he struggled to free his sword.

The second volunteer, a great hulk of a man, bore down on Alomar, brandishing a long-sword. And Alomar still hadn't retrieved his own weapon from the dead tester.

He stumbled back over shards of bowl, and fell.

The hulk slammed his sword down but Alomar rolled away.

The blade clanged on stone, sent sparks flying.

Again and again, Alomar rolled out of the way but was unable to get up, his attacker was too quick, too close, too good! This one kept his mouth shut, offering no access to his vulnerable vitals.

Alomar snatched his poniard, threw it and it bounced, flew off the man's body, issuing a hollow coppery sound.

A third volunteer was soaking under a bloody shower, he noticed, glancing over his shoulder as he rolled yet again.

Ulran watched the fight with half a mind; the other half was gauging distances, while he rattled his chains threateningly to dissuade the slowly encroaching soldiers. None seemed anxious to attack him – they'd wait, let the invulnerable ones do that. Besides, they all seemed to be enjoying the fight.

Now, Alomar grabbed a broken wooden pole, twisted and swung it round at his assailant's legs.

The invulnerable hulk overbalanced, fell against more scaffolding which rocked then fell apart, tumbling another bowl to the flagstones, the jagged pieces glancing off the hulk's coppery body as if mere hailstones.

Alomar jabbed the pole into the man's belly.

Doubling up, winded, the hulk offered his chin as a tempting target.

Alomar jerked his knee up and his hands down hard; there should have been a fatal, satisfying crack of bone, but instead the man lunged, growling and it seemed that everyone present held their breath as Alomar reeled back, gripping the sword blade that protruded from his abdomen.

He stared at it, and smiled. "*At last!*" he shouted then with an enormous clatter he fell backwards amid broken wood and pottery.

Grinning amidst the cheers from the soldiers, Yip-nef Dom's invulnerable warrior leapt forward and grabbed his sword hilt and pushed it deeper into Courdour Alomar.

But instead of blood gushing out, blinding white beams of light sprayed in all directions.

No-one ever knew where the words came from but in every skull they resonated, terrifying in their power and unconcealed rage: "*How DARE you sully the blood of the Wings of the Overlord!*" The incandescent light travelled up the sword and suddenly the invulnerable warrior looked thin and terribly weak. Within an instant, he was a green-tinged skeleton, crumpling to the floor, and his sword had exploded into harmless stardust and vanished.

Alomar painfully eased himself up. "*Damn!*" was all he said as he pulled his sword from the tester's mouth.

Before anyone could react to the strange turn of events, Ulran snatched a shagunblend lamp to his right and threw it at the prospective third invulnerable warrior.

His aim was good: the warrior slipped on the blood and sand; he fell over and screamed, beating his head as his long hair burned and crackled. As he writhed he upset and smashed a bowl into a thousand gory shards.

Ulran's ears buzzed with the red tellars' plight as his lethal chains swathed a path through the soldiers, yet not a sound did the birds make.

Through the fighting formation he had glimpsed the king, now wielding Ulran's own sword and shouting encouragement to his men. He must retrieve that sword – for if he died it would be returned to its source.

Slashing and slaying with his left sword-hand, Alomar immediately appreciated the need for an escape route for the birds. In the few pauses as the soldiers held back to get second wind and fresh courage, Alomar whirled his sling-shot and the small stones from his belt-pouch whistled high, raucously, shattering window after window.

Spears rained down from the swaying platforms, but claimed more soldiers and left Ulran and Alomar unscathed.

Men with smashed skulls fell to right and left as Ulran used a borrowed sword to plough through them, his blood singing. His legs darted out and his lethal feet penetrated through shields and silenced hearts.

Now his wounds were forgotten, of the past. Later, if he lived, pain would return, doubtless redoubled. But this was *now*!

Broken and bleeding, the soldiers lay in his wake and groaned or hobbled away, beaten.

"Stop them!" screamed the king, louder, closer.

Only four soldiers stood between the scaffolding, bowls and Ulran. Beyond, cringed the figure of Yip-nef Dom.

Ulran wrenched free a dying soldier's shield and flung it over the soldiers' heads and the bowls.

The king saw it coming and ducked, but lost his footing on a pool of the red tellar's blood.

Yip-nef Dom fell forward, his face paling. The sword of Ulran rang out loudly, sounding above the din of Alomar's battle and the screams of the dying.

As Ulran fought his way through the four soldiers and toppled the scaffolding and bowls, he saw reinforcements.

Obviously, the remainder of the chosen five hundred: they emerged from the doorway behind the dais. Iayen was pointing in Ulran's direction, her crooked features black with hatred, mouth flecked with spittle.

Alomar met them head-on.

Por-al Row stared at the innman, incantations drooling off his fleshy wet lips. Abruptly he flicked his hands out, and green powder sprayed into Ulran's eyes.

Though his eyes streamed and his ring-scored face stung, the innman did not falter. Discarding his borrowed sword, he went for the alchemist.

Blanching, Por-al Row withdrew from his sleeve a curved sacrificial knife. He slashed out but missed, offering an opening which Ulran grabbed.

The innman's fingers locked onto the alchemist's thin wrist.

Alomar fought an incredible holding action on the far side of the royal platform. Already he had thrown a couple of knives at the cages and severed the fastenings.

Some red tellars had broken free and toppled the soldiers from their wobbling platforms, midst shrieks and howls. A few other red tellars helped Alomar surge against the soldiers at the doorways behind the dais. They pushed them back and back until only a couple could fight through each doorway at a time. Iayen had long since gone.

Ulran's eyes bored into the enchanter.

Por-al Row felt the knife press against his stomach, cut into the folds of his black robe: there was nothing he could do, his eyes were transfixed, mesmerised by the innman's; a swirling emptiness engulfed him, identical to the sensation that fleetingly overcame him in the mountains. As the blade sank deep into his belly Por-al Row smiled, at last appreciating the Overlord's terrible irony. He was incapable of feeling the pain, the outrage, and the frustration.

Ulran let go of the knife.

The enchanter slumped to the dais and suddenly emerged from his entranced state. At the top of his voice he cried the Overlord's name out loud and stared wide-eyed at the knife that protruded from his body.

Alomar fought on, sneezing again and rubbing watery eyes. Ulran joined him after picking up another discarded sword on his way. Later, if possible, he would search for his own weapon.

The odds were seemingly impossible. Then an uncanny lull occurred as a high-pitched continuous screech thrummed in everyone's heads though not their ears. As one, the birds looked upon the crying form of Por-al Row, perpetrator of the red tellars' plight.

At least twenty of the great birds swooped down and back up again, curved beaks digging and biting into the alchemist. Eerily, the birds descended and rent him time and again without a sound. Only a low whisper, from the doomed man himself. Then the birds broke off and left the pulsing bloody whining shape upon the royal platform.

And from the window ledge above swooped the largest bird in the salon, a white sekor emblazoned on its throat.

Scalrin swooped down.

***

Talons deep in the enchanter's chest, Scalrin lifted the man, effortlessly, high above the dais, massive wings flapping and thrumming, dislodging torches onto the matting, setting the floor alight. As the man cried for release, Scalrin's beak jerked forward and down, once, and penetrated the skull, silencing Por-al Row forever.

The body was discarded at once and landed with a dull thud amidst the burning matting, and this seemed to be a signal to the other red tellars. There was little fight left in the onlooking soldiers as the birds lined the window-ledges, flickering yellow eyes cast upon the soldiers, waiting.

One by one, the soldiers dropped their weapons.

Alomar nodded his approval. "Very wise, very wise indeed," he said. "Perhaps there is hope for your people, after all."

More royal guards burst into the salon through the broken double doors.

"We have no quarrel with Arisa!" Ulran called. He strode through the flaming dais and looked down at Yip-nef Dom who lay sprawled upon the ruins of terracotta bowls and spilt blood.

He knelt down.

All eyes were on him as he retrieved his own sword from under the king's head. "Look," he said, pointing. The chains on his wrists rattled but were forgotten. "See for yourselves! The king died by accident, by the Overlord's hand, not ours."

The sergeant-at-arms knelt down and nodded agreement.

Clearly, the sword's pommel had struck the king's chin, breaking his neck with the upward force as the sword hit the floor.

Still kneeling, Ulran kissed the hilt and felt whole again.

At that moment, a cheering and bedraggled mob charged in, led by Bindar. The royal guards backed to the right, wary, swords still unsheathed.

Ulran held up his hand. "No more killing, Bindar! The day is yours!"

The crowd cheered and abruptly broke into two, forming an aisle.

Along this limped the ragged figure of Yip-dor Fla, bruised and battered, his eyes blinking in the light. "Royal guards, soldiers of the king – the people's uprising has vanquished Yip-nef Dom's lackeys!"

A loud cheer broke out.

Alomar stood by Ulran's side and surveyed the carnage they had wrought. "This day would have made Fhord proud," he said quietly.

"Yes," said Ulran, saddened.

"The king is dead! Long live the king!" It was a cliché, but none the less heartfelt for all that.

One by one the red tellars clustered at the shattered windows. Some shared the task of carrying their dead brethren. No red tellar corpses would be left behind. They edged their way out, to fly off to freedom.

Scalrin was the last to depart.

Ulran watched, waved, and the great bird was gone.

Morton Faulkner

EPILOGUE
FIRST SAPIN-SAPINMA OF LAMOUS

"... or else I'll send for the Black Hat!"
– Mother's threat to naughty child

Alomar sneezed and hissed an imprecation upon the deceased king and the infamous Tower of Ash that – according to Yip-dor Fla – would shortly be destroyed.

The coronation banquet was fitting, with Ulran on the king's right, Alomar on his left; near Alomar sat the returned Essalar and his wife and Bindar who had been newly installed in his beer-hall.

The feast had gone well with much merriment and wine.

Now Yip-dor Fla stood with goblet raised.

The murmur of voices dwindled and the returned king spoke: "I declare Ulran of the Red Tellar and Courdour Alomar innocent of killing your late king! There shall be harboured no grudge against these men, through whose suffering we have all seen a fresh new day, the dawning of a renaissance in Arisa!"

Cheers rose like a wave and moisture was upon the king's eyelids. "All plans for the conquest of Lornwater have been dismantled. Let it be understood, this city has no quarrel with any other.

"Once Arisa was great, leading Floreskand in every way. It is my vow to make Arisa a good and memorable city, one to which all enlightened people will want to flock!"

More cheers, banging of flagons and goblets.

"The black days are finished, my people!"

***

Later, replete, Ulran and Alomar had a private audience with Yip-dor Fla.

"It sorrows me that you must leave so soon, my friends," said the king.

"Lornwater's civil war is still raging, sire," Ulran explained. "I must join my son. My place is by his side."

Yip-dor Fla looked to Alomar. "And you, warrior?"

"Adventure beckons. Always to find a new quest, a new trail. I am impatient to feel Borsalac's withers between my legs again!"

"I am sorry that Yip-nef and Iayen saw fit to deprive you of your eyelids, Alomar. Surely, my surgeons can help – they'd–"

"No, sire." Shaking his shaggy black head, the immortal warrior grinned and successfully held back an incipient sneeze. "It bothers me little – I don't sleep."

Alomar's mischievous grin puzzled Yip-dor Fla but the king refrained from delving deeper.

At this exposal Ulran wondered if Lorgen were more than mere legend.

"Besides, Edu-seren's done enough to recompense, by treating my arm," and Alomar patted the heavily bandaged limb.

"What of Iayen?" asked Ulran

The king's face turned grave. "That troubles me that she should have fled without trace. And if as you say she *is* with child by Yip-nef, then, perhaps I have not heard the last of her." He sighed, settled back into his chair. "But that is my problem, not yours. You've done more than enough for me *and* Arisa!"

"Your provisions and horses are waiting in the courtyard," said First-Captain Dab-su Hruma. "The city almost went to battle stations when the Kellan-Mesqa rode up to the Varteron Gate!"

"The Hansenand are here?" queried Ulran.

Dab-su shook his head. "No, they would not linger, saying only that they must ride on, but had heard of your quest's success and left your horses. I must say, they are fine beasts. The palfrey, she is–"

"Sarolee – Fhord's horse. Would you like to keep her?"

"But – I have plenty still to learn, Ulran, yes, I accept your gift, knowing how much Sarolee must mean to you."

***

While the festivities progressed and dusk approached, Ulran and Alomar rode through Arisa's Varteron Gate and down the winding track to the plains.

Though unsaid between them, each brooded over the sense of loss they experienced as their horses cantered over the grassland.

"It feels strange," said Alomar, finally shaping their feelings into words. "Without her, without Fhord..."

"Yes, it does," Ulran replied softly.

They rode to the varteron in silence.

***

Dusk fell. Still in sight of the flashing white and coloured lights of Arisa's celebrations, the pair halted. Ulran was painfully reminded of Fhord's glorious departure from this mortal coil.

"I hope your city is not too troubled, Ulran – but alas I cannot abide city life of any sort." Alomar shrugged. "And besides, I know you won't need any help from me!"

"You'll continue to seek the Navel of the World?"

"Aye, I'll do that – I may look upon the black-white again, see if it has anything to tell me." He swerved Borsalac round and rode, cloak flurrying, down the grassy rise, to the ranvarron.

Ulran swung Versayr towards his beloved Lornwater, many launmarks to the ranmeron. He had decided not to stop this first night, if his wounds could stand up to the riding. He was anxious to be alongside Ranell again. His thoughts about his son were interrupted, a familiar voice impinged: a soft, gentle, almost jovial voice.

He reined in Versayr and shook his head: he knew there was nobody within a launmark.

"Now I *know* I was right about you," said the voice, quite clearly.

Still nothing, no-one.

"Where are you?" he asked and felt a little foolish, talking to thin air! He shook his head, annoyed with what he thought was his mind playing tricks: could it be the wound? That had definitely been Fhord's voice. But it couldn't be, no matter how real it seemed.

"Look above you."

Ulran did so, and gazed upon the bloodiest of setting suns.

He comprehended.

Fhord was home.

The innman smiled to himself, eyes afire with the red sunset.

As Ulran turned Versayr for Lornwater again, a final parting shot reached him, as soft-spoken as the last: "No need to hurry, Ulran. Ranell is handling the situation well."

Drawn once more, Ulran looked up at the setting orb.

A shooting star crossed the sky and the voice said, "It is only to be expected from the son of a Kormish Warrior."

She had been to Sianlar. "Farewell, *Friend* Fhord."

***

The blazing sunset was now on Ulran's right and seemed to linger. Then he espied a silhouette upon a brow ahead, the rider's distinctive floppy hat quite unmistakable.

As the innman reined in beside the immortal warrior, they both turned in their creaking saddles and eyed the last of the setting sun.

Ulran felt sure he glimpsed Fhord's face in the dying orb and superimposed over her image was that of a man, perhaps Slane.

And then the sun's orb sank, leaving the orange afterglow that seemed strangely warming.

Floreskand: Wings

AFTERWORD

For five terrible years did the Three Cities' Civil War rage...
– Tsukcoldol Almanack

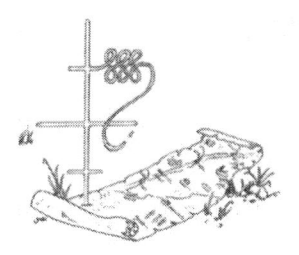

The end of WINGS

KING, the the beginning of the history of the Three Cities' Civil War of 2050-2055, including the involvement of Ulran, Courdour Alomar and Ranell, will be released from the Royal Institute of Records shortly. Other histories include MADURAVA and PROPHECY.

Morton Faulkner

GLOSSARY A
Names, places and meanings

AC	Arisan Calendar. Recorded history began 0001AC. Originated and introduced during the fifth year of King Zal-aba Men's reign. The Calendar was backdated to his first year on the throne. (See Glossary D).
Altohey	One of four Manderranmeron Fault volcanoes.
angkorite	Hermit of religious leanings
anjis newt	Most common of the two newt species. Feeds on worms, crustaceans and insects.
Arion	Arable land within the Sonalume Mountains, accessible through the Arion Gap which is guarded by Arisa, and also through the hazardous Astrey Caron Pass.
Arisa	Oldest city, founded 001AC. Also referred to as the Prime City
Astle	One of four Manderranmeron Fault volcanoes.
Astrey Caron	Discoverer of a dangerous pass through the Sonalume Mountains, linking the dunsaron plains of Floreskand with Arion. Discovered in 86BAC
BAC	Before Arisan Calendar
Below	Hell, colloquially the Underworld
biter	Vicious icy wind usually coming from the ranmeron, found in the Sonalume Mountains.
Book of the Dead	Floreskand has two versions: Manderon and Ranmeron
cawcaw	bird
carst	Monetary value. 10 carst = 1 sphand.
cherese	Gecko
city	Large populated towns of over one launmark square; must be walled to be classified as cities.
cycle	Comprising 20 orms: one day. Virtually archaic.
dahal-nasqed	Cicada-like insects remarkable for their chirping sound; common throughout Floreskand; also known as night-devil.
Danumne	One of the four Manderranmeron Fault volcanoes.
Daqsekor	The Overlord; name seldom uttered aloud due to its assumed potency.
dates	Unless stated otherwise, all dates are AC.

day	Used in preference to archaic cycle.
dead money	A pento, given to every person at birth and retained until death; used symbolically as payment for last rites and funeral. No self-respecting thief would steal Dead Money.
Devastators	Nomadic tribesmen, also known as Kellan-Mesqa. Original aborigines of Floreskand; the names of rivers, lakes, mountains etc derive in the main from these people. Comprise six separate hordes: Hansenand, Baronculer, Selveleaf, Aquileja, and Mussoreal; the sixth horde, the Tramaloma, have ceased their nomadic way of life and inhabit Taalland. Each horde is also sub-divided into montars, each administered quite separately.
dacorm	Time measurement. 100 dacorms in 1 orm. (1 dacorm = 43 seconds)
devil	Unnamed malicious spirit; night creatures generally.
dogs	Apart from the domesticated canine, there are wild-dogs: forest-dogs, small, fast and vicious; plains-dogs: larger and hunt in packs; and their larger relative, the wolves, who inhabit the foothills of mountains and rarely tread the lowlands.
Doltra Complex	Prestige building in Lornwater's Second City, named after its architect.
Drop, the	Colloquial name for the Varteron Edge (q.v.).
ebon-diamond	Largest diamond found in Floreskand, held in the palace of Arisa. The only known black diamond in existence.
Edge, the	The moment between life and death.
Endawn	Manderon city founded in 56AC.
fane	Temple.
Floreskand	Land contained between the manderon range of Tanalume Mountains, the Varteron Edge, the dunsaron range of Sonalume Mountains and ranmeron Shomshurakand Barrier.
Floreskandian symbol	Mark of the Royal Institute of Records, Lornwater (q.v.), whose archives have been used for this odyssey.

Forshnorer Forest	Where tree-dwellers live
Free Cities	Cities of Floreskand, referred to as such by the Ranmeron Empire.
galnear	Century.
gamen	Hundred soldiers plus one officer.
garrotmen	Guardians of the Forests of Ironwood; also known as garrotters. Poachers are usually garrotted. The Fourth Toumen.
gild	Guild. The vast majority of common people belong to some kind of gild, be it religious, merchant, or craft. Most infamous illegal gild is the assassins' Gild. Merchant Gilds regulate trade monopoly. Gildsmen form the greater part of the militia. Gildsmen also take up vendettas on behalf of members' families.
glo-moths	Caged insects used for illumination in places where shagunblend fumes may be overpowering.
Goldalese	City founded in 995AC.
haemoleaf	Leaf possessing healing ability for raw wounds. Only found outside Floreskand, thus extremely rare, if not mythical.
Harladawn	A manderon city of Agrash Teen. Comprises two separate walled cities: *Harl* on the manderon bank and *Dawn* on the ranmeron bank of Agrash Teen. Founded in 220AC.
honey-loaf	Sweetened bread, baked by the Devastators beneath camp fires.
Inn, The	The inn on the shores of the Lake (q.v.).
innman	Landlord or innkeeper; always the owner of the inn, not his staff or managers.
ironwood	Strongest known wood. After special treatment and lacquering, virtually unbreakable and as strong as iron, hence its name.
Jahdemor	Lord of Day; the god of light and strength.
Janoven	Fabled port by the equally fabulous Sea. In Renjhoriskand, manderon of the Tanalume Mountains.
jhet-fibre	Exceedingly rare if not mythical cloth, woven specially by seamstresses from the Fane of the Overlord.
Kellan-Mesqa	See Devastators.
Khamharic victory	A victory gained at too great a cost, such as that

	gained (1227AC) by Lornwater's General Somoror Khamha over the Hansenand Kellan-Mesqa.
Korm	Mythical controllers of the Kormish Warriors; believed to be only three in number.
Kormish Warriors	Mythical warriors of the Overlord. No Kormish Warrior, according to legend, knows to what end he works. Certain exceptional Warriors are permitted to be free agents, though always available if the Overlord requires them.
Lake, The	Lornwater Lake. Unnamed, because of the mystery and dread surrounding this stretch of water. All other lakes in the land save this one have been named by Kellan-Mesqa and are referred to as taals (q.v.).
launmark	Measurement of length. (1 launmark = 1400yds)
Lhoretsorel	Famed sorcerer, reputed author of the Book of Concealed Mystery.
Lornwater	Also called the Three Cities, comprising The *Old City*, the *Second City*, and the *New City*. Founded in 959AC.
madarkin	Hot seasonal wind from the varteron.
madurava	Compass. Floreskandian compasses are enormous. There are no portable ones. They are kept in Madurava Houses, usually one per city. (See Glossary C).
Manderranmeron Fault	Geological fault running the length of Floreskand and containing the four fault volcanoes: Danumne, Astle, Altohey and Olarian.
mark	Floreskandian measurement of length.
marnmark	Measurement of length. (10 launmarks = 1 marnmark. (1 marnmark = 8 miles)
melog	A blasphemous creature, magically created from inanimate matter.
mercenary	A legal gild, aka the Brethren of the Sword.
Meshanel	Jahdemor's prophet (786-900AC).
messengers, The	Riders who convey news between cities using staging posts; known as Roumers.
mid-moon	Midnight – referred to as such regardless of the visibility of the moon.
mid-sun	Mid-day.

mindsaur	Leaves, shoots or resin of the saur plant, smoked as an intoxicant.
mists, the	Reference to the ranmeron borders of Floreskand, perpetually enshrouded by mists. Shomshurakand Barrier.
montars	Individual groups of Kellan-Mesqa, part of a horde, autonomous; small party of Devastators.
Moon	Eye of Nikkonslor.
moon	Month, in the context of time.
mort-taal	Ox-bow or cut-off taal.
names	Surname is said first, then the chosen or personal name; thus, Canishmel Bis refers to Bis (chosen) Canishmel (surname).
niedem newt	Crested, poisonous, its venom found mainly in the skin, muscle and blood and its eggs. Poison acts on nerves, preventing impulses from being transmitted to the muscle. Apart from insects, feeds on anjis newts.
night-devils	Dahal-nasqed.
Nikkonslor	Lord of Night.
Olarian	Volcano of Manderranmeron Fault.
orm	Time measurement; 20 orms per cycle. (1 orm = 1hr 12mins).
othenal	Mineral tar, found in the Othenal district of Renjhoriskand; similar to that derived from shagunblend.
paper	See reedpaper.
parchment	Common alternative to reedpaper.
Prime	The original, the biggest, the tallest, etc.
quarter	Seven days, in the context of time.
Quotamantir	The great sorcerer from KClenand. (Born ? – Died ?) Prominent 542-556AC.
Ranmeron Empire	Situated at the edge of the Mists; culturally different to the cities of Floreskand. Tarakanda.
reedpaper	Expensive paper, used exclusively by the affluent.
Royal Institute of Records	Situated on High Road, Lornwater's Second City. Previously the Mythological Studies Institute, founded by King Datrek in 1293. Comprises: mythological studies, general studies, storyteller and historical records Departments.
roumers, the	Also referred to as the messengers.

Sardan	Secret sect.
scribe	Fane clerk. Any recorder of archives.
sekor	Type of flower, with octagonal petals; regarded with religious significance, each god being given a different coloured sekor as an emblem.
set	Direction of wind.
shagunblend	Combustible tar-like substance; a method of illumination.
Shomshurakand	Mysterious land of mists beyond Carlash Teen.
Shomshurakand Barrier	Mists bordering Ranmeron Empire and Shomshurakand
Sianlar	City founded in 1160. The Fane of the Overlord was built here in 1241; situated on the Varteron Edge and has become a place of pilgrimage.
smalt	Glass derived from the treatment of cobalt ore.
sormakin	Seasonal wind from the ranmeron, bringing mist up from Shomshurakand.
Soveram	Mountain in Sonalume range, overlooking Arion and possessing two peaks, Soveram Marle and Soveram Torne, the latter peaks also known as the Twin Mountain.
stioner	Practitioner of stionery.
stionery	Weather prediction. Derived from a small chameleon called a stion, which changes colour with atmospheric pressure changes.
storytellers	Gild of tale tellers, graded in excellence by the pastel colours of their cloaks.
taal	Lake.
Taalland	Country of lakes; contain warm water and an abundance of fish.
Tanalumes	Mountain range 1200 launmarks manderon of Taalland. Believed to be an impenetrable barrier in the year 2050AC.
tangakol	Devastator shaman.
Tanlin, the	The Holy Book: The Book of the Living.
Tarakanda	The Ranmeron Empire.
teen	River.
toran	Ancestral home.
toumen	In military terms, 10,000 men.
troop	Usually refers to 50 soldiers or horsemen; half a

	gamen (q.v.).
tukluk	Serrated knife, brainchild of the Gild of Mercenaries.
underpeople	People who are never seen or heard; feared, perhaps mythical, inhabitants of the waterlogged disused mines of Lornwater.
Varteron Edge	The edge of the Floreskandian plateau; the Drop.
watchmen	City-wall or palace wall sentries, wearing distinctive plaid cloaks; policemen.
wordmasters	Most Floreskandians are illiterate. Professional readers and writers aka Wordsmiths sell their services; respected throughout society.
xadra	Grimoire; a manual of black magic.
xagga	Many-stringed musical instrument with flat shallow sound-box, popular in Arion.

Floreskand: Wings

GLOSSARY B
List of characters

Traditionally the surname comes first, followed by the given name.

Aba-pet Fara, female assassin
Aeleg, aide to Ulran
An-Sep, a thaumaturge
Aska, long-lost sister to Ulran

Badol Melomar, head and innman of the Open House Combine
Banstrike, Lornwater Watchman
Bashen Corl, head of a housestead
Berstram, Red Tellar man
Borsalac, Courdour Alomar's horse

Cantonera, Lord, Soemoff
Cobrora Fhord, an ascetic city dweller
Conofrack Jasebours, father of Ulran
Cor-aba Grie, financier
Courdour Alomar, long-lived warrior
Cursh, Lornwater Watchman

Dab-su Hruma, captain, Arisa
Den-orl Pin, officer in charge of the royal stables
Dyr, son of Bashen Corl

Edu-seren Grippore, Arisan surgeon
Elar, mother of Ulran
Ephanel, enlistee for Red Tellar Inn
Etor, a Kellan-Mesqa warrior

Fahurar Grie, an Arisan thief
Fascar Dek, gildmaster of precious metals, city's Great Gildmaster
Fet-usa Fin, a trader in weapons and poisons
Foo-sep, General, Arisa

Gel-en Bindar, innkeeper and rebel from Arisa
Grayatta Essalar, Arisan merchant

Grayatta Sapella, wife of Essalar

Iayen, daughter of King Yip-nef Dom
Illasa, Sister; Sardan witch with allegiance to Nemond Adama

Jan-re Osa, freed female slave
Jaryar, spouse of Courdour Alomar
Jentor, gildmaster for the assassins' gild
Jikkos, queen, wife of King Saurosen

Krailek, enlistee for Red Tellar Inn

Laorge, retainer in Toran Nebulous

Marosa, a queen from myth
Meetel, enlistee for Red Tellar Inn
Mirmellor Dhal, an experienced poisoner

Neran, daughter-in-law of Bashen Corl, wife of Dyr
Nostor Vata

Olelsang, gildmaster of the saddle-makers gild

Por-al Row, alchemist of Arisa
Pro-dem Hom, speech writer for the king
Pro-dem Zimera, widow of Hom

Rakcra, a Kellan-Mesqa warrior
Reall Demorat, a champion duellist
Ranell, son of Ulran
Rashen Pellore, a mercenary
Regloma Troglan, a champion duellist

Sarolee, Cobrora Fhord's horse
Saurosen, king of Lornwater
Scalrin, a red tellar
Ska-ama, madam of the House of Velvet, Lornwater
Slane, son of Bashen Corl
Solendoral, a Kellan-Mesqa warrior

Tanellor, Lord, Duke of Oxor
Trellen, Red Tellar man

Floreskand: Wings

Trulan, the royal torturer of Yip-nef Dom

Ulran, innman of the Red Tellar Inn
Usa, long-lost sister to Ulran

Versayr, Ulran's horse

Welde Dep, special investigations watchman, Lornwater
Wolderiq, a Kellan-Mesqa warrior
Woura, a Kellan-Mesqa woman
Wral, wife of Laorge

Yip-dor Fla, cousin to Yip-nef Dom
Yip-nef Dom, King of Arisa
Yoan, wife of Bashen Corl
Yorda, enlistee for Red Tellar Inn

Zen-il, Prime Watchman, Lornwater

Glossary C
Madurava – compass bearings

There are eight points on the Floreskandian Compass (madurava) which are read in a clockwise direction:

Manderon	-	north
Dunsaron	-	east
Ranmeron	-	south
Varteron	-	west
Mandunron	-	North-east
Dunranron	-	South-east
Ranvarron	-	South-west
Varmanron	-	North-west

Floreskand: Wings

Glossary D
The Arisan Calendar

There are 13 moons of 28-day periods in a year. Each moon is named after a constellation:
1. Sekous
2. Viratous
3. Dandulous
4. Ramous
5. Centirous
6. Juvous
7. Fornious
8. Darous
9. Lamous
10. Sortulous
11. Anticous
12. Petulous
13. Airmous

Each moon is divided into Quarters. There are 7 days and 7 nights in each Quarter.

Days:	**Nights:**
Sabin	Sabinma
Dekin	Dekinma
Sidin	Sidinma
Dloin	Dloinma
Sufin	Sufinma
Durin	Durinma
Sapin	Sapinma

These days are numbered One to Four, depending on which Quarter they are in;
thus the 16th day of the 4th month in 1470 would be written as follows:
Third Dekin of Ramous, 1470AC.

Glossary E
Lords and Gods - religious structure

There are three major religions in Floreskand:
1) The Overlord (orthodox)
2) The Hidden God; worshipped in Tarakanda.
3) The Inner God; followed by those who don't believe in outside influences.

In the orthodox religion of Floreskand, there are 3 tiers of gods:
1) The Overlord is the Highest God
2) The Great Lords and Lady; siblings; gods of the second rank
3) The High Lords are gods of the third rank

Overlord	- Daqsekor
Great lord of Day	- Jahdemor
Great lord of Night	- Nikkonslor
Great lady of Land	- Arqitor
High lord of Light	- Brilansor
High lord of Dark	- Bridansor

The Less Lords (more commonly lesslords) are spirit messengers/workers of the gods and demi-gods. Arqitor is the most powerful after the Overlord, being the balance between her brothers Jahdemor and Nikkonslor. She also has her own spirits in the Madurava. Jahdemor and Arqitor have their white lesslords. Nikkonslor and Arqitor have their black lesslords.

Lesslords of	*White*	*Black*
winds	Sansor	*Lamsor*
water	Alasor	Mussor
fire	Osasor	Honsor
mountains	Sursor	Frasor
war	Dassor	Baosor
woods	Amasor	Chasor
roads	Inasor	Labsor
valleys	Ronsor	Trasor
animals	Marsor	Tassor
birds	Opasor	Vensor

Under each lesslord is a host of lesser spirits. Nobles believe themselves related to the gods, and are thus referred to as Lords.
Gods of emotions are linked to the physical world.

Floreskand: Wings

Next from the Royal Institute of Records, Lornwater

FLORESKAND: KING

Morton Faulkner

When Ulran and Cobrora Fhord left Lornwater on their quest to resolve the mystery of the red tellars (*Floreskand: Wings*), the city was ripe for rebellion against King Saurosen, holder of the Black Sword.

In charge of the Red Tellar Inn, Ulran's son Ranell is drawn into a conspiracy with nobles to support Prince Haltese, the king's heir, to overthrow the tyrant. Inevitably, as a mining disaster and a murder in a holy fane stoke the fires of discontent, open rebellion swamps the streets.

Conflict turns into civil war, where the three cities' streets become a battleground. Conflict is not confined to Lornwater, however. There's fighting below ground in the mysterious tunnels and caves of the Underpeople, and within the forest that surrounds the city, and ultimately in the swamps and lakes of Taalland.

Subterfuge, betrayal, conspiracy, intrigue, greed, revenge and a thirst for power motivate rich and poor individuals, whether that's Lord Tanellor, Baron Laan, Gildmaster Olelsang, Lord-General Launette, ex-slave-girl Jan-re Osa, Captain Aurelan Crossis, Sergeant Bayuan Aco or miner Rujon.

Muddying the fight are not only bizarre creatures – the vicious garstigg, the ravenous lugarzos or the deadly flensigg – but also the mystics from the Sardan sect, Brother Clen, Sisters Hara, Illasa and Nostor Vata.

At stake is the Black Sword, the powerful symbol that entitles the holder to take the throne of Lornwater.

By Gordon Faulkner
MANAGING STRESS WITH QIGONG

The ancient Chinese health system of Qigong combines physical postures with breathing techniques to promote harmony between the body and the mind. It is quickly gaining popularity in the West as a natural yet powerful way of combating stress and its related effects.

This step-by-step guide to managing stress using Qigong begins by looking at our response to stress from both an Eastern and a Western perspective. It then presents a program of specially-designed stress relief exercises, followed by a series of gentler stress prevention exercises, many of which can be carried out either seated or standing.

The author provides easy-to-follow instructions for each of the steps, and the postures and movements are explained with the aid of photographs.

Designed specifically to fit in around a busy lifestyle, the Qigong program set out in this book will help to reduce stress, decrease anxiety, and restore energy.

This practical book will help anyone who is prone to stress, regardless of their level of ability or experience of Qigong. It will also be a useful resource for Taijiquan and Qigong instructors, alternative therapists, and other professionals working with clients who are affected by stress.

Small selection of reviews

A truly knowledgeable book that's both easy to read and easy to understand. Excellent. I'd be interested to know the name of any western teacher that has an equal or greater knowledge of the subject, I don't think there is one!!

A technically excellent and very well written book. The exercises are easy to follow and learn from the clear text and photographs

Paranormal books by Nik Morton published by Manatee

GIFTS FROM A DEAD RACE
... and other stories

Collected short stories – Volume 1
Science fiction, ghost, horror, and fantasy

Brave firemen still do their job though suffering radiation poisoning after a nuclear war; but to what purpose? Maybe a simple little thing can save the world from an alien plague... The first murder in space – can it be justified? Are dogs and trees and children as innocuous as they seem? If you're going to burgle a house, make sure you know who lives there – or else. The credit crunch can only get worse – worth an arm and a leg? Criminals should be nice to little old ladies, or else. A birth on the moon? Sounds marvellous, or then again, maybe not. He lost his memory – then found he was buried alive, reliving his life! What if you had to celebrate Christmas two days early? Would the children notice? He had the last laugh when the Doctor misused his incredible discovery. He found that out the hard way that drink and driving don't mix. The plague waited thirty-six years to show itself, and then went global.

'Nik Morton's 'A Gigantic Leap' re-imagines a piece of Soviet history and wonders what might happen if the American paranoia about space-born germs had been justified. It's a gently told story, narrated by an old man who has seen too much in his hard life. Then in the last few paragraphs, the stress and alarm build up nicely. All of the international panic and national security issues occur in the background, though, so as not to spoil the calm flow of the story. It's nicely done.'

'Spend it Now, Pay Later' is an unsettling and timely story of a single mother caught in an economic depression who jumps at an opportunity to get herself out of debt and build a future for her daughter ... Morton has over thirty years' publishing experience behind him and this latest story - a taut, nightmarish allegory from first word to last - is proof of his highly honed craftsmanship.'

Morton Faulkner

MISSION: PRAGUE

Tana Standish, Psychic Spy
in Czechoslovakia, 1975

It's 1975 and Czechoslovakia's people are still kicking against the Soviet invasion.

Tana Standish, a British psychic spy, is called in to repair the underground network.

But there's a traitor at work.

And there's an establishment in Kazakhstan, where Yakunin, one of their gifted psychics, has detected her presence in Czechoslovakia. As he gets to know her, his loyalties become strained: does he hunt her or save her?

When Tana's captured in a secret Soviet complex, London sends in Keith Tyson in a desperate attempt to get her out - or to silence her - before she breaks under interrogation.

'Interestingly, Morton sells it as a true story passed to him by an agent and published as fiction, a literary ploy often used by master thriller writer Jack Higgins. Let's just say that it works better than Higgins.'
–Danny Collins, author of *The Bloodiest Battles*

'...The best scenes are the one-on-one confrontations, claustrophobic closed room battles of expert second-guessing. One particular superb scene is beautifully choreographed and delivered, dragging the reader into the sweat-soaked reality of being stalked by a stronger killer...' – *Murder Mayhem & More*

MISSION: TEHRAN

Tana Standish, Psychic Spy
in Iran, 1978

1978. Iran is in ferment and the British Intelligence Service wants Tana Standish's assessment. It appears that CIA agents are painting too rosy a picture, perhaps because they're colluding with the state torturers.

Allegiances and loyalties are strained as Tana's mission becomes deadly and personal. Old friends are snatched, tortured and killed by SAVAK, the Shah's secret police. She has to use all her skills as a secret agent and psychic to stay one step ahead of the oppressors and traitors.

As the country stumbles towards the Islamic Revolution, the Shah's grip on power weakens. There's real concern for the MI6 listening post near the Afghan border. Only Tana Standish is available to investigate; yet it's possible she could be walking into a trap, as the deadly female Spetsnaz fighter Aksakov has been sent to abduct Tana. Meanwhile, in Kazakhstan, the sympathetic Yakunin, the psychic spy tracking Tana, is being side-lined by a killer psychic, capable of weakening Tana at the critical moment in combat with Aksakov. Can Yakunin save Tana without being discovered?

In the troubled streets of Iran's ancient cities and amidst the frozen wastes on the Afghan border, Tana makes new friends and new enemies...

'This is a substantial book, not the sort of thriller you skip through without paying careful attention and it's quite lengthy with several tangled subplots. It carefully balances the psy aspects of the story with more down to earth concerns – like the increasingly apparent discord between MI6 and the CIA, the grimy reality of undercover action in hostile territory. Morton knows how to write a kick-ass action sequence, too, with fight scenes that rival the best of Bourne or Bond.'

MISSION: KHYBER

Tana Standish, Psychic Spy
in Afghanistan, 1979-1980

In the aftermath of *Mission: Tehran*, psychic spy Tana Standish crossed into Afghanistan, accompanied by agent Alan Swann. Their rendezvous with Mike Clayton was delayed and while they waited for him in Herat, Tana befriends a Soviet forces family, intent on discovering details about the presence of General Pavlovsky. They're then caught in a devastating civil uprising....

Inexorably, the Soviets are being drawn into the politics of Afghanistan. And Clayton, Swann and Tana are linked with the heroic Massoud, the tyrant President Amin and the mujahedeen. Tana makes new friends and new enemies in her constant fight against injustice.

Professor Bublyk is still trying to locate Tana – and the missing Spetsnaz agent Aksakov. Distrustful of the psychic Yakunin, he recruits killer Klimov. Together, they imprison Yakunin in order to draw Tana out to rescue him.

Tana is aware that it must be a trap. But she owes her life to Yakunin, even though they have not met...

A tense cat-and-mouse battle of wits stretches the length and breadth of the country – to the far reaches of the Wakhan corridor, the Special Psychiatric Hospital in Dushanbe, Tajikistan, and ultimately to the Khyber Pass.

'If you read crime fiction to immerse yourself in a sense of place and time then *Mission: Khyber* will be perfect for you. Almost every chapter provides a potted history of a region and its people, from an archaeological perspective through to the religious upheavals which fuel unrest to this day. This is a spy story with a history lesson sneaked inside it.' - extract from a 4-star Amazon review by Rowena Hoseason, Hall of Fame top 100 reviewer

CHILL OF THE SHADOW

In her search for truth she found love – with a vampire!

This cross-genre thriller is set in present-day Malta and has echoes from pre-history and also the eighteenth century Knights of Malta.

Malta may be an island of sun and sand, but there's a dark side to it too. It all started when some fishermen pulled a corpse out of the sea... Or maybe it was five years ago, in the cave of Ghar Dalam?

Spellman, an American black magician, has designs on a handpicked bunch of Maltese politicians, bending their will to his master's. A few sacrifices, that's all it takes. And he's helped by Zondadari, a rather nasty vampire.

Maltese-American investigative journalist Maria Caruana's in denial. She can't believe Count Zondadari is a vampire. She won't admit it. Such creatures don't exist, surely? She won't admit she's in love with him, either...

Detective Sergeant Attard doesn't like caves or anything remotely supernatural. Now he teams up with Maria to unravel the mysterious disappearance of young pregnant women. They're also helped by the priest, Father Joseph.

And there are caves, supernatural deaths and a haunting exorcism.

Just what every holiday island needs, really.

Where there is light, there is shadow...

'... a strong structure and is full of rich writing and action. The plot has page turning twists and the main characters are likeable, especially the female lead. I hadn't read a vampire book in a while and was reminded of how intensely gruesome they can be. While this one has its squeamish moments it's not atypical for the genre, and I can't help liking a well written book! The Malta setting was perfect, making this a great escape read.'

Printed in Great Britain
by Amazon